THE SKY PEOPLE

Summer Ends Now (short stories)
Freedom

THE SKY PEOPLE

JOHN EMERY

SOHO

ACKNOWLEDGMENTS

I would like to thank my two chief eyewitness informants: Mr. John R. Black (Patrol Officer, Lt. Col. ANGAU, now of Marion Bay, South Australia), and Mr. Robert Emery (Planter, Lt. NGVR, now of Kingston S.E., South Australia); and also the late Mr. Michael J. Leahy of Zenag, New Guinea, for the use of his diaries and other archival material.

Thanks to the Literature Board of the Australia Council for the grants to research and write this novel.

A portion of "This Is My Strife" by Rainer Maria Rilke reprinted from *Translations from the Poetry of Rainer Maria Rilke* by M.D. Herter Norton, by permission of W.W. Norton & Company, Inc. Copyright 1938 by W.W. Norton & Company, Inc. Copyright renewed 1966 by W.W. Norton & Company, Inc. "Walkin' My Baby Back Home" by Fred E. Ahlert & Roy Turk. Copyright © 1930 by Chappell & Co., Inc. Copyright renewed. International Copyright secured. All rights reserved. Used by permission. "Rainbow on the River" by Louis Alter and Paul F. Webster, Copyright © 1936 (renewed 1964). Leo Feist, Inc. All rights of Leo Feist Inc., assigned to SBK Catalogue Partnership. All rights controlled and administered by SBK Catalog, Inc. All rights reserved. International copyright secured; used by permission.

Copyright © 1984 by J.C. Emery and A.J. Emery. All rights reserved under International and Pan American Copyright Conventions.

Published in the United States of America by
Soho Press, Inc.
1 Union Square
New York, NY 10003

Library of Congress Cataloging-in-Publication Data

Emery, John, 1947–
The sky people.

1. New Guinea—History—Fiction.   I. Title.
PR9619.3.E47S59   1988   823   87-26525

ISBN 0–939149–10–9

Manufactured in the United States of America
FIRST U.S. EDITION

For my parents
Bob, who went to New Guinea in 1933, and
Heather, who went in 1946,
thus starting the events that culminated
with this book.

THE SKY PEOPLE

· CHAPTER ONE ·

NICHOLLS

The sky had changed from the pale violet of false dawn to the intense blue of the tropical day. Steaming vapour rose from the mountain ridges. Sweat already beaded Nicholls' face as he wrote in his diary. His flesh was burned mahogany brown. Survival had made his eyes watchful. As he wrote, he occasionally glanced up at his men.

The carriers and police waited patiently for his word. Only the white gold prospector showed his irritation. But Nicholls' word, as Australian Trust Territory's Patrol Officer for this area of New Guinea, was law.

The Administration required him to record the facts of each day on Patrol. But somewhere during the years he had spent in the jungle he had begun to weave his own thoughts around the bald record of murder and intrigue that it was his lot—as policeman, anthropologist, and magistrate—to record. Fifty men waited on his command to move out, but until he had assembled his thoughts in order on paper, read them through, corrected their grammar, he knew he could not give that command. So he wrote on, feeling the film of sweat forming between his pressing fingers and the pen, as the sun climbed higher and the last of the night's fog drained down towards the Central Highlands plateau.

Diary: 30th April, 1937

The feeling of heightened awareness, of sharper emotions, of more vivid recognition of objects, that I had when I arrived in these Highlands, on my first trip, a good five years ago, has returned to me this morning.

1

Perhaps it was the waking before daylight, in the cold, biting wind that came from the north, the mercury at thirty-three degrees on the grass. I struggled out of the warmth, waking my dog, who yawned and stretched and shook herself out. When I emerged from the tent, I could see the fire was almost dead. I stopped to return it to life, and Lik Lik roused Wallace's dog, Major.

They ran ahead of me silently, seeking out the scents of the brand-new morning, to the top of the ridge, where the full force of the wind sliced through us. But where we were rewarded with the sight of the sunrise.

The dogs ran on down the slope. If you could call that precipice a slope. It was a knife-edge. One slip and the dogs would have begun rolling, and not stopped until they slammed into the jungle that began several hundred feet below us. I stayed. All the valleys were filled with thick white fog, through which the mountain peaks for a hundred miles around broke in dark masses. I could see the distant limestone escarpment shine as the rising sun struck it. I could almost hear it, so powerful was the beam of light. The sun was golden as it broke through the mist. The sky above was cloudless, growing bluer as the night fell away. I stood there, breathless. Then I breathed in and, as the air charged my lungs and fired my body, I filled with ecstacy.

To be alone on the roof of the world, standing on a knife-edge that slides down into gorges thousands of feet deep, into tumultuous rivers towards which we must wind our tortuous way, down a track hacked from the living forest, that will grow back at our passing, swallowing us without trace.

As the fog drained away, spirals of woodsmoke began to slice through it: verticals opposed to its horizontal movement. Lost in that mist was an entire culture. And the ecstacy turned, instantly, to fear. Those humble hearth-fires were not those of a peaceful and downtrodden peasantry. They were the fires of warriors, of a civilization devoted almost entirely to killing. And I was about to move amongst them, with my wits more than my firepower to protect me.

Standing there, as the sun sharpened focus, I could pick the track we would have to follow, slicing through the jungle on the ridge-side. It vanished into the vegetation, but I marked its bearings. That act of conscious, logical thought banished the terror. I called to Lik Lik, and both dogs lifted their heads and yapped and hauled themselves up the slope to me. Wallace's Major, a friendly old dog, rubbed himself between my legs. Lik Lik watched, uncertain if she should protest or not. So I patted her and turned back for camp.

2

It was well astir when I returned. For the sake of propriety, Wallace would have the girl out of his tent before I was up, on most mornings. But he was late this morning. She was just leaving: bejewelled with her discs of mother-of-pearl, and her pig-fat. She smiled at me, cheekily, and let me have a good look at her fine, firm breasts and her thighs. But for the ornaments, she was naked. I heard Wallace, from inside his tent, tell her sharply to be off. Then his head appeared and he saw me.

He looked abashed. I laughed, and waved to him, and he relaxed. The social division between Patrol Officer and prospector is a clear one, and an awkward one to live with on a journey like this. Last night we were drunk together, he and I, and he offered me her services. I declined, but in declining thought of the act itself.

She sauntered across to join the other girls. Wallace likes to travel with a few home comforts—as he puts it. And there is wisdom in his approach. The girls are eager to go, quite often. Good prices are paid, and the villages often feel honoured— assuming all the girls go to satisfy the legendary powers of the European. But of course most girls will be consorts to his own labourers, easing the rigours of the journey for them.

Wallace's line was preparing to pull out. His boys were taking leave of mine—the sorrow more on my side than theirs. The girls have been most liberal with their favours, judging by the giggling and grunting that has emanated from their tents most nights.

In a way, it will be a welcome break to be separate again. The sounds of carnal revelry can make sleep difficult. But, beyond that, two Europeans together make a club that instinctively isolates itself from the locals. Only by travelling alone, living with the people, speaking their language, listening to their affairs, can you carry out real "Native Administration". The rest is just flag-waving. And Wallace is not really my sort. Few prospectors are. They see this country, and its people, as something that stands in the way of their true goal: gold. Something to be used to obtain that end. Oh, they're brave enough, or foolhardy. I've seen enough of them dying, and dead, to know how tough they are.

We breakfasted together. We've had a good passage. He's prospected his creeks, and I've carried out the surveys I've wanted. We've helped each other more than hindered. But I'm afraid that his travelling with my patrol will give, to the more susceptible natives, some semi-official status to his ventures. Which they do not have

He's headed back along our travelled route, with the intention,

3

so he says, of dropping down into the plateau, along his most favoured stream. But I suspect he has the Dutch border in his sights. The myth of El Dorado dies hard. Edie Creek looked like it was just that, for some. But there are always prospectors who miss out on the big one, and console themselves that "next time" it will be theirs. They look for the hardest journey, the most dangerous people, and say: "Right! It must be there. No one has looked there yet." And so they head off.

That's Wallace's type, and it is why I do like him, and respect him. Gold is the reason he gives. But, like me, it is the intoxication of the journey that is the reward. But if he gets into trouble over there, I won't be going after him. I'll wait along the rivers and fish his body out as it floats by. If there's enough of it to recognize. European and Melanesian skeletons are not all that damned dissimilar—despite what the racists back in Rabaul maintain. But it's time to break camp. Enough of this rambling.

Diary: Evening, Same Day

We're out in the open now. Five thousand feet lower than this morning. Dusk is near. Looking back, I can see the escarpment we traversed today. The low angle of the sun is picking out in relief the mountain ridges. Here, on the plateau, smoke is spiralling up from innumerable native homes scattered all over the grass terraces. I sit here writing, with a mug of tea, my boots off, my feet up, watching my boys sprawled in their camp, idly gossiping, smoking— by the gestures I assume Baranuma is remembering, with extravagant praise, the attributes of one of his paramours. There is a village a mile off. As yet, they have not sent a deputation out to meet us. So I'm taking advantage of the added peace of mind to collate a few notes.

The first must concern the disquieting rumours I am picking up, concerning the alleged activities of a group of European prospectors who appear to have passed through some time in the last month.

Rumours are always rumours, but they have their basis in something which occurs. The rumours suggest this party is intent on genocide: which means they have killed at least one native in cold blood. The rumours also speak of pillaging of villages and the forced abduction of women, neither of which can be dismissed easily. I will be interested to hear what the local villagers have to add to the story.

Wallace could throw no light on the stories—or didn't want to.

4

Prospectors know enough to stick together in some matters. Next week, it could be him faced with a similar accusation, and needing all the character witnesses he can find. If he does go over the border, it will pay me to question him on his return.

Bena Bena cannibalism. It seems to me that cannibalism is endemic to a society with chronic protein shortage. In fact, without it, the society would not be able to colonize its district. The problem is exacerbated by the obvious solution to the protein crisis—pigs—being regarded more as currency than as pork, and having magico-religious significance. Overpopulation must be kept in check, hence the interminable warfare built around the complex "payback" system, that literally ensures there will never be peace. Agriculture is practised, but the staples are over-abundant in carbohydrates and little else—and the cannibalistic solution is so easy that other solutions are not sought out.

And so the culture-knot is developed. It appears, at first glance, so complex, so intertwined: to destroy the symbolic role of the pig will destroy the religion; to wipe out payback killings will start the whole Malthusian population explosion; to wipe out cannibalism will starve the people, force them to re-evaluate the pig (and hence the bride-price system, the power of the Big Man—the most important social stabilizing force, the festivals that bring different tribal groups closer . . . and so on). The knot is so complex. At first glance, so life-denying. At closer examination essential to life-support. And yet, it can be undone by pulling one simple string. And I am the man charged with pulling that string. I am the man who is supposed to outlaw killing (and I will have to kill to do that). I must say: "This killing is bad. This one was bad, but understandable. This one was necessary. Because you have killed badly and unnecessarily I will take you to Rabaul, where I will kill you."

Preparation. The inedible parts of the body will be buried, and that grave will be considered the resting place of the unfortunate person's spirit. Death, of course, will have been by enemy action, for all death is regarded as the work of the enemy. "Natural causes" are not recognized. If they do not fall in battle, in ambush, then it is the work of magic. The skin is burnt off in an open fire until it presents a yellowish-white appearance. The meat is cut into small pieces. Bamboo pots are prepared by cutting off a joint of bamboo, and the meat is boiled in them with a small amount of water. The meat is usually left a day, and eaten cold. The bones are picked over, marrow sucked out, and casually thrown away.

5

"That's Nicholls' seat."

Don Harris stared at the drunk who was standing over him. He looked hastily around the Madang Administration mess. Two store clerks were eating in a far corner. The other white-clothed tables were empty. Through the window he could see the glitter of sun on the ocean.

"I beg your pardon?" he said.

"That's Nicholls' seat. You know, old Fire and Brimstone Nicholls. You can't sit there."

"Why not? Where's Nicholls?"

The drunk smiled. Don was trying to place him, but couldn't. His body was too soft to be a Patrol Officer's. The drunk leaned heavily on the white tablecloth. Don could see a Boy watching nervously from the servery. Don smiled reassuringly, and the Boy grinned and nodded and turned away.

"Nicholls is up somewhere in the bush, having arrows shot up his arse."

"So why can't I sit here?"

"Because, in this mess, a man's seat is a man's seat. Now..." the drunk looked around. "There's Black's seat. There's Morris's. Over there is where Bellamy sits when he comes in to get away from his missus."

"Where's yours?" Don asked quickly.

The drunk grinned and waved a finger.

"That would be telling, wouldn't it? Now, we're going to have to find you a seat, Mr . . .?"

"Harris. Don Harris. I'm a Cadet Patrol Officer."

"Mr Harris. My name is Dudley Simmonds, and I am Comptroller of Customs, Collector of Excises, Registrar of Births, Marriages and Deaths, and any-damn-thing else you'd care to name. Oh, I'm also Head of the Department of Highways, Madang Division."

"We haven't got any highways."

"Oh, yes we have. What do you think that road up the north coast is, eh? Now, where can we seat you, Mr Harris."

"How about over by the window there?"

"No, the Administrator Himself has been known to sit there."

6

"Mr McNicol?"

"Just between you and me, boy, his real name is Ramshackle McNackers. Only flunkies call him Mr McNicol."

"You're drunk, Mr Simmonds."

Don pushed his seat back and collected his plate of fish-and-rice and followed the Comptroller of Customs to another seat.

"Here we are, this one's vacant."

Don sat down.

"Who sits here?" he asked.

"Greathead. But he won't mind. He's dead." Simmonds leaned closer. "Got himself ambushed going into a village up in the bush." Simmonds sat down and watched Don eat.

"Why is your head bandaged?" he demanded.

"I got shot up crossing a creek with Morris."

"Morris shot you?" Simmonds suddenly brightened up and stared eagerly at him.

"No. A native."

"Oh, that all." He lost interest in Don and stared around the room.

The big ceiling fans chopped at the muggy heat. Don touched the bandage. It would come off tomorrow and he could see if he had been scarred. He rather hoped he had. Now that the excitement of the event was over, it would be nice to have a souvenir. He imagined walking into a pub back home in Adelaide and having someone, a girl, ask him: "How on earth did you get that scar, Mr Harris?"

"I copped an arrow. Bit of a dust-up with some head-hunters when I was on patrol. We were looking for a murderer and got ambushed."

In his mind he swaggered to the bar. Older men made way for him, glancing quickly at him, sideways. The girl was on his arm.

"I haven't seen you around, Harris?"

"Eh?" He returned to reality. The Administration Mess at Madang, on the North Coast of New Guinea, being cross-examined by a drunk clerk.

"Your face, it is unfamiliar to me."

"I've been on patrol since I arrived."

"Going back out again?"

7

"I rather hope so," Don said.

Simmonds shook his head. "You're mad," he said. "But then so are all your mates. Anyhow, welcome to Madang."

He extended his hand. Don took it and nodded eagerly. Simmonds squeezed hard and stood up.

"Must be off," he said. "Time and tide wait for no man."

Alone, Don poked at the grey, unappetizing mixture of boiled fish and rice. When he had finished he walked out onto the verandah and looked down at the harbour.

The sun was setting. For a moment he could see the inner lagoon, the docks, the giant copra shed and Carpenter's big concrete and iron store; beyond them the islands with palm fronds trailing on the calm, almost oily water. Then darkness enveloped him and the scene. It seemed to rise up out of the ground. He had an image of flying-foxes wheeling in the air, setting out on the nightly hunt. Then he turned and walked through the half-light, down the steps and along to the row of huts.

He let himself into his own quarters and found the matches by the door. He lit the lamp and trimmed the wick and placed it on the deal table by his bed. He sat down on the bed and looked at the publications on the table.

Native Labour Ordinances.

Report of the Administrator of the Australian Trust Territory of New Guinea to the League of Nations, 1935.

Agriculture in Tropical Territories: a government report.

He grimaced and lay back on the bed and folded his hands behind his head.

Nicholls, he thought. Fire and Brimstone Nicholls.

He wondered what nickname they would bestow upon him. Blood and guts? Quickdraw Harris? Don the Pirate? For a moment he felt a stab of fear. He remembered the name bequeathed to the Administrator. Oh, God, he thought. Spare me that sort of thing.

Outside, blackness swallowed all. Now the fishermen came out, sliding their canoes into the still water, holding aloft vivid torches of burning reeds as they poled into the lagoon, the light calling the fish to the surface. Along the coast the village fires burned red. And, clustered together, squares of

8

yellow light showed where "the Mastas" were preparing to live through another night of poker, billiards, bridge, and plain and simple drinking.

Beyond the coastal plain, the swamps and wandering river estuaries, rose the mountains, sudden and sharp, falling back in blackness upon blackness, each tier closing another door on the Mastas. Mountain ridge villages huddled against the fearsome night, waiting attack. In the blackness sorcery replaced courage as the measure of a man.

The mountains were cold and the people huddled closer in the smoke-filled houses. And beyond the last barrier of mountain, the last tier of the steps that led from the coast and the twentieth century into the Stone Age, a Masta slept in his tent, curled tight in his down-filled bag. About him his Patrol slept, too. Awake, the sentries faced out toward the blackness, shivering in the cold, waiting for attack, their fingers frozen with anticipation to the stocks of their Lee Enfield .303 rifles.

Don Harris stared at the mirror, and the mirror stared back. He touched his chin, feeling the youthful, blond stubble. Cadet Black was no older than him, but with his bushy beard seemed a real old trooper. He fingered the plaster on his head.

What the hell, he thought. He lifted a corner and tugged.

And there it was, white and jagged. It had cut into his eyebrow. But, instead of giving him a battle-scarred look, the scar raised his eyebrow, giving him a look of surprise.

He frowned, and the scar-tissue crinkled. That was better. If he drew his eyelids down, over the blue eyes that he considered too pale . . . now his face lost its youthful symmetry. Maybe he wouldn't have to grow the beard, after all.

He rubbed his chin again. He shaved about once every two days. Growing the beard would have been a fulltime occupation. And, if it had been as fair as his hair, no one would have been able to see it.

He nodded to the frowning reflection. It would have to do.

9

Diary: 1st May, 1937

The rumours have been given credence. The mystery of the village that did not come to greet us is solved. Wallace is dead.

Baranuma woke me out of a dream, last night. All day the thought of a poem had been teasing me, something that summed up my feelings as I stood on the escarpment. It came in the dream. John Keats: "On First Looking into Chapman's Homer". I woke to the sight of Baranuma's fear—for he is far more at home on the coast now, dealing with his role as my servant amongst the Rabaul-racists, than back out here in the "big-bush".

One of Wallace's Boys had staggered into our camp, more dead than alive, with arrow wounds in the back and thigh. He was in a very bad way, for he had carried out a considerable feat of endurance to make it down the escarpment, the rotted-human-bone arrow still lodged in his knee, working its poison into him. I don't think he will last. It was obvious that Wallace had been ambushed, and equally obvious that we could not move until daylight.

But my camp was well and truly awake. I doubled the guard, and told Sergeant Bukato to issue ammunition to the Police Boys. I operated on the wounded man as best I could, and located and removed the arrowhead. His back wound is less severe, but the action of staggering twenty miles with that thing lodged into the flexing part of his leg, has probably spelt his end. If he had lain up, perhaps? Who knows? But Masta Wallace told him to run and warn the Kiap, and run he did.

I sent a runner to Mount Hagen base, but it'll be a good two days before he reaches there—if he makes it. I suspect the whole country's now up in arms, and I equally suspect it's the result of whatever war party of prospectors passed through here.

We got cracking at first light. It was a long, hard haul up that escarpment. I left the wounded man with the carriers and two Police Boys. We needed to travel quick and light, with as much armament as possible. I kept remembering what I had written about Wallace. The irony stared me in the face as I panted up the track. We got to the remains of the old camp and picked up his trail pretty quickly.

He hadn't gone far—confirming my suspicions that he was merely going through the motions of heading downhill, waiting until I was gone, and then heading west for his El Dorado.

10

Which he has found. We got to his camp an hour before sundown. His gear was scattered over a wide area, well and truly looted. Rice and meat lay where it had fallen. We found his .44 revolver, the muzzle choked with mud, two spent bullets, one misfired, and three in the chambers. The grass was trampled in a circle around the camp and the tent riddled with arrows that had come from all directions. I'd say he'd been quietly surrounded, and then rushed.

Baranuma, who was keeping a discreet distance, ostensibly as a lookout, discovered the body, halfway up a ridge, about a thousand feet from the camp. There was a single-barrel shotgun lying beside him, the hammer cocked and a cartridge in the barrel. An unused cartridge lay beside him. I found his cartridge-belt further down the slope. He must have dropped it and hadn't the time to pick it up. He was fully dressed, but his boots were undone, and they must have slowed him down enough to get him. There were three arrows in him, two in his back. When I rolled him over, I found the third. They had had the presence of mind to split the force and send someone up the hill. It was a good piece of tactical thinking and made me sharpen my wits.

I fired off two revolver shots, to let any survivors know we were there. But I didn't have much hope, not if they'd circled him properly. I set my guard, and then Baranuma and I quartered the area with a tape and searched systematically.

We found her at the top of the hill. She lay face-up, still wearing her mother-of-pearl. When they had finished raping her they had forced an arrow up her vagina. The blood was caked along her thighs. Her eyes were wide open, enormous with terror. I turned her over. They had also inserted one up her anus. It, too, had bled.

I vomited. Baranuma walked away. He was green. He found two of Wallace's boys, but they were altogether finished. I got myself back under control and began making mental notes. How far she had run. Her position in relation to the camp. Her wounds. There was also an arrow in her side. That's what had stopped her.

We carried out the rest of that grim search in silence. We found another three of his boys. There had been thirty in all, plus four girls. I didn't want to find them, and was glad I didn't—but that wouldn't have made it any easier for them. I remembered the Gadzup raid, and those dismembered figures I had at first thought were dead, chained to the tree, until I saw the eyes, driven insane by their slow butchery—being held alive as fresh meat, to be sliced up when required.

Was that what Keats had in mind when he wrote:
Then felt I like some watcher of the skies

11

When a new planet swims into his ken . . .?

After sunset, two of Wallace's Boys crept into the camp. One was wounded in the hand, the other was intact. In the hissing light of the hurricane lamp, on a naked slope of the new planet, I took their statements.

Statement of Hagu, Labourer Indentured to David Wallace

After we left the Kiap we walked until mid-afternoon. The Masta stopped us and said we would make camp. He then told us we were going into the mountains. We were very afraid, and said so, but he talked to us and said it would be for a short time only, and that we had nothing to fear. We would get more girls and lots of gold-lip shell. We would become rich men. He then left us to go to the village of Parap to meet the Lu-lui, and buy some food. His servant, Gain, went with him.

They came back very soon, and we could see there had been trouble. The Masta said there was a misunderstanding and he had had to show the Lu-lui who was boss. He had not got any food.

Gain was afraid. He told us that the Lu-lui had been very cheeky to the Masta, and that the whole village was armed. The Lu-lui had told the Masta that he would not supply food to any more Europeans, because of the killings. The Masta asked what killings, and the Lu-lui said he knew and was only pretending that he didn't. They argued, and the Masta pulled out his revolver and hit the Lu-lui in the face. Armed warriors immediately came forward, but the Lu-lui stopped them. He told the Masta to leave. The Masta kicked him hard, and left.

The Masta said he wouldn't let the Lu-lui get away with insulting him, and that we would wait until the next day, and then show him who was boss.

But they attacked as the sun went down. The Masta was in his tent with his woman. She ran out first. We all grabbed our bows, and Gain came out with his shotgun. The Masta took the shotgun off him and told him to run for the Kiap.

They shot Gain in the back, as he was running. But he kept going. The Masta yelled at us to run for the top of the ridge, while he held the attackers off. We all ran. I saw some of us hit. His woman ran first and I think she got to the top of the hill.

I ran. I saw the Masta trying to do up his boots. Then he got shot in the back. He fired his revolver, and killed one attacker. He looked up to me and yelled a warning. A warrior was about to fire

12

his bow. I jumped and he only got me in the hand. The Masta was yelling for us to hide. I ran into the thick grass.

The others ran for the hill, but the attackers were already there. I heard the Masta yelling for his woman. Then he fired the shotgun. Then he got hit in the stomach and went down.

I saw them run up to camp. They killed the Masta's dog and took it with them. They cut open the packs and took food and mirrors and trade-beads. They were very excited when they found the steel tomahawks. I could hear a woman screaming on top of the hill. Then she stopped. The warriors came down the hill and left. When it was safe, I ran away.

Nicholls hung the shaving mirror on the tent ridge-pole. He angled it carefully, tapping it with his fingers. He frowned at his reflection, not studying it, simply frowning as a thought passed by. He looked around.

He'd not had time to shave that morning, or all that day. Now the camp was bright with unused energy, fear, even excitement. He rubbed his chin and looked to Baranuma, his servant, who had hooked the kerosene tin of water from the fire and was lugging it to him. Steam rose from it. Nicholls watched the strain in his Boy's face. He knew Baranuma did not enjoy ambush and fighting. He was not a "typical" Highlander in that regard. Maybe that difference was responsible for his abilities to think like a white man.

Nicholls glanced past him. The other Boys were roaming about the camp, unsure of themselves. Sergeant Bukato was drilling his men in an effort to keep their tension, their adrenalin, both on the boil and useful if an attack should come. It was the carrier Boys who were the hardest to handle. There were thirty of them, all recruited from the coast, unused to the High country, brought up with both the reality of attack from hills dwellers and the fantasies of their mothers, the scare-stories used in every society to keep kids in line: be good or the cannibals from the hills will get you.

Baranuma placed the bucket at his feet. Nicholls nodded to him, abstractedly, picturing how the Boys were feeling right now—three weeks' walk from home, surrounded by traditional enemies; the memory of the bodies of Wallace, of his woman, of his Boys, fresh in their minds. He groped for the razor and felt its edge. He stropped it lightly against his palm.

13

Evening was near. Clouds gathered along the distant mountains. The grassland slopes rose around them, like the shoulders of animals. The green vivid, almost rotten in colour. He stretched his chin and felt the flesh of his neck. With his left hand he pummelled the shaving brush into the soap dish that hung against the side of the bucket. He could hear the roar of the stream that ran at the base of their hill. Its sound might possibly have covered the noise of Wallace's ambushers, he thought.

He began to shave. The action cleared his mind. He studied his face. It had acquired lines around the eyes, from squinting into the raw sun of the Highlands, and lines beside the mouth—lines of tension and suspicion. As he watched, his right eyelid flickered. He tried to stop it, but it fluttered again. He concentrated hard, and nicked himself.

He swore and ignored the tell-tale eye. He was all right for a man of thirty-five, he told himself. His black hair was half-grey, but it would look better next time he was in civilization and had it cut. He did not subscribe to the image of the bearded warrior—the Romantic vision of the Patrol Officer favoured by some.

He thought more in terms of a commissioned officer of a battle-tested regiment. The sort of officer who shaved every day, in the trenches, in the mud, up here on the fringes of the jungle—as an example to his men.

True, he did not command a company, nor a platoon, nor a section for that matter, of Britain's finest—or even Australia's toughest. He commanded fifty of the most cynical people in the world: Melanesian natives, from scattered coastal hamlets, from offshore islands, from the Sepik swamps, and from these very Highlands. But they were tougher even than the Australians who had fought the Boers on the Boers' own terms. And they were as loyal as the King's household cavalry.

Now he started on the cheek, slicing the rough, black bristle from his face. He thrust his jaw forward, narrowing his dark brown eyes. There was a filament of tissue in the corner of each eye. Not glaucoma, but simply nature erecting a barrier against the penetration of the harsh light of the tropics. But it gave him a prematurely aged look.

The sun touched the distant mountains and he glanced

14

momentarily towards it. Shadows came rushing across the velvet hills now; silent and swift. Even up here, on the top of the island, there were mountain ranges rising behind mountain ranges. Perhaps that was the key to his love of the island. Its mystery was never revealed. You climbed every ridge, and beyond it was another, more remote, more untouchable. And so you went on climbing.

He smiled and returned to his shaving. Baranuma was back at the fire, attending to the meal. Soon Nicholls could put his feet up, pour himself a whisky, and open a fresh page of his journal.

He turned his face and commenced work on the other cheek.

Diary: 1st May, 1937

Now it is night. We're camped on top of the hill, where she died. Where Wallace thought safety lay. We've buried them all. I think we are safe here. We've cut the growth back, giving us clear fire-lines. All weapons are issued. Another two of Wallace's Boys have limped in. We'll keep two-hour shifts. I'm on at midnight. Must get some sleep.

Wallace's diary. So that's what he thought of me. I admit my embarrassment, and I admit the truth of his observations. That's why they hurt. But I don't believe we can do anything about our basic personalities. We can shape around them, but that core is too solid, formed too well in early life. He is right about my being tempted by his lifestyle . . . but his death verifies my feelings about his attitudes to the locals. He believed in the invincibility of the white man, and that is the final mistake.

Noises.

So we are to be subject to attack by vilification. They are out there now, screaming abuse, telling my men just what will be done with them after the attack. They think there are women with us, too. I don't think they will attack. I'm very tired.

2.15 am. The worst is over. The abuse has slackened off. A few arrows loosed at us. My men are good men. They're scared. I'm scared. But we're sticking to our posts. And for what? Ten shillings a month for them. And the glory. We mustn't forget the glory. I'm too jumpy to sleep.

15

Wallace's diary mentions a German team, led by Herman Ludwig. I can remember questioning Ludwig about infraction of the Native Labour Ordinance, a year ago. Nasty piece of work. Wallace suggests confirmation of the native rumours. Quoting a few extracts.

No word of Ludwig. Rumours are that he's had some trouble with the nigs, which'd hardly be surprising. He's a bit of a bash-artist at the best of times.

Ludwig kai-kaing with us. He's very nervous. Reckons the nigs are after him. He could be right, too. Damned if I like his manner, or that of his mates. Germans all. Bloody Lutherans should never have been allowed into the country, filling the poor ignorant kanaka with Christianity, bad rice, and worse ideas—making them think there's only one thing worse than the devil and that's an English-speaking prospector. I noticed a couple of young Marys in his camp. They were in chains. I didn't say anything. His ideas are sound, and his samples even sounder. There is gold out there. But I won't travel with him, that's for sure. I'll pick up an Australian Patrol, and go in with them, and meet him over the border.

There was light over the distant mountains. The sun would be in the sky soon. He shivered, rubbing his arms, stamping his feet. One of the other men looked at him and raised an eyebrow. Barum grinned. They were cold. Waiting was what made them cold.

There was mist below them, muffling the roar of the stream. As yet it was too early for the birds to begin calling. The stars had faded and there was only light cloud against the mountains.

They had kept warm during the night through the effort of screaming abuse at the Kiap and his party. They had run and stamped and shouted, hurling their invective across the hilltops. They were keen with excitement, excitement that displayed itself in the inventiveness of the abuse. Their insults touched on the sexual habits of the Kiap's mother—assuming he had one and had not emerged, grunting, from the arse of a pig. They derided the black men who were with the Kiap.

16

Sure, the Kiap might well be some returned, wandering, lost Spirit of the Dead; but that made the others simply his rubbishmen, cleaners of his shit, drinking his piss instead of water. They probably couldn't raise a decent Snake amongst the lot of them. They had the sort of Snakes that didn't sniff out the hole in a woman, but buried themselves in holes in the ground. Well, those Snakes would soon be cut off their living flesh.

Now they were quiet. The time of insult had passed. The time of action was close. The Kiap's party, the party of Sky People, had not replied. So, if they were Sky Gods, then they were a particularly weak group. They were not like the others that had been through the valley: Sky People who killed before you could begin to work up a good insult. Sky People who took pigs and women and vegetables and offered no trade—unless death itself was a trade. Perhaps that was all they had to trade. Perhaps, coming from the Land of the Dead, that was their only currency.

But this party had not responded. They had huddled in their little, portable houses, shivering with fear, clutching their sticks.

Their presence represented a manifestation of the Power— whether of the Earth Goddess or the Sky Gods was debated. They could even represent a new force in the cosmos, an until now unknown third party to the Spirit World.

Whatever their origins, their genealogy, the important thing was to use them in the battle for supremacy in the valley— just like a man used his knowledge of the emanations of the Earth Goddess' forces, and made his gestures to her in his spot to ensure crops and pigs; and placated the Sky Gods and the trackless spirits of the dead to ensure they did not return to louse up the workings of village politics.

Perhaps, even, the Spirit World was at war. The Sky People could be warriors of the Sky Gods, sent to attack the Earth Spirits of the Earth Goddess. Or, they could be Her troops, returning from successful ventures in the heavens.

"Should we get them now, before they are awake?" one of the men asked Barum.

The others waited on his word. He was the acknowledged fight-leader. He had the sort of mind that could work out

17

strategy. While other men were still debating whether to hang
the fighting stones from the rafters he was up on a hilltop,
staring at the land, noting where a man could creep close to
the enemy; how a party of ambushers could outflank an
advancing war party and, while the business of insult and
abuse went on, move in close enough to attack.

Even the Sky People recognized his talent. For, some years
previously, when Mastas Mick and Jim had been the first Sky
Gods to descend on the mountain valleys, they had issued
Barum with the ceremonial hat with the bright and beautiful
emblem on it. They declared him "Lu-lui", keeper of the
"book".

"No," he said, "they're so weak we can take them any time."

"Samura would have attacked by now."

There was a sudden tension among the men. No one looked
at the man who had spoken that. Slowly, Barum turned to
stare him down.

"What courage was there in his act, eh? He might as well
have gone and killed his own children and pretended that was
as 'brave' as slaying the prospector."

"He would not have taken the prospector without our
help," one of Barum's friends mumbled.

"That's right," Barum said. "The attack by the Gafu would
have failed if we had not been there. And now we must face
the Sky People alone, while Samura and the rest of his cowards
hide out on their ridge-top."

"So, let's take him now. Quickly, before he can do us any
harm."

"It's too late! Look!"

As they watched a man, a black man, emerged from a little,
portable house, shivering, rubbing his hands together. He
went off to one side. He hawked up phlegm—the sound
carrying clear and sharp to the watching warriors. He eased
his Snake out and aimed it at the soil. The watchers grinned.

Barum rubbed his jaw. It was bruised and tender where the
prospector had hit it with his stick. He had deserved to die, as
the previous prospector should have died—but that one had
proved too tough even for the boastful Samura. Barum
wondered if this Sky God would have any women amongst his
party.

18

"Now's the time," someone said.

Barum grinned and nodded.

"Half of us," he said. "You," he touched one of his men, "take the lead. I will take the rest around the hill to the other side. Go quietly. Don't show yourself. If those sticks are like the others they can kill you at a good distance, beyond bowshot . . ."

"He's looking up here!"

They fell silent. They watched the man stare at their hilltop. Then he yawned and stretched. He hid his Snake back in his clothes and turned his back to them. A lucky bowshot could have brought him down. To turn like that meant he couldn't have seen them.

The warriors glanced at each other. The bond of the fight held them. They could feel it flow between them. Barum nodded thoughtfully and the first assault force moved around the hill. He watched them go and then pointed with his chin in the opposite direction.

Diary: 2nd May, 1937, Evening

Baranuma woke me. I don't remember any sleep. I woke fully dressed, with a bad taste in my mouth. It was first light. Baranuma's eyes were enormous.

He had gone out for a leak, prior to stoking up the fire. He had seen armed warriors on the next hill. They were keeping low. He thought they meant business. He had kept cool and strolled nonchalantly back to the tent. I knew if I showed myself they would know we had twigged them. I sent him to wake Sergeant Bukato and get him to organize our resistance.

Lik Lik could sense the fear in the air. She was whimpering on my bed. I eased her off and eased on my boots. I thought about her playmate, Wallace's old dog: Major. He was probably inside the bellies of the men now advancing on us.

Is this how "stout Cortez" woke up, the day after he stared at the Pacific? "Silent, upon a peak in Darien"? I thought, as I laced my boots, that it was someone like me, not the poet, who would understand Cortez's thoughts. And that I was closer, this moment, to knowledge of Ulysses' feelings than Chapman, or Keats, or

19

Homer for that matter. Across the years the warriors salute each other.

God, the junk we fill our minds with to avoid thinking of our own, approaching death!

I checked my revolver and made sure I had ammunition ready.

Baranuma returned. Bukato and four of the Police had rolled out the back of their tent. The rest of the Police were crawling to the perimeters of the camp. Baranuma fondled the whimpering dog. I could see Baranuma's fear, too. I caressed his head, like he caressed the dog's. He tried to smile at me.

God I hate murdering . . . [at this point, in his diary, Nicholls scratched out "murdering" and wrote "killing"] . . . killing the poor bastards. But they're warriors. In the end what they understand is force of arms.

And they must understand that justice will be done. No matter how bad were Ludwig and his party, their own acts cannot be countenanced. I will bring Ludwig to book. He will stand trial for crimes against the law.

Our law. Anglo-Saxon law.

They rushed us. They were good. They came from two directions. But we were better. Bukato and his group cut the first attackers down, killing two of them immediately. The noise, the smoke, the stink of cordite, turned them on their heels and they ran, screaming, dropping the weapons.

The other group came in behind us. They were screaming. But they saw what happened to their friends and their resolve wavered, fatally for them. I shot one with my revolver, a young fellow. I saw the look of surprise on his face. I think they feel surprise more than pain, because they just aren't expecting to be killed at a distance like that. He fell against the old man, the leader by the look of him. One of the Police Boys stopped another one. The old man threw himself to the ground and his mates did likewise.

Now it is night and we are camped in their village. We sustained a few injuries: only two serious though. But there are already two stretcher cases from Wallace's Boys. I might need to send a stretcher-party back to Mount Hagen.

The locals are now suitably abashed, and have had first-hand experience of our weaponry. It never fails to impress.

Such skirmishes as this will go on wherever Patrols make contact. They have to understand we are not the weaklings they think we are. There is no other way about it—unless you, yourself, want to join that large troop of dead Kiaps who held their fire too long, and now will fire no more.

20

The old man is the appointed Lu-lui. I must speak to Jim Taylor next time I see him about the suitability of the man for the position. Of course—Anglo-Saxon law—he is innocent until proven guilty beyond reasonable doubt. As yet I have no evidence that it was he who slew Wallace and his party. Let's hope I can get something out of him when I interview him in the morning.

What a European can never credit is the way they regard war as we might regard a cricket or football match! The Lu-lui has already come to express his admiration for our battle-prowess. We spoke in the Mount Hagen tongue. He talked as if we had just finished a minor round football match! As if my ruck had been superior to his and that, alone, had made the difference. As if, next time, with his best players back in the team . . .

Now he has arranged a celebratory feast of truce and has offered me a woman. I have tried to explain my position. But . . . when in Rome.

I guess it has always been like this. When cultures meet. First they fight. Then they eat. Then they fuck. So Ulysses met Circe.

"Silent, upon a peak in Darien"?

Baranuma was grinning. From his position, squatting behind Masta Nicholls' tent, he had an excellent view of the proceedings. The Masta had resisted the awesome temptations of the prospector's girl. How he would never know— certainly there were clear advantages in not giving up all your seed to women; for if magic were to be done, then women were the force to reckon with, and a dollop of your sperm was something that could cause incalculable harm in the wrong hands. But a man had a lot of force down there between his legs. He couldn't walk around all his life with it unspent, his nuts getting larger and larger, until they were so swollen he couldn't walk. No. You had to take the risk some time, even when in alien country, amongst potential enemies, and the Masta's force was surely much greater than any that could be mustered here in the mountains.

21

When was he going to get on with it? Here, he had her now, not as plump as the prospector's woman, but nice all the same. Admittedly she was glistening with pig-fat — a thing not necessary on the coast, where the climate was better, and you didn't freeze those valuable nuts off. Baranuma had forgotten how cold the mountains were; how your balls could ache with it, unless liberally smeared with grease.

The Masta was offering her a drink. She was gagging on it, giggling and choking at the same time. He was touching her, but only with his fingertips. There was a certain reluctance to come to grips with the issue at hand.

Then he let go of her and looked up and Baranuma froze, for the Masta was looking straight through the tent, into him. Was he being seen? The Masta could read minds, that was known. Had he heard Baranuma's lewd thoughts? But then he bellowed:

"Baranuma! Baranuma!"

Baranuma slid away from the tent as softly as he could. His bare feet made no sound. He waited a moment, brushed down his lap-lap, and walked to the tent entrance.

"Masta?" he inquired, as innocently as he could.

"Wash-wash," Nicholls said, glaring at him, trying to keep up the dignity it was a European's duty to keep up before natives. "One-fella Mary, pek-pek bilong him . . ." He wrinkled his nose to indicate the problem.

There was a gleam of amusement in his servant's eyes. Nicholls frowned and the amusement slid away. The polite facade returned.

What I want. Nicholls thought, is a clean woman. I don't care if she's black, white, or brindle. I just want to be able to touch her without my hand slipping off, and without the stench of rancid, weeks-old pig-fat. I know that without it they'd freeze to death, but she can put a fresh layer on tomorrow. Tonight she's mine. I won the right to her in battle, and by God I'm going to enjoy it.

She stood uncertainly in the tent, trying to follow the interchange between the Masta and his servant. She had no Pidgin. Nicholls did not speak her dialect, and he was damned if he'd have a translator in bed with them. He smiled at her

22

reassuringly, as his servant went in search of hot water. She smiled back nervously.

Nicholls indicated the Johnny Walker bottle and she giggled, shaking her head. She was about twenty, he decided. She had received her first lot of initiatory tattoos on her cheeks. Her face had shed the puppy-fat of a diet overladen with carbo-hydrates. She had a prominent nose and cheekbones to match. There was an old bruise across her cheek. He reached out to touch it and she flinched. He smiled to reassure her. There was no evidence of fracture. A boyfriend must have caught her one, he decided. Her breasts were—and his eyes returned eagerly to them—full and firm, with large nipples. He wanted to kiss them, but restrained himself, waiting for Baranuma to return with hot water and soap.

Still smiling at her, pantomiming relaxation and enjoyment, he picked up the bottle and poured himself another shot. He added some water, and sipped the drink. The image of a girl rose up in his memory. He was dancing with her at a hotel in Sydney, ten years before. He recalled, vividly, the texture of her dress, the wave in her hair, and the scent of her perfume. He remembered her silk stockings.

Baranuma arrived. His face was very grave. The girl stared in fear at the bucket of water. What magic was the Masta about to do? Baranuma looked to him, waiting to see who had the honour. Nicholls shrugged and set his glass down and took the bucket.

"That will be all, Baranuma," he said, stiffly. His servant nodded, his eyes straying to the girl, and backed out of the tent.

Nicholls wrung out the soapy rag and grabbed the girl. She shrieked when it touched her, and struggled against him. He smiled at her, tried to soothe her, and kept washing. She screamed desperately. My God, he thought. They'll think I'm killing her.

"It's all right," he said. "I only want to clean you up. Savvy? We wash. It makes it much nicer."

Baranuma's sides were hurting. How he had avoided screaming with laughter he didn't know. Now he rolled on

23

the ground, safely in the dark, his fist against his mouth, the tears running down his eyes. But he couldn't tear himself away from the scene. Weakly, he dragged himself back to the tent, and applied his eye again to the opened seam.

The Masta had subdued her now. He was soaping her behind. Her fear was giving way to a certain interest in the proceedings. He had to admit that the Masta had the right touch. He knew the way to a woman's heart: right up between her thighs.

Now he had finished that part of the operation. He paused for a drink. Again, he offered her one. To his surprise, she accepted. Again, she choked on it, but she kept it down, enjoying its afterglow. She was staring with obvious intent at the Masta's crutch as he stripped his trousers off.

Ah, there it was. Her eyes were wide. She, of all her generation, had the honour to see for herself the legendary White-snake, that was supposed to travel of its own free will as the Masta slept, to sneak into the houses of young women and have at them in their sleep

Nicholls found her interest in his member disconcerting. True, it was harder than it had ever been, almost vertical in its desire to be into her. And her obvious interest was not decreasing it. She knelt down and took it in her hands, rubbing it lightly, causing him to tense against her touch.

"Oh, God," he moaned.

He did not hear, from outside his tent, the quickly-choked snicker. He motioned her up and laid her out on the stretcher, spreading her thighs with his hands.

Baranuma had stopped laughing. Quietly, he loosened his lap-lap and found his own rigid penis. He sighed and began to caress it, watching as the Masta ran his tongue over her breast. Mastas had a strange fetish for the breasts of young women, nuzzling into them like infants after milk. But if milk was their desire, then they always chose the wrong women.

But, enough speculation. The Masta sank into her and she moaned and wrapped her legs around him. They were still a bit greasy. There was still a certain odour to them. But what the hell, a man led by his Snake is blind, they say. And the Masta was well and truly led now. He was bucking and

24

groaning, his sounds carrying out into the night . . . to the delight of his own men who stood next to the critically listening villagers, assessing the performance of the Kiap.

And Nicholls could hold back no longer. He roared and let go his load and she screamed back. The stretcher collapsed under their threshing, and they floundered together on the ground. All the tension left him, all the fear, and he rediscovered the ecstacy he had felt only three mornings ago, silent upon that Highlands peak.

Afterwards, he remembered the image of the white girl. He realized he had not seen her at all. He had only remembered her clothes. He had never seen her flesh, never touched it, and never plumbed its depths.

She looked at him anxiously, and he grinned and slapped her thigh, and she relaxed against him, but kept her legs firmly clamped together. She shivered.

Realizing the problem, Nicholls wrapped her in a blanket. She smiled her thanks, but kept her legs drawn up—not from any modesty, but to protect the valuable load of Masta's power.

She would go outside in a moment to urinate. One of the women would be waiting, with a swab, and they would have a real hold over the Masta. The men had failed with fighting. The women would not fail with magic.

Barum waited for the Kiap to come. He was trusting that his opposite number from the Gafu, Samura, had cleared away the last of the bodies of the prospector's men. Barum was reasonably sure that the Kiap's inquiries into their whereabouts would not be exhaustive. This particular Kiap had been in the Highlands a fair amount of time now. He had acquired a working knowledge of Highland ways. He thought like a Highlander, which made him dangerous. But it also made him predictable. Who could predict what a Kiap who thought only like Kiaps and Mastas would do?

Barum was at ease with his world. From where he sat, beside the men's house, he could see over the palisades to

25

the top of the tower he had erected at that point where he judged the forces of the earth were felt most keenly. Other men had disagreed with the siting of the spot, but he knew it to be right. And now the tower guided those forces into his land, into his pigs, bringing him good fortune. The legs of the tower sank into the belly of the Earth Goddess. He anointed them with red earth for her, and she sent him her power. So that sitting here, waiting for the Masta, he could feel it coming to him through the soil.

That power which had increased his pig herds made him a Big Man. The Biggest in the district. Which was why Masta Jim had conferred on him the title of Lu-lui, giving him a cap and a badge and the book, and had carried out certain ceremonies with him. The ceremonies, though unintelligible, clearly marked him for more power. Now, in festivities with the neighbouring people, he was expected to bear much of the brunt of the cost of entertainment. His pig-largess had won him respect throughout the valley, and with that respect had come more power in his own lands.

With power came responsibility. The responsibility for the ambush was his. And the ambush had not gone well. But in Highlands fighting a war is rarely finished. A battle had been lost. Lessons had been learnt from it. Now trade relations could be assumed between the warring parties. While trade went on, the manoeuvring for the next attack could begin.

The Masta appeared from his tent. He carried his armament with him. Barum watched him look around at the palisade that enclosed the village; at the doors of the women's houses, many of them still boarded up—anticipating trouble; then at his own men, arrayed behind the rope they had strung out that night, watching coolly and calmly. Barum could see they were seasoned fighters.

The Masta's dog ran after him, and was called back by one of his men, an unarmed man who took it back to the Masta's personal tent. Presumably his servant. Barum smiled and squirmed his haunches on the ground, getting ready for the next form of assault.

He wondered how his daughter had got on with the Masta, whose loose-legged walk through the village attested to a vigorous night's sexual combat. Again, it might look as if the Masta had won that round. But it was what happened behind the scenes that dictated the final outcome. Barum was certain the women had obtained what they needed to work their magic.

He rose as Nicholls approached, and extended his hand.

"Good morning, Masta," Barum said, with suitable deference, knowing this was the style Nicholls favoured. He spoke in the dialect of his cousins, those who had known the Sky People much longer than he.

"Good morning, Lu-lui," Nicholls replied, watching his face closely, trying to read the man's thoughts behind the polite mask he now wore. "You wish to speak the language of Mount Hagen?"

"They are my cousins. I know the tongue."

"I don't know yours, yet," Nicholls said. "But I shall learn it." He grinned. "After last night, I have an incentive."

"She was good?"

"Excellent, Lu-lui . . ." Nicholls gestured with his hand, a gesture of friendship. "My name is Nicholls, Masta Nicholls."

His host nodded and smiled, as courteously as he did. "Barum," he said. "That is my name."

Barum withdrew his hand from Nicholls' and took him by the elbow, motioning him to sit on the step by the men's house. Barum himself sat on the earth, that he could better feel the power there.

"There are different groups amongst the Sky People?" he asked.

"The Sky People are no different to Valley people," Nicholls said, sitting, watching him closely. "We have our differences. We have wars."

"When the Sky People first came, it was thought they were different to men."

Nicholls frowned, searching for a way to steer the conversation down the paths he wanted it to go. He glanced around the village, masking his reactions to it. That which looked picturesque from a distance, with its woven and thatched cottages, its patchwork quilt of cultivated fields, and the roving, grunting pigs—that had caused people like Frank Hides to eulogize on a "lost civilization" in these

27

hidden valleys, people of "Semitic" profiles, that had caused a flurry of activity amongst the "lost tribe of Israel" theorists— stank when you were in it. The ground was foul with pig faeces, with urine, with the ashes of ancient fires. Hookworm was rife, and hygiene unknown.

But that was probably the case amongst the tribes of Israel, too.

"The Sky People, the Australian Administration, are different to your people, Barum. In our laws, we do not sanction the killing of innocent people."

Barum breathed out, touching the earth with the palm of his hand. Nicholls watched the gesture, mildly irritated by it.

"I am here to talk about murder, Barum. Not death in legitimate fighting. Not warfare . . ."

"You are here to talk about the murder of the Highlands people by the prospectors?"

Nicholls studied the calm, brown eyes in the bearded, seamed face. He could not begin to guess the man's age. The nose was sharply hooked. You could call it "Semitic". But the tattoos? And the colour? Deepest, darkest mahogany. He forced himself to relax, to enter a state of mind where he could feel the levels, the paths of thought that this man from the Stone Age was pursuing.

"The rape and murder of a girl, Lu-lui. The murder of an Australian prospector, called Wallace—who may have abused and assaulted you, but whose conduct did not warrant killing. The disappearance of the people who were with Wallace . . ."

The calm brown eyes watched. The man's head was slightly cocked, listening. Again his hand extended, palm flat, and touched the soil. Nicholls found himself watching it. And was again irritated by the seeming pointlessness of the gesture.

"I will tell you everything, Masta. I will begin by talking about the prospector. Not the one you refer to, but the one who came before him. A demon . . ."

Nicholls let the man have his say. They sat in the shade of casuarina trees, that screened out the heat of the Highlands sun. The shadows were permanent in the village. Several pigs grunted their way towards the two men. Looking up at the sound of voices they fled from Nicholls' alien appearance.

28

"We were afraid for our lives, Masta. He came and laughed at us and killed a man. Here, in the village. The man's wife, his children, were watching. He forced others to go with him, against their wills, knowing he was going into the country of cannibals, way up in the mountains, beyond all civilization.

"So, when this other prospector arrived, asking for him—'A party of prospectors, led by a thin man with a red beard'— when your Wallace asked this, and then began to behave as though he, too, were a killer, what were we to do?

"We held a meeting with our neighbours and determined a course of action."

Nicholls interrupted. "Which neighbours?"

Barum blinked, waving his hand. "The people of Gafu village. The people of Kinan."

"And at this meeting, you determined to rape and torture innocent women?"

Barum shrugged. "I know nothing of this. My people shot their arrows at Wallace's tent, just to frighten him. We then fell back. We know nothing of this other business."

"So you deny all knowledge of what happened on the hill? With the woman?"

Barum looked at him steadily. "I have told you what took place. What other people did, I cannot say."

"What happened to the bodies?"

"I cannot say."

The clear, brown eyes stared into Nicholls' own. Little runners of glaucoma could just be seen at the edges. If the man lived another ten years, he would be blind. But Nicholls felt he was already at his prime, perhaps past it, and in this land death came before the age of sixty.

"I know nothing of bodies, Masta. Perhaps you should speak to the Gafu people."

"And the Gafu will tell me: 'It was like this, Masta. At the attack, we surrounded the tent. The people of Parap, they rushed up the hill after the girl . . .'."

Barum nodded sagely. "That is true, Masta, very true. The Gafu are acknowledged masters of lying. They are very treacherous, those people. Only because I have this wife from there do I bother to associate with them. And she is no

29

better than the rest of them, let me tell you . . ."

"I don't want to know about your blasted wife!" In irritation, Nicholls had switched to English. He frowned. Barum watched him steadily, anticipating his next line of questioning, waiting with an answer already formed, his hand resting lightly, knuckles against the earth. Nicholls stood up.

Sergeant Bukato checked his men, seeing that they were well-stationed behind the rope barricade that enclosed the huts allocated to the Patrol. The rope was not a physical barrier, but it served to mark where the authority of the Kiap began.

Sergeant Bukato was on edge, sensing the nearness of a fight. He had survived more attacks than any other man in the Constabulary, beginning his life with the Europeans amongst the German missionaries and plantation owners of the Madang coast, before the Great War and the change to Australian administration.

There were no children to be seen. That was the vital clue. The women's houses were all boarded up. They might be in there, but it was more likely they had been removed to safety. The only children left were youths, young fighting men, watching from various buildings with their fathers, all seemingly casually dispersed, but all giving off the scent of adrenalin. All waiting on a signal.

Sergeant Bukato thought that the Masta's decision to talk was the wrong one. These people's guilt was clear. They admitted it. Now they must learn the consequences. The jails of Rabaul and Salamaua were overflowing with murderers waiting trial or execution. Save the extra work of charging them, getting them to the coast, onto a ship, over the waters.

Sergeant Bukato saw the Kiap rise. He heard his angry voice. He pushed the safety off his rifle. The Lu-lui was watching closely. Again Bukato glanced around his men. The Kiap's personal servant was crouched behind a hut, clutching the Kiap's dog. Their eyes met and the servant looked away. Sergeant Bukato permitted himself half a sneer.

Barum could feel the eyes of the village on him. The moment was at hand. He knew that if he did not order it now, they would rush later, of their own accord, when the Patrol was spread out through the fields. He was reasonably certain that being in the village would restrict the Masta's movements.

Barum knew they could not win. But it was also important to act. He stood and raised his arm as Nicholls turned and began to walk back to his own men.

Sergeant Bukato saw the gesture and dropped onto one knee, his rifle coming up automatically to his shoulder.

"Masta!" he yelled.

Nicholls saw him kneel and, before he shouted, was already running, throwing himself into his lines.

"Don't shoot!" he yelled.

Suddenly the village was full of men. Plumed heads. Flashing pearl-shell. Spears in hands that, a moment before, had been empty. Feet drumming on the earth.

"Fire over their heads!" Nicholls ordered, seeing Bukato was going to fire, no matter what.

The sound of the rifles halted the yelling stampede. The memory of the damage inflicted by these weapons in the previous clash was all too clear. Sergeant Bukato swung his gun down, second barrel primed, aimed straight into the hesitating charge.

"You! Sergeant!" Nicholl's voice was fierce.

The white man and the old sergeant stared at each other. Neither smiled.

"I'll have your balls if you fire, Bukato."

"Yes, sir," the sergeant said. Then he grinned. "The Lu-lui's having trouble."

Bukato pointed with his chin. Nicholls looked. Barum, laughing at Nicholls' ignominious scramble for safety, had been caught short by the sudden sound of the guns. His belly had gone to water. No shot had hit him, but fear had evacuated his bowel, where he stood.

31

His warriors had all dispersed.

"Let's get out of here, sergeant," Nicholls said.

"Yes, sir."

The two men stood and moved back amongst their troops. Baranuma hurried to Nicholls with his dog. Sergeant Bukato watched sardonically as the Kiap fondled the anxious animal's ears.

Diary: 3rd May, 1937

It is clear that there is substance to the rumours of Ludwig's atrocities. How else can I explain the suicidal hostility of that village? According to the records, Jim Taylor made first contact with these people two years ago. It would have been Taylor and Black. Mick Leahy no doubt has sniffed around, bringing his brand of "shoot, and then shake hands" diplomacy. But all Australian contact has been strictly according to Hoyle. We observed the rules, and they observed the rules.

We had to run the gauntlet to get clear of the village. The warriors lined the razorbacks, screaming obscenities at us. Bukato wanted to take a party up behind them, and I had the Dickens of a job restraining him. His blood is up. In a way, I fear that man. We have taken him from some unknown native hell—some personal tragedy I can sense, but not fathom, and not discover in any records left us by the Germans—and trained him in the considerable European art of armed combat. He has brought to it the lore of jungle fighting, and the sensitivity of a man possessed. I do not "control" his actions. At best, I "guide" them. Heaven help us if he were to go renegade.

The poor old Lu-lui! The ignominy of it. A man can train his eyes not to show fear, his nostrils not to quiver, his nerves not to jump. But the final reflex is the bowel spasm.

Now, safely in camp, I can admit something to myself. I no longer enjoy the fighting. As I walked away from the Lu-lui, my back to him, knowing he was quite capable of planting a spear in it, that the only thing preventing that action was his respect for the gesture. My back "crawling", the flesh hunkering in readiness for

32

the blow, the hairs waving like psychic tentacles, trying to sense the arrow notched to the bow, the hand lifting the spear from the ground. Things I have done before. My eyes on Bukato's solid, reliable face. Aware of Baranuma cowering in the hut, clutching Lik Lik to his chest—let her take the arrow first. Things that, yes, I have enjoyed before—the clarity of the totally concentrated mind. The sexual thrill of discovering you are still alive. And that's something no strategist will admit to. The hoarse shout. The bunched reflexes heaving me forward, into my lines. All around me the smells of fear: sweat and urine . . .

I've had enough.

But I know no other trade. I am a Kiap. I dispense "Native Administration". I put my body on the line that divides the Stone Age from Western civilization. The two will eventually accommodate themselves to each other. They will come together, like the meshing of giant cogs. The grease between the cogs: Patrol Officers, Cadets, Prospectors, Native Police.

It is becoming obvious to me that no one would take this job on unless there was something inside him, something dark, unrecognized. In a sense, we play with death. Our own death. We are born as misfits to our own peaceful, slumbering culture. We cannot fit. We are the outsiders amongst schoolmates, at university, even in the Army. We begin to scour the countryside for somewhere that will welcome us. All of us have a history of movement, of search: from country to country, or trade to trade. We are never still. We are seeking.

And, here, we find a world more violent than our most secret dreams. Here, we can play our game with death.

There is no difference between me and the Lu-lui who organized the killing and pack rape of the girl. There is no difference between me and Ludwig. There is no difference between me and Sergeant Bukato. I know that because of the eager way I seek them out. I want to embrace them, but fear to embrace them. And so I kill them instead.

It is time to stop writing. If I plunge any deeper I will lose the will to survive. I don't want my motives to be so obvious to myself.

One thing, though. If I return to this valley—and there is no way I can't return—if I return, I shall have need of that extra protection. What I asked Lee Chiang to make when I was last in Rabaul, that I told myself was only a "game" . . . Well, what is it now? Prophecy? Admission of failure of my nerve? Recognition that it is time I got out of this "game", and that I can't get out of it . . . Stop writing!

33

· CHAPTER TWO ·

So, predictably, the Australian wasn't going to make it. Well, that was hardly a surprise. They could manage without him. Like all of his countrymen, in the final analysis he was unreliable. And Ludwig felt a surge of anger. The country was his: his people's. Germans had settled it. Germans had traded, planted, farmed, mined. German missionaries had attempted to bring the word of God to the heathen. And then, in 1914, a tinpot squad of Australians had taken the Rabaul radio station, and that was that. They had won by knowing which side to be on in the larger arena. And the same now as then. As the blacks became cheekier, so the Australians shifted their allegiance to them, away from Europe. They were prepared to sell out their own race.

Ludwig could feel the force of the conspiracy, that extended from Sydney to Rabaul, to the League of Nations, waiting to read the mealy-mouthed reports on the Australian "Trust Territory". It embraced Lae and Madang on the coast. It crept up the trails, to Bulolo and Wau, even to Mount Hagen outpost . . . and all those good German names: Wilhelm, Bismarck, all appropriated by these sons of bitches. The conspiracy followed him towards the border, towards Dutch territory, so he could feel it as he stood by the river, waiting for the Australian, and knowing he would not arrive. That he had buckled under the pressure of the watching eyes and told the Kiap.

Still, the Kiap would not come into Uncontrolled Territory after him. And it was only there, on the border, in the real wilds, that you could trace the gold to its final source.

His son, Walter, had understood that—even more instinctively than himself. But Walter had been born on the trail. After his mother died he had been raised on the trail of gold. His toys were gold.

34

The memory of his dead son made him shiver, despite the brooding, clammy heat. He wiped his brow and tugged at his straggling red beard. He checked behind him, along the track. Rudi and Paul waited patiently. They were good men, but they weren't his own blood. In the end, it was only blood you could trust.

In the end, he had failed his son.

And the eyes flickered through the trees, in the deeper shadows. They gave him no peace. He woke at night, out of dark dreams, to find them staring in his face. The eyes of dead men. The eyes of the waiting, breathing, living blacks.

He swung back to his line and gestured. They were on their feet immediately, straining at their loads. He had no trouble with labour now they were in cannibal territory. No need for chains. The only safety was the safety of the line. Of the shotguns.

He shivered again. The chill was on him. He could recognize the beginnings of a malaria bout. Tonight he would hole up and sweat it out. Tonight they would be at the junction of the rivers, and he would be ready to make the decision: from which stream did the alluvium come? From which headwater sprang the mother-lode?

He commenced walking. Behind him, the line swayed forward, heads bowed against the fifty-pound packs, head-straps cutting a permanent stripe across foreheads, clasping staffs hewn from the bush to help force their legs onward. Rudi and Paul spaced along the line, each covering a different flank with the ever-swivelling barrels of their guns.

The river was brown and swift and ugly. It could not be crossed. They followed the native path along its bank, knowing it had to lead to trouble, but knowing there was no other way through the jungle. Ready to meet trouble with trouble of their own making. Ludwig was confident that the bush telegraph would have passed on the message of his coming, and with it the message of his abilities as a warrior.

Rudi was the furthest back of the Germans. There were two carriers behind him, men toiling against the added burden of fear, aware with each step they took that it could easily be their last. Men keyed to the limit for a week now, unable to sleep from the strain on their nerves, jumping at

35

their own shadows, and ready to believe that the Masta could indeed see eyes out there. That they, themselves, could see eyes.

Johnnie Johnson saw the smoke column on the horizon and corrected his course. The cross-wind he had picked up in the Ramu Valley eased off once you were into the mountains. And once you were over the plateau then the wind tended northerly. He was flying a Ford Tri-Motor. The view forward, through the arc of the prop, was of hills rising from the plateau; distant, circling mountains. He located Mount Wilhelm and again checked his course.

His eyes moved ceaselessly across the gauges, through the window to the wings, and back. He flew as much with his body as his eyes. His thighs listened to the vibrating metal body of the plane. His hands read the shiver in the wings and tail. He didn't bother with a map any more. This was old, familiar territory, flown for four years now—since Jim Taylor had set up air-support for his foot-patrols.

Taylor's men had organized a feast and a sing-sing on a piece of flat land near Mount Hagen. A thousand pairs of feet arrived, stamped and danced; their owners sang, ate and fornicated. Finally there was no grass left, and the earth was beaten hard as concrete. On that piece of earth the first plane in these Highlands had landed.

It was still an event, he could tell as he banked over the strip. A crowd had assembled. Warriors in plumes and mother-of-pearl. Women and children agape. He checked the wind speed and direction from the smoke column again and swung out wide for his approach.

Mount Hagen strip was a relatively easy piece of landing, though it was over five thousand feet and the air had lost a certain amount of its substance. The Ford Tri-Motor was the largest plane he'd brought down on this drome. It was rather like landing a very large brick on a very small handkerchief. But the drome at Wau was only marginally larger, and

36

it was on the sloping side of a hill. Here his approach was unhindered and the site was flat. He brought Tri-Motor Fords and Junkers down at Wau every week.

He felt the tail-wheel touch, and then the forward wheels settled, and the Ford bounced and was down. He ran it from side to side, angling for a view past the upturned nose.

The brave warriors lay face down on the earth, hands over their heads, feathered finery in disarray. The women and children had fled. Johnnie smiled and swung to approach the cluster of still-standing people: two Europeans and their Boys.

He cut the motors and listened to them cough. Number three was pre-igniting and running rich. He figured it wasn't anything to get excited about. Better a rich mixture than one too lean.

He had been expecting the stretchers. He had been called off the normal Lae–Wau freight run for a "mercy-dash". He could see that a Patrol had been well and truly carved up. But it gave him a shock to see it was Edward Nicholls waiting, crouched by the stretchers, reassuring one of the Boys as the monstrous Baloose rumbled towards them. Nicholls had the reputation of invincibility.

The Mount Hagen base Kiap, Andy Williams, was grinning and waving, unable to contain his excitement at seeing a new white face, even when a disaster had brought it to him. As the props coughed to a standstill he ran under the wing and clawed at the door.

"Johnnie!" he shouted. "Hiya, Johnnie!"

Johnnie unwound his scarf and pulled his helmet over his head and grinned at him, fanning out his beard from where the chin-strap had constricted it.

"Morning, Mr Williams. Just passing by. Thought I'd drop in."

"Did you bring my whisky?"

Johnnie eased himself down, taking Williams' hand.

"And a loaf of bread," he replied. "It's a regular food flight. Two cases of Johnny Walker. One loaf of bread."

"Boy!" Williams bawled. "Hurryup, saquip! Dispela bokis, now e got Wiski. Catchim easy!"

Johnson walked over to where Nicholls was hunched.

37

"What happened?" he asked.

Nicholls' head came up slowly from the wounded Boy, whose enormous eyes stared at the man who had just walked out of the Baloose. Nicholls too, stared at him, seeing him as alien; someone who leapt from place to place, never settling in, never finding out what drew men into the jungle, content to lounge at the various clubs along the coast and on New Britain.

"A prospector called Wallace got bushwacked," he said, slowly. "Then we got carved up when we went in after him."

"David Wallace?"

Nicholls nodded. His mind slowly focusing on Johnson, on the technology he blithely carried with him. Nicholls felt as though he, himself, was the man from the Stone Age, and Johnson the true man of the twentieth century.

"I was drinking with him back in Lae a month ago, before he took off. Said he was going to meet up with that mad German, what's-his-name?" Johnson said.

"Ludwig. Herman Ludwig."

"Did you bring Wallace out?"

"He would have gone off. We buried him. Do you know his family?"

"He came from Queensland, I remember. Didn't he used to work for the Railways down there? Some sort of clerk?"

Nicholls nodded distractedly.

Andy Williams frowned nervously, watching his whisky being unloaded. He glanced to where Johnson and Nicholls both now squatted on the ground beside the stretcher. Nicholls was rocking back on his heels, unconsciously trying to move away from Johnson. Andy smiled. Nicholls was a man who was only at ease away from civilization. Any hint of its dread influence, as in Johnson's command of the latest technology, made him nervous.

With the prospector dead and the locals on the warpath, Andy had a lot of work on his hands. Life had been so boring lately that he had been pining for a break in the routine. Well now he had it. And he didn't want it. He suddenly could think of a dozen things he had been meaning to do, that would have to be put off as he followed up the rumours and accusations that would now sweep over the Highlands plateau; that it was his job to begin to sift through, in search of the impossible: the truth.

The bravest of the warriors had regained their feet now, and were moving cautiously to the big plane as it stood in the field, its head reared up and its belly exposed beneath the glistening, corrugated wings.

They approached with weapons at the ready. Their eyes swept the smooth underbelly, seeing for themselves what had been told them by others, and which they had dismissed as tall tales and rumours, but which was now confirmed.

It had no sex organs.

But others were known to exist. It had to reproduce itself.

Alternative explanation. It was created by the Sky People themselves, in their land beyond the mountains. It was created and ordered to fly the pale men over the mountains in order to return to the Highlands people their own dead.

They approached it with respect and did not touch it. They stared with awe at the black men who worked for the Kiaps. Calmly, smoking their long cheroots of black tobacco, they opened its mouth and stepped into its belly, dragging with them the bodies of men wounded in the fighting— presumably food for the great bird.

Johnnie Johnson watched the refuelling of his plane from the forty-four gallon drums at the side of the strip. He looked past the plane, at the sky, calculating the cloud density and how it had changed since his arrival. The wind was quiet. There was rain on the northern horizon, moving across one of the hills, but it wasn't going to reach them for a while. He knew Andy Williams would dearly like him to stay, if only for an hour.

Even with the airstrip providing the feeling of communion with the rest of civilization, this was still the arsehole of New Guinea; and New Guinea was the arsehole of the world. From here Madang looked like civilization, and Rabaul was a cosmopolitan city.

Tomorrow night, in fact, Johnnie would be in Madang, where a liner was visiting, and on the liner white women who liked nothing more than a quick flight over the land of the headhunters in a nice, modern aeroplane, and then a long, slow fuck with some modern buccaneer like himself. He grinned in anticipation.

"Well, Johnnie, I guess I'll be seeing you." Williams' voice was full of loneliness. Johnnie clapped him on the back.

"You'll be out of here soon, sport, back to the coast and its flesh-pots."

"Not for six bloody months," Williams said, watching the pilot cross to the fuel drums and check that the hoses had been correctly stowed, and the fuel tank properly recapped.

Lesson one for pilot survival in the tropics. Always check what a coon has done.

The warriors fell back when the pilot approached the Baloose. They stared at his costume, noting the goggles he wore on top of his head-dress, and the dirty scarf. These were no doubt important in the ceremony of flight. They watched him walk around it, speaking to it, touching its wings and peering under its belly. They realized he was soothing it before flight, perhaps even apologizing to it for riding it through the sky.

They watched the tall, stooped Kiap stand and follow the last stretcher inside it, noting how even he radiated dis-ease at the prospect of climbing inside.

Andy Williams watched the three motors fire up, noting the thick puff of black smoke from number three. He could see Johnson carefully watching as it cleared itself. Through the window, Johnson caught his eye and gave him the thumbs up. He signalled back ruefully.

Again the warriors had prostrated themselves as the Baloose lumbered across the field. But Andy had seen them do it so often it had ceased to be amusing. He checked that no one was in the direct path of the plane, and then turned and walked away. He refused to look up as the plane's engine note changed on take-off. He ran his hand, instead, over a case of whisky. He would celebrate the arrival and departure with a quick snort. Or two.

On the plane, Nicholls stayed with the wounded men, reassuring them as, wide-eyed, they stared around the booming, shivering interior. He caught Baranuma's eye and smiled. His servant smiled back.

Baranuma had been just as frightened at first, but he had not shown that fear. He had reasoned that, if going in the Baloose was what gave Mastas their power, then he could only gain by following.

And his equanimity in the face of technology had impressed people like Jim Taylor, and then Nicholls. Any local who appeared halfway capable of understanding their world, or even desirous of understanding it, was welcome as a servant... one day as a partner.

Satisfied that his men were as comfortable as could be expected, Nicholls hunched his way forward into the cockpit. Johnson glanced sideways at him and nodded to the empty seat, and Nicholls slid into it.

Up here, the roar of the forward motor prevented speech. But it gave a tremendous air of security, of safety, to know that one motor could cut out and the plane would still fly, almost as if nothing had happened to it. For to ditch in this country meant, quite simply, death, even if you did bring your plane down safely.

Nicholls stared down at the brown, racing rivers, the white waters of rapids and the long ribbons of waterfalls. The jungle was a uniform mass of rotting brown. They passed over a hilltop that had been cleared. Centred on it was a village of matchwood houses. The odds were that these people had never met with a European. The odds were also that they would regard survivors of any plane crash as so much fresh meat. He stretched out in the seat and opened his diary and, clipping it to the map-board, began to write.

Writing, for Nicholls, was far more than the regulation storage of information for future recollection, as required for Administration and legal purposes. All Patrol Officers were required to keep diaries, and he knew many non-Administration people in the Territory who did likewise. They were all lonely men up here; all outsiders. He suspected that the diary was their only confidant. Tight-lipped, laconic, stoic they went about daily life, living always on the edge of being killed, or killing; every day confronting the marvellous, the fantastic Stone Age world with twentieth century technology; the world of Honour and Shame with Anglo-Saxon law.

Diary: 7th May, 1937

Ludwig is down there somewhere. I can feel it. He has carved a path across the country, from Lae to past Mount Hagen, in the process breaking every law known to mankind, both civilized and savage. He has put us back fifty years in our contact with the Uncontrolled Territories . . .

He felt the angle of flight change, as did the engine note. He looked out the window, at an escarpment of rock, white in the sun. A river fell out of the side of the mountain, tumbling in space before thundering into the jungle at its base. They were angling for the valley of that river, to give them a lower crossing height of the ranges. Brown water. White water. Rivers so powerful they hurled giant boulders down their course, sweeping away men, breaking their legs if they tried to cross.

Johnnie Johnson located the distant Ramu Valley, into which the valley they followed fed. He felt the touch of the sea-breeze that pushed its way a hundred miles inland, to surprise the hot, slogging Patrols on the ground, and set the plane, in the air, bucking in turbulence. He glanced at Nicholls and nodded.

Nicholls nodded back, feeling the plane catch the change in the air. Then, not knowing what to do with this sudden intimacy, he returned to his diary.

We took three days to reach Hagen. My runner had got through, for Williams met us on the track in. He was all agog with the rumours.

42

Then, when we got back to Base, he was just as agog with his new toy: the brand-new wireless, that can give him contact with Madang and Rabaul, and even the damnable Hit Parade on the shortwave!

He got me through to Bellamy, in Madang. Naturally, Bellamy "concurred" that flight was the wiser policy in this instance. Bellamy's been fleeing all his life. Naturally he thought a firm show of strength would be necessary in the near future. When he got back to me the second time, it was with some garbled message about a Cadet. Harris. Harris would bring up a second detachment of Police.

Harris will get slaughtered . . .

He broke off again. Writing in the plane made him feel dizzy. He was aware of the last words he had written. He closed the diary and tried to think.

He had left Sergeant Bukato in charge of his Police Boys, waiting at Mount Hagen. There was no sense in their returning to Madang, then flying to Hagen again. Bukato would drill them and drill them and run them through weapons practice until they ached.

It had taken a bit of an effort to get Baranuma onto the plane. Only the prospect of being left under Bukato's direct orders shifted him in the end. Those two were like chalk and cheese. The problem was compounded by Baranuma's family living close to Mount Hagen. On arriving there, he had promptly gone bush. No threat from Nicholls could make him give up the chance of seeing his family.

And Nicholls couldn't have issued any threat. The sight of a man eager to be with his kin again was too much for him. It reminded him of his own family, and the realization that it, too, was something he had fled. If something dark and violent was dragging him into the jungle, they were something pushing from behind.

Your origins were something you could not change, try as you might.

43

CHAPTER THREE

All the windows in the seaward wall of Bellamy's Madang
office were open, picking up as much of the breeze as they
could. Nicholls could see across the bay to the island. In the
sheltered water two native outrigger canoes patrolled the
submerged reef, the fishermen poised at the bows, spears at
an angle to the water. The corrugated iron sheds at the
wharf reflected back the blinding sun. He could see all the
way to the point, where the Madang Hotel's buildings
sprawled to the water's edge. Anchored out to sea, beyond
the reefs and bars at the entrance to the harbour, and only
half-visible behind the inshore islands, was a large, white
P&O liner. Her launch was anchored at the wharf, beside
the boat that had brought the Administrator over from
Rabaul.

Richard Bellamy, the District Officer, sat at his desk,
watching his Patrol Officer pacing the narrow confines of
the office, staring hauntedly out to sea, as if somehow he
might be able to leap through the glass and vanish.

The Administrator of the Trust Territory of New Guinea,
Ramsay McNicol, entered the room and sat down. He also
watched Nicholls. He glanced at Bellamy, not quite knowing
how to attract Nicholl's attention.

"This is a bad business, Bellamy," he said, by way of
preamble.

It worked. Nicholls turned and stared, abstractedly, at the
two men.

The Administrator's background was the first thing you
saw, when you looked at him, Bellamy thought. You saw his
upright posture, his slightly frowning, judgemental expression;
almost churlish. You saw he wore a suit and tie. You knew
he had been a school headmaster. You knew that his military
career was at least at brigade level. And you knew, from a

more recent guardedness, an anger hidden by diffidence and irony, that his present position was not necessarily of his own choosing—a political compromise, a case of being "kicked upstairs" to administer Australia's only colony, the one it wanted, above all else, to forget.

McNicol caught Bellamy's thoughtful stare and frowned towards the haggard Patrol Officer. Whether Nicholls knew it or not, he had a tic around his right eye. His pacing spoke of impatience, even impetuousness—yet his reputation was for thoroughness and meticulous attention to detail.

McNicol's job seemed simple enough. He was charged with not making waves, and not asking Canberra for money. The latter was simple: copra prices were high and gold kept on being discovered. The former wasn't: because copra prices were high and gold kept on being discovered.

He studied the hand-scrawled document that Bellamy had given him and decided that Nicholls probably prided himself on being "direct". Very well, he would ask Nicholls a direct question.

"You call this a skirmish, Nicholls, and yet you killed three men?"

Nicholls stopped his pacing and swung around.

"They had already murdered Wallace and half his party."

"You established that this village . . . Parap . . . was responsible for those deaths?"

"They are implicated, sir. They admitted shooting at Wallace."

"But they didn't admit hitting him?"

Nicholls looked away. He clenched and unclenched his fist.

"God damn it, Nicholls!" the Administrator said. "You're supposed to be a careful man."

"I'm still alive, sir. That indicates how careful I am."

"Meaning what?"

"Meaning Wallace and his . . . his people . . . aren't."

Bellamy saw something cross Nicholls' face, a memory from the incident. He came to the Patrol Officer's defence.

"Unfortunately," Bellamy said to McNicol, "such firebrands as Mick Leahy have been proved right. A show of force does work wonders with the natives."

45

"Mick Leahy is still alive," Nicholls growled. "That is the final argument for his methods."

"Mick Leahy is not accountable to the Australian Parliament," McNicol said. "I am. He doesn't run the risk of being pilloried in the Sydney newspapers, and denounced by the Australian Labor Party. I do." He paused and stared again at the Patrol Officer. At first he had taken him for a well-used forty-five. But there was a chance he was not yet forty. He almost had the look of one of the boys stumbling out of the trenches: aged in everything but their dislike of authority.

"Australia has discovered its social conscience," he added, in a conciliatory manner. "Unfortunately, Edward, you and I are it."

One of the canoes executed a turn. It drew their eyes. They waited until the boat was on course again, and then the glances of the three men intersected. Bellamy smiled. The Administrator smiled. Nicholls still stared, his expression one of waning anger.

"Sir," he said, "when I am operating in the field, I need to know your position on this matter. I need to know under what conditions you would countenance the use of maximum force."

"Under conditions of direst necessity, Nicholls. A necessity decided upon by the senior man in the field at the time. When you return to the field, you will take a much junior man with you. You will both use the utmost discretion."

He rose and buttoned his coat. It proved uncomfortable and he unbuttoned it again.

"Nicholls," he said, "ultimately, I must trust your judgement. I have been more fortunate than you in my war. Then the home government was eager to hear of the death of the 'enemy'. Now, times have changed."

"Yes, sir."

"I would like your typed report ready before I sail, in two days' time. By then I expect that you, Cadet Harris, and the new troops will be heading back to Mount Hagen by plane. Upon reaching Hagen you will continue your investigation into the Ludwig affair—creating what I hope will be an open-and-shut case against the gentleman, and producing the man himself, to stand trial."

46

He went to button his coat and remembered he had only just unbuttoned it.

"Having found him guilty, it will be necessary to hang him. Having hanged him, we will be applauded by the League of Nations, vilified by the local planters, and denounced in Federal Parliament by the Labor Party . . . who in the meantime will be denouncing us for letting a killer of natives run free."

He walked to the door and paused by it.

"You will also apprehend those natives involved in the murder of Wallace and his people. Those found guilty will also be hanged. This time, the local planters will cheer us, and again the Labor Party will denounce us."

Watching him, Bellamy realized that beneath the calm discipline and the conservative ethos was a sardonic sense of humour.

"Bellamy," the Administrator said, "we have been invited to dine aboard the P&O liner, *Ontranto*, by her Captain. Yourself and Mrs Bellamy. And you, Nicholls."

"Thank you, sir," said Bellamy, getting up, glancing to the frowning Nicholls. "What time, sir?"

"Seven-thirty, for eight." They both waited on Nicholls.

"Not if I'm typing up this report," he mumbled. He caught a warning frown from Bellamy and forced himself to smile and look at the Administrator.

"Thank you for the invitation, sir. But I would like to second Mr Harris, the Cadet, in my stead, owing to pressure of work."

The Administrator stared at him, flatly, then inclined his head in assent, opened the door, and was gone.

In the silence Nicholls and Bellamy regarded each other. Bellamy shook his head and returned to his chair, swivelling in it until he could put his feet on the desk—like a schoolboy after the Head has left the room. He grimaced at Nicholls.

"You should have stayed in the bush, Edward."

Nicholls' anger returned. "What the hell would he know about it!"

Bellamy studied him quietly and smiled sympathetically.

"The work's getting to you, isn't it, Edward?"

Nicholls started hastily, wondering if Bellamy was privy to his thoughts.

47

"What do you mean?"

"Exactly what I said. The work's getting to you. It gets to everyone, Edward."

"I'm all right," Nicholls growled, refusing to be drawn.

Bellamy stared thoughtfully at him. In this business you lost men in one of two ways. The best way was the way the prospector, Wallace, had gone. The other way was also from ambush; but ambush from within. Somehow, some of your faculties, your talents, that had served you so well and had brought you to this place, and promoted you to your job as Patrol Officer, pushed themselves too far out of line with the rest of your spirit. You became a caricature of yourself; at first, a harmless buffoon—perhaps you drank too much, in a funny, droll sort of way—perhaps you evinced a desire to "go native", and took up with a native girl and horrified the Camp Wives by parading her at functions—or you began to declare that the processes of justice were too slow, too likely to be subverted by clever southern lawyers, and that justice had to be done quickly and surely, in front of the people themselves, and you would probably slap an imaginary pistol holster as you said, "just like you punish a child".

That would be Nicholls' way.

Bellamy knew his own way. He was measuring his life as a race between a necessary promotion into the policy-making bureau, and duty-free Johnny Walker at fifteen shillings a bottle.

"At this moment," Bellamy said, "we have to proceed with a great deal of caution."

"We have to be firm, sir," Nicholls replied, becoming agitated as he saw Bellamy begin to play his role of conciliator, diplomat with an eye on an Administrator's post. He hunched forward with urgency. "The Highlands are at flashpoint, sir. Wallace won't be the only one to go, believe me. And once word gets back to the racists in Rabaul about his death, there will be a howling for blood like we haven't heard for a long time . . ."

"I know, Edward. That's why I'm not giving you any furlough. That's why I'm throwing you back into the thick of it, immediately."

There was a moment when Nicholls remembered his fear,

the feeling down his spine the moment before Bukato had shouted and he had hurled himself towards the safety of his lines. The moment before the rifle spoke. The moment in his camp, later, discovering the truth about himself as he wrote.

But he was a Patrol Officer: a Kiap.

It was expected of him.

"So, why send me back with a fresh kid, Richard? Why not, say, Black?"

"He's not that fresh, Edward."

Bellamy got up, opened a locker and took out his Johnny Walker bottle. He held it up, towards Nicholls. Nicholls considered, and nodded. Bellamy smiled and found two glasses.

"The trouble with being Administrator is: either you trust someone else to read all the Reports, and precis them for you; or you read them yourself. McNicol is of the latter school. The problem with that is: there are just too damned many."

He handed over the glass. They motioned to each other with the glasses, the social remnants of a toast.

"He hasn't read Morris's report on the latest trip up the Rai coast. He and Harris were jumped. Harris took an arrow over the eye, but kept his head and brought down the bowman. They got clear with no other casualties. Oh, except Morris's personal Boy got an arrow up the bum."

"How recent was this?"

"While you were gone."

"Do you think it was associated with the Ludwig business?"

"Morris is collecting evidence. But, at this stage, I think we can safely say there is a connection—if only in that rumours of a rampaging white man are making the villagers very twitchy."

Nicholls drank his whisky and watched the boats. One part of him wanted to go down to the shore and throw himself in, to drift slowly over the reef, cool and washed clean of murder and intrigue. To eat fresh fish, watching the flares of night fishers across the bay, hearing their sing-sing drifting over the water; waking on clean sheets, to freshly-ironed clothes. But there was another part that wanted the

49

ecstacy of the mountains, the sharpened sense of fear as his body moved through the ambushes of words, of ground-spears, and of sharp-smelling, pagan sex.

He stared at the empty glass and put it on Bellamy's desk.

"Thanks for the drink, Richard," he said.

"Sure you won't change your mind about tonight?"

He shook his head. "If young Harris wants to get on, he'd better get some practice at his social obligations."

"And if you want to get out, Edward?"

The question caught him off guard. His smile slipped. He looked hastily away.

"I'd better get onto the report," he mumbled.

Bellamy watched him leave. The door closed softly. Bellamy shrugged and sat again on his swivel chair. He spun it to the window. As he watched, one of the figures at the prow of a canoe leaned backwards, his spear raising, then leaned forward, the spear entering the water, and threw himself headlong into the bay, his arm powering the spear down into the unseen fish.

Bellamy smiled.

They were at the bottom of a gorge. It was so steep they could not camp there. The tents were above them, on a narrow razorback ridge. They were in granite country, and Ludwig maintained that granite country was gold country.

The stream raced, grey and brown, through the red rock. Above them the granite broke through the tangled hillside vegetation, streaked white with quartz. The narrow arc of sky was dark blue. Rudi could not see the camp from his position at the end of the sluice-race. He could see Ludwig, halfway up the ridge, shotgun cradled in his arms. Paul was watching the camp, and so was invisible.

He had decided that Ludwig's natives knew far more about gold-mining than he did. All that was necessary was for him to stand there, looking knowledgeable, nodding when they showed him a piece of rock. Ludwig's natives could teach the press-ganged natives all that was necessary to work the race—to keep the water coming and keep the gravel churning over the wooden baffles. Rudi's job was to collect the minute flakes of gold that came their way and store them in an empty tobacco tin.

He could already feel some sort of fever beginning to consume him. His flesh was now scarred with leech bites, mosquito bites, ant and spider bites, rashes from stinging vegetation. He had worked up a lather of sweat descending the loose rock from the camp to the stream—a drop of three hundred metres almost vertically down—and now the chill at the bottom of the gorge, where the sun was visible only two hours a day, was freezing that sweat to him. He shivered.

He was not born to this life, like Ludwig, like Paul. He had been an indentured clerk in Berlin when inflation got the better of the company he worked for. He could have scrabbled for another job, doing the same sort of thing, but the shock of redundancy had made him thoughtful. And then adventurous. He had signed as accountant to a gold-mining company in a place he knew only as an address on despatch documents and receipts: "North Coast of New Guinea".

The North Coast was very beautiful, with black beaches, volcanoes riding offshore, their tips in cloud. The road along the coast was flat and well-made, flashing under coconut fronds that meshed overhead. He could have been very comfortable on the North Coast.

But the gold-mining company consisted of two white men: Herman Ludwig and Paul Josephi. It had no office, though it did "own" a strip of land near the Madang harbour, on which the two men squatted, with their Boys and their equipment. In fact it was not even a gold-mining company. It was a gold-prospecting company, and between the two was a world of difference.

He should have got out then, the moment he saw that gaunt, red-bearded man squatting on the heels of his unlaced boots, drinking what Rudi had thought was coffee from a tin pannikin, but which was actually rum. The Lutheran Mission's coastal boat was at the wharf. He had only just vacated his spot on the deck. It was sailing on to Finschhafen and Lae.

The Head Boy gave a shout and plunged his hand into the swirling mud of the sluice-box. Rudi blinked and, despite himself, leaned forward. All the other Boys crowded around as the Head Boy yelled and lifted his hand from the gravel and water and held up a rock. High up on the ridge, Ludwig saw the gesture and knew what it meant. He waved to Rudi and Rudi stepped over to take it from the Boy.

This was the direct cause of his being there, he thought. A heavy piece of rock. He turned it over. It was predominantly quartz. But laced through fine cracks in that stone was an intrusion, an impurity, of dull yellow.

The Boy was watching him eagerly, waiting for praise. Rudi nodded to him, smiling, trying to think of something he could say in his crude Pidgin and finding nothing. He slapped the Boy on the shoulder and pocketed the stone. He could see Ludwig waving and he leapt across the stream, not caring that his trailing foot missed the bank and floundered in the water.

He threw himself at the hillside, clawing up with the help of hanging vines, scarring his hands on thorns. He beat through the web of a giant spider, red with a yellow cross on its back. He slipped and fell and had to scramble on hands and knees.

Ludwig took the rock and grunted. He peered at it suspiciously.

"Well?" Rudi said. "It is, isn't it?"

Ludwig grunted again and held it into the light—like a housewife, Rudi thought, investigating a cabbage she suspects is stale.

"It could be," Ludwig admitted reluctantly.

"Could? I thought this was what you were after? Don't you know what it looks like?"

Ludwig stared at him abstractedly, frowning.

"It could be reef copper," he admitted finally.

"God!" Rudi yelled. "You've lied to me all the way from Germany! I'm not an accountant with you. I'm a labourer! I have no salary, just 'percentage'! Twenty per cent of nothing is still nothing! Now you tell me you don't know what you're looking for?"

"I know what I'm looking for, son." Ludwig's eyes were steady and unblinking. Watching them Rudi could not visualize him as the man who would, in his fever, be screaming and raving, waving his pistol around, with Paul holding him. Paul shaking the pistol hand and swearing, keeping it pointed into the air and clawing Ludwig's finger away from the trigger, while Ludwig screamed about the "filthy niggers! the murdering heathens! the black bitches!"

"I know what I'm looking for. And this could be it. Now we'll just walk up to the camp and pour a little acid on it and watch what happens. If it is reef gold then it's come down this creek from higher up."

"Do you mean we will have to go further into the jungle?"

"If you want twenty per cent of something, my son, then you will definitely be going further up." Ludwig examined the hillsides around them. "You can't tell in this jungle," he said. "You could be standing on the reef and not know it."

Rudi wiped the sweat and blood from his palms onto his trousers and pushed up the hill.

"Hurry up," he called back to Ludwig. "Let's see what the acid says."

"Paul!" Ludwig shouted, as they reached the summit, the narrow, flat-topped ridge. "Paul!"

The smoke of their cooking fire was caught in the trees. Even here the vegetation was dense. Sunlight filtered through the smoke, blue and grey. Through the trees Rudi could see more ridges, similar to their own. The whole world was mountains from which there was no escape.

"He might be with the Marys," Rudi said, trying to keep the repugnance out of his voice.

"Find him," Ludwig said. "I'll test this sample."

The girls did not need to be chained any more, now they were out of all controlled territory. The same with the carriers that Ludwig had pressed into service. The jungle and the headhunters acted as chains now. The only hope for survival of any one member of the team lay in survival of them all, Rudi thought.

53

He walked to the Boys' cooking fire and stopped.

Paul and two of the girls lay beside it. They stared up at the treetops. Their throats had been slashed open. The blood soaked their bodies, Paul's clothes, the damp ground. They had been arranged beside the fire, feet towards it, like three spokes of a wheel.

Rudi turned and ran.

· CHAPTER FOUR ·

From the deck of the liner, Madang was a tropical paradise, with wharf lights glimmering across the black, still waters, with the lights of houses yellow on black. And, of course, the picturesque native villages spread along the water's edge, with the sound of singing rising and falling across the water, the cries of children and the barking of dogs. A peaceful paradise of lazy tropical bliss.

Jennifer touched her friend's hand and pointed to the slowly moving light of a night fisherman, and beyond it the lights of a launch. She felt the returned pressure from Gloria. They said nothing, both immersed in the romance of the moment. Then, behind them, the ship's bell tolled, adding to the romanticism; its echo shimmered back to them, and they turned to get ready for dinner.

The light of the night fisherman bobbed in the wake from the launch. Don Harris turned, watching it fall behind them. In the glare of the torch he could see the fisherman, bronzed by the light, arm upraised. He smiled and looked ahead, to the lights of the ship.

A ship riding at night in tropical waters is probably the most romantic sight on earth, he thought. The heavy calm of the tropics, the black sheen of the water, the fading cries from villages along the shore, and then the ship rising like a city out of the water, white and majestic, spilling out warm, yellow light from a thousand portholes, its decks bathed in light; lights like jewels from bow to stern.

Turning again, he could see the District Officer, Bellamy, and his wife, the faded Mrs Bellamy. The husband faced into

55

the breeze of their passage. She sat, hands folded on her lap, staring quietly at her shoes. She seemed, to Don, to be immune to the romance of the night. He turned his attention back to the ship.

During the day, as he and Constable Giram had sorted through the stores for the new patrol, he had seen the ship's launch come ashore and a party of passengers disembark and, with eager cries, descend on the sleepy town. They discovered the German cemetery, the giant staghorn ferns high overhead in the trees, the flying-foxes hanging by their toes. They walked out to the hotel and a few swam over the coral reef. The others clung to the shore in fear of sharks and crocodiles.

In the distance Don had seen two young women in the party. Stripping off their sun-dresses they revealed tight, one-piece bathing costumes. Hand in hand they stepped, giggling, into the warm, clear water.

And a fierce current passed through the town. Every male eye, from every vantage point, turned. In the native labour compound, in the shade of the concrete-floored store, on the verandah of the mess, and in the Administration store— where Don, staring, became aware that Giram was staring also, aware of the new focus of the young Masta's attention.

Giram had noticed the desire in the Masta's face, and the way it had made him forgetful. The Masta was no older than himself and, like him, was a stranger in this town. They were both single, both intent upon making their fortunes. Yet the Masta rejected him.

Pondering this, as he and all black men did, often, he wandered out past the Madang Hotel that evening—taking care to avoid the hotel itself, and the suspicious eyes of the clustered Mastas. He stood there on the headland, above the thin strip of beach, and looked out to the glittering steel ship, and beyond the ship to the ocean.

Home was out there, over the horizon, on the island the Mastas now called "New Britain", that the Germans had called "Neupommern", and that his people had not called anything but "home". It was the centre of the universe, after all.

His home was on the inside of the great harbour, inside the home of the Guria—the earth-dwelling snake that every now and then flexed, and twisted, shaking the earth, even killing people. In the bay, just out from his home, was the Guria's mouth. His father could still remember when it had belched out fire and steam, rocks and mud, and villagers had died, and before their eyes an island had grown from the waters.

Even here, across the water, he could sometimes feel the Guria twisting. It was less severe, of course, coming from so far away, but it served to set off the shattering homesickness he felt.

Since the Germans had declared that the great harbour was their "capital" the Guria had not spoken so loudly, contenting itself with grumbling beneath the earth. It was a measure of the power of the Lord Jesus Christ, so the missionaries avowed, that the Guria had been silenced.

Now he stared into the early night, half-conscious that he was exposing himself to danger—something a meticulous Police Boy did not do unnecessarily—by being here, on the edge of the jungle, but unable to move as the longing for home swept over him.

He should not have left. But there was also a guria inside him. It knotted his stomach up. At the mission school they taught him to read the Bible, in Pidgin. They stressed the importance of the white man's ways, the worship of the Lord Jesus Christ, who made all men equal.

Except black men. Somewhere, in the Bible, it was stressed that black men were inferior. Hearing this, a guria had growled inside him. He had looked around, and observed there were no differences between himself and the missionaries—except the colour of their skins, and the power the whites had. He looked further, and saw that, outside the mission, the Germans were no longer in charge. A new race of white men had taken their place.

Perhaps they would be different, he thought. Perhaps their Bible did not stress the inferiority of people like himself.

57

And here he was, with a uniform, knowing how to use a rifle, knowing how to drill, to march; the intimate of white men; slowly and surely gaining knowledge, and through knowledge, power. But he was unable to stop feeling homesick.

"A beautiful evening, brother."

The whispered voice made him jump. The man had approached him soundlessly, materializing like a sorcerer out of the dark jungle. He whipped around, and stared at the man's intense, burning eyes.

"The sun has set, and you look to your home. You are sick with longing for it."

The man's thought-reading ability alarmed him further. But he carried no arms.

"What do you want?"

The man shrugged peaceably.

"To pass the evening with a Policeman." He reached out and touched Giram's tunic, smiling at him all the while.

"There must be a lot of power in possessing such a tunic. Power over simple village girls, for example. Power to smooth the way for local people, and gain a few riches for yourself."

Giram relaxed. The man was someone who had broken one of the whiteman's innumerable laws. He was looking for a Police Boy to bribe, to intercede for him.

"What have you done?" he asked sharply, in the proper manner of someone with power, to a supplicant.

"I want nothing." The man's manner was too smooth for a wrongdoer. "I want only to touch your tunic. Tell me about the Mastas you serve. They are all drinking whisky? They are conversing with their God?"

"Masta Nicholls is writing up his Patrol Report. Masta Harris has gone to the big ship with the Kiap and the Missus."

"They are all out there, on the water?"

Giram nodded uncertainly. He had a feeling that the knowledge the man had just gained from him could be used against the Mastas, and thus against himself.

"They have so much power," the man said, musingly, his hand still fingering the tunic. "But they will not share it. Why do you think that is so?"

58

"Our fathers before us were foolish," Giram said, voicing one explanation. "When the Cargo was shared out, they took wooden canoes, while the white men took steel ships. The steel ships could travel further, to the Sky People in Sydney, even to London and the King himself."

"That is one idea," the man said, nodding. "It is also possible that the power would be available for us, if we knew where to look. In books, for instance."

Giram smiled, shaking his head. The man's ignorance put him at ease. "Not in the Bible," he said. "The knowledge is not there."

"Maybe they have not translated the important books of the Bible? They tell us about Noah, about Ham, about Jesus Christ. But Noah built a wooden boat, didn't he? And where did Jesus Christ gain His power?"

The man let go of his clothes and looked, himself, out to the ship.

As they had talked, the last light had left the sky. In the pitch, velvet blackness, the ship burned fiercely with light.

"Maybe," he said, "if we were to find those other Books, and translate them into our own tongues, then we could build such a ship. And, having built it, sail to Sydney, or to wherever it is the Sky People go for the Cargo."

"That would be a hard job," said Giram.

The man nodded, still watching the ship.

"And the Mastas are out there, eh? Out on the steel ship? Perhaps they are making Cargo?"

Giram did not reply. He was unhappy about having told the man so much. He backed away, then turned and ran as fast as he could into the blackness beside the jungle.

Alo watched him go. When he was out of sight Alo laughed, and stepped back, as quietly as he had arrived, into the jungle. He remained there, motionless, invisible, until he was sure no one else was about. Then he reappeared. This time he carried a billum made of string and his steel tomahawk.

59

He walked quietly after Giram, like him avoiding the noise and the light of the hotel. As he walked, he dropped his axe into the billum, and took out a thin, sharpened wire. It was a killing wire. Originally it had sounded a note on a musical machine in a North Coast chapel. "Big bokis with teeth. Na, you fight him, he cry out" was the description they gave the box. The missionary called it "piano". As the humidity wrecked it, so Alo removed what he needed.

The killing wire was far more effective than the axe, because it could be used in such a way that there was no mark on the victim. And that was the kind of killing a sorcerer needed to do in order to maintain his power.

He skirted the cluster of Administration buildings, and walked up the track to the District Officer's house.

> The homeless man finds it too late to build.
> The lonely man will keep his loneliness,
> Will lie awake, will read, will write long letters,
> Will wander to and fro under the trees
> Restlessly, while the leaves run from the wind.

Awaiting Nicholls on his return from patrol was a pile of mail. It included two new books of verse he had ordered from London. One by Rilke, a German he had read of with interest, the other by an old favourite, Housman.

He sat reading now, in his room in the Administration hostel. Instead of whisky, he drank coffee. He wore a silk dressing-gown, made for him by a Rabaul Chinese tailor. Lost in the poetry, he had forgotten himself as Kiap.

> This is my strife:
> dedicate to desire
> through all days to roam.
> Then strong and wide,
> with a thousand root-fibres
> deep into life to gripe —
> and through pain
> far beyond life to ripen,
> far beyond time!

The words caused him almost physical pain. He closed the book. The intensity of poetry pierced him, and he wished, yet again, that he had the gift: to summon up words like that, to distill them down to their essence, so they could strike like arrows into other people's hearts.

And then what? Well, then, to reach other people. To have them understand who he was and what his life meant, to get beyond the dreadful self-consciousness of speech, the clumsy order of words as first thought they tripped off your tongue, giving wrong impressions to your meaning as you struggled to articulate.

Like today, in the office with Bellamy and the Administrator, both men whom, in their ways, he admired. Given that McNicol was a politician and Bellamy was . . . well, Bellamy was himself in ten years, but saddled with a dipsomaniac wife.

Nicholls rose and went to the door of his room. About to yell for his servant, he remembered that Baranuma had the night off, was out somewhere, like everyone else in town, carousing. Nicholls stepped to the verandah and looked, against his will, out to the lights of the ship, half-hidden by the growth on an island.

Then his sixth sense made him aware of someone. He turned fractionally, using his peripheral vision, sharpened by many nights in the "big bush", to pick out the movement. A solitary native was moving along the road.

Nicholls relaxed. For a moment he had entered into the state of mind of patrol. But he could see only one native, carrying a billum, strolling along the edge of the road— probably heading for an assignation with some woman from a different village, while her husband was out fishing.

Nicholls did not return to his reading. He stared at the other parcel, tied neatly with string. Reluctantly, he opened his knife and stared at the blade. He glanced around the room and sat on the bed, looking at the parcel.

He touched it, pursing his lips. He was aware again of the muscular flicker at his right eye. He got up and went to the mirror and watched it.

He could not stop it. He placed his fingertip on it and felt the flutter there, like an insect pinned. He realized that both Bellamy and McNicol would have seen it.

The tic made up his mind for him. He returned to the bed and cut the string on the parcel.

It had been made by the same tailor who had made his dressing-gown and his shirts. He had ordered it, almost as a game, when he had last been on furlough in Rabaul. He had been reading . . . was it Tacitus? Some Roman general.

He had conceived the idea of a general-purpose armour, to be worn on patrol, in tight situations. He had not told any of his contemporaries about it. But he had sketched his idea and taken it to Lee Chiang, who had read it with his usual immobile, Oriental eyes, and had looked Nicholls over, not speculatively, not as if he were a coward, but simply as a tailor looks over his client. Satisfied, he had nodded and said, "Yes, sir."

Nicholls took off his dressing-gown. "It's not cowardice," he told himself. "If this device saves lives, it will be invaluable to the Administration. I'm simply testing it, working out the details."

But the other part of his brain laughed. He ignored it.

The armour had thin sheet metal as its core, taken from biscuit tins, and cut to flex with the body. Cotton waste was packed on top of the tin, tightly wadded, then quilted with calico. Cotton straps came over the shoulders, and under the groin. It covered him from throat to genitals.

He walked across the room. It was not flexible enough. He walked stiffly, like a marionette. He would have to alter the core, he thought. The tin would have to be further jointed. But the more it was jointed, the more readily an arrow could penetrate.

He took it off and laid it on the bed and looked at it, thoughtfully.

He remembered prints of Japanese and Chinese warriors wearing such armour, but presumably without the added benefit of tin. However, it was the tin that made it so inflexible. That was the conundrum. There was also the heat factor.

He removed his shirts from their drawer and laid the armour carefully at the bottom, then repacked the shirts. He didn't want Baranuma to find it.

62

He pushed his poetry books aside and stared at the typewriter he had borrowed from the store. There was a piece of paper screwed into it, and a heading typed up.

REPORT ON PATROL INTO THE WESTERN HIGHLANDS, APRIL–MAY, 1937

The rest of the page was blank.

The ship's orchestra, a cross between a dance-band and a string-ensemble, was playing Mozart. The humidity had selectively detuned the piano, and made the tuning of other stringed instruments difficult. The music had a slightly atonal edge.

The dining-room was white, with cedar panelling. Big tropic fans turned lazily overhead. If you listened hard you could hear the ship's generators rumbling, providing the magic of electricity—something Patricia Bellamy had almost forgotten in the twelve months of their Madang posting.

Used to soft, yellow lamplight, she felt uneasy in the brightness. Doubly uneasy. Although she had chosen her best "little black dress", she was aware that the two girls sitting with them at the Captain's table wore fashions that placed it just enough out of vogue to be ridiculous.

Looking around the room she could see other women similarly attired to this pair. None were as pretty as they, which was the obvious reason for their elevation to this table, as company for the invited single men: the moon-eyed Cadet, Don Harris, and the exciting aviator, Johnnie Johnson. The four of them were deep in conversation, whilst her husband talked politics with the Administrator and the Captain.

The drink waiter extended the wine bottle to her and, gratefully, she accepted the top-up. There was no doubt that liquor relaxed her, that without it she would go stark, raving mad; living as they did in this tight, alien world on the edge of the wilderness. She turned her attention to the two "single men".

63

The Cadet was only a boy. Life had a lot of shaping to do on him, yet. The acquisition of an arrow-scar over his right eye was the first step in that process. But, as yet, he had made no compromises. He had not discovered the limitations of his dreams.

That he was a dreamer was clear from his hunched shoulders, almost in imitation of Nicholls. But he did not possess the advantage of Nicholls' height. His boy's body was still slim. She wondered how slim.

Johnson, though, was different He was her husband's contemporary. Sitting across from him, poor Richard came off the worse. Johnson was a good six feet, and solidly built, with an extravagant, woolly beard that flared out, like an old-time bushranger—as in many ways he was. He possessed self-assurance, something any woman found irresistible. He never plunged too deeply into things. He came, he saw, he conquered. His clothes had a romantic threadbareness.

He was not smoothly handsome like the dreadful Errol Flynn, whom so many Administration wives had drooled over—who spent longer on his toilet than most women, adjusting his knee-boots so, his kerchief thus, and parading the effect down the main street of Port Moresby, looking for some lonely woman, her husband away in the bush, to seduce.

One of the girls became aware of Patricia's exclusion from the conversation. She was the bolder of the pair, her hair cut in a fashionable bob. She wore more make-up than Patricia considered necessary. But she turned to her with a warm smile.

"We swam over the reef today, Mrs Bellamy. It was wonderful. Have you ever seen it?"

"No," she replied. "We've been here twelve months, but I've never been swimming."

She didn't add that the stares of the men, both black and white, were what kept her from doing so.

"Oh, the coral was wonderful, and the fish."

"But no puk-puks?" Johnson called to her, reminding her of his presence.

The girl looked puzzled.

"He means crocodiles," Patricia explained. "It's Pidgin-talk."

64

"Oh, that's just a joke, isn't it? About the crocodiles?"

Johnson winked at Patricia, who blushed and looked away.

"An infant was taken from a beach village, only last month," Don Harris told her. "It was attributed either to sorcery or to a crocodile."

Both girls shuddered. Don leaned his elbows on the table, eager to continue the tale.

"We caught one here, a few months back, and cut it open. Do you know what was inside?"

"Please," said the girl, whose name was Gloria. "Please, spare me."

He was suddenly contrite, sitting back, not knowing how to woo her.

"It's a wild place all right," Johnson boomed, moving in. "The only way to see it is from an aeroplane."

Both girls, Gloria across the table, and Jennifer at his side, turned to him.

"It's safe and comfortable. You can cover in one hour as much territory as these boys," he nodded to Don, "cover in two weeks—during which time they're getting shot at, contracting malaria, and finding they can't get Life Insurance."

Jennifer touched his hand with hers. "Is it possible to take an aeroplane flight, Mr Johnson?"

Gloria glared at her. She was afraid she was going to be stuck with the boy. Jennifer had been lucky enough to have been seated next to the aviator, and that was her only advantage—but she was playing it to the hilt.

He closed his hand over hers. "Anything is possible," he told her. "Guinea Airways won't stand for any joy-riding, surely?" Don said, petulantly. Johnson took his eyes from the girl's and stared at him. "Guinea Airways does what I tell them," he said."

"Anyhow they and I will be parting company within the month. I'm setting up my own seaplane service to the other islands." He returned his attention to the girl. "How about we fly out to a coral lagoon and I'll show you what the Pacific Islands are really all about?"

Don retreated into silence, biting his lip. Gloria felt sorry for him, but pity was no building-block for a shipboard romance. Jennifer was considering the pilot's proposition.

"I've got to fly Mr Harris up into the bush in the next day or two," he went on. "There'll be room for a passenger . . ." he looked over to Gloria, "or two," he added. Her heart rose at her inclusion.

"We'll have a pretty full payload," the Cadet mumbled.

"Not in the Ford," Johnson said. He winked to Gloria, and she smiled back. "We could take the ship's orchestra as well."

Gloria laughed. She caught Jennifer's eyebrow twitch, and ignored her. She wasn't giving up without a good fight.

"The thing I can't understand, Mr McNicol," the Captain was saying, "is the failure of your people to take the Japanese threat seriously."

"We're keeping a close watch, Captain, I assure you."

"You'll be needing more than a watch, Mr McNicol. They've denounced the Anglo-Japanese Treaty, withdrawn from the League of Nations, grabbed Manchukuo, and refused to limit naval shipbuilding . . ."

"You're very up on their activities, Captain," Bellamy said, trying to take the heat off McNicol.

"And so I should be. Everywhere we sail in these waters are Japanese fishing boats—not sampans. Modern mother ships, trawlers. Floating fish-processing factories."

McNicol and Bellamy stared at each other, neither willing to be drawn by the Captain. For all McNicol knew, he could be a Japanese agent. The Pacific was rife with rumours and counter-rumours. An American aviatrix, Miss Earhardt, supposed to be on her way to New Guinea right now, was rumoured to be taking photographs for the American government. A Chinese tailor in Rabaul was supposed to be sending back sketch-maps to the Japanese government.

McNicol looked around the dining-room, observing the Cadet staring unhappily at his plate, Johnson holding forth

66

to the ladies—as was his want—and beyond their table, the other cruise passengers. His eyes came back to the D.O.'s wife, realizing she was embarrassed at being dressed out of step with the women on the cruise. If it comforted her, the wives of the Coastal planters at another table, taking advantage of this rare visit for a night out with their husbands—getting them away from their native women—felt the same.

He shook his head. He had a lot to learn about the country—and more to learn about the breed of white man who inhabited it. He had made one patrol up the Sepik so far, and was eagerly planning a cross-country jaunt: from Mount Hagen to the headwaters of that river. The report of the fighting out from Hagen distressed him considerably, delaying the mounting of that expedition. Now, to top it, the Captain was reminding him, deliberately or accidentally, of something the Australian government wanted absolutely nothing to do with—and which occupied at least six inches of his office filing system: the Japanese expansion into the Pacific.

"The Japanese army mutinied in February," the Captain went on, "killing Cabinet Ministers. As far as I know, the mutineers have gone unpunished?"

McNicol nodded. He, too, had heard nothing of any repercussions.

"And now, according to the Press, Japan has over twenty naval ships of significant tonnage in the Pacific. The British have three, and no cruisers."

"The Americans have the Japanese outgunned at the moment," McNicol said.

The Captain blinked and stared at him. McNicol realized that the man was seriously worried. He was not in anyone's employ—save that of the Peninsula and Orient Line. He was the Administrator of a floating dominion, concerned for its safety.

"Is that a fact?" the Captain said, an edge of sarcasm to his voice. "I'm certainly glad to hear it. And where would this huge American fleet be stationed Mr McNicol? Somewhere handy?"

"Pearl Harbour," he mumbled.

67

The Captain stared at Bellamy, who smiled uneasily.

"Pearl Harbour," he repeated. "Japan could take Rabaul, then Madang, and over the mountains to Port Moresby." He blinked again, his hands sketching the procedure. "Darwin . . . they could drive to Sydney before the American fleet had taken on its complement of ice-cream before sailing."

"What about the Australian fleet?" Bellamy asked.

"What Australian fleet?" the Captain replied.

McNicol and Bellamy stared at each other. McNicol allowed himself an undiplomatic shrug.

"Japanese language courses are the only answer, Mr Bellamy," he said. "Captain Wilson, would you like some more rice wine?"

The Captain stared at him, and then laughed.

He was now in the Kiap's house. He moved silently through its shadows, awed by the power around him—the machines that could make sounds, that could talk to you by themselves, or call up other Kiaps in places beyond the horizon. And, above all, by the power collected between cardboard covers, in books.

Alo's father, too, had been a sorcerer. Alo was his apprentice. But his father had been hanged by the German Kiap. The whole village, including all his father's children, had been forced to watch as the Kiap paraded his father before them, the missionary read some powerful words from the unexpurgated Bible, and his father had dropped through the floor of the structure the village had been made to build. His eyes bulged out of his head, his tongue distending, black and swollen, and his penis engorged. He swung there, naked, hands bound, and dead.

Alo had not cried.

Now, he quickly searched the bookcase, looking for the familiar cover of the Bible. He found it with little difficulty, and opened it. He did not recognize the marks in it, which meant they were probably in "English", the language of

68

power. He dropped the book into his billum and turned his head.

Standing in the doorway was a tall dark man, wearing a blue, wrap-around lap-lap: the uniform of a houseboy. Alo smiled and stood up. He saw the houseboy carried a small gun, but his eyes clearly indicated he did not know how to use it.

"The German Administration may have been ruthless, but it was efficient," the planter was saying, leaning against the Captain for support as he addressed McNicol. He caught Gloria listening and tried to wink at her, but was too drunk and succeeded only in blinking.

"What has the Australian Administration done to discipline the lazy savages, eh? Nothing. Look at how the country is falling into ruin. Do you know, once . . ." he wobbled, and frowned, wondering if the ship was moving . . . "once you could drive from here to Bogia. Now, you're lucky if you can start the car, as some bloody coon's probably stolen the crank-handle!"

Gloria turned away from him, and watched Jennifer dancing with Johnson. They danced well to the orchestra's foxtrot. She could feel the lad watching her, and tried not to look at him. Despite his story of ambush by savage head-hunters, and the new scar on his forehead, she did not find him attractive. He was too like the private school boys she had known back in Melbourne, whom she had fled on this crazy escapade with her best friend from her pre-nursing days.

The lad cleared his throat and leaned to her. "Miss . . ." he had forgotten her surname. She did not help him with it, but sat, smiling. He bumbled on. "Would you care to dance?"

She considered the dance floor. Then she relented. Why not? She was certain she could resist what other advances he made.

"Thank you," she said, in reply, and waited for him to help her up.

69

Although the houseboy had pulled the trigger, the gun had not gone off. When it failed to explode, like it should, killing the intruder dead, he knew he was not faced with an ordinary man, but with a sorcerer. He dropped the gun and turned to flee.

Alo caught him behind the ear, on the nerve, and the Boy dropped in his tracks. He waited to hear if anyone would come to investigate. Then he picked up the revolver and dropped it in the billum, next to the Bible. He knelt down and unrolled the wire.

Carefully, he probed the still-breathing body. He located the spot he wanted, over the liver, and pushed the wire into the flesh. It slid in easily, leaving no mark. He pushed it through the tissue, feeling it slide into fat and muscle, and then into the man's internal organs.

There was a noise outside. Leaving the wire in place, he rose and crossed to the window. The Police Boy he had spoken to was standing outside, staring at the building. Alo drew back into the shadows.

The Police Boy walked to the door, and knocked on it. Alo glanced at the body. It was still twitching. He moved to it and knelt on it to prevent any sound. The muscles tightened and spasmed beneath him.

Constable Giram stepped back from the District Officer's door. He had hoped to find at least a servant home, but all was quiet. They must have sneaked off to a village for a bit of a spree once the Masta and Missus left. He considered mounting guard on the building himself.

Then the sound of singing came from further down the track. The song was European. He glanced back. Several Mastas were returning home from carousing at the Hotel.

Giram slid into the bush.

Alo waited, listening as the whites staggered past, full of whisky. Then he withdrew his wire and tidied the boy's lap-lap. He coiled the wire and returned it to his billum. It was greasy and would need cleaning. He glanced around the room and checked that nothing had been disturbed. He waited until the whites were out of earshot, and then left, as

70

soundlessly as he had entered. Giram did not see or hear him.

The body lay quite still. It did not bleed.

"God," the D.O.'s wife said, "I'm getting out of touch."

"Pardon, dear?" Both the D.O. and his Missus seemed to have forgotten Don, sitting uncomfortably in front of them in the launch, not knowing where to look. Bellamy bent to her lips to hear her over the rumble of the motor and the whip of the wind.

"I'm out of touch. I'm so unfashionable."

He squeezed her shoulder and looked up at Don and winked. "You're divine," he said. "Black never dates, you know."

"The colour mightn't," she said, "but the cut does."

"We'll take our leave soon," he said. "Three months. Go to Melbourne. See the kids."

She snuggled against him, feeling a slight melancholy against the warm familiarity of his body.

"I wonder what they're doing?" she said.

"Sound asleep. We pay enough in school fees to guarantee a good night's sleep, I hope."

"I miss them."

He nodded, and spoke across to Don.

"God, that planter's a boor," he said.

"Which one?" Don asked.

Patricia laughed. "All of them."

"No. You know. He was ear-bashing the Skipper and McNicol, and falling down the front of that girl's dress . . ."

"She was nice," Patricia said. "At first I didn't like her . . ."

"One of those who came up after the War, walked straight onto an expropriated German plantation, and has let it slide steadily downhill ever since. Did you hear him about the Bogia Road! The reason it's deteriorated is because the likes of him don't send a few boys out with bush knives to slash it."

"McNicol looked tired."

71

"He is. No matter what he does, he'll be attacked, viciously, by one side or another whose self-interest is threatened."

They fell silent. She leaned her head into his shoulder and he ran his hand through her hair.

Don watched them. He was still trying to understand what had happened with Gloria. They had danced. She was as light as a feather in his arms. Her perfume was tantalizing, the touch of her clothes erotic. She looked into his eyes and laughed. She returned the pressures of his hand. He had suggested a "breath of fresh air". Johnson and the other girl were nowhere to be seen.

Outside, the moonlight running silver across the bay, a breeze heavy with salt and ozone, the music now remote and softly muffled, its off-key nature more pronounced with distance, he had put his arm around her, his fingertips just touching her breast. It was like a night at a school dance—he felt the summer winds coming down from the Adelaide Hills as he and some squatter's daughter danced the same dance to the same tune, the same mime of fingers and fumbles—but she turned in his arms, kissed him fleetingly, and ducked under his embrace.

"Let's walk," she said. And walk they did, around the deck, in the moonlight, coming occasionally upon couples clinging together. By a lifeboat they had found Johnnie Johnson and Jennifer. They were joined at the waist, her skirt up, his trousers down, so his bum gleamed white. Gloria had jerked Don angrily away, but the other girl's moans had pursued them along the deck. Gloria's hand tugged him away from the others, but the rest of her body seemed to want to be back there. Finally she had said she felt sick and he had let her go.

Now he sat at the stern of the boat, looking back, again seeing the great ship, still strung with jewelled lights, still calling to him—even though its romance was now tarnished.

"No," he thought. "Not tarnished. Revealed for what it is. Simple lust. But why wouldn't she accept at least that from me? I'm as good in that department as Johnson."

But he couldn't continue the lie to himself. Squatters' daughters don't come across that easily. He had arrived in the Islands a virgin and, until he could readjust his vision to accept the native girls as desirable, he knew he was going to remain a virgin . . .

She was clothed in the kirtle of clinging white, cut low upon her bosom, and bound in at the waist with the barbaric double-headed snake, and her rippling hair fell in heavy masses almost to her feet . . . For a moment she stood still, her hands raised high above her head, and as she stood the white robe slipped from her down to her golden girdle, baring the blinding loveliness of her form. She stood there . . .

Rider Haggard. Not so much the words as the images he had seen when he read *She*, came to him. They had reappeared when he had read the newspaper accounts of Jack Hides' expedition over the escarpment, across the entire Island of New Guinea, and Papua—and how, high up in the hidden central plateau, lost from contact with civilization for generations, he had stumbled into an agricultural civilization of "whites". Villages, tilled fields, neat hedges, well-made roads.

Well, no one else had ever found exactly what Hides found.

Now Don would be able to see it at first hand. As near as he could judge, the punitive Patrol he would be part of was going into the same general area. And with the legendary Edward Nicholls: misanthrope, misogynist, some said misguided—the mentor of the "second-wave" of Patrol Officers. The "first-wave" had established contact, uneasily, with difficulty. Now, guided by the latest anthropological thought, wary of the League of Nations Charter, in full knowledge of the atrocities committed in every previous encounter between European civilization and tribal societies, there was a chance for one small nation, Australia, to bring civilization to a lost corner of the world.

Everyone else had failed: Spain, Portugal, France, and even Britain. The Americans refused to try—contenting themselves with sniping at those who did attempt the task, and manufacturing the trade-beads for exchange. What had happened when the British had landed in Australia must never be replicated. People like McNicol and Edward Nicholls and Don Harris himself were dedicating themselves to

73

preventing it from happening. In all of history, the Australians were the one people who had learned from the mistakes of their own past.

Well, thought Don, that's what we like to believe.

"Who is he?" Baranuma asked, somewhat thickly, squinting through the tobacco haze at the newcomer, who seemed to have materialized out of the night to join their party.

"I don't know," replied the Administrator's personal servant, handing the bottle back to Baranuma. "I think he's a local."

"Well, then, give him a drink."

But the stranger waved the bottle aside, looking carefully around the dimly-lit hut, in which the personal servants of most of the town's Europeans were getting thoroughly plastered.

"Hey, Boy," the Administrator's servant asked, "you come from where?"

"Oh, I'm a local, that's all: just a bush kanaka."

They studied his unbecoming modesty, his lack of clothing, the billum he carried with him.

Baranuma took another tug at the white rum bottle. The spirit scoured his gullet, but he prevented himself from coughing. It was a test of white-manhood to handle this poison, and he was determined to pass the test.

"Hey, bush kanaka, you got any kia in that billum?" someone else called.

"Leave him alone. We got food. We got biscuits, now. We got cake."

"Ahh! That Masta's kia, pek-pek bilong beenatung, that's all. You got any taro there, boy?"

The man grinned and reached into the billum and pulled out a stick of sugar-cane. His interrogator accepted it and chewed it eagerly.

"You gentlemen all work for the Mastas?" he asked, and

paused until someone nodded. "I'm just a bush kanaka. I was visiting a sick uncle in a village on the coast and stayed too late, talking. Now, I must walk home."

"Watch out, bush kanaka. Spirits come out at night, you should know that. Some ghost'll gobble you up."

They all laughed.

Then, clearly, they heard the sound of the returning motor-launch.

"Jesus Christ," mumbled the Administrator's servant, in exact copy of McNicol off-duty. He stood up quickly. The others, with the exception of Baranuma, did likewise.

"Where you all going?" he demanded. "The party's just warming up."

"Where do you think we're going, eh? We going home to open the door for the Masta and the Missus and tuck them into bed."

"They'll see you're drunk."

"They'll be so drunk themselves they won't know what they're seeing."

"They won't know if it's the missus they're feeling up, or the houseboy."

"That's because it'll be both."

"Come on. Jesus Christ, where's my cap! Masta always wants me to wear this bloody cap!"

Baranuma grinned at the stranger through the melee, and the stranger smiled back.

"How about you?" Baranuma asked. "How about you and me have a party?"

"Good night, Baranuma. Stick it up Nicholls' arse when you see him."

"Good night," he said. "You stick it up the King when you see him."

"You gentlemen move in very high society," the stranger observed, watching them depart.

"Ahh, they talk big," Baranuma said. "They're just bush kanakas, deep down inside, like you and me. Their fathers all ate long pig. Come on, have a drink. What's your name?"

But the stranger did not say his name, and he declined the drink. He looked very steadily at Baranuma, aping his posture on the floor, the way he leaned forward and gestured,

75

even the rhythm of his breathing. After a while he began to talk, softly, but with a voice full of resonance.

"It's been a long day," the stranger said. "A very long day. And you have drunk a lot of drink. Your friends have all had a good time, and you have spread largess over them. They think you are a very Big man. Big with gifts, with generosity. You have done well. Now, you are tired."

He was tired, too. He yawned. The stranger shared the yawn. His voice sounded tired.

"They will spread the news of your Bigness. Your fame will grow. It will attract good fortune." Baranuma smiled, and the stranger smiled the same smile. "Women will seek you out, to extract some of that fortune from you. You will demand a huge bride-price. For you are a Big man. A Rich man."

He spoke every one of Baranuma's favourite dreams.

"One day, a white woman will get off a huge ship. She, too, will have heard of your prowess: not just your riches, but the size of your organ . . ." He paused, and Baranuma squirmed his thighs. The stranger's thighs squirmed.

"She will seek you out and throw herself at your feet. She will beg you to marry her. But, you will already have a fine, black wife. You will take her on as a secondary wife, for her relatives will bring you your own steel ship . . ."

Baranuma did not hear any more of the story, for he was asleep.

"Where's that Boy of mine?" Bellamy asked, of no one. "I told him to meet us here with a lantern."

"He'll be asleep," Patricia said. "He'll have sneaked your whisky, got drunk, and fallen asleep. Come on, it's moonlight. We can walk."

"The lazy bugger," he said. "No. He wouldn't do that, not Peter. He's a good Boy."

"Gee, it's great, being out late,
Walking my baby back home," she sang.

76

They fell in step, walking flank to flank, up the hill towards the darkness of the bush, and their house.

"Goodnight, sir!" Harris called behind them.

"Goodnight, Don," he said, over his shoulder.

"Goodnight, Don," she said, yawning.

A native appeared before them. He wore a rumpled lap-lap and a peaked cap. He was staggering from one side of the road to the other.

"Hullo," Bellamy said. "It's McNicol's Boy."

"He's drunk, Richard. He's as full as a boot."

" 'Night, Massa. Missus."

"Good night, my boy."

"He's as drunk as a skunk."

"Who isn't? Come on."

"Yes, but . . ."

"But what?"

"But nothing. Kiss me."

When they were through with kissing, they walked on to their house. Bellamy was feeling good, relieved that what could have been a potential disaster for Patricia, a welling-up of all her fear and insecurity in the presence of the Administrator and the slick girls from the cities, had turned into such a pleasant evening, with the promise of a more pleasant time back in their bed.

The Boy was still not around when they got home. Bellamy let them in.

"Peter!" he shouted. "Where the devil are you?"

He stood aside to let her through. She stumbled on something and bent down to touch it.

"Peter?" he called.

Then she screamed.

Bellamy saw his servant's body.

His wife began to shake. Her screaming did not stop. It built higher and higher; louder and louder.

"Patricia!" he shouted. He grabbed her and shook her, but she took no heed of him. He clamped his hand over her mouth, so the scream became a harsh moan. Her eyes were rolling, showing their whites.

"It's all right," he said. "He's just dead. It's only the Boy."

The moaning subsided, and he released her.

"Someone's been here," she whispered. Her face was ashen. She was now stone sober.

"I don't think so," he said, kneeling by the body. Hearing a noise, he glanced up. She had begun to tremble again. "It was probably a heart attack," he added. He stood up and grabbed her—like you grab a child in a tantrum, wrapping his body around her.

"They've been watching us, Richard. I've seen them. It's us they're after. I can feel it whenever I go outside. It's us they want to kill."

"Hush, dear. Hush. Come on. Quieten down. No one will kill a D.O. or his Missus, you know that. Hush now." He began to walk her across the room.

"I hate it," she whispered, sobbing. "I hate this place." She saw the body again. "Peter?" she said. "Peter?"

"He's dead, dear. I think it was a heart attack. We'll have the Coroner examine him, but he won't find anything else."

The sobbing was subsiding. He walked her through the living room, past the bookcases and his desk, to the bedroom. He lifted the mosquito net and helped her onto the bed.

"Don't go," she said. "Please, Dickie. Don't go."

"I'm going to have to cover the body."

"Leave it! Please, don't leave me."

· CHAPTER FIVE ·

Baranuma had not been admitted to the ranks of men by the time the Sky People first came. He was only a child, who spent his time playing with his age-mates in the garden, well within the safe limits of their territory. Looking up from the gardens, it was possible to see the men standing, silent and still, watchful on the borders. And around him, the women and girls squatting on the soil, turning it over with their digging sticks; or harvesting taro, or leading pigs to some choice area of foraging.

He had never given thought to the world outside their valley. Very few people did. They exchanged pigs with their neighbours, sure, but that was no reason to trust them. The world was contained in the bowl formed by mountains and escarpments, usually lost in cloud and mist. A river ran through it. It came from somewhere, and went somewhere else.

His father was a Big Man and he shared in the honour of that, as did other close relatives. His mother was the third wife of the Big Man. He had six in all, and was negotiating to buy himself another from a neighbouring village. With six wives and a brood of daughters he had the largest labour force in the valley. With that much labour, he had a guaranteed steady flow of produce for his pigs. With the pigs he had financial security and, beyond that, the power of investment capital. He bought into other men's schemes, contributing to bride-prices, and thus securing regular interest payments — plus, of course, secured their obligation to return favours when he should need them. He was able to trade for gold-lip mother-of-pearl shell — securing for himself only perfect specimens, no worm holes, no faded colours. He had access to almost unlimited land-use, for he had demonstrated he was a superior raiser of pigs, and any land lent him would repay in pig meat very quickly. He was able to stake promising young men with a sow, on condition of the usual rates of interest in piglets.

Baranuma's father was not a renowned warrior. But the cultivation of pigs was in no way inferior to warfare. There were Big Men whose prowess lay in warfare. They brought honour to the village that way—and they kept it safe from the marauders. But when fighting was done, after a local death had been avenged or, more seriously, when an assault on their land-holdings had been repelled (and, on occasion, when their warriors had launched a bold attack that had secured the village some more territory), then there was no point to peace if the people could not bask in the glory that a Big Man of trade and pigs could bring them.

They would declare a feast, send out invitations to the neighbours, a few sample-pigs—not the best, but not inferior stock—and prepare for the feast and the exchange. Then Baranuma's fat, glistening porkers would be led out to be pole-axed to the awe and chagrin of their neighbours—whose own pigs would seem, by comparison, scrawny, worm-riddled, victims of sorcery and poor feed.

He did not know his father well. He was the man seen always in the distance, sitting with his colleagues, listening to propositions for the investment of his wealth, walking through his gardens frowning at the evidence of garden sorcery. Or, at his most unapproachable, in the full regalia of a man of his standing—bedecked with mother-of-pearl and bird of paradise feathers—his wealth displayed for all to see, acknowledged business leader of the village, and of the whole valley.

Baranuma was coming to see that he could be expected to follow in his father's footsteps—if he could prove himself capable of it. If he could trade and scheme and plan in advance, he could fight his way up through the intricate web of relationships, of deals, of the ever-present fear of sorcery, to a similar position.

He could daydream about it, as he played in the gardens. And in the daydream, when he had bought and sold his way to that position of eminence, with a dozen wives in his fields, leading his pigs, then he would look across the field and see an old man watching. That old man would walk, stiff with age, down the track, through the gate in the fence, treading carefully amongst the planted vines, stopping to admire a sow and her brood; and then he would come over to Baranuma, lounging in the shade, and look into his eyes and smile, and place his hand on Baranuma's shoulder. And Baranuma would know, at last, that his father respected him.

The day of the Sky People, he had still been a boy. Clouds were building up along the escarpment. Rain was in the air. It was muggy, but not too hot. The whole valley was afire with the news of the Sky People. The tall, wraithlike, pale emissaries from the Land of the Dead.

The excitement in the village was far greater than that of any feasting; even greater than that of battle. The people had never been overly preoccupied with religion. The Earth Goddess existed. Big Men had developed means of communicating with her, and she had rewarded them. Sorcerers studied the power that lay in her bosom, and used it for their clandestine ends.

Sorcerers killed people. Dead people vanished. They went beyond the mountains. Sometimes their ghosts returned, to accuse sorcerers or to demand mourning. Sometimes, in dreams, people had seen the Sky People themselves, the emissaries of the Land of the Dead leading the Dead across the sky.

And now they were here. Suddenly everything had acquired a new meaning, or was losing its old meaning. Perhaps the Earth Goddess was not the strongest power. Perhaps they had been mistaken in spilling their blood on her. She had always existed in counterpoint to the Sky People and the Sky Gods, the two poles of the cosmos. Because she directly controlled the gardens, and hence the economy, she was regarded as the stronger. But, now . . .?

The boys ran frantically along the track. Ahead they could see the warriors massing, equipped with killing spears and poison-tipped arrows. The women were coming behind, more slowly, hampered by the infants, by pigs. The warriors had gone to greet the Sky People and to see if they wanted to do trade. They were armed, just in case.

Baranuma and his mates reached the line of warriors. He looked for his father. He was standing in the rear ranks of the warriors. He was positioned with a good, quick escape route. Baranuma felt suddenly ashamed of him.

But then he saw the Sky People appear down the track, coming around a bend in the kunai slopes.

It was exactly as described. There were two of the wraiths. And with them a line of dead men, who walked in a trance, leaning forwards, heavy loads on their backs, staring dully at the waiting line of warriors.

He saw the two wraiths stop. They called out something. He then saw that some of the dead black men were not dead. They carried no loads. They carried sticks. These sticks must be "guns". At the sight of them, the warriors murmured among themselves. They knew about guns. They notched their arrows.

The dead men had halted. They leaned forward against the weight of their loads. Were they loads of accumulated shame from past lives? Baranuma watched them closely. He could see their fear. Perhaps they were the "rubbishmen" of many villages; the men who in their lives acquired few pigs, no gold-lip shell, who brought no glory to the village. This, then, was their punishment.

The Sky People and the black men who were not dead felt some fear, but it was the fear of warriors before battle. The fear of the dead men was the fear of women.

One of the Sky Persons stepped forward, ahead of his troops. The villagers murmured at this show of courage. Baranuma watched closely, giving his father a quick and critical glance. This was not a situation his father could exploit. Sure enough, he was edging to the rear of the crowd. A warrior let him pass: scornfully. Baranuma felt a flush of anger.

The Sky Person spoke. He did not speak their exact language. He spoke one of its near relatives, one of the valley languages, that made him understandable enough.

"We come in peace," he said. He looked along the line of warriors and, suddenly, his eyes encountered the eyes of a

82

fifteen-year old boy. The boy watched him solemnly, but sharply. There was no fear in his eyes, and none of the dazed look of men confronting gods. It was the sort of look only a child can give you: assessing, knowing, waiting.

"We come in trade," the Sky Person said.

Something made Baranuma break eye-contact with him. He looked back and met his father's gaze. His father's face was no longer blank: it was grey with fear.

His father had seen that his days as Number One Big Man were numbered.

Any man in the valley was a pawn of the elemental forces. He tried to conjure with them, to call them to his assistance, to discover the secrets of power from them. He had been more successful than most. And he made regular offerings to the Earth Goddess of his own blood—from his nose, from his penis. But he was still only a man.

The Sky People were not men. They were the Power incarnate. He had only to look at them to read it in their haughty demeanour. Their voices spoke of trade, but their faces spoke of Power. He saw the look of scorn on the face of one of his sons. He turned and walked away, head down, his eyes clouded with tears.

Baranuma turned back to the Sky Person, wild with anger at his father. The warriors waited, still murmuring. The Sky Person waited, haughty, regal, wondering what effect his words had made. Baranuma took a deep breath and stepped through the ranks.

"I will trade with you," he said.

And behind him, the murmuring became laughter. He puffed out his chest, like a warrior, and stared into the Sky Person's pale eyes.

Patrol Officer Jim Taylor stared at the boy, and smiled. Wherever they went, there was always at least one monkey who would ignore the fear of his parents, or the customs of his people; who would initiate the first contact, breaking the explosive tension into laughter. He handed his shotgun back to his sergeant and knelt on one knee.

"You are the paramount Big Man of this village?" he asked the boy.

And the line of warriors erupted into explosive laughter.

But Baranuma frowned. He held the Sky Person's eyes.

"I will trade with you," he said.

The Sky Person examined him more closely.

"What do you have to trade?"

"What do you want?" Baranuma replied.

"We require food. Taro. Whatever vegetables you have. And a pig."

"And what will you trade?" Baranuma demanded.

The Sky Person stood up. He reached out and placed his hand on Baranuma's shoulder. A murmur ran through the ranks of villagers. Baranuma glanced back and waved to them, reassuring them. He would not be abducted.

"Gold-lip shell?" the Sky Person asked.

"Let me see the quality." Baranuma kept his head, though his heart was pounding faster. The touch of the man's hand had told him that this was not a wraith. It was a man, like himself, like his father. The touch gave him a strange, warm feeling.

"And, in return, let me see your produce," the Sky Person replied, humour in his voice, turning Baranuma to look at one of the dead men. He met the dead man's empty, exhausted eyes. The Sky Person gestured and the dead man released his load from his back and opened it. Baranuma stared into a sack of gold-lip shell. Incalculable riches.

His mind worked ferociously. He had no produce of his own. He certainly had no pigs. But his father had both; he would have to borrow against credit. But he was not yet a man, not yet of an age when he would expect to do business. But these times were new. New times meant new rules.

"I'll be right back," he said, pulling free of the Sky Person's grasp and diving through the crowd.

Taylor watched him go with relief. Fear was always with you on patrol. Most of all when you confronted new people. Children could be relied upon to break the ice — if it were to be broken. He glanced back to his colleague, the prospector Mick Leahy. Mick grinned at him, his face streaming sweat.

"She'll be right, now," Mick said.

Taylor nodded, suddenly weary, in his weariness remembering his men. He spoke to his sergeant of police.

"Get the Boys to unload," he said. "We'll set up camp on that knoll."

84

And his carriers, the dead men, dropped their fifty-pound packs, that they carried each day, all day, ascending from the coast to the plateau; a climb of ten thousand feet through swamp and jungle, prey to marauding bands of headhunters and vicious mosquitoes. They collapsed beside their packs.

Taylor let them rest. He turned his attention to the warriors. One of them had stepped forward. It was time for international diplomacy.

Baranuma found his father walking, dazed, along the track. He spoke to him anxiously, gruff with anger. His father answered dreamily. Yes, he was willing to advance his son some credit, at the usual rates. Yes, repayment in gold-lip shell was entirely satisfactory. But, no, he would not advance him a pig. He could have vegetables, and that was all.

Baranuma let him turn off the track, and watched him stumble in an irrigation ditch. He had no more time for anger, or for sadness. He had business to do. He ran to the shade-house where the women had been collecting taro roots, and began to scoop them into a billum.

Seeing he could not buy a pig, he would have to steal one. But everyone would know it was not his. They would assume it was his father's. Did that matter any more? Would they tell his father? Would his father notice, or care? Was his father now dead and his estate waiting to be distributed to his heirs?

There was only one way to find out.

"Baranuma? Baranuma!"

His name sounded somewhere far away. He struggled out of sleep.

"What the hell have you been doing?"

It was the Masta's voice. He shook his head to clear it, but the action had the reverse effect, sending shivers of pain through it, like a guria. He groaned.

"You bugger," there was amusement in Nicholls' voice. "You've been drinking."

"Ah, no, Masta . . ."

"God, it looks like you had quite a party. Was McNicol's boy here, too?"

85

"Ah, Masta, lik lik drink, that's all."

Now he could see Nicholls' face. It was struggling to suppress a grin. Baranuma shook his head a second time, and it hurt just the same.

"There's only one genuine cure for a hangover, my boy, and that's sweat. You get yourself together and I'll find something to make you sweat."

Baranuma groaned again and looked around his room. He wrinkled his nose in disgust, seeing the empty bottles and the remains of the long cheroots that had been smoked. There was even a betel-nut stain in one corner. He looked for the half-empty bottle of rum, thinking that one little nip would restore his equilibrium, but it was nowhere to be seen. One of the others must have taken it. He groaned again, and tried to stand.

Nicholls walked to the Administration buildings, laughing to himself. He walked jauntily. He couldn't help but feel superior to everyone this morning. All the town's whites and, by the look of it, half the blacks, had been ruining themselves last night as he slogged over the Patrol Report.

There was a piece of hallowed tropical lore that, to survive, you had to drink: hard. Not only that, you had to drink "pure spirit"—not wine or beer. If only the natives knew it, they could win their island back by the simple process of not drinking—and waiting while the whites drank themselves to death.

But he knew it wouldn't happen. Whatever the European did, the native aped, in the mistaken belief that thus he would become the European's equal—not realizing that, morally, he was that equal, and the European's refusal to recognize this was purely political: nothing more.

It was not yet 9 a.m., but Bellamy already looked harassed when Nicholls arrived. Sitting in a chair by the louvred windows was a blond-haired youth who was going through a written list of items, presumably the check-list of patrol requisites. Nicholls studied him covertly.

"Nicholls," Bellamy said. "I don't think you've actually met your number two yet."

The boy looked up eagerly, smiling. Nicholls looked away from his young, blue eyes.

"This is Don Harris, Edward." As Nicholls took the proffered hand Bellamy added, "And, of course, Edward Nicholls." Nicholls looked up and met the steady gaze. He studied the healed scar on the boy's forehead.

"I've heard all about you, sir," the boy said.

Nicholls frowned.

"What, in particular?"

"Your ideas, your methods. Your success in the Highlands."

Nicholls shied from his familiarity.

"My success I attribute to Clauswitz, whom I had read and the opposition hadn't."

The boy laughed. Bellamy was edging towards the door.

"Look, chaps," he said, "I've got to leave you to it. I'm in a frightful pickle at home. My boy dropped down dead last night."

"Good Lord! Natural causes?"

"As far as I can tell. There's not a mark on him. No sign of a struggle, or anything. Probably his heart. We found him by the door. He must have been coming out to get some help."

"Most of the other boys were down with Baranuma, getting a skinful," Nicholls said. "I'm surprised he wasn't there, too."

"Patricia asked him to stay home and keep an eye on things. There've been a few prowlers of late."

"And he actually stayed home?"

Bellamy nodded. "He was a good Boy. We'll miss him. Which is why I must scoot now. I've got to find someone to replace him."

"Ask Baranuma. He's bound to have a cousin."

Bellamy nodded, still distracted, and left them.

Nicholls stared after him, then glanced at Harris.

"His relatives will say it was sorcery," he said, "and demand a payback." He thought for a moment, frowning.

"Something wrong, sir?"

87

"No. A feeling, that's all." He studied the boy again. "Do you trust your instincts, Harris?"

The boy nodded, unsurely.

"Mine say that something funny was going on last night. I felt it just before I started writing up the Report. But you can't listen to your sixth sense and worry about grammar at the same time."

"No, sir."

"Did you enjoy dinner last night?"

"Not really, sir. Too much of the stuffed-shirt brigade, and some silly women from South, carrying on with that bloody pilot."

"Johnson?" Nicholls grinned. "We'll get on, I think: distrust pilots, Administrators, and white women."

"In that order, sir?"

"That's the order you'll meet them in."

"And what about the black women?"

Nicholls studied him a moment. The question seemed innocent enough. He decided to play it at face value.

"Fuck 'em," he said. "But never marry them. How are you getting on with the stores list?"

The lad handed it to him wordlessly. Nicholls read it quickly.

Ammunition
Axes
Aspirin
Beads
Butter
Bandages
Bacon

He skimmed the list, down to . . .

Vaseline
Vinegar
Writing pads

"I think I'd like to double up on all medical supplies," he said. He looked up and met Harris's eyes. "Just in case," he said.

"You think we'll be mixing it with them?"

Nicholls noticed that the comment about women had made the lad stop calling him "Sir".

"You've mixed it before, haven't you, Harris?"

"That's right. On my last patrol, up the Rai Coast."

Nicholls grunted thoughtfully. "Well, get over to the medical store and see about some more bandages, and morphine. Clean the store out."

Harris hesitated.

"Clean it out, sir? What about the other Patrols?"

"The other Patrols have a fifty per cent chance of getting into trouble. We have a one hundred per cent chance."

He saw the recognition dawn on Harris's face.

"This is a Punitive Patrol, Harris, thinly disguised as a legal inquiry."

"Yes, sir."

Nicholls looked back to the check-list. He heard the door close as Harris went out.

Alo had woken well before Piccaninny Dawn. The drunk was snoring. He had risen and collected his billum. Seeing the bottle beside the sleeping drunk's outstretched hand, he had taken it, uncapped it, and had a nip.

The rum had blasted him awake, fuelling him with warmth. He had grinned, recapped the bottle, and added it to the collection of curios in his billum. Then he left.

He walked south along the coastal track, pausing to skirt villages when he came to them. Dogs, sensing his presence, barked into the jungle. Tamed jungle hens squawked uneasily. But he made no sound. As he walked, the coast grew visible.

He could see the offshore islands, peaks hidden in cloud; he could see the still water on the black, sandy beaches. He walked effortlessly and quickly, knowing the distance he had to cover to reach safety. The sun came up over the ocean, flaming red.

He reached the river's mouth by the time the sun was overhead. The river was strong, filling the ocean with muddy water poured in a rush from the mountains. In the mouth of the river were many small islands.

89

The locals kept away from these islands as they were the spawning and breeding grounds of crocodiles. Great, log-like beasts could sometimes be seen sunning themselves on the muddy banks, or slumbering in the shallows, eyes half-open, watching for food.

But Alo was a member of The Great Crocodile Association — a secret society of sorcerers whose emblem was the crocodile —and who understood the beast better than anyone else.

He looked along the bank, shadowed by crowding vegetation, and saw one beast asleep, half in, half out of the water.

Alo had sunk his canoe in the pool formed beside the roots of a giant tree. He retrieved it and upended it to flush out the water. The paddle was tied inside.

He checked the rushing water. Another good reason for the locals' avoiding this estuary was the fierce current. But he knew the incoming tide would weaken its effects—just as it would float that animate log out into the stream, eager to search out fish on the rising tide.

The rippled surface of the water changed as the outrush met the inrush and the current slowed. He slung his billum into the canoe and stepped aboard, pushing the canoe into the stream.

He steered the frail craft into the centre of the stream. It bucked on the clashing water, and his feet shifted balance, holding the canoe flat on the rippled surface. He searched the surface closely, looking for the spot where a hidden snag smoothed out the power of the water and made navigation possible.

With a slow sigh, the log on the bank stretched out a chubby, child-like leg that ended in claws, and dragged itself into the water.

He found the smooth water and swung his paddle, turning the canoe out to sea, pushing it past the islands cluttering the estuary.

Looking back, he could see the crocodile drifting now on the tide, head submerged, watching for fish. As he watched, a shiver ran down its tail, and it lunged into the depths. He turned back to the sea horizon.

Beyond the estuary was another island, one that the

crocodiles rarely used. It was beyond the fish-rich estuary waters, and exposed to the wind and the open sea. His father's father had discovered it, and noted how the locals regarded it as one of the crocodile islands and steadfastly avoided it. It seemed the right spot for a sorcerer to keep as his retreat.

His father's father had constructed a hut in the centre of the low scrub that covered the rocky outcrop. His father had rebuilt that hut with Alo's help, when he was a boy. Now he made himself comfortable outside the hut and examined his haul.

He could sense the power within the black-bound book. It was like the fierce power of the river he had just left. The power of the revolver was nothing compared to the book's power. For the book could tell him how to obtain revolvers.

He opened the book, as he had seen the missionaries do, and contemplated its meaning.

Once upon a time, the "meaning" of the world was not debated. It simply was. People lived in it. These people were all dark-skinned. The centre of the world was right here, on the coast. If you came from, say, Karkar, you naturally said that was the centre. If from Bok, well that was the centre.

Now, up and down the coast, there was intense debate about the origins of the world and the people in it.

Most people spoke of two ancestors: Kilibob and Manup. Some said they were brothers, though others denied this. But one of them, brother or not, had led some of the world's people down into the Underworld, the world of the Guria, and had shown them, there, how to make Cargo. These people, because they had to enter the Underworld, had died and become white-skinned.

The other brother (and to his despair, as Alo journeyed up and down the coast listening to and comparing these stories, it became obvious that no one could say with certainty which brother . . . assuming they were brothers) did not make the journey. For various reasons he remained on the surface, and his people remained alive, and black, and denied the access to Cargo.

By rights the returned, white-fleshed dead should have shared their Cargo, and the Cargo-knowledge. But the journey, death, the return, all had ruined their minds. Even though relatives could clearly recognize the face and mannerisms of a lost son, that son—now white-fleshed—would look right through them, content to sit with the other white-fleshed dead men, not understanding local languages or customs, not even knowing how to throw a fish-spear.

So when the missionaries came, telling everyone that they, and they alone, were there to share with them, through the spirit of the Lord Jesus Christ, who also had died and been reborn, all of Jesus Christ's power and his Cargo, then the people came running.

Villages were left to ruin. Ceremonies to invoke their own spirits were forgotten. Old and sacred implements were destroyed at the missionaries' urging. The people were "baptized". They denounced the gods of tree and river, beach and island. Only the Guria occasionally rumbled, reminding them of what they had betrayed. But even he was subdued.

They sat in the "churches" eagerly listening as the "words of power" were spoken. The missionaries promised "equality". They said "all men are brothers". The people glanced at one another, smiling. Yes, at last some people had returned with their minds intact. Now, any moment, the "words of power" would be revealed.

But they never were.

The people began to drift away from the missionaries and their humbug. Only to find that, in the meantime, somehow, they had become carriers and copra workers and house-servants. And their wives and daughters were whores.

So Alo and his Crocodile brothers worked. They confronted the "meaning" of the changed world, the "meaning" of traditional stories, and the "meaning" of the Bible. They observed the power that lay with the white-skins: the power of the gun. This power was never explained in the Bible.

The only possible answer to this omission was: the white-skins had hidden the relevant passages of the Bible. These were not translated. They had tapped the source of the world's energy, and kept it for themselves.

Alo put the Bible aside and fingered the revolver. He had seen them work. A renegade Police Boy had shown someone

92

in Rabaul how they worked, and that person had told someone else . . . pantomiming the mechanism with his hands . . . and that explanation had been carried all up and down the coast, and inland.

He caressed the cold steel, and put his finger inside the trigger guard. Grinning, he pointed it out to sea, shut his eyes, and pulled the trigger.

Nothing happened. He opened his eyes and stared at it again, remembering how it had refused to work for the houseboy.

He went over it carefully, probing each indentation in the surface. Above the trigger guard was a small catch. His finger poked it and it moved. He felt a mechanism click. He tested the trigger and there was more "give" in it. He aimed it out to sea and pulled.

His heart jolted as the gun leapt in his hand and roared. He pulled again, and again, laughing, until it stopped firing.

He touched the barrel and burnt his finger. He sniffed the heavy smell of cordite. He remembered the pantomime of the revolver. At this point it was necessary to recharge it with magic. But he did not have the necessary magic. He felt an urge to throw the thing into the depths. That was what an ordinary man would do. But, being a sorcerer, he put it in his billum and sat there, wondering how he could acquire the necessary magic to make it fire again.

The geckoes scuttled across the lounge-room wall. Patricia watched them, immobile herself. From outside came the sound of insects. Rustlings that once had set her nerves on edge. But now she was at the stage of pure calm, before misery, of three Gilbey's dry gins.

Richard was working on the screened verandah. From her seat she could see the pool of light surrounding him — the insects beating hopelessly against the wire in an effort to reach that light. Moths six inches long. Giant stick insects. Spiders spread as wide as Richard's hand. She stared at them and sipped.

As if synchronized to her movement, his hand lifted its glass too. She could see the honey colour of the whisky. She knew he was reading everything he could on a man named Ludwig: Patrol Reports, native gossip, old Court Reports for infringements of the Native Labour Ordinance, and the Report and newspaper clippings on the murder of his only son by tribesmen in Uncontrolled Territory, in 1930.

She tried to imagine what it would be like. The imagining was all too easy. Her own son was twelve, Ludwig's would have been about sixteen. A boy beginning to look like a man. The bond, which only a parent can understand, between two people—different to, and more powerful than, any bond between man and woman.

There was a dull ache in her belly at the thought of young Richard. But he and his sister were at school in Australia. Not just thousands of miles away, but thousands of years away, several civilizations away. To reach them she would have to take a plane across the mountains to Port Moresby, then a ship to Sydney, and then a train to Melbourne . . . and from there a tram. The distances stretched out in her mind, endless and unendurable.

Richard's hand moved across the table, the light falling on it. It slid the papers away. It came back to rub his forehead. She saw the tension in his neck and the pain in her belly grew larger. She carefully placed her glass on the thin, teak table beside her chair. She pushed herself up. The humidity always made her breathless.

He felt her arms across his shoulders and sat still. Her fingers touched his forehead, then her breasts were against his back. He reached up and felt her hair. Her lips brushed his.

"Richard," she said.

He leaned back against her and they looked, together, at the insects that threw themselves at the screen, thudding with real force. He turned out the lamp.

There was a man watching them from the edge of the bush. Her heart thumped. She felt Richard stiffen. His hand cautioned her. With the light out, they could see their watcher better than he could see them. He would have been invisible, but for the gleam of sweat on his dark, brown flesh.

He watched, immobile. His eyes locked on theirs. He was unarmed.

"I think we'll go inside, love," Richard said, quietly.

"Yes," she replied, drawing back from him, but unable to tear her gaze from the watcher.

Richard stood up. Almost unconsciously he glanced at the locks on the screens and the doors. He turned and smiled at her, but she could see the tension behind it. She smiled back, as bravely. He put his arm around her and led her inside, his free hand picking up his glass.

"Sit on that chair," he whispered to her, and she obeyed instantly, like a frightened child. He rummaged in the drawer by his bed.

"Damn it," he muttered. "My revolver should be here."

She stared at the opened drawer, then at the door into the living-room.

Still muttering, he left her alone in the bedroom. She began to shake. She clamped her arms to prevent it. She could hear him checking the doors and windows. Then she heard him pouring a drink.

"Here," he said, on his return, and handed her a glass of neat whisky. She downed it, spluttering, and was now totally drunk, totally immune to feeling. Floating, she watched him return to his search for the revolver.

"They're always watching," he said. "You know that. Women make too much about being watched." He was speaking as much for his own benefit as for hers. "Where did I put that damned gun? I wonder if the wretched Boy pinched it?"

"Or someone else," she said.

He glared at her, then tried to smile, to not agitate her.

"We are living here only on sufferance," she said, with an intense effort to get each word right. "It's not just insects that want to get through the windows, to get at the light."

"Do you want me to apply for a transfer? Eh?"

She said nothing. She looked down at her skirt, at the stain of perspiration along her thighs.

95

· CHAPTER SIX ·

Dawn in the village of Parap. The sun, coming over the blue mountains, lit the valleys of mist streaming white through the passes that fell away to the unseen, unknown ocean. The village, shrouded in the shadows of casuarinas, was quiet. Then the first board at the door of a woman's house was released. Grunting impatiently, the first pig stumbled into the light. Other boards were loosed and the village street filled with pigs, snuffling in the debris of the night's meal. The children began to emerge, yawning, blinking, looking up into the overhanging trees at the birds that, having called the sun over the mountains, now fell silent.

Barum's eldest daughter, Merin, emerged, hunched over, squeezing through the door of her mother's house. She did not glance at the trees, or down through the grove to the scarp falling away into the valley. She scrabbled on the ground for a few sticks and began to stoke up the embers smouldering beside the door. She glanced up, once, to the men's house, but its door was still fastened.

"Hurry up!" her mother said sharply, from inside. "Get that fire going and go for the water, quickly. And take the baby with you. He's driving me crazy!"

She grunted in reply, kneeling by the coals, fanning them into life. She felt her mother emerging from the house, puffing with the exertion. She, too, knelt by the fire, holding in her hand left-over sweet potato from the night. Wordlessly, Merin took them from her and slid them into the coals. Behind them, the baby began to cry again and another child, a ten-year old girl, appeared in the doorway, dragging him with her.

Their mother snatched the infant before any damage could come its way. The infant grabbed for her breast. He nuzzled into her, his cries giving way to the sound of suckling. She sat back on her heels, smiling at the baby.

Merin sat back, too, watching the door of the men's house as the boards at the door shivered, then clattered free, and the first of the teenage boys emerged into the shadowed light of the village.

When the women were all gone to the gardens, taking their pigs and children with them, the village was silent. The trees kept out the increasing heat of the day and the fierce, white light of the plateau. The men were able to relax and stretch out around their clubhouse. They were silent a while, all thinking the same thing, waiting for the discussion to begin.

Barum let the silence ride a little longer. His eyes moved from man to man, evaluating each individual's mental processes. He did not want to open the discussion; he wanted to steer it without making his presence too obvious. He did not want to be seen as the initiator of any more bungled heroics.

His brother-in-law, Pari, aware of Barum's eyes on him, began the discussion. He knew the role Barum wished to play and, being an outsider to the village, marrying into it from a far mountain-slope village, he was anxious to consolidate his position within his new clan.

"It's going to be a good crop of sweet potato," he observed casually. "That's why I shifted here, you know. The vines grow much better on this soil, than back home . . ." he let his voice trail off. The others meditated on his statement. The fact that he had migrated to join his wife, rather than the reverse, was indication of the ascendance of the village of Parap in the eyes of others.

"If it gets harvested," someone replied, opening up one area of worry.

"And why shouldn't it?" replied a third, filling in the next move.

"The times are not propitious."

"The times are all right," someone else said. "It's the people in them that are causing the trouble."

97

He was an old man and they knew what he would say next.

"I don't know what's happening to this village," he continued. "The young, today . . ." he drew his hand out in an uncertain gesture, unable to see beyond it with his glaucoma-blind eyes. "In my time, if there were people causing trouble . . ." his hand continued the gesture, turning into a club, a stone axe.

No one defended the current generation. The listening boys were there only as listeners, not as debaters. Everyone looked to the ground. In their minds were the images of the men who had died at the hands of the Sky People. Barum let the image stay with them a while longer. Then, judging the time to be ripe, he spoke.

"Sometimes . . ." he paused, letting their attention focus on him, "sometimes, when an enemy is too strong, it is better to move more slowly."

The old man snorted and scuffed angrily at the dirt.

"Barum moved fairly swiftly the last time the Sky People fired," someone else muttered. There was a ripple of laughter.

"You planning on shitting them to death, Barum, next time you meet?"

He laughed, too.

"Yes," he said. "They scared me. They scared a lot of people. They've got a lot of power."

"I'll tell you all something," the old man muttered. "What you need is sorcery. But there's no good sorcerers left any more." He shook his head sorrowfully.

"How can we work sorcery on Dead Men? On spirits from the Sky?"

"Do we want to work sorcery on them?" Barum said, with some surprise, looking up as if the idea was new to him.

"We want to keep them away from our women and our pigs. If it takes sorcery, let's use sorcery."

"Maybe a fight would be better," Barum mused. "We did well against the prospector, because we hit him quickly."

"We're not hitting anyone else like that. You know, like me, that the Kiap's gone to see the Baloose and be flown away in it, and it'll bring him back with more troops, and more guns."

The talk became confused now, as different men voiced their opinions. Two of the boys were sent for refreshments. The others listened to their elders intently. Agitated men stood up, gesturing to make their points, beating their breasts as they harangued the others—who listened, half to the argument, half to the style of oration.

The talk crystallized into three factions: those for sorcery, those for a fight, and those for simple flight. Within the factions, sub-groups developed the ideas further. What kind of sorcery? How would they get the necessary body excrements? How did sorcery measure up as an act of war? What would its ramifications be with their allies, and their enemies? The fight proponents discussed possible allies, and re-examined the campaign against the prospector—and with it, the retaliation of the Kiap. That attack played into the hands of those arguing for flight. They, in turn, speculated on flinging themselves on the mercy of some other community, perhaps trading some land for access to a mountain slope on which they could hide.

Barum listened to all points of view, placing a word here and there: lightly scoffing at the idea of flight; soberly acknowledging the enemy's superior firepower to the hawks; admitting that, yes, sorcery did have its attractions.

By the time the first of the women returned, exhausted, from the gardens, the talk was unanimous. Sorcery would work best. The Sky People were supreme sorcerers, though, and it would take great sorcery to bring them down.

"They have one weak point," Barum said, and all eyes came back to him.

He pushed aside his bark girdle and pointed at his genitals. He looked around the group. The eyes watched him, puzzled.

"My daughter, Merin, was sent to look after the Kiap, wasn't she?" No one said anything, watching him. "She did a good job. And, being the daughter of a prudent man, she collected a little memento of the occasion . . . just in case, you understand?"

The puzzled frowns began to give way to smiles, then chuckles, then an obscene joke at the white man's expense. Barum knew he had carried the day.

Returning from the garden, tired and irritated, holding the baby on her hip and leading a pig by the cord on its foot, Merin felt the shade of the village trees and stopped to enjoy the first plunge into the coolness, like stepping into a stream. She closed her eyes.

When she opened them, she was aware of the men ahead of her. They stared as she walked past them. No one gave her a rude greeting, or made a copulatory gesture. Instead, they watched her quietly, speculatively. She saw her father and smiled at him, but his return smile was slow in coming. She frowned and walked on, head down.

Something was up, she thought.

There was a song—"Satin Doll" was the title—and for some reason Gloria could not get it out of her head. She had a melody, but no words other than the title. The band had played it on the ship, the night she had met the man now sitting in the pilot's seat of the huge aeroplane. Jennifer had won him, that night, and now sat beside him. The booming interior of the plane was screened from them by a piece of sacking—presumably erected by Johnson to hide the girls from the "official" gaze of the Patrol Officers, and also protect them from the lust of the Native Police. Why did they stare at white women the way they did? We wear more clothes than their own Marys, she thought.

The plane banked, and she could see islands in the distance, rising out of the shimmering, blue sea. As the plane turned back to the mainland she saw the whole coast of New Guinea. The vivid, vibrant green and the anonymous folds of the mountains stretching into the sea frightened her. They were like drapery over a hidden, violent animal. Rivers spat white and brown mud into that peaceful sea. Then the plane crossed the coast and she could see the jungle close up as they began the climb along a braided river valley.

"We follow the Ramu!" Johnson shouted to them, through his beard. "We go up the valley until we find the pass, then we haul ourselves over it. You'll see Mount Wilhelm way out to your left, the highest peak on the whole island . . ."

"What happens if we crash?" she asked him.

He stared over his shoulder at her, momentarily flying blind. Jennifer shivered, her hand unconsciously reaching for the controls.

"We die," he said.

Then he laughed and looked ahead, taking Jennifer's hand and smiling at her, settling her hand and his own on her knee. Gloria noticed that, even here, flying above the jungle, Jennifer wore stockings.

Baranuma sat, composed, smoking a cigarette, watching the efforts of the newer Police to hide their fear. The Senior Constable, young Giram, had obviously never flown before. He was petrified. But he tried hard to hide it. Baranuma approved his actions.

Although they were the same age, Baranuma had years of experience with the Europeans. He had probably been the first Highlands-born man to step into the belly of the Baloose. And he had been as close to shitting with fear then as any time since. But he had not shown it. He had made it through the ordeal, and now could reap the benefits.

He shifted his attention to the new, young Kiap. Masta Harris. Baranuma had a bad feeling about him. He was frowning now, trying to see through the hessian screen that Johnson had put up to keep the view of the girls' legs from the rear of the plane. Using a Highlands analogy: the pilot was a Big Man amongst the Europeans, perhaps because of his daily contact with the Baloose. Because he was a true "Sky Person". As such he had first pick of the eligible girls. Masta Harris was ideally situated to become a Big Man, but he had no grasp of the Power. He didn't have Nicholls' basic cunning, or Nicholls' fierce scorn for the rest of his own people. Masta Harris was too eager to please, and that was not the path to becoming a Big Man. You had to make it on your own, adapting the forces of nature, the Power, as each situation called for it. If Masta Harris wanted one of those girls, he had to come up with something better than what Johnson was offering: a flight in the Baloose.

Masta Harris was still a boy. And you should never send a boy to do men's work.

The river beneath them was a ragged streamer, criss-crossing itself in silver braids. The jungle closed in on both sides. They flew over villages hewn out of the jungle, perched precariously on razorback mountains. Looking down, she saw the people looking up in awe and fear.

Then Johnson took one hand from the controls and pointed. The plane shifted with his slight loss of control. He laughed and corrected. This time he pointed with his chin, native-fashion.

"Cecil Holmes went down there!" he shouted.

Both girls looked. Beside the river rose vertical hills, like the hills in stylized Chinese paintings—like enormous loaves of bread, mouldy with jungle. On the side of one was a small gash, bright at its centre and blackened up the hill.

"A bad storm," he said. "Cec flew straight into it."

They now saw that the glint was of metal crumpled up and thrown against the mountainside.

"The fire cooked him!" the pilot went on. "They got there and all they had to do was sit down, wait for him to cool down a bit, and then eat him."

The girls looked at each other and shuddered.

They had been so close! Ludwig had held it in his hand! He had looked across the ridge to the granite boulders breaking

102

through the trees, knowing that those boulders covered the reef.

And now Paul was dead, and two of the Marys were dead, and the new man would not last—he did not have what was necessary for Island work. Five of the Boys had slipped away from the expedition. They would be dead by now. The eyes were out there, in the jungle dankness, watching, waiting, planning their next strike.

The expedition was back on the main river now. Ludwig knew its course quite well, and he knew there was no more than three or four days' hard walking to get them back to relative safety—where the niggers had had a taste of the white man's medicine and were relatively docile. He knew they could make it.

Ludwig was leading the party. His personal Boy was stationed fifth. Rudi was bringing up the tail, with two carriers following him. Ludwig was thinking that he knew where It was, this time. He would outfit a larger party. He would seek active government assistance: a Patrol Officer and a gang of Police Boys with .303 rifles.

He pushed himself harder, forcing the pace along the track that ran beside the river. He was aware that the death of Paul had been a warning from whatever headhunters inhabited this territory, and the headhunters would still be out there, would not leave them until they came to the limit of their domain. So he pushed.

No one complained. They had dropped most of their prospecting gear, carrying only necessary food and equipment, and their weapons. The Boys were as eager as Ludwig and Rudi to force the distance, all thinking now of the open country where they should have met with Wallace as if it were home and safety.

Karap was the last man. He was a family man from the Ramu valley. He had thought that, when the red-bearded prospector arrived, they would sign paper in the usual manner. But not this one. He had arrived in their village with his two silent, armed deputies, and pointed. With each point two black guards, blacker than any man he had seen, had stepped forward and grabbed the man pointed at. One man's

103

wife had shouted at them. The Masta had pointed his pistol at her, it shouted, and she died on the spot. Karap's wife had not shouted. Instead, she had hidden with her children.

And now he trembled at the rear of the line, watching the bush with each step, stumbling because he was too frightened to watch where he placed his feet. The pack seemed to have grown into his back over the long march. He had almost forgotten what life was like without it. When they halted at night, the sensation of flying that came with the removal of it was unpleasant, the rush of blood back into his shoulders painful.

Now he was seeing the eyes that the Masta cursed at night. They hung in the darkest shadows: unwavering, staring eyes. He stared back at them, willing them to go away. They returned his stare, unblinking.

The path angled sharply around a bend in the river. The air was roaring with the thunder of the powerful stream as it slammed against the rocks. The rest of the line had turned the corner. Karap placed his foot carefully on the rock, still watching the eyes as they floated beside him.

And he was dead. The hands held him tight, choking off his cry, sliding him softly to the ground. The bamboo knife whipping open first his windpipe then, on the second slash, going in deep, through the tendons, and catching the jugular; so that thick, red blood burst from him, hot and sticky to the sure, skilled hands of his killer.

They let the river have him, they were not hunting for food. They had no use for his pack. They slid back into the jungle.

They got the next man on the next bend. They knew every inch of this track. They had opened it up, and kept it open. Their village was spread along a ridge-top nearby and they were going to keep the prospector and his party from coming too near it. They had no intention of letting their women and children go to meet the Sky People with his aid.

Rudi toiled in silence. His ears were fear-sharp. His eyes were steady. It was three days since Paul had been killed. Two nights of fear, lying in a circle in the forest, no fires, little sleep, waiting and listening—knowing the headhunters were out there, were playing games with them. Knowing Ludwig was close to the edge, seeing "eyes" wherever he looked; hearing sounds. Rudi's ability with the Pidgin language was improving rapidly as he became the only man who could keep the Boys, the carriers, the two terrified women, together.

He was thinking that it must have been a devil in him that had sent him to New Guinea, and shown him the red-headed man. He felt he could remember the devil laughing as Rudi realized what he had signed up for. He could remember the moment when he knew he should have gone back to the steel safety of the trading boat, but when he had instead stepped forward and introduced himself to Ludwig.

His concentration lapsed and he stumbled. He hunched over, conscious of the man toiling behind him, not wanting to bring him down as well.

But there was no one behind. Rudi stared at the empty track. The fear caught him in the gut, cramping his bowel. He pulled back the hammer on his shotgun and opened his mouth to scream.

The arrow tore out his throat, cutting off the scream. But the bowman had not anticipated his dying reflex. Rudi pitched forward and his spasming muscles jerked the trigger and the bowman took the full force of the shot in the chest.

Panic swept along the line. The women screamed shrilly, beating their hands about their heads. Ludwig flung himself off the track, disappearing into the thick grass. He heard his Boy's shotgun bark once. He wondered if Rudi were still alive. He had an image of violent eyes, wide-open and staring with blood lust, hurling down on his panic-stricken carriers. He saw a stone axe come down on a woman's head, splitting it open. He saw the axeman scream with delight and swing at the Boy.

But the Boy had got another cartridge into his old single-shot. The man folded up, flayed with shot, his belly torn out and splattered across the bushes.

A spear, hand-held, was jammed into the Boy's kidneys and his eyes opened wide with the shock of it. His hands clawed desperately, trying to cling to life. The attackers rushed past him. One fired low, and the arrow took the remaining girl in the calf. She stopped screaming as she collapsed, lying on the ground quietly as the men reached her.

Ludwig took aim carefully and shot the warrior who was first at her. The others scattered.

"Masta!" she screamed and dragged herself off the track, pulling herself upright. The warriors saw her going and regrouped. One of them caught the movement of Ludwig in the grass and hurled a spear. The others yelled again and ran for him.

He shot one more. The girl flung herself through the undergrowth, stumbling to the river. Ludwig realized it was the only way out. He hurled his empty pistol at the screaming faces, and followed her in.

He went under as far as he could. The river was alive. It grabbed him and threw him forward with savage force. He tried to keep himself under, but it forced him up. He saw them screaming on the bank, hurling their rage at him. Then he was past. It slammed him against a log and he choked on water. He got his head clear and saw the girl being thrown about. He knew the river took another turn up ahead, ramming into a solid wall of rock. He let his body go limp and gave himself up to the Lord.

"Did you see them?" the resident Kiap whispered to Harris, nudging him in the ribs. The Ford Tri-Motor lumbered back down the grass strip and heaved itself into the bright afternoon sun. "Did you see those Popsies? Mmmm!"

Don turned with him to watch the plane dip its wings in farewell and turn for the run back over the mountains, down the Ramu Valley, back to Madang and civilization. He nodded stiffly to the Resident, Andy Williams.

"Yes," he said, "I had dinner with them. There's a P & O ship in harbour . . ."

"Don't tell me. Don't tell me. God, I don't want to know

106

about it. I'm carving notches on my bed: 160 days till I get down to Sydney. Look, where's your Kiap?"

"He's sorting out the Police Boys. He wants to push off as soon as possible."

"That's Nicholls. He's got a jungle-fixation. Very serious. Look, you come with me."

He grabbed Don's arm, by the elbow, and marched him up the hill towards the square bungalow that stood on its crest in stark, geometric contrast to the round, thatched huts of the plateau around them. Its galvanized-iron and fibrolite flared back the sun—each piece flown in by plane.

"Nicholls is too keen," Williams said, "and that'll be his undoing. But don't tell him I told you. Keep it to yourself. He's a hard man if you cross him. Just don't let him push you too far."

Don nodded, smiling politely. Williams had a crazed gleam in his eye. He escorted his guest up the steps, almost rubbing his hands together with glee.

"I'm fixing us some dinner," he said. "Let's have some talk, listen to the wireless, you know . . ."

Don looked out from the verandah to where he could see Nicholls talking to some of the Boys.

"My brother can supply all the food they want," Baranuma informed Giram. "He's got good pigs: no worms. Fat pigs." He spread his hands to indicate how juicy. "He'll kill them, too."

Nicholls was watching Giram, to see how he would react. Giram was aware of how important it was not to show fear or confusion. Here he was, in the Highlands, home of the traditional enemies of the coastal people—headhunters, murderers and rapists who plundered peaceful villages.

"They're big on business up here," Nicholls told him. The phrase meant nothing.

"Bisnis?" he repeated.

Baranuma nodded enthusiastically. "Don't buy from any-one else, just you buy your stores from my brother. I guarantee it with my family ties."

107

"For God's sake!" Nicholls said. "A pig's a pig. Just remember, we leave at first light tomorrow. Just us. No relatives, brothers, cousins. And, above all, no girls!"

"Savvy Masta," Baranuma said, half-mockingly.

Giram watched the Kiap glare at his servant. He admired Baranuma's ability to keep astride the uncomfortable line between obedience and servility. Baranuma was the man to emulate, that was clear.

"I'll be eating with the Kiap here tonight, savvy?" Nicholls said. "You've got the night off, Baranuma. But you're not to hike away to your village. If you want to see your family, have them come here. We want a fast start in the morning."

"Oh, Masta." Baranuma looked forlorn. Giram saw Nicholls weaken in his resolve, and then get tough again.

"It's no good," he said. "The last time you did that, you were gone a week. This is a very serious patrol."

Baranuma shrugged and nodded. Nicholls grunted and headed back to the Kiap's square house. Baranuma looked at Giram and grinned.

"Come on," he said. "To hell with him. I'll introduce you to my brother."

They had listened to the shortwave wireless playing the "Hit Parade". When the signal faded and reception was lost, they discussed politics. Andy Williams was keen, also, to discuss Popsies. He did not hold with Nicholls that the modern girl was a scatterbrained fool, her only aim being to snare a man. Somewhere in the middle of the discussion they realized the wireless reception had faded for good, but their host was not to be put off that easily. He dragged out his collection of gramophone records and set the room jumping with Benny Goodman playing "Louise". He had a standing order with W. R. Carpenter's to import gramophone records for him, and the plane had brought him the latest offerings from Goodman and from Artie Shaw.

Now, high in the mountains, a Big Band sax section rolled out its riffs against the black night and the distant laughter of

108

the Boys at their own sing-sing. Andy Williams pushed his chair back and surveyed his guests genially.

"All right," he said. "All right. You liked my roast pork. You approved the way I deep-fried the taro. You definitely gave my banana trifle the nod. But now I want you to try something that is really number one."

He got up, grinning at them with suppressed glee. They watched him, so agreeably surprised by his skills in the kitchen they were prepared to tolerate whatever game he wished to play. He turned the record over and wound the gramophone again. He disappeared from the arc of yellow light cast by the lantern.

"Where's he gone?" Don asked.

Nicholls shook his head.

"Do you think he's all right?" Don said.

"He knows how to survive on his own."

"How's that?"

"Do exactly what you want to do, and do it to the hilt."

Don stared in surprise at Nicholls' vehemence. Nicholls flushed guiltily and got up and looked irritably at the gramophone, now spreading "Begin the Beguine" across the lamplit air. But he did not tamper with it.

From the table-top beside the gramophone he took the file Williams had compiled on native sightings of Ludwig. He returned to the table with it and showed its cover-title to Don, who nodded abstractedly, listening to the music, anticipating the melody as he remembered similar records, the same feeling, from nights in Adelaide with his fellow art-students, arguing, getting drunk, half-heartedly sketching one another.

"Ludwig," Nicholls said, and sat down heavily.

He opened the file and began to skip through it.

"Do you think he's insane?" Don asked him.

"He's a German."

Nicholls read on. The record hissed on its final grooves. Don waited for Nicholls to elaborate, but he didn't. He prompted.

"And?"

"That means he believes in the Evolution of Historic Destiny, and therefore the ultimate rightness of his own

109

acts—as all Historical Evolutionists believe that History and Evolution have culminated in themselves. If they didn't believe that, there'd be no reason in supporting the rest of the philosophy."

"That sounds a bit judgemental, sir."

Nicholls looked up at him. He reminded Don, at that moment, of a schoolteacher, not a warrior.

"After all," Nicholls added, "the aim of philosophy is not to explain the world, but to change it."

Don could almost feel, through his slacks, the hard boards of the student seats in the Barr-Smith Library of the University of Adelaide. The stupefying boredom of too much study, words passing before his eyes, not entering his mind; the consciousness of exams like a stopwatch in the back of his head.

"You sound like a lecturer I once had," he said.

"Don't underestimate Edward Nicholls!"

They both looked up to the kitchen doorway, through which Williams was calling.

"Did you know about his articles in *Oceania*?"

"No," Don said, staring at the older man, who now looked down, embarrassed with ill-concealed pride. "Really, sir? What did you write about?"

"Just the usual stuff us Patrol Officers see." Now he looked up. "The differences between the races, between even people of the same race who inhabit valleys fifty miles apart."

"You hold with Racial Theory, do you, sir?"

There was silence for a moment, they both listened to the record rumbling as the needle ground on through the final grooves.

"Turn that damned thing off," Nicholls said, jerking his head at it.

Don pushed his chair back and lifted the needle from the groove. The spring was almost wound down. He watched the record roll to a halt, and read the title upside down: "Indian Love Call".

"Different races have different traits," Nicholls said. "There's no getting away from that. It's the basis of anthropology. And, in describing those traits, one doesn't necessarily condemn them."

110

"But you speak like a Historic Evolutionist, don't you, sir?"

"I believe that societies evolve. Yes. I believe that law evolves—it has to, through trial and error. And, if law evolves, then Anglo-Saxon law is superior to Prussian law, and even that is better than Melanesian law."

Don glanced to the kitchen. He could hear furtive scrapings and mutterings coming from there. He frowned, concentrating on the argument, suddenly plunged into just such a discussion as he had enjoyed as a student, surprised that it had arisen like this, in the Highlands night, to the music of Artie Shaw. There was something wrong with Nicholls' argument. A movement in the doorway caught his eye and he looked up. Williams was standing there, poised and listening, bearing a tray.

"Hang on," Don said. "If you're talking about a strict time-scale of Evolution, then Prussian law is far in advance of ours. Anglo-Saxon law has its basis in Roman law."

"I'm talking about law as practised today, in British territory," Nicholls was clearly annoyed.

"Then you're talking about a body of cases, a series of decisions, of precedents, of legal tricks that can overturn what was once thought established 'law' in the twinkling of an eye. Your argument falls to pieces, sir."

"Damned finely argued," said Andy. "Now you don't get an argument like that when you spend your day asking old men if they pinched their neighbour's pig or if it just accidentally fell down dead outside their house."

He was conscious of Nicholl's irritation at having been out-talked on such a point. He knew Nicholls prided himself on his intellectual achievements.

"I see you've got my report there," he said, still holding himself out of the lamp-light. "I'm afraid it's a pretty pragmatic document," he added apologetically to Don.

"No," Nicholls grunted. "Utilitarian, Andy." He brightened up. "What the hell are you standing in the dark for?"

"Coffee, gentlemen."

With a master's timing, he stepped forward, thrusting the tray ahead of him. They were suddenly aware of the aroma of fresh coffee.

111

"Williams!" Nicholls said, leaning forward as Andy poured from an old, blackened pot. "What have we here?"

"*Coffea arabica*," Andy said. "Gentlemen. They said it couldn't be done."

He sat down in triumph.

"I got the seedlings sent over from the plantation at Wau. I've had my boys planting out plots and now they're harvesting the three-year-old bushes. I even think I've got a few interested in moving out of pork and into coffee."

Nicholls sipped it appreciatively.

"I didn't even know there was a plantation at Wau," he said. "But I haven't been up that way for a while." He nodded to Don. "The only strain that has been tried on the coast is *robusta*. The pundits have been saying that coffee just wouldn't grow in these Highlands."

"It's damned good," Don said.

It was actually a bit oily. But it was fresh, and it was served with pride and a great deal of finesse.

"You're in the wrong business Andy," Nicholls said. "You should be a restaurateur."

"By God, we could do with one in these islands," Andy said, with feeling. "The poor bloody coons have given up eating real food for biscuits and tinned beef."

"It's the price they pay for being colonized by Australians," Nicholls said. "We learnt to cook from the British, and got it all wrong then." He placed his cup back by the pot and looked at the pot meaningfully. "But this is damned fine coffee."

Andy took the hint and refilled the cup. "To hell with the Service," he said as he poured. "I'm going to become a coffee baron. Instead of 350 pounds a year I'll be on a thousand; maybe two."

"Good luck to you," Nicholls said. "We need agriculture up here, if we're to stabilize the economy. A coffee baron like you can help the locals become coffee barons."

"As long as there's a few Boys left to work my plantation. Don, another cup?"

Don nodded. Andy was aware of having closed him out with their coffee talk. He wanted to keep the evening flowing smoothly. He was afraid of conflict erupting between this pair.

112

"Listen," he said, "I heard you had a bit of a dust-up along the Rai Coast."

"Oh, it was nothing much," Don said.

"They were ambushed," Nicholls said. "This boy got them out of trouble."

"Really? Come on, Don. Tell us your version. I've only heard the bush telegraph account so far."

"Go on," said Nicholls, leaning back in his chair with his coffee, reluctant to give up the evening and study the Ludwig file. "Tell him the truth about it. He's only heard Madang lies so far."

"Well, I was with Morris, as you know." He hesitated, glancing quickly at Nicholls, aware that he was about to criticize another officer.

"Actually, I think he was a bit hasty, taking us forward like he did, when all the signs were out that they were pretty stirred up. You know, they'd been following the patrol for days, hurling insults and arrows coated with their own faeces."

He was conscious of their attention. They were men, listening to an equal discussing the problems of a very difficult job they shared. He wasn't a student any more, arguing some European theory with other students who would never test that theory in the way it had evolved—in bloodshed and violence and fear. He was aware that arguing with Nicholls was different to arguing with his student contemporaries. Nicholls' philosophy had been tested with his own blood. And, as he began to tell his tale, he realized that the same could be said of him and his theories. He realized that, whatever theoretical differences he shared with Nicholls, the older man respected his ability to get the job done.

And that was what counted, in the long run.

After three days of non-stop harassment by violently angry coastal warriors, they had woken to find themselves alone, save for their own Boys and Police. Their haranguers had melted into the forest. Don had been unsure of continuing, fearing the warriors had withdrawn for an all-out assault. But Morris was sure they had tired of the game, had decided

113

the Patrol was too heavily armed and, having yelled enough insults to satisfy their pride, they had gone home to tend their gardens and admire their pigs. The Patrol had pressed on.

A raging creek had halted them. Morris instructed the Boys to fell a couple of trees to bridge it, but the torrent whisked the trees away when they fell. The creek was in flood from torrential downpours high in the mountains.

Everyone was keyed up and nervous. Morris bawled the Boys out for misfelling the trees. The Boys became sullen. In anger, Morris had dropped a tree himself, and it had fallen onto the far bank. But it sagged in the middle and the stream began to bank up behind it, pushing its crown towards the water until it wedged against a stump on the other side.

Satisfied that it was wedged tight, Morris had taken a rope around his own waist. With Don holding the other end, he had waded into the torrent. It was a foolhardy action, as the stream was strong enough to be rolling boulders along its bed. Morris had been grabbed by the waters and had struggled to hang onto the creaking, bending sapling. Immersed in the spectacle of waiting for the Kiap to be swept to his death, no one was keeping sentry watch.

He made it to the other side, and yelled for the Boys to follow him over. Fairly naturally, they were reluctant to do so. Finally his own servant made the trip. He lost his lap-lap in the crossing, and emerged dripping wet and naked. Even Morris was forced to laugh.

Then, the servant was on the ground, clutching his thigh, from which an arrow protruded. Don swung around, immediately, flicking the safety on his rifle.

He turned directly into the sight of a grim-faced warrior, bow already back-stretched. Even as he swung the rifle up and yelled at the Boys to take cover, he could see the warrior's hand releasing the bow-string. Don did not flinch. He stood there, taking aim, and the arrow struck him as he pulled the trigger.

At first he thought he was blinded, as his sight disappeared in a torrent of warm blood. Clutching his face, he staggered forward. There were cries all around him now, and he could hear the booming of rifles and shotguns. He pitched forward, blindly helpless, clawing at his face, and collided with a tree.

On the ground, he scraped the blood away long enough to see another warrior coming for him with a steel axe. He shouted and someone, he did not see who, got the man. His sight restored, he realized he was lying in the blood of the man who had wounded him, whom he had killed with his rifle shot. Ants were beginning to swarm on them both. He got to his feet, slapping them off his neck.

The fight was over as quickly as it began. The attackers melted back into the bush, leaving three dead. One of the carrier Boys had died. Morris's Boy was badly wounded. With one of the Kiaps also wounded, that made a quite respectable tally for the attackers.

"We waited an hour," Don concluded. "But they had gone. Morris carried his Boy back across the stream. God knows how. My head was hurting like hell and I was deathly afraid that they had poisoned the arrow. If they had, of course, I'd have been a goner in a day or two."

He paused. The others still watched him, their eyes on his face. Again he felt the closeness of the three of them. He had a vision that History would negate what they were doing. Theoreticians in many universities would deplore the death of "innocent" savages, as the tribesmen became the proletariat of the New World. Here he was, trying to uphold the older order, at the point of a gun. No. He was trying to ease the friction of the impossible-to-avoid clash between the different worlds. It didn't matter. He and Nicholls and Williams understood the truth of the matter. They had acted correctly. The historians would only ever get their actions half-understood; and that the wrong half.

Williams pushed his chair back and got up and went out to the verandah to check what the Boys were doing. He looked beyond them, to the blackness of the mountains against the blackness of the sky.

Nicholls stared soberly at Don.

"It was word of Ludwig's exploits that stirred them up," he said, "I'll stake my reputation on it. If we let him get away

115

with these murders, then we can all pack up and go home."

"What's changed?" Don asked him. "Has he killed more people than, say, Mick Leahy on his first contacts?"

"Times have changed," Nicholls said. "This is 1937, not 1927. What Mick did was necessary in his time. If he hadn't, he'd be dead today, instead of giving lectures in New York and London on his successes."

Nicholls emptied the almost-cold coffee-pot into his cup.

"The League of Nations is watching us like a hawk. They'd dearly like to take our mandate to govern away from us. And you know who'd be in the running to get it back?"

"The Germans?" Don saw Williams moving back into the room, still nervously watching the night.

"That's right," Nicholls said. "Let the Germans in and they'll do a deal with the Japanese, and there they are, right on Australia's doorstep. Not that the Australian Government gives a damn."

Andy sat down again and smiled nervously. Don wondered if he was conscious of his fear of the night, or if it was something that had grown in solitude, to the point of becoming part of him—a fear that it would be uncomfortable to live without.

"What about the Americans?" Andy asked.

"What about them?" Nicholls spoke angrily. "Look how late they got involved in the Great War. If Germany and Japan wanted they could take the whole of New Guinea in ... say, two weeks."

"You know some of the missionaries have been putting out pro-Hitler material?" Williams asked him.

Nicholls nodded. "I think it's pretty mild stuff. You know, just homesick Germans."

"I heard on the wireless talk of Germany wanting to start a Negro Empire by winning back its colonies in Africa," Don said.

"They've got a religious war going, up here," Williams said. "There was a fight between the Lutherans and the Catholics, over Goroka way. The Lutheran priest got his boys to burn down the Catholic church." He laughed.

"And we're supposed to put down sorcery," Nicholls said, pushing his chair back. "I'm going to turn in and read your

116

report, Andy. You'd better get some shut-eye, too, Don. We'll want an early start tomorrow."

Don heard the use of his Christian name, and realized that his relationship with Nicholls was changing.

Diary: 13th May, 1937

He surprised me with his arguments. At first, I thought he was just clever. But he has guts, too. There's still something unformed about him though. Something has been harmed inside him. Not allowed to grow. And that's why he's here, seeking to make it up.

Into my heart an air that kills
From yon far country blows . . .
That is the land of lost content . . .
Where I went and cannot come again.

And that's why we're all here, isn't it? That's why he makes me uncomfortable. I can see myself in him.

Now it's late night and the wind has picked up and is blowing cold from the slopes of the high mountains. The Boys are shivering in their thin blankets, huddled by the fires. There's rain on the wind. Mist on the mountains. Far, far distant thunder on some granite peak.

The wind buffets these thin walls, and gets under the raised floor. The house confronts the wind. An alien house fighting the primal wind. Not one part of the walls or roof of this house is native to these mountains. The wind can feel it, and attacks. The house resists with its technological cleverness. Nails, not rope bindings. Fibrolite manufactured in a southern factory, not platted wall-matting made by the women. Galvanized iron cast in Port Kembla foundries. The house draws to it the sounds of hotel ballroom dance-bands. Voices of armchair pundits emerge, discussing war and trade.

Far away is the sound of youths and girls singing the unison songs native to the mountains, but no one in the house can hear. Sorcerers plot death and the inhabitants do not feel the tremors of that plotting. A distant guria shivers the ground and the house trembles.

117

When I first came to these mountains, when I was a Cadet and Jim Taylor was the great God, the feared Kiap, then I did feel like the character in Keats' poem. I guess I came to believe I was Ulysses. Here I was, a long way from home, charting the unknown world with a frail band of trusted men. Every step we took put us further into the world of sorcerers, into contact with Cyclops and Scylla and Charybdis. Arrows rained down on us. Maidens lured us with their charms, leading us towards treachery and ambush. I watched my men fall, one by one — to arrows and infections and influenza. I thought I would never find sweet homecoming. Everywhere I went, pig-sacrifice was made, the gods were invoked, the restless dead clamoured to rise up at our presence.

And then, enter a young man, come looking for me. Was his name Telemachus? No. Don Harris. And, equally, there was no Penelope. But I still can't help it. I still feel this mythic quality to what I am doing. It is so much larger than the life I would have expected to lead if I had remained in Australia.

Maybe it's understandable, then, that the fear growing inside me is larger than ordinary fear. It is beginning to knot up my guts.

And I glance to my case and know that, hidden in it, is my antidote to that fear. But, instead of relief, I feel shame. What will Harris say when he sees me wearing my armour? Will he laugh with the Boys at my expense? Will he return here and sit down with Williams and regale him with stories of me, frightened out of my wits while he stands still, not moving as they attack and he fires?

Nicholls stopped writing and put down his pen and stared at the case. He listened to the wind plucking at the walls of the Kiap's house. He listened to the creaking of floorboards, wondering if it was caused by Harris or Williams, and deciding it was the wind.

He got up and stood by his case and looked into it.

He went to the window and pulled the shade aside and looked out.

He could see nothing but blackness.

He returned to the case and lifted out the suit of armour and laid it on his bed. He could taste fear in his mouth. He touched the cotton covering

I can't go on, he told himself.

Another voice in his head snapped back: Keep going! You're not a coward! Keep walking!

118

I'm terrified.

You're not a child! Your fears are unfounded! You're a man. Act like a man!

God, he thought. What's happening to me? Is this the crack-up?

He dug into a side-pocket of the case and lifted out his flask. He poured a healthy shot into a glass and downed it in two gulps.

He shook his head as the whisky eased him. He smiled at his dilemma and screwed the cap back on the flask and replaced it. Then he returned the armour to the case and began to undress for bed.

One thing, he told himself, they're not going to attack the Haus Kiap.

Instead of walking the ten miles to his village, Baranuma had waited for some of his family to walk in to see him at the Kiap's settlement.

His next brother and two young cousins had come. A sister was there, too, but had disappeared to flirt with the Boys on the line. They sat by the fire, hunched against the wind on their backs, warmed by the watered-down rum he supplied.

"Father did not come?" he said, to the fire.

"He isn't feeling well," his brother said, watching the fire too.

"Sorcery," one of the cousins said. "He's just wasting away. One of the Biggest of Big Men . . . now . . ."

"You should come and see him, Baranuma," his brother said. "You need to patch up your fight with him before it's too late."

Baranuma shrugged uncomfortably. "I'll patch it up when I have something to show him," he said. "When I can show him a black man as strong as a white man."

"And when will that be? When Jesus Christ comes back? When they give us their power?" There was anger behind his brother's sarcasm.

119

He looked up, and into his brother's troubled, angry eyes. He looked at the two younger cousins.

"We've got our own power," he said. "They haven't got any more 'power' than us. What they've got is guns."

"That's enough power for me."

"Yes, but they don't want to use that power!" In his excitement he grabbed his brother's arm. "You don't understand. Look, if they wanted to, they could destroy us all, every one of us, with those guns. But they don't. Why not?"

"Jesus Christ has saved their souls?"

Baranuma laughed.

"Jesus Christ means nothing to your average white man. Nicholls cares nothing for Jesus Christ. No, there's only one sort of person they know they need, to help them here."

The three young men huddled closer to him and waited.

"Us," he said. "You, me, Highlanders, Coastal people. We live here. They don't know how to. Without us, they are useless. And they know it."

He sat back.

"So what do you advise?" his brother asked, his face now troubled.

"Help them, yes. But, while you're helping them, make certain you're helping yourself. Use them to settle your disputes with other people. Learn from them whatever is useful."

He had never seen it as clearly as when he said it to his brother. He laughed and stood up, and felt the wind on his kidneys. The wind filled him with vigour. It was the wind of his boyhood here in the mountains, that he had forgotten in his sojourn to the coast. He had been away too long. He reached down and caressed his brother's head.

"I am going to be so Big," he said, "you'll have to wait outside my door to see me, like the Administrator in Rabaul."

His brother laughed and caressed his thigh.

"Brother," he said, "I've missed you. Everyone else is so gloomy since the whites came. Stay with us and make us laugh."

"Not yet," he said. "I've got a few things to do first."

120

Don lay in his sleeping bag, on the horse-hair mattress. The mattress, like the house he was lying within, had been flown up from the coast in a 'plane. It had been shipped to Lae from Sydney. It had been made somewhere in Australia, like the iron, the fibrolite, the coffee pot, the glasses from which they drank, the plates from which they ate.

Lying there he realized how alien he was to this country. He felt himself as part of the leading edge of a wedge, or of a plough slicing into new soil. He was almost asleep when he remembered that it was this new land that had first intruded into his own safe, suburban world, not he into it. It had called him when he had been nothing but a callow student, five years ago. It had called to him through the instrumentality of an axe.

An axe in an exhibition of Primitive art and artifacts.

The head of the axe was an olive-green stone, carefully polished and shaped. It was bound to a balanced wooden handle with plaited cane. The handle was cross-hatched with a burnt-on design.

He had looked at it for a long time, and then moved on to the next exhibit.

Wooden sculpture. From the Ramu valley, New Guinea.

Beak style.

The figure was almost inhuman, but human enough to be unnerving. It was less than a foot tall, and the head had been shaped to resemble a bird's skull, with a long, tapering beak, the tip of which looked like nothing but a circumcised penis. The eyes looked down craftily. They were outlined with concentric circles, like the "worry" lines on a mature person's forehead. The head was by far the largest feature of it.

He tried to walk on past it, but it drew him back. He stared at it. It had that same feeling to it that certain recent European art had. The feeling of almost telling you something very deep, very profound, and very frightening.

He decided it was the fact that the eyes did not meet yours.

121

He looked around the rest of the exhibition, in the Exhibition Hall of the South Australian School of Art. Other painted panels and sculptures had a similar quality, and the eyes in them looked slightly askance, or were blind eyes simply outlined and left to suggestion to fill in.

He turned back to the figure and looked at it again. It was by far the most "secretive". Furtive. It drew him back to the axe and he read the card lying before it.

> Stone fighting axe. Traded from Chimbu Gorge. The design pattern, though abstract, reflects certain anthropomorphic features.

He looked more closely at the design on the handle. It was of a highly elongated human figure, arms wide, legs wide, with a long, thin penis stretching on down the axis of the handle.

He looked at the other students wandering through the exhibition. The lecture accompanying it had mentioned nothing about the sexual nature of the display. But, the more he looked at it, the more . . . obscene was the only word. It filled him with a nervousness. The hooded eyes and pecking, beak mouths. The stylization: the lecturer referred to current German art as an example of similar attempts to express human emotion through caricature. The exaggerated genitals. The gaping womb from which a penis-like head was emerging, in a swollen-bellied caricature of a woman giving birth.

And the axe. Its lines cool and clean. The balance obvious from the proportions. Polished lovingly. Handle detailed with care. Designed, quite simply, to kill. He touched the glass between it and himself.

He dawdled his way home. An early summer heatwave had Adelaide in its grip and he moved from patch of shade to patch of shade. There were a few swagmen by the river. Normally they would have intrigued him, but that day he kept his distance. They seemed malevolent in their hunched attitude, crouched together, sharing a bitter joke. He was grateful for the shade as he walked into Stanley Street. He could have ridden from North Terrace, but he enjoyed walking, even in the heat.

The suburban houses had seemed strange, all of a sudden. Their white, blank fronts. The drawn blinds and curtains. The dusty small gardens. No one else was in the street. It was like a de Chirico street scene. He kept anticipating violence.

But all that had happened was that his father was late home from the cricket. The evil Jardine had almost killed the Australian batsmen by ordering Larwood to bowl his Bodyliners. Father felt that Larwood hadn't wanted to, but that Jardine, obsessed with winning, had demanded it of him.

Don drank a cup of tea and watched his father, a small man, balding, with an impressive moustache to make up for the receding hair. He blinked nervously as he told the tale. Don realized that part of him relished the violence that had suddenly flared in that most gentlemanly, and boring, of sports: cricket. Part of his father wanted to see blood, and hear the splintering of bone.

His mother didn't seem to know what to do with all the energy suddenly simmering in the parlour. She uncomfortably shifted lace doilies. She stood up and straightened a print. She fidgeted with her hair in front of the mirror. His father didn't notice. It was time the Australian Cricket Board of Control put their foot down. This was a deliberate policy to wreck the game. It was probably linked to Sir Otto Niemeyer's appointment by Scullin, that had led the country directly into ruin.

"That was in 1929, dad," he said. "Three years ago."

His father stared at him.

"Are you contradicting me?"

"No," he said. "You're contradicting yourself."

"Have you been seeing about getting a job?" his father counter-attacked.

"Yes," he lied. "As you just pointed out, there aren't any, thanks to the Conspiracy of Bankers."

"Don, what's got into you?" his mother asked, now watching him shrewdly.

123

He stared back at her, seeing a plain, dumpy woman with a bitter mouth.

"It's hot," he said. "It's as hot as hell. I'm going for a walk."

"Don!"

"Leave him, mother. He's not worth it."

"Safety and failure! That's what middle-class life in Adelaide represents!" He was pleasantly drunk. His friends were, too. "People come to settle here who are too afraid to face the challenges of the outside world. But, by refusing to take the risks, they elect creeping failure . . ."

"Who are you talking about?" the girl said.

He didn't know her. He stared at her, and shook his head.

"What do you mean?"

"You sound like you're angry at someone, for something personal."

He got up and struggled away from the group. They were strung along the slate verandah of someone's home. A house a little higher up the hill, picking up a little more of whatever breeze became available to blow the heat out to sea.

"I don't know what she means," he mumbled, to no one in particular. No one noticed him. The girl had turned her attention to another argument. He stared back at her. She was cool and aloof, very pretty. She had a condescending manner. He disliked her intensely.

She'd also been right.

"You silly old bugger!" he had told his absent father. "You frightened little man!"

124

· CHAPTER SEVEN ·

"There are two Sky People staying with the Kiap," the young man reported. "One of them was here before."

"Masta Nicholls, the Kiap?" Barum asked.

The young man nodded, though he looked a bit uncertain. All the Sky People tended to look the same to him.

"The other is younger," he offered. "He has a new scar here." He touched his forehead. "The Police said he got it fighting the people on the Coast."

"Those women," the man beside Barum said scornfully. "The more I hear about them, the more I think we're wasting our time up here. We could clean them up in no time."

"What about Police?" Barum said, ignoring Samura's typical statement.

The young man held up the fingers of both hands and Barum frowned and looked over to Samura, his opposite number from the next village, Gafu.

All the men were crowded into their Lodge house, with a number of the Gafu. The fire smoked, and most of them were smoking trade-tobacco cheroots. The air was heavy, pressing down on them with its weight, like the foreboding of a battle.

The Gafu clung in a group by the door. The two peoples had an uneasy truce at the moment, an agreement on pig exchange, and a common frontier on which no one had been killed for several seasons.

Samura shrugged at the number of Police.

"They will all have guns," Barum explained.

"I know about guns," the other man said. "And I know that your women are getting some kind of sorcery ready; that they have power over this Masta Kiap."

125

"Sorcery is good," Barum said, "but it is better with some forethought. If we split the party up, it will be better for us. There will be less of us dead, and more of them."

"Who planned the raid on the prospector?" Samura demanded, looking around the smoky room and raising his voice to orate. His men grinned at him.

"Who thought to attack from two different directions? To draw him out of his tent, where he was banging away at his woman? Eh?"

Barum's men mumbled their approval and support. Some of the Parap grumbled, and Barum glared at them to silence them.

"This isn't a talking contest," he said, and his men grinned at the sharpness of his wit. "We're planning a war. You were lucky in the last one. Sure, you set it up, and let us take the counter-attack from Nicholls. It was not just us who then provided him with a woman. It was me." He glared at Samura, who shrugged. "My daughter."

"Didn't you have the prospector's woman?" Samura countered.

This time Barum shrugged.

"We all did," he said.

They were silent, staring at each other.

Samura was thinking that the Parap were in an untenable position. No matter what happened, they would be attacked. Whereas the Gafu could pull back to the top of a high ridge, where the Patrol would never flush them out. Old Barum was losing his grip. He was trying to get the best of the bargaining, but he was so clearly in the weaker position.

"When a man gets too Big," Barum said, "then the sorcerers take notice of him. They begin to think it would be good for them if they brought him down. That's why a truly Big man appears just a little bit Small."

"Who are we working sorcery on? Me, or the Kiap?"

Barum kept his cool. He spoke softly, so the listeners had to strain to hear. He deliberately contrasted himself with Samura's bombast.

"We work sorcery on Nicholls, but we split the party up. We don't know this new man. He may be impervious to the sorcery. We watch him and learn about him."

126

Samura cocked his head on the side and thought a moment longer. He could see no danger for himself. He nodded.

"We split them up," he said. "You will keep the younger one here. You will send Nicholls to us, with the promise of finding whatever it is he seeks."

Barum nodded.

"Then you can eat his testicles," Samura said. "I will send them to you personally."

Barum let the insult of cannibalism appear to slide off him. He walked to the door.

"Oh," he said, as he got two of the young men to unfasten the boards, "you keep his skull, and eat his brains. You need them far more than me."

The Gafu left amongst the laughter of the Parap.

When they had disappeared into the blackness beyond the village sentries, Barum strolled down to his wife's house. He stood some distance off, and waited for her to come out.

A similar meeting was going on in there, with all the village women bunched together—but with no representatives of the Gafu. A girl looked out and saw him and called inside and his wife appeared, stooping, through the doorway. She carried a bundle of leaves with her.

"Is it done?" she asked him.

He nodded and pointed with his chin at the leaves. She smiled, and opened them.

What had once been ejaculated into their daughter's thighs was now a glaze on the leaves. She looked up and smiled at her husband.

"What will we do with her?" he asked. "With Merin?"

"She did it once with Nicholls, she can do it once with the other one," she said.

"We hide her from Nicholls, and tell him she's married into the Gafu. That will give him the reason to go there."

The practicality of women always scared him.

"How do you know what we've agreed?"

"That was the plan you wanted. And you always get what you want amongst the men," she said, with her smile.

He laughed and grabbed her by the thighs.

"Let me go," she said, but wriggling her body against him, teasing him with it. "I have to finish the sorcery."

127

"You never finish it with me," he moaned, clutching his penis.

She laughed and turned back to her house.

"Such a Big man," she said, mockingly.

From Mount Hagen outpost they began the walk into New Territory. Don's previous Patrol had been on the coast, where your obstacles were swamps and rivers, mosquitoes and leeches, and the constricting jungle. Here they walked in grasslands. There were no mosquitoes. But there was the head-high kunai grass, razor-sharp as you threaded through it. And there were the ridges.

The grasslands were like rumpled blankets, he thought, from a giant's bed. Green, vividly green, with distant mountains purple and blue. The air ringingly clear. And ringing on the air were the calls of the grassland people following their progress.

From ridge-top to ridge-top echoed the yodelling shouts, falling away to burst out anew from the next hill-top watcher. Musical cries dying in the echoless air.

Don would halt, panting hard, his chest close to bursting, his clothes wringing with perspiration—and knowing that the evening cold would chill that moisture on his body. He would look back at the caterpillar of men struggling up the absurdly steep slope, all like him, knowing that when they crested it they would begin the equally back-breaking slide down the other side. Fifteen Policemen now, forty carriers, himself and Nicholls.

No one spoke, saving all energy for the effort of placing one foot above the other, leaning into it, lifting the weight of body, or body and pack.

On the ridge-tops, the local peoples waited to watch the legends pass. Proud men with spade-shaped black beards, long noses and high cheekbones. Rounded, beguiling women who giggled and flirted shamelessly, distracting the Police Boys from their solemn duties, even making the carriers leave off panting to smile and ease their burden with an

128

obscenity. Small boys who ran amongst the line, daring each other to pass closer and closer to the pale, white Sky People. The people were not tall, but the men were immensely muscular.

But it was the women Don kept noticing, with their pert breasts, small bellies above the scrap of cloth between their thighs. Their brown flesh glistened with oil. They wore bracelets and necklaces. Some carried piglets, or led young pigs on foot-ropes. Young mothers held their babies up high to watch him pass.

But when he got close to them he drew back mentally. Their cheeks were tattooed. The glistening flesh was greased with animal fat, rancid in the creases of elbows and knees. What they wore was, truly, bark or grass tucked between their legs. He could smell the fat and the clinging odours of old cooking fires, ash, smoke, the constant presence of pigs. He could see the older women now, with their weary dugs and cynical faces, dust and fat ground into their flesh. Some had lopped off joints of fingers. Their mouths grinned, broken-toothed.

He retreated into his memory. He retrieved the adventure tales of his youth. Edgar Rice Burroughs, Rider Haggard. The image of *She* kept returning to him.

> . . . clothed in the kirtle of clinging white, cut low upon her bosom, and bound in at the waist with the barbaric double-headed snake . . . the white robe slipped from her down to her golden girdle . . .

There was plenty of time for his imagination to wander on the long walk. They walked three days. His feet fell into an automatic step: the upward thrust of calf muscles, its corollary the strain in his hamstrings as he descended the ridges. The miles of kunai grass became the same mile, endlessly repeated. The yodelling announcements of their advance became part of the background, noticed only if they ceased. The people became one more irritation to be endured, like sweat and foot-blisters.

"What am I doing here?" he began to ask himself. "At this moment in time I could be anywhere in the world. I could be in Paris or London, or back home in Adelaide. I could be in Sydney. I could have gone to the Antarctic with Mawson.

129

"There was a time when all these possibilities were there. I was free to choose. I had discovered that what I had thought was a talent for painting was in fact a talent for draught-manship. I was a great copyist. I could have chosen to be a commercial artist, but I knew I didn't want to work in some department store, reproducing the lines of next season's look. That discovery had freed me of the necessity to be at art school.

"I could have chosen to pick up at university. I could have read law, like my father. Instead, I read adventure novels— as my mother read romantic novels. That was my undoing."

A rainy Adelaide evening in August. The same streets that had baked in December were now cold and windswept. But Don walked, hands hunched in his pockets. At one level walking because he was afraid to return home and confront his father with his decision to leave art school. He had already left his freshman year at university unfinished. He had wanted to take a job, but no job had presented itself to him—and he had not presented himself to many. Art school began as a fill-in, while waiting for the mythical job to arrive. As the country was in the depths of Depression, there weren't likely to be many coming his way.

The rain clung in his hair. It fell in a light, but constant mist. His top-coat was wet but the damp had not penetrated through his clothes. His shoes were wet in the puddles. He should have been depressed, but he was elated.

Freedom. He had never possessed it before. Now, he could do anything. He could talk his father into staking him in a trip to Paris. He had friends who had gone to Melbourne. He could look them up. He could join the great army of swagmen and drift down to Melbourne, taking his time to see the country on the way, living off the land as they did. He could return to that law degree, work his heart out for it. If he applied himself he could discover the delights of study. Tomorrow he might find a job. He could even go to New Guinea and chase up the dreams of life amongst the primitives that had been excited by the exhibition he had seen the previous summer, and the newspaper articles that attended

130

on the exhibition—Champion and Jim Taylor and Jack Hides, the prospecting Leahy Brothers.

Freedom, he suddenly realized, lay in choice. By cutting himself loose from a false dream he had exposed himself to it. Now, what would he do with it?

"Freedom is a total illusion," he told himself, feeling the pain now in the back of his calves from the descent of a ridge. "You think you possess it when you stop doing something and look up and realize there are other things you are equally capable of doing. For that moment you are transfixed by the illusion. I could be anything I want to be, you tell yourself. But then you choose.

"I will go to Paris. Right. You buy your ticket. You pack your trunk. Now, your ship leaves from Adelaide via Fremantle, so you'll never get to see your friends in Melbourne. You won't get to walk the Coorong. No, I'd better not go to Paris.

"You register at the university. Paris is five years away, if at all. By the time you graduate you'll probably be married, your father will have lined up a position for you . . . no, don't register.

"And then you choose. Heart leaping in your mouth you receive the envelope in reply to your query. 'Vacancies exist . . .' Now, you can see your Melbourne friends on the way. But, you will never see Paris or London at the age of twenty.

"Freedom doesn't exist. Because, in being free, you are only free to choose. And, having chosen, you are no longer free."

Coming back to present time, he realized they were walking onto the top of a ridge, and that the inhabitants of that ridge had turned out to view them. The image of *She* was still fading in his mind when he saw the girls, with their upturned breasts and glistening thighs. But instead of golden girdles and white robes they wore bark between their thighs. Their naked flesh was covered with rancid pig-fat; their cheeks were tattooed in raised, swirling patterns. Their crinkled hair was caked with mud and fat.

131

The older women, the mothers, had breasts that lay flat on their chests, bodies prematurely aged to look like wrinkled bark. Children as old as three years grasped at those flattened dugs. Even piglets had access to them.

"Why did you come up here?" he asked Nicholls over lunch.

The question seemed to rock the older man. He stared quickly at Don, then looked away. He wasn't used to, and didn't want, intrusions into his personal life.

"I left university," he said, after a pause, during which he studied his troops and, beyond them, the villagers now seated on the grass to watch the Sky People eat in their strange fashion.

"Which university?" Don asked, boring straight in, ignoring Nicholls' discomfort.

This is why I hate two-man patrols, Nicholls thought. They force you into intimacy. With an extra man this would not happen.

"Adelaide," he said.

"Really? I was at Adelaide for a term."

Nicholls stared at him, saying nothing.

"What were you studying?" Don asked.

"History."

"And you gave it up to come here?"

Nicholls examined the tin of meat he was eating from. He poked his fork into it and hooked out a piece of pressed ham. He chewed on it. It was tasteless.

"I got sick," he said, "of listening to academics who had never left the library explaining how battles were won and lost, and passing value judgements on the soldiers and making moral judgements of the generals. It seemed to me that, in studying history, they had made sure they would never discover what it was all about."

"And that is?"

"People living their lives."

Now Don picked at his pressed ham, feeling Nicholls' eyes on him. Nicholls looked away and studied the villagers again. After a while, he grinned. Don looked at him expectantly.

"She's all right," Nicholls said.

"What?"

"Not what, my boy. Who. That girl, sitting over to the left. Yes. She knows I'm pointing at her. Look at her squirm."

Don stared at him in amazement. Nicholls turned back to him and studied his shock.

"Haven't you had a native girl?" he asked, seemingly innocently.

Don shook his head.

"You should. They're better than whites. They've got no inhibitions when it comes to sex. They make no demands on you."

He studied Don's open-mouthed wonder.

"This isn't Rabaul, my boy. The white women aren't in charge out here. Come on, admit that, while you were walking, just occasionally your thoughts turned to below your belt. Eh?"

"I guess so."

"What were you thinking?"

Now Nicholls attacked Don's privacy, with glee.

"About a girl, I guess."

"Back home?"

"Yes."

"White?"

"Yes."

"Blonde?"

"I suppose."

"Everyone up here fantasizes about blondes. But there aren't any. That's why they're fantasies."

"You have . . . had one of these girls?"

"Yes."

"Do . . . does Bellamy know?"

"I presume he does. If I hadn't bedded a few, I'd be the first white man up here who hasn't. Bellamy would too, if he could get away from his neurotic wife."

Nicholls studied Harris's discomfort. He had made the attack simply to get him off his back. Having native women seemed a minor sort of confession—as compared to, say, confessions of fear and inadequacy, and the confession of his suit of armour.

"Would you like me to line you up with one?"

133

"Hardly."

"You'll change. I'll give you another week."

Nicholls stood up and looked around. He caught Sergeant Bukato's eye and gestured for the men to be on their feet.

"I've got a girl waiting for me," he said, "up ahead. She is a beauty, let me tell you."

Don heard him laughing as he hurried down the line.

After three nights Ludwig was still alive. He knew it was three nights because, three times, the delirium of his fever had clamped down around him, black upon black, and the cold that the distant light had driven away returned to him. All he could do was feed into the fire more of the hut's furnishings and huddle closer to it, shivering violently, fighting to keep his mind above the fever, above the visions, above the blackness.

He presumed the others were dead. Once in the tumble down the river he had come into contact with something that wrapped against him, brushed him with its tentacles, and tried to cling to him. He had fought it aside, desperate to get his own mouth back to the booming, spray-drenched surface. The drowning try and take you with them, he remembered from somewhere, when he was a youth perhaps. He had hit out at the clinging organism, and then together with it had hurtled into the chute of churning water that slammed against the rock at the bend in the river. Whatever it was, perhaps one of their attackers, perhaps one of his carriers, or the girl, took the brunt of the assault. Ludwig felt himself lifted up by unseen hands, hands of water, and then his head slammed against something, whether rock or bough he never knew, and he went limp.

The limpness had saved him, letting his body be taken by the water on its own course around the rocks. Great lungs-full of water poured into his slack mouth, reviving him. He choked it up, too weak to struggle, dazed to the point where

134

he was nothing but an extension of his environment, swirling and churning with it around and over the slippery rocks onto which less fluid matter impacted.

The rocks had broken the ferocity of the water's descent through the mountain forest. The river flowed fiercely now, but with less agitation, like a rippling sluice-race to a gold-mine. The one he knew best, at Bulolo, winding five miles around the mountain, pouring its brown water on until the sudden drop that smashed into the alluvium.

Was this river about to perform such an act? he had thought. To drop suddenly from the edge of a mountain? The panic revived him and he flailed out and caught at something. It could have been a dead man's hand. He let go of it quickly.

He remembered that he had walked along this river for four days on the way in. There had been rapids but no waterfalls. They had walked along it a day on the return journey. The equivalent of three days' walking would see him safe.

It was near dark when he got himself out of the river. The track no longer ran beside it. Six hours' transport down-stream had taken him further than two days' walking upstream. He was in a moss forest, which meant he was still very high. Dead trees were covered in all manner of lichen, the ground carpeted in thick moss. He made no sound, and there was nothing else to make a sound. It was like being dead. The heat of the day was going rapidly and the cold mountain night moving in on him.

He still had his holstered knife, and with it he cut away his torn, bloodied and soaked clothes. As he worked, his teeth clenched tight to keep his concentration focused on the act of cutting, of freeing himself, he began to shiver. Part of his mind reminded him of his malaria.

If he stayed in the open night, he would die. It was that simple. He forced his body to its feet. Walking would generate some heat. He wrapped his arms around himself. He had his belt and knife. His boots were ruined, his clothes useless. That was all right, because he was still alive. He had that on everyone else. He blundered into the silent, dead forest, his teeth chattering loudly, moaning, forcing his lungs to keep working, his legs to keep pounding, driving him away from the sound of the river, into the darkness.

That part of his mind concerned with survival was very sharp and clear; the rest was blurred. It focused in on the act of living. That act now demanded much intelligence, much cunning. He holstered his knife and strapped the belt against his shivering belly. The match-pouch was intact, and presumably dry.

Then the mountain seemed to wake itself up, become alive, and yell out loud. It reverberated with thunder. There was a jagged rip of lightning, and rain fell out of the damp, cold air.

He did not think a track could cross the river. So, therefore, it should continue to run parallel to it. That meant he needed to walk perpendicular to the river, in order to reach the track. It was so simple! This was how you stayed alive. Simple logic and mathematics. The sort a boy learned.

He could see it again, so clearly. The river pouring through the narrow, steep gorge. The coons standing by the sluice-box. The brown water skudding over it, sliding across the baffles, dropping its magic load of alluvial gold. And his son standing beside him. No more than a boy. Silent, naked, brown and strong. Watching him he felt a surge of love.

His feet, in darkness, with no boots to shield them, told him he had arrived on the beaten earth of the track. He turned downhill automatically, his sharp brain guiding him, while the muzzy part fed him images of Walter—looking up from the sluice-box, having seen within the brown foam a flash of gold. Looking up and laughing.

His sharp brain told him there were huts ahead. It cautioned him, taking over full control now. His shuddering hand found the knife holster, but the hand could not extract it.

The village had been deserted long ago. The huts were slowly returning to jungle. The rain fell on them, quietly, in full flood, spreading a river of mud across the bare village hearths. One hut was bigger than the rest. Presumably the men's house, where they had lain, smoking, sweating, planning the deaths of prospectors and innocent children. On the hut ridgepole he caught the pale gleam of bone. He crouched down and pitched himself into the total blackness of the hut.

136

The rain stopped falling on him. He could hear it outside. The shivering was total madness now, sending him scurrying across the floor. But there were no other animal noises. No pythons. No rats. Where was the hearth? He found it, centrally located. His body knocked against the hut's furnishings, the rows of bunks on which the men had lain, boasting of their treachery.

The fever assisted him, jerking his hands across the rotting wood, sending some of it scattering into the blackness, but enough of it onto the hearth. He was sweating now, his forehead hot, his body cold as he concentrated. He sat himself down and clamped his elbows at his sides, but they still shook too much. So he lay on his side, pinning his arm down, and then took hold of his right hand with his left, and guided it to the match-pouch.

It seemed like forever, but he opened the pouch and felt the rough edge of the matchbox. He had to rest. He closed his eyes and immediately the fever consumed him. He jerked them open again and stared into the blackness, seeing only blackness.

Realizing it was the first time since that day in the mountain gorge with his son that he had not seen the eyes when he looked into shadows.

His fingers pincered the matchbox. Then a tremor shook him and the matches cascaded into the black. He was weeping. He scrabbled blindly on the earth, and found the precious slivers of wood with their phosphorous heads. He clamped three of them together and struck them against the box.

A flame blossomed. He forced it forwards, into the rotten wood on the hearth. It wavered, dying down. A shivering fit took him, and his fingers spasmed and the match disappeared.

He cried. The sharp, intelligent side of his brain let go and he fell into the swamp. Now the eyes returned, laughing, taunting.

"You heathen bastards!" he croaked. Anger forced his mind to clear. He found the matchbox and clamped his hand on it and waved it at them. He dragged himself closer to the hearth and forced the box deep into the pile of wood.

He spread his body against the earth floor and sought the

137

spilt matches. He found slivers of wood, of bone. His fingers had to search them, feeling for the tip that would tell him: "This is a match, this can keep you alive". He found three.

His shuddering fingers flared the trio of matches across the box and splattered them into the wood. The wood sprang into three pinpoints of light. One died immediately, but the other two flared brighter, and rose up through the dry, rotted wood. Warmth and light grew, like a miracle, out of the coldness and the dark.

And Ludwig slept, his body curled into the warmth, shaking with the fever. Outside, the rain fell easily and effortlessly.

In the village of Parap life had come to a halt as reports of the approaching expedition filtered in to them. There seemed no point to working the fields, to repairing houses or even plaiting bark for clothes. In the men's house the clutter of ceremonial masks, weapons, possum fur as yet untreated, flutes, axes and other everyday goods mounted up as the men came in, dropped what they had carried, and lay there, hands behind their heads, staring up at the rafters, saying nothing, but all seeing in their minds that long snake wending towards them: the Patrol.

If there was anything worth doing, it was to be with your family. It was custom that a man not touch his infant children until the fontanelle had closed and the skull was hard. Until that time, the child lived entirely with its mother, totally cossetted by her—for fear that excess crying would drive the child's spirit out through that soft spot on the top of the head, and so kill the child.

But now men sat awkwardly beside their wives' houses, not yet breaking convention to the point of entering them, and with uneasy delight held those small, squalling bodies to their own. The infants, feeling their fathers' hesitancy, cried more loudly, and the mothers and grandmothers and mothers-in-law crowded uneasily close, tensing for the moment when the child's spirit would leave.

138

And the infants and fathers slowly worked out relationships. The infants staring with their huge eyes at the strange, fur-faced creatures that had usurped their mothers. The fathers staring with wonder at the miracle of life that could be held in your hands.

Barum played with his latest infant a little. He was mostly content to be close as the women and girls played with it. He found himself, instead, watching his eldest daughter, the troublesome Merin.

He remembered that first birth. His wife had been taken to the little house he had built her in the forest. Her belly was huge. Fear was written all over her face. The midwife shooed him away and he wandered uneasily amongst the other men, who teased him gently, and caressed him when it was obvious how much he worried.

He did all he could. He undid every knot on every article he owned, that the child's cord be free of knots. He opened boxes, that the way out should be smooth and free. He greased himself and stood in flowing water, that the child might come slipping and sliding easily.

It was impossible not to hear the cries from the hut, or to see the midwife scurrying about, appearing and disappearing with herbs and potions. The men built a fire and, as darkness fell, he sat by it—never hunching up, sitting erect, standing often, keeping his body open to assist her.

Then he had felt a searing pain in his back and belly and doubled over. They grabbed him, to keep him out of the fire, and began to massage him—as, at the same time in the hut, the midwife was massaging her; sure, experienced fingers drawing the baby down into the pelvic arch.

At the right moment, they forced him to his feet, making him squat, as she was squatting—and urged him to push. And, with the sun about to come over the mountains, the air crackling cold, the stars black and heavy, he had heard the wonderful cry from that little hut.

Now that child was a woman, playing with the latest baby, seeming engrossed solely in that operation. Was she thinking about the coming encounter with the white men? She had to be. He thought often of it, as did every other person in the village.

139

She had not been a good child. A perverse spirit seemed to inhabit her, making her crawl too early, stand too early, walk and talk before the proper times. She was hungry for knowledge, demanding it from her mother, her grandmother, from anyone who would give it.

Then, one day, she had got away from her mother, in a staggering run, and flung herself into his arms. He would always remember the feeling of that thrashing, squirming body, the life in it as strong as a stream, while the women wailed and rolled their eyes to the sky.

Now she felt him looking at her and glanced up, smiling uncertainly. He returned the uncertain smile, not knowing what to say to her.

"I'd better see what the men are doing," he said, and she nodded, watching his back as he walked away.

She handed the infant to his grandmother and stood. Merin wanted to run after her father, but there was always something holding her back, that held back all children in their relationships with their fathers. They might hug and kiss their age-mates all they liked, and tenderly embrace old relatives, but with their own fathers there was discomfort and uncertainty.

She remembered the singing parties, with all her age-mates, boys and girls, clustered in one house, hands clasped sweatily, bodies pressed together. The girl they were singing for, about to leave for marriage into another village, was herself. The voices rose up in a reverberating wall of sound.

Solo voice.
    Fetch the water from the stream.

The roaring response of all the others.
    Cut the leaves and bring the food.

The flute-like solo of a girl's voice.
    Chop the firewood, heat the stones.

140

The reply.
Unfold the mats, spread out the leaves.

The total thunder of all voices.
We sing for her as we feast;
from the mountain peaks to the water in streams.
From sky to the earth.
She leaves her people.
Her mother cries
as she goes so far.

And the fluting voice again, rising like a single bird-song from the roar of a mountain stream.
Our bellies cry happily for food,
for pork, for potatoes, for green vegetables.

The reply.
But our hearts are like stone,
they sink like the dying sun.

In previous parties she would have merged into the warm, comforting crush of bodies, mingling her voice with the others until her consciousness of herself would have disappeared also, and she would have been one with them, united in song. But this night there was a barrier between them. She could never return to the world of her girlhood. Even its grinding chores, the work in the fields, the long haul from stream to village with bamboo tubes of water, the endless chewing of bark and plaiting it into net for clothes and bags, the grinding of needles on stone, all the irritating endless work a young girl got stuck with, seemed pleasant in memory.

She pushed her way out of the pitch blackness of the house, into the clear, sharp air. The singing rose up behind her, both doleful and exciting, spiralling into the night on girls' voices, descending into the depths with the thunder of the boys'.

She remembered the morning she awoke and found her thighs sticky with blood. Knowing what it was she called to her mother, excited and nervous, for the spirit of moisture at last had come to dwell in her.

141

Solemnly, gravely, she was washed and oiled by the women of her family. Her forehead was adorned with bands of emerald beetle-shells. Her throat and wrists with pearl. The glittering plumes of bird of paradise were placed in her head-dress. She was led into the centre of the village, before all the people—men, women, and children—and her father came forward slowly, immensely proud.

He placed his hands on her hips and pointed her to face the whole body of the people.

"This is our daughter," he said, slowly, measuring each syllable. She could feel the pride in his hands. "She has become a woman, a fertile woman who will produce children. Sons in abundance. Daughters, too. She is strong and clever. Her fingers make plants grow where none grew before. When she lifts up an infant he ceases to cry immediately."

He raised his head, and his voice, to the rims of the valley.

"Hear me, you men of Gafu, of Kianan . . ." As he named each village, he turned her to face it. "Hear me, you men of far Enop. Our daughter is now a woman and ready for betrothal. But her price is high, for she is an exceptional woman, born of exceptional people, and will produce exceptional children. Hear me, all you men of this valley, and of the far mountain-slopes, and prepare your bride-price, sow your plants, fatten your pigs, collect your salt and your axes, and begin your journey to our home."

Then, on her wedding day, she had been dressed up so she was more like a toy than a person: a stiff plaything for other people. Her hair and her flesh were freshly, darkly greased, and hung about with loop after loop of red and yellow beads. On her forehead a circlet of emerald beetles holding two soaring plumes of bird of paradise feathers, scarlet and golden showers of the finest feathers ever seen. On her chest five rows of mother-of-pearl, gold-lip, ground and polished to gleaming perfection.

She had stared out from her entourage as the party made ready to carry her across the land of her people, over the stream, to the land of her husband. Barum's men were already loading up the trussed pigs, the containers of gold-lip shell, the feathers and other finery that were part of the bride-price. The flutes keened and roared. The kundu drums

142

sounded. The people fell into procession, Barum's daughter carried high, the stiff figurehead rising above the garden vines, the planted red and yellow flowers along the road, the hedges and bushes of her childhood.

She had been immobile with shock, unable to move in her costume, transported almost against her will down the familiar path. She recognized the gate-posts to the family garden that her father had carved with birds. The straight line of fence-posts, some sprouting. The bushes she and her mother had planted, that bore good fruit. The rows of laboriously cultivated vegetables. The casuarinas growing tall in fallow fields.

She didn't know whose shoulders she rode upon. All around her the music soared, like twin birds, male and female, interlocking, plummeting and soaring. Then her escort was shouting as they plunged through the stream, coming up the other side, towards the gathered crowd of her husband-to-be's relatives, already thundering the ground with their feet, shouting out the welcome song.

> Like the streams that rush we know not where
> from mountain to mountain,
> we come and go, seeking like birds
> a nest in the trees, a nest on the ground.
> We say goodbye to our fathers, journeying
> into the valleys, following the rushing streams.

The bass boom of male voices ceased and the treble of women's continued.

> Seeking husbands we leave our mothers.
> Seeking children, we leave our sisters.
> Like the cassowary we run over the plains,
> skirts bobbing, weaving our way.

And all together.
> We welcome a new sister, we welcome
> a new wife, to sit with the women, to
> give new life to our village.

143

The only work being done at Parap was the cleaning of the dance-ground. It was on an area levelled on the side of a hill, just down from the men's house. Trenches were being dug for the ovens. Rest houses from previous celebrations were being repaired, and some new ones constructed.

Barum made his way to the site and examined the work with a critical eye. It was not just the Sky People he was aiming to impress. All those other villages with kin married into the Parap had been invited to an exchange of gifts and pigs. It was the time to renew old ties and treaties, and for the current crop of youngsters to inspect each other and begin the task of choosing a mate.

So that, watching the preparations, he remembered his daughter's wedding to that rubbishman from the Gafu. How someone like that had got around his daughter, he did not know. Extricating the family from their obligations had been expensive, and they had lost face over the whole deal. Which made the prospect of outsmarting Samura and the Gafu loudmouths even more pleasant.

"There's no way the coast can prepare you for the Highlands," Don said, as he and Nicholls sat on the ground, waiting for Sergeant Bukato and Constable Giram to finish their reconnaissance of the village ahead of them.

"The girls are better, up here," Nicholls said.

"I don't know how you can say that."

"You've been giving it some thought, then?"

"A little, yes."

"Come on, man. If we're going to talk, we can at least be honest. What's the point in hiding your meaning in this situation?"

Don examined the situation. A grassy knoll on which the Patrol had camped, drawn in a circle, with the Police on guard on the periphery. Mountains ringing them in the

144

distance. Between them and the mountains, a wooded ridge above which drifted blue smoke. Within the deep shade of the trees could be seen a village. On the slopes of the ridge were isolated huts amongst the gardens. But no one moved. All the villagers were waiting for the Sky People to move.

"I think if any man examined his thoughts, at any moment, he would find sex beneath whatever the subject was," Don admitted.

"True enough," Nicholls said. "So, why don't you avail yourself of it?"

"You want me to be like you, don't you?" Don said, with a sudden insight. "If I'm as corrupt as you, you'll feel less guilty."

Nicholls laughed. "I feel anger, sadness . . ." He hesitated. He wanted to follow his own precept and talk openly, but not too openly. "I feel fear," he added, casually, glancing quickly at the younger man. Harris didn't react to the confession. "But I never feel guilt."

"Never?"

"Not over sex," Nicholls amended. "I feel bad about some of the . . . contact."

"Killing?"

"Yes, that. Sometimes."

Don could feel Nicholls holding something back. In his own mind he could see his own "contact", the death of the bowman who had wounded him.

"It happened so quickly," Don said, remembering. "I didn't have time to think. He was there, about to shoot me. I shot him. Afterwards, I was so elated to be alive that I didn't think about the killing."

"Did you feel fear?"

"Not at the time. Afterwards, when I started to think about it, back in Madang . . ."

"Thoughts had in Madang should not be held against you," Nicholls said.

"What do you mean?"

"Civilization corrupts; and colonial civilization corrupts absolutely."

Don stared at the older man. He sat with his arms encircling his knees. While he spoke, his eyes quartered the landscape

145

ceaselessly—foreground, middleground, background—sweeping across each item that could conceal a man.

"Do you expect attack?" Don asked.

"Some time," Nicholls said. "Maybe not right now. But, some time in the next week, someone is going to test us. If not the Parap, then some of their mates on the next ridge."

"Now that scares me," Don said.

Nicholls examined him.

"Really?"

"Doesn't it you?"

"It makes me cautious," he said. In his mind he rehearsed saying it: I am terrified of dying up here, clubbed to death, speared, rotting with poison; all the ways they can kill you, that they have killed Patrol Officers. Instead, he sniffed the air.

"If they were going to fight us," he said, "they wouldn't be cooking pork." He stood up, seeing his scouts returning.

"There's no danger?" Don asked.

"Only from the pork. It'll be half-cooked, at best, and full of worms."

He grinned down at Don. Don, staring up at him, thought that the prospect of battle seemed to enliven him. It's not sex he wants up here, Don thought. It's fighting. He stood up, his legs suddenly wobbly.

Merin could hear warriors on the road. They would be dressed for a ceremonial occasion, not for war—in their best head-dresses, plumed with bird of paradise, their largest and best shells hanging on necklaces. But they would be armed for a fight.

She could hear the keening of the bamboo flutes, informing any passers-by that here was a party intent on ceremony, on gift-exchange, on dancing. A party of wealth and largess, led by her father, who had donated two of his best hand-reared pigs, that now were trussed, live, to poles carried by the rushing men. The pigs' eyes were glazed, froth flickered

146

around their mouths, as they were rushed to their death, unable to move . . . like her, she realized, in her wedding finery. People and pigs out of control, in the grip of something beyond themselves, chanting as they ran, stamping their feet in thunder, drowning out thought and fear in the rush towards death.

The sound carried across the valley to the stream where she herded the remainder of her father's pigs. The animals ignored the noise, snuffling along the bank, tossing up roots with their snouts. She held a small piglet in her arms as she walked, absentmindedly stroking him.

The day was pleasantly warm, the morning sky cloudless. She could see the distant peaks clearly. She stroked the piglet and thought nothing, losing herself in the rush of nearby water, the circling of a hawk high overhead, the familiar domestic grunting of her charges.

There was something wrong with the way she felt. It took her a while to discover it. Her mind would not settle comfortably on any familiar image. It shivered and jumped, anxious to avoid confronting itself. It felt cold, as if a layer of fat had been stripped from it.

She remembered the night with the Kiap, and the cold of it.

Just as fat was both cloying, and also gave warmth, so this feeling she had lived with, that was now missing, had protected her and smothered her.

She stood still, on the edge of the stream, aware that she was close to the limit of her people's territory. There was only one sentry posted today. She could see his head as he sat against a tree, bored, chewing a length of sugar-cane. From across the stream was where a killer would come — either singly, or in a party of warriors.

Was there an ambush ahead of her? Was a war party making use of the noise of celebrations to mask its advance on the village, to suddenly attack the remaining women and children, butchering them, and then falling back? Would they find her on their way back and have her?

And the answer was no. The Sky People were here. The Kiap had ordered them to end warfare and killing; and was prepared to kill them in order to see his command was

147

obeyed. In order to meet the strength of the Kiap with comparable strength, the whole valley was now united. There would be no more inter-village fighting while the Sky People were here.

The feeling she discovered missing was the feeling of fear.

She cuddled her piglet closer, feeling it squirm with pleasure. The feeling was at the pit of her stomach, and spreading upwards, cold and frightening. She was afraid of it. She was afraid of the lack of fear.

The men felt no fear as they raced along the road. They felt nothing but the intoxication of the run. The only one who kept his head clear was their leader in this rush: Barum. An old man of fifty, he was still agile, still able to lead the rush, still full of seed. He was still sure enough of his power to let the Gafu think senility was approaching him.

He was thinking that the best thing that could happen was that the Sky People leave the valley and return to their place of origin. That was the best thing, and it would not happen. Now the people of the valley must look to the second-best thing.

Sure, Barum would help Samura set up the ambush for Nicholls, just as he had with the prospector. The death of the Sky People would carry great status for the people involved. But it would also bring very certain retribution — as the death of the prospector had brought Nicholls and his armed troops.

The Gafu could have Nicholls. The finger of accusation could point straight to them. That was all right by Barum. Any force of Sky People seeking vengeance would have to cross his land, and he would assist them to get at those hilltop dwelling cousins of cannibals. But he would take the glory of having set the battle up.

And while all that was going on, he would have the other one, the younger one with the arrow scar. He would bind him to the Parap through gift-exchange and favours. Nicholls was an old hand, too smart to fall for the reciprocity of exchange; too powerful to meet his obligations for having a Big Man's daughter for the night. But the younger one would be ensnared like any boy, through sex, marriage, and obligation.

"Here they come," Nicholls said.

They stood together at the edge of their bivouac. Nicholls glanced around quickly, seeing where his Police Boys were stationed, and where the anxious carriers were grouped. He checked his old dog, held tight by his servant, Baranuma, her ears back, like everyone else watching the approaching stampede.

They came in a rush of plumes, of dancing feet and thundering drums, chanting wildly. As they ran, they swung their spears out and notched arrows to their bows. Their eyes glazed over, their nervous systems overloaded with adrenalin, pounding drums, the hyperventilation of their chants, the smack of their feet on the road.

"Kill!" they screamed. "Kill the enemy from the Sky! Kill the thieves of pigs! Kill the rapists! Kill!"

Don felt his bowels loosen. He watched the barbed spear-ends and loaded bows. The bone tips, festered in rotting corpses, would kill by infection or by the trauma of entry. His hand moved for the holster of his Service revolver.

"Don't move," Nicholls rasped. "Don't move an inch. If they wanted to kill us, they'd do it by ambush."

Nicholls stood with his feet apart, his arms folded on his chest.

"Stare straight ahead," he said, from the corner of his mouth.

Don could feel the thunder of the earth, and he could feel the line of sight of those spears, all congregating on his chest. He was conscious of Nicholls beside him, impervious to fear in his white trousers and white shirt.

149

"Jesus . . ." Don said.

Then the warriors were on them. He could see each individual, tossing plume. He could see the kill-crazed eyes, the froth at their lips. He could smell the stink of rancid fat and of sweat. He shut his eyes.

There was silence. He opened them. He was staring at a line of grinning, swaying faces. An old man stepped forward and held out his hand to Nicholls. He spoke in a dialect Don could not understand.

Nicholls shook the proffered hand. But all the eyes were on Don Harris, taunting him, laughing at the moment of fear he had displayed. He stared back, his face flushed and hot, refusing to let them laugh him down.

"Welcome back, Masta Nicholls," Barum was saying. "In honour of your visit let me present you with these two pigs from my own herd."

"Thank you, Barum. Thank you very much."

Nicholls watched the older man's shrewd face, but it gave him nothing more than welcome. Then Barum's eyes shifted momentarily, to quickly assess Harris, and Nicholls caught the scent of something else, some level of activity below what was presented on the surface, a conspiracy that gave him a surge of fear.

"They are magnificent animals," he said, glancing at the two trussed porkers, rigid on their poles, decorated with plumes and leaves. "You will, of course, do us the honour of sharing them with us?"

"Thank you, Masta Nicholls. That would be an honour. But these pigs are for you alone. It would take more than two to feed this brood of empty bellies. For them, we will slaughter more, perhaps not as magnificent as these two creatures, which I must admit are the finest I have seen for many seasons . . ."

"Thank you, Barum, old friend and ally. This is indeed a generous offer. We will share food with you, and you will accept these gifts in exchange. Great gifts from the Australian government: steel axes, mirrors, gold-lip shell."

You're a tricky bastard, Barum thought. But not tricky enough. Those steel axes will be used to chop off your own head by those savages across the stream. Your gold-lip shell

150

will be full of worm-holes, I suppose. For someone from the Spirit World, you're very human.

It occurred to him that the Spirit World could be simply using these pale ordinary mortals to carry out its work. It was possible that Nicholls and his young, and scared, companion were being swept along by forces over which they had no control—like trussed pigs on a pole, carried to the fires.

"The women are waiting," he said, watching Nicholls' face. "The fires are lit and the pigs already cooking. We have invited the other people of the valley to come and meet, to dance and to talk.

Nicholls' face had flickered at the word "women". Barum knew he was not thinking in the plural. He was thinking of a singular woman.

Behind that flicker. Barum could see something else. Nicholls was a dead man. Death was in the back of his eyes, sitting on his hunched shoulders. Nicholls was aware that the sorcery had begun. Because he could think like someone from the valley, so he was susceptible to the valley's sorcery. A man's greatest strength is always his weak point.

"Thank you, Barum," Nicholls said. "We will be honoured to eat with you. Now, let me introduce another Kiap; Kiap Don Harris."

Barum was thinking that, if the Sky People were only ordinary mortals, swept up by the Power, then they were doing all right, traipsing around the country, living off the best food they could commandeer, the best women, stealing away young boys to return with them to wherever they came from. Then he turned and studied the other Kiap.

Don felt himself the subject of scrutiny by the shrewdest eyes he had ever met, their corners wrinkled, humour lurking in them, but also ruthlessness and strength. He summoned up all his own energy, driving the fear out of his eyes, and stretched out his hand.

151

· CHAPTER EIGHT ·

The world has, as to time and space, a beginning.

The world is, as to time and space, infinite.

Everything in the world consists of elements that are simple.

There is nothing simple, but everything is composite.

There are in the world causes through freedom.

There is no freedom, but all is nature.

In the series of the world-causes there is some necessary being.

There is nothing necessary in the world, but in this series all is contingent.

The world a ball, turning. Night and day chasing each other across the turning ball. Wakefulness and sleep. Life and death. Male and female.

All the great oppositions chased themselves across the field of his eyes. The words of Hegel, transcribed from a schoolbook by his own father, snaked through the turning opposites, a thread trying to link them.

Rain, ceaseless rain, falling easily, effortlessly out of the grey sky, into the deep, grey lagoon; into the sodden grey forests that fell into the lagoon from the volcano slopes. The silent niggers flitting through the rain, stacking the copra bags on the little jetty, their faces impervious to the rain as it fell off the sheen of their brown bodies. His father's hand on the white, blank page of the exercise book, pointing to where he was to transcribe the words.

And Ludwig seeing the rain, and its satin touch on brown flesh; recognizing the woman, standing there, who occupied his father's nights now that his mother had been buried in the sodden grey soil, during a break in the long, silent rain.

Then present time broke through, but like a dream interfering with reality. He was conscious of smoke hurting his eyes and cold beginning to seep into his naked body. He was shivering violently, jerking back and forth, his fingers dancing. He clenched the earth and felt it against his cheek. He looked along it to the dull winking of coal-like eyes. The dancing fingers felt for and found the wood and slithered it against the coals.

Flame danced on the wood, winking and glittering, running towards him. He curled his body in closer to its tiny heat.

His body curled to her body. She lifted him with her as she stood and moved to the verandah. Together, they could see the green jungle falling into the still, acid blue water of the lagoon. Blue smoke hung in the rim of the volcano as they watched.

The screams erupted out of the servant's hut. He felt the spasm of fear from his mother, as her hands jerked tightly against him, holding him closer to her body. Then she pushed him away and was holding him up, so he could see what was happening.

The woman was shrieking as she ran, holding her head with her hands, as he had seen others of the brown-skinned women do when they were frightened. The man was close behind her, yelling out his anger violently. Something glittered in his fist.

His mother lifted him higher as she strained forward. Her own anger was chasing the fear away. She was wanting him to watch with her, to observe and learn.

The man was shouting at the woman. She was screaming. Whatever he was accusing her of, she was denying. But Ludwig could hear the lie in her voice. The denial was false. The accusations had the indignant ring of truth. She slipped as she ran for the Masta's house, and the blade in the man's fist sank easily, effortlessly, into her kidneys.

There was his father, running, shouting too, his pistol waving ahead of him; but the man took no notice of it. The man's teeth were as bare and bright and sharp as the knife blade that slid in and out, in and out, with dark blood bursting from the slit-like wound. His father pointed the pistol as he ran and smoke came from it, then the sound. The man jumped, but kept sliding his knife in and out. The woman had ceased shrieking, and was now moaning. Ludwig's mother was shivering with excitement, with anger, with fear, still holding him out, his knees against the verandah rail, showing him what was happening.

The pistol jumped and smoked again, but this shot missed. The man pulled his blade one last time from the wound and stood up and waited for his father with it.

His father stopped running and steadied himself. Other natives were running, but when they saw the two men face each other, they stopped and waited. All eyes focused on the two men.

The native took a step, the blade before him, red and silver. On the ground, the woman twitched and shivered, like someone with fever. The native accused his father with the blade and with his grimacing mouth.

His father did not deny the accusation. He raised his left arm and laid the pistol across it and sighted on the man. The man drew back, the muscles down his spine and his legs tensed, and he hurled himself forward.

The pistol shot smoke, jerked. The sound was sharp and flat. The man dropped his knife and skidded on his face to his father's feet. His father stared at him, then looked around. The other natives stopped looking and turned away. His father looked up to the verandah and saw his wife and son watching.

"Take him away!" he shouted at her. "Why are you watching?"

"I want him to see her," she said.

Ludwig felt the pressure ease on his knees. His mother turned, now cradling him close. Instead of his father, he saw the grain of the wood in the walls. His mother was sobbing. In the background, the other native women commenced to cry.

The flames built a pyramid of light. He smiled and turned on his side, letting it warm his back. He stared at the flickering shadows on the far wall. His own shape was outlined, shivering and fading as the flames rose and fell. He

154

stretched out his hand and examined the fingers. The tremor had almost ceased. His head was clear of fever dreams. He smiled and closed his eyes.

Sleep, he thought. Let me sleep.

When Merin heard drums, and then the singing, a wave of loneliness encompassed her. In her mind she could see the dance-ground. Her clansmen would take the field first, in their tall, proud dance-frames; their heads tossing the plumed feathers like tall grass in the wind; their faces almost masks in the paint and ornamentation — but not quite masks, each painted face a ritual stylization of its wearer, carefully drawn to suggest to the female watchers the vigour, the strength, the access to power that this man possessed.

They would swing onto the dance-ground, drums held across their bodies, legs pounding thunder-rhythms, their mouths open as they burst out the songs, the sweat gathering across the discs of muscle on their chests, running into the corrugations of muscle on their bellies. The women and girls drawing in their breath at the sight of all that male sex before them, its scent and its boastful, upraised power.

Then the visiting men would join in, their faces more serious, intent on winning the hearts of the watching girls, drawing them into their webs and away from their fathers' clans.

Now the dancing in earnest, bodies thrusting forward, lines of chanting dancers forming and swaying until some girl could bear it no longer and would leap up, her own hips swaying, her own legs pounding, and join the men.

Women's voices joining the men in high-pitched ululations, creating the counterpoint that was at the heart of their world. Bass and soprano, hot and cold, male and female, Earth Mother and Sky Gods.

Once, a long time ago, when the people lived in the mountains, life was very difficult. There were no pigs, and no fields of

155

vegetables. They lived on bush-rats and on nuts and the roots of bushes. Some of the nuts drove men crazy.

One of the men, driven crazy by eating the amug nut, lay on the ground and, in a sexual frenzy, copulated with it, thinking he was copulating with the Earth Mother herself. His friends laughed at him and tried to get him to stand up, but he was strong with his frenzy and kept on pushing himself into the ground: in and out, and in and out. Like someone with a digging stick turning the soil before they place the seeds in it.

Which is what he did. He shot his seed into the soil.

And immediately he came to his senses, and stood up, shamefaced, aware that the others were laughing at him, and he hurriedly kicked soil over his spilled seed, and went away.

But something happened in that spot. It ripened with the sun and was fed with the rains. And one day, when he returned to it, he found an infant girl half-buried in the soil, still anchored to it with her cord, like the root of a bush. He cut the cord and removed her from the earth and took her home with him.

He hid her away from the others, in a little hut he made for her, and she grew very quickly into a comely young woman. He kept her in the hut and lay with her all the time, until she became pregnant.

But she gave birth to a vegetable, not to a child. He grew very angry and killed her, when he saw what she had done, and he buried her body and the roots of the vegetables with her.

But the roots grew and produced the sweet potato. And, where he had buried her, he found one day a small animal, a piglet. He began to feed the sweet potato to the piglet and it grew bigger and bigger . . .

Stories grandmothers tell their grandchildren as they sit with them beside the fields, watching the mothers working. Stories children listen to, wanting to believe, while knowing they are exaggerations—but which part is the exaggeration, and which part the truth? Were there once people like that woman?

156

Now she was discovering the literal truth. She was such a woman. She was the one who lay down and opened her legs and whom the Sky Gods sent down their emissaries to lie with, for the benefit of the people.

She was the outcaste. She had been pushed outside the normal life a woman led and turned into a woman from a story.

Her husband had come into the house he had built her, nervously, glancing around with uncertainty. They had been married two years, and she had acquired all the detritus of everyday living. Several pigs lay at ease in one corner. Hanging from the walls were net bags she had made, some of her best clothes, some for unprepared possum skins, some with lime gourds of ointment, herbs, make-up.

It was to these he crossed.

"What do you want?" she demanded, sharply, backing towards the pigs' corner. One of them grunted in displeasure at her closeness.

He heaved a gourd to the ground, spilling its contents. She knelt down and quickly tried to gather the contents before the pigs got up and nosed the spilled powders into the dirt.

"Which one is it in?" he demanded.

"What do you mean?" She looked up at him, puzzled, and noticed the glaze on his eyes and the tremor of his lips.

"You know what I mean. The sorcery ointment. What you use to keep me from having you like I should."

"There is no such thing," she said. "You're intoxicated. Go away."

He glared down at her and she shrank back from his wild anger.

"I'm not a complete fool," he said. "I know what's going on. I know what is being said, about the lack of swelling in your belly."

"Children take time to grow. It takes a lot of watering of the seed before it germinates."

"I know all about that. I'm not a fool. So why do you stop me planting the seed? Let alone watering it?"

157

She felt more at ease now that the subject was the common one between them: his impotence. She pushed herself off her knees and smiled at him.

But he did not respond as she had expected. His nostrils flared as she moved closer to him. He leaned back and swung.

She caught the blow across the cheek and reeled into the wall. She fell backwards into the pigs, who squealed and kicked her with their hooves. They ran for the doorway and plunged into the street, squealing indignantly, and advertising the domestic dispute to the deafest of the old women.

He was breathing hard and rubbing his hand where he had hit her. His eyes slipped in and out of focus.

"You've eaten too much amug," she said. "Go away and come back later."

"You've eaten whatever you women use to make yourselves sterile. I know about it. I'm no fool. All the men know the grandmothers take you into the mountains to find the right bushes . . ."

She did not deny it, as it was true. He drew breath loudly.

"Then what do you do but lie around here all day, painting your face like a young girl, so the men can see you when you walk about, so they'll follow you down to the stream . . ."

"Go away and sleep it off," she said thickly, her lips swelling.

He hit her again. Blood poured from her nose.

"The men laugh at me, don't they? The old women wag their chins. They giggle as I walk past. Where are the children? they ask. What sorcery is she working on him?"

"No one has children in the first few years," she said.

"So, you admit taking the drug?"

She shook her head to clear it. Once, there had been a violently heavy bleeding, with thick, clotted blood and tissue. Her mother-in-law had looked after her as she lay, unable to move for two days. They both knew what it meant. No woman could survive if she had children every time. She would be worn to death.

But he interpreted the shake of her head as a denial. Enraged by her lying, he kicked her in the belly. He saw her mouth open and her eyes roll. There was surprise on her

158

face as she pitched forward. He became aware of a crowd of women at the door.

"Go away!" he yelled at them. "This is something between her and me."

"Get out of her house," one of the women said.

He looked, and saw it was his mother. She stooped and entered the house, glanced at his prostrate wife, and took his elbow.

"Come on," she said gently. "Come on, you've had too much of a good time with your friends. Your mind is not clear at the moment. Come outside and sit for a while."

He struggled half-heartedly, but let her drag him outside.

Merin watched the mother lead the son, like a girl leads a tamed boar on a leg-rope. None of the women paid any attention to her. The crowd disappeared from her door and she moaned to herself.

He had been such a strong dancer, from a strong family. He spoke Big. He strutted his finery with arrogance. Seeing him dancing, she had almost swooned with excitement.

But, married to him, he was a different man. It worried her that the sight of her did not arouse him. Her breasts were firm, her belly did not protrude, her buttocks were lean. She had all the hallmarks of beauty. She painted her face for him. The drugs she used were the opposite of what he accused her of using. They were the ones that should have engorged him at the sight of her.

Groaning, she hobbled upright. She had no relatives in this village. The other women would prevent him killing her, she knew, but they would be indifferent to him beating her. She cried as she leaned against the wall. She wanted to be a little girl again, one who had not bled, who had nothing but girls' tasks to perform, and who had a father close by to keep men away. She cried and hobbled out of the hut, into the bright sunlight of the village—harsh and hot, not like the cool shadows of her home.

In amongst the thunder of the drums and the shouting, singing voices, Barum was thinking of his daughter. He kept

159

his face carefully composed, staring ahead at the display, the configuration of loyalties, old enmities and new alliances revealed in the pattern of the dance. He was vaguely aware that fighting must not break out before the Sky People. He was conscious of the various taboos on contact that should be observed—that enemies with unresolved conflicts should not share sleeping quarters, even though they might share relatives through marriage; and the location and building of rest houses had been designed to allow the maximum flexibility in this regard. But these thoughts only teased at the main current of his mind.

What he thought of most vividly was the hill-slope down to the stream, the far gardens, the day when he had been on guard-duty in the shade of the trees by that stream.

In that drowsy heat the cicadas had kept up a background whirr of noise. Hawks floated lazily on the upcurrents from the distant, blue mountains. The heat-haze shimmered. Nothing moved in the quietness of midday. Then, there was a splash in the creek. He jerked awake and listened. There was another splash. Whoever was fording the creek did so clumsily, not like a warrior intent on ambush.

But it could be a ruse to draw him away from the trees and expose him to an arrow shot. Rumours were circulating, reports of contact with a dangerous party of Sky People who had shot and killed villagers in distant valleys, and had enslaved others for a march into the most distant mountains.

He half-rose and scanned the creekside. He could detect no untoward movement. He waited and heard the splashing again, now more desperate, like someone floundering in the water. It could possibly be someone wounded and now close to death. He crouched forward, keeping his head below the level of the grass, and moved down to the stream.

A woman had collapsed in the water. She was struggling to keep her face out of the powerful current, trying to kneel, but so exhausted that her arms kept buckling under her, pitching her forward. The current tugged her sideways, threatening to toss her on her side and drown her.

But she could easily have been a decoy, a captured girl put out as bait. He waited, still checking the streamside. Then she looked up.

160

He was on his feet without thinking. He dropped his bow and ran the last distance and leapt into the water, stumbling as the current gripped him, and floundered to her.

"Merin!" he called. "Child. My child."

She cringed, not recognizing him, dazzled by sun and exhaustion. Her face was badly bruised, blood crusted from her nose to her chin.

"It's me," he said. "Your father."

Her face showed the delight. She reached up her arms to him and he took them. He knelt beside her. The water banked against them both, swaying them together. She was crying. He wrapped his arms around her and stood up, lifting her from the water's embrace.

"I want to come home," she whispered.

He nodded, now conscious that a war-party could be hot on her heels, come to demand her return to her husband. He turned and carried her from the stream.

"We are seeking the prospector Ludwig," Nicholls said. "The man who started all the trouble in this valley. And we are also seeking the killers of the innocent prospector Wallace. The killers of him and his woman and his men."

Barum stared blankly at the Kiap. The noise of the festivities was a background roar. Nicholls watched him closely, frowning at the lack of comprehension on Barum's face.

Barum's mind returned, reluctantly, to present time. He studied the face of the man beside Nicholls. It held a look of disgust, the look all Sky People wore on first contact. As always, it was intermingled with curiosity; and something else, a longing. They looked like captives waiting to die, watching ordinary life go on, he thought; knowing they will never be part of it again.

"We have been collecting evidence against Ludwig! We are preparing a case!" Nicholls said, loudly, slightly irritated. Barum collected himself and turned to the Kiap.

"The red-haired one is in the mountains over there," Barum pointed with his chin.

"He's been seen?" Barum noted Nicholls' eagerness. Guilelessly, he fed him the information.

"The people over the stream, the Gafu, can tell you more than me. I heard from them that his party had been seen in the north mountains. You will have to ask them."

"Thank you," Nicholls said. "I'll do that."

Barum watched him look at his assistant, whose attention had been captured by the girls, shaking their charms at the men of their choice as the dance progressed. Nicholls' eyes went there, too. Barum waited for the inquiry.

"Ummm," Nicholls said, not looking at Barum, but addressing him. "There was a young woman, the last time I was here . . ."

"Yes?"

Nicholls glanced quickly at him. There was both desire and shame in his face.

"She entertained me . . ."

"She is no longer with us." He tried to sound disinterested, but was aware of the anger behind his voice.

"She's dead?" Nicholls misread the anger.

Barum touched the earth with the flat of his hand and reassured himself with its contact. He breathed in and out, and replied evenly.

"Worse than that. She ran away to the Gafu, after a dance, and had an affair with some rubbishman of theirs. She's too afraid to return home and face her punishment. You will undoubtedly find her over there."

The earth seemed to press back at him, to reassure him.

Nicholls nodded, feigning indifference. The younger Sky Person spoke to him in their language, questioning. Barum heard in reply the word he was beginning to recognize, "Ludwig". Nicholls indicated the Gafu slopes with his head.

"How's it going?" Don asked Nicholls as he turned away from the old village headman.

"There's a lead on Ludwig. He's over on the next mountain range."

"So we'll push on?" Don's head was whirling with the noise and the heat and the half-cooked, fatty pork.

"It's not far to the next village." Don was aware of something hidden in Nicholls' careful voice. "We'll split the force, I think. You stay here and get on with the census and some mapping. I'll take most of the Police Boys with me and collect what I can about Ludwig."

Don felt a guilty surge of relief, that he would not be pressing on into the unknown. Then he became aware of the wrinkled, monkey-like face of the headman, holding out for him some choice delicacies: pig entrails. He smiled falsely and took them. The man watched him closely. He put some in his mouth and fought his nausea. He chewed, eyes locked with the old man. He kept the vile stuff in his cheeks and feigned swallowing.

The old man looked away and Don spat it into his hand and deposited it on the steadily-growing pile beside him.

He was becoming more and more disorientated, by nausea and by the din, the heat, the discomfort of sitting on soil reeking of human and pig faeces, and by boredom.

He had watched the exchange of pigs for steel axes and mirrors. Then he had sat through the interminable exchange between the locals and the visitors—as each tried to impress the other with his largess, with the vigour of his scrawny pigs. He saw only avarice in their eyes, and cunning, as they evaluated the worth of each animal—like farmers at a country stockyard. Then he had watched the squealing animals led out to be bludgeoned to death before his eyes. The jerking, barely dead bodies were improperly bled, slit open, half-heartedly gutted, and tossed onto the firestone-filled trenches. They steamed and blistered immediately. They were covered with leaves and with earth, and the smell of roasting flesh, skin, and hair began to seep up through the ground.

As some of the locals filled these trenches, others were opening different trenches and dragging out still steaming branches and thick leaves, and then the bloated pig corpses, now half-cooked. They tossed the steaming flesh onto the

163

shit and ash covered ground and began to slice it up, to pick through the gizzards. Screaming children fought for tasty morsels of intestine. Men tore at the meat with their teeth. The women grabbed great hunks and chewed at it, their faces contorted by the tough sinews.

In amongst all of this, long and eloquently bombastic speeches were made, by the host, the Lu-lui as was his title, and by other notables. All Don could follow were the boastful intonations and gestures, presuming they spoke in praise of themselves and to the detriment of parties not present.

He found a relief from it in imagining each speaker as a well-known mainland politician at the hustings, and supplied his own speeches—in denunciation of Labour or Capital and in praise of the incumbent party.

Then the dancers burst onto the ground, hitting it with a physical shock. The men were almost unrecognizable as human. They were aliens from another planet. Their legs were tassled with cassowary feathers, their hips girdled with slashing grass skirts. From their backs rose huge, ten foot high frames of wood and feathers, vivid with colour in crude geometric designs and stripes. Their faces were painted, foreheads hidden by iridescent green bands of jewellery. Discs of mother-of-pearl blazed on their chests. Through their noses hung more circles of pearl and bone, disfiguring what could be seen of their faces. Some wore bracelets and necklaces of teeth—he presumed dog-teeth, but could not be sure. Tossing on every head were the plumes of thousands of birds of paradise, butchered solely to provide feathers for this outlandish display.

Each man carried a simple megaphone-drum, and beat on it continuously, to no recognizable rhythm. Their feet beat out a similar staccato thunder on the ground. Their voices screamed and thundered.

The display was at once horrifying and repellent. And it was vividly, intensely sexually exciting. Simultaneously his head swam with nausea and his groin shivered with excitement.

The strutting bodies, gleaming with oil, flung themselves at the watchers, grass skirts concealing and revealing powerful

164

male genitals. Each step the men took sent ripples through their stocky, muscled legs, and made their gleaming torsos flex and pound.

Each step was aimed for effect, directed to the groups of women who watched entranced, until suddenly there burst from them a collective, orgiastic cry and they leapt onto the dance-ground themselves, flinging their bodies in parody of a woman's sexual movements, and the dance lurched into its next stage of excitement.

He tried to deny the sexual feeling, but could not. He crossed and uncrossed his legs, but the movement only excited his engorged penis the more.

The women's voices, joining with the men's, set up a weird counterpoint, beyond any musical comprehension he had. All he could recognize were the bass and the treble of it, held together by the pounding of the drums.

The women were not ornately displayed, but they did not need to be. They showed a fine sense of understatement. A clean grass skirt, a few circles of jewellery, oiled bodies, and firm full breasts. They let their hips and thighs speak for them, shamelessly.

He remembered how Nicholls said these women would do "anything". He understood now. They did everything a man wanted a woman to do, but which no woman from the civilized world would consent to. They were shamelessly sexual, not innocent, not acting out of ignorance—each movement was a deliberate provocation, aimed at the men to draw from them another thrust of the pelvis, another strain of legs and back. As they drew him into their dance, their ugliness disappeared. They were not the clean, shimmering creatures of his fantasies, they were something far more powerfully erotic; sexuality divorced from an object. He felt immersed in a stream of libido.

The dance was also an act of endurance. It thundered on, hour after hour. Most of the women retreated, leaving the men to fight it out between themselves, but always watching from the sidelines. As he watched, the women became individuals, and he saw them singling out individuals amongst the men—coolly appraising their dance techniques, their wealth display, their endurance and strength. In the shadows

165

beyond the firelight, assignations took place. Male and female figures clasped hands and darted into the night. Closer at hand the chaperons, the old men and women, dozed in the fire's warmth.

"Ulysses," a voice beside him said.

"What?"

He became conscious of Nicholls' erect figure, stiff with judgement, with held-in desires, with the full authority of civilization. He turned to Don.

"I was thinking about Ulysses, how extraordinarily similar our journey is to his odyssey."

"Oh. I don't know it all that well."

"The sacrifices that are made, of steaming blood into the steaming earth, and the shades of the dead rising up to meet him. Cattle, sheep, pigs, rams . . . the sacrificed domestic animal. The bewitching goddesses he must battle with his skill and guile. And the journey itself, through treachery and strange, magical happenings. Our journey, too."

Don grunted and nodded his head. Nicholls had forced him back to consciousness. He presumed Nicholls had kept a tight hold on his faculties by making these analogies, by looking for these similarities that he could anchor himself to and so translate the experience into something safely literary, mythic and imagined.

But Don had been in the sway of the realness of it. The reality of the Stone Age, the dawn of mankind, existing at the same time as the twentieth century. The night teeming with palpable spirits. The Earth Goddess at his feet, the blood of sacrificial victims soaking into her. The thunder of unleashed sex, like nothing he could have imagined.

He had been looking into a well, down inside his own belly, into a volcano. There in its depths was a lagoon. Something was rising from the depths of that lagoon, like a huge crocodile.

"Time to go," Nicholls said. "We've graced them enough with our presence."

"What? Oh." He struggled to stand, muscles cramped and locked, aware of his erection and aware that the monkey-faced old man was grinning at him, at it. The old man

166

extended a hand and, to his shock, ran it inside his thigh, clasping him firmly. He jumped backwards.

"Come on," Nicholls said, "Telemachus."

"Who?"

"Ulysses' son, who came to save him."

"That old bastard goosed me."

"It means he likes you."

"I know that! But I don't like him."

Nicholls grinned at him as he led the way clear.

The thunder fell away, and with it the spell. Black night returned. Don felt the cold of it gratefully, as his own, familiar senses returned to him. He was glad to be European. Glad he did not have to look any longer into that pit of fierce desire. He sucked in the cold air as he stumbled after Nicholls. Ahead of them was a light; clear lantern light. European light.

Baranuma stood at the entrance of their house, holding the lantern. His face showed a mixture of worry and scorn, then relief as they returned. Nicholls mumbled something to him as he entered. Baranuma looked towards the sounds of revelry. His eyes met Don's and his lips curled.

"Bush kanakas," he said dismissively, and then stood back to allow Don to enter the hut.

He stood outside the stockade. Tonight there was no likelihood of attack. Samura heard the distant thunder of the dancing across the valley. He smiled, thinking of old Barum sitting beside the two Sky People—a wizened old turd between two dry sticks.

There was a debt to be paid out, one that both he and Barum recognized, if only tacitly, in all their dealings. The debt went back to the generation before their grandfathers', when people were expanding across the valley, pushing against each other's borders. The Gafu, the pre-eminent people of the valley, fought against the immigrants who, driven from their own lands in distant mountains, demanded land from Samura's kin.

167

To influence the negotiations, the interlopers ambushed a party of women and children, and killed them all. In the after-shock of the attack, Samura's people had agreed to give up some land.

Now the murdering Parap controlled the best soil in the valley, grew the biggest pigs, and made the most noise at their festivities. When Samura went to them, he masked his feelings with a false smile. He had not yet hung the ancient fighting stones from the rafters of the men's house, but when the business with the Sky People was finished, then he would personally tear out the tree of peace he had planted with the Old Turd. He would return home, here, to the stockade on the high ridge, and lift up those ancient symbols of war, show them to all the people, and hang them there, like a pair of giant testicles, announcing the return of virility, the return of masculinity, and the return of war.

Women held the power amongst the Parap. The forces of men, the hot, dry, aerial Sky Gods were in decline down there — and maybe that was why the Sky People had arrived, in response to this imbalance of forces. For wherever you went in the valley, you felt the coldness, the moisture, of the earth-bound Mother.

The Sky Gods controlled the upper body of a man: his mind and his voice, his chest and arms. The Earth Goddess controlled the sex, the legs; birth, death and decay.

Up here, on the ridge, the advancing Sky People would meet battle with true, male warriors. But they would be weakened from their stay amongst the women down below. Their legs would be unsteady, their sexual power diminished from intercourse with women. They would be ripe for harvest.

Samura no longer regarded the Sky People as super-human. They had genitals, they had sexual desires. Wherever they fitted in the scheme of things, it was not all that much higher than men. And, in the ultimate test, they died just like men.

He grinned and spat and turned back to see the sentry watching not him, but the far gleam of fire and the distant music.

"They dance before dying," he called, and waited while the sentry unhooked the boards to let him back in. Even

168

though there was no danger, tradition died hard. The boards would remain in place.

With Nicholls' death, he would rise in prestige above the Old Turd. People all over the valleys and mountains would hear the story. But when the Sky People came for retribution, they would have to pass first through the Gafu's illegally-taken valley to get to him. And on the way they would find Nicholls' remains, and those of his troops, scattered amongst the garden huts of the murderers of Samura's kin.

Samura walked to the men's house, feeling the Power all around him now.

Her father crouched by the dying fire, holding out his hands for warmth. His chest and face and knees soaked it up gratefully, but his back shivered.

Feathers were scattered about the dance-ground, as if giant birds had mated there. The air smelled of a mixture of woodsmoke and pork. The fires had burned to embers, all except the one he had stoked and now sat before, shivering. As she watched, he half-turned, to warm his back, and saw her watching him.

He smiled at Merin and indicated the fire.

"They went to sleep hours ago," he said. "These Sky People have no stamina."

She stepped to the warmth.

"Where are the others?" she asked.

He gestured at the guest-houses.

"I was cold," she said. "I couldn't sleep."

"It's a cold night."

They stared together into the flames. She picked up a stick and thrust it into the fire and watched it burn. He remembered the cold night of her birth.

"Must I . . ." she asked.

He spoke quickly, sensing what she wanted to say. "When you left your husband," he said, "that bum-boy of rubbishmen, his uncle, the Old Turd Samura, demanded immediate repayment of your bride-price."

169

She lifted the burning stick out and brought it close to her face.

"Immediate," he stressed. "Not repayment over time, as you would expect in a case like that."

"He beat me."

He shrugged. "Many wives get beaten," he said. "They accept it."

"Why?" she said, lowering the stick and looking at him. "Do you accept that these Sky People can order you around? Some men do. Why should I accept what some other women do?"

He chuckled and reached out and clasped her thigh. She sat down beside him and returned her stick to the fire. The flames consumed it.

"They're ugly," she said. "Skinny. No chests. Legs like sticks. White like something you'd find under a log."

"They're powerful," he said. "They are as powerful as tomorrow. While we are as powerful as yesterday."

"We never used to talk about tomorrow," she said. "What we used to talk about was the day in hand: pigs, crops, children. Now we talk about yesterday, worry about tomorrow. What happened to today?"

"It's gone."

She shivered in the heat.

"You have a debt," he said. "It must be paid out."

Amongst any group of women whose chief desire is marriage, the presence of a divorced woman is not welcome. In the old days, she thought, and realized she was thinking about "yesterday", a woman who was branded "unfaithful" could be killed. The rumours were that she had betrayed her husband and that was why he threw her out—not "that was why she left him".

She felt very angry, staring into the fire. The truth of what had happened had never been discussed. Instead, the lies had been spread by her husband's relatives. Her father had not chosen to combat those lies. He had chosen, instead, to buy her out of trouble.

In the old days, a wronged husband could ambush the woman and drag her home with him, or rape her on the spot.

And the old days had only ended when Nicholls came into

170

the valley, in pursuit of the prospectors—the one that had died and the one that was good at killing. Nicholls' superior firepower brought the old days to an end.

She lit another stick, angrily, watching it burn with a burst of fury. She could feel her father beside her, not watching her now, immersed in his own thoughts; his hand, in a characteristic gesture, flat on the earth.

She remembered him sitting like that while the arguments raged. Three men dead in one skirmish, and they had not even got close to the Sky Person. The bodies of the prospector's party only partly disposed of, and that tall, skinny, pale wraith already seeking vengeance.

What could they do to stop him? What payment could they make? How many pigs? How many women would he demand for his pleasure? How far would they be devalued in having consorted with him?

The women had listened on the outskirts of the meetings. Sometimes the men were boastful. They had speared the prospector. Sometimes they were afraid. The Sky Person's guns were every bit as ferocious as had been described.

Watching the men, she had seen them in a new light. They were no longer the fierce, strong warriors of the dance-ground and battlefield. They were the boastful bullies who burst into a woman's house and abused her for their own impotence. They hid behind masks of their own devising, masks they had come to believe were their real faces. Now, with their supremacy in the world ended, they milled like helpless ants around their exposed nest, frantic with worry, snapping their pincers at whoever ventured close, waving their arms and pretending that there was still point to talk, to oratory, to the cult of their own invincibility.

She had pushed through the ranks of women, and then through the boys. The men, feeling her elbow her way to the centre of the group, tried to muscle her out. So she stopped where she was, behind one solid, muscular back, and spoke in the first silence.

"I'll go to him," she said. "I've got nothing to lose."

"Let her through," her father said, invisible to her, seated on the ground.

The back shifted from before her. Eyes watched her

171

suspiciously, nervously, and with a touch of awe. She found him sitting at the centre, with old Samura, Biggest man from her ex-husband's people, standing by him, eyeing her with scorn and lust.

"This adulteress?" he said.

Her father's hand left the ground and had hold of Samura's scrotum.

"My daughter," he said, quietly, but his teeth clenched against the anger, staring at her, so she knew half the anger was at herself, for having given rise to the rumours.

Samura did not show the pain, but he took his time before replying.

"Your daughter," he said. "The wife of a clansman of mine."

"Ex-wife."

"Her bride-price has been paid by us."

"It will be returned." Her father's eyes never left her, though his hand had released its grip on Samura.

"You are arguing how to handle this Sky Person," she said, "and you are wondering how to choose a woman to go to him. I'll save you the choice. I'll go."

"For what?" Samura leered at her. "For the goodness of the act?"

"For my bride-price," she said. "Seeing as none of you men can stop him, it is up to a woman. And seeing as your Gafu women are so restrained in their sex-lives that they wouldn't know what to do with a Sky Person's snake . . ."

The men of her village began to chuckle. Samura stared at her, not knowing how to react.

"She speaks well," her father said. "It is my blood you hear speaking. She will go to the Sky Person for all of us in the valley, Gafu, Parap, whoever. And in exchange the bride-price will be waived."

"She is making no sacrifice," Samura said. "She can hardly wait to get to him. Her hole is already dripping. There is no need to waive any repayment."

"Half her bride-price," her father said.

"All right," the other man said. "We would never be able to get back more than half from you. And half is reasonable for an adulteress."

172

"A woman's husband should be able to prevent her from straying," her father said. "He should be able to pin her to the mat. Can she help it if her husband could not rise to the occasion?"

The villagers began to chuckle again. Samura grimaced.

"You have a quick wit, old man," he said. "It's a pity your spears were not as quick."

The flame had died on the stick, leaving a dull, angry glow that moved slowly towards her hand. She lifted it and blew on it, but the flame did not reappear. She dropped it into the fire and leaned her head on her father's arm.

"If you do this," he said, "you will be known throughout the mountains. We will be the people who stopped the Sky People in their tracks."

She pulled away from him.

"If I do it," she said, "I do it because, despite his looks—and looks have deceived me before—he is a strong warrior. And because he has control of tomorrow, while you can only mumble about yesterday."

She stood up and stared down at him. His face was expressionless. Then he grinned.

"You think like a man," he said. "And so, you can be played like a man. It's your strength, and your weakness."

She glared at him, too angry to speak. He caressed her thigh and she flinched away from him. She saw the sadness invade his face, but she was too angry to stop it. She turned and walked down the hill, not looking back at her father.

Now in daylight, Don thought, the scene could be Europe. Whatever happened last night was a dream; something out of Freud; something pathological. He stared at the dusty lanes and the distant blue mountains; the variegated fields, some lying fallow, some being revived under a regime of

173

legumes, or cultivated by foraging pigs turning the soil with their snouts; or being tilled by the women, sitting cross-legged, with digging sticks in their hands, weeding and planting.

He shaved carefully and closely. He wet his hair and combed it. Baranuma had polished his boots. He rolled the sleeves of his shirt to the elbows. Methodically he prepared himself, as a European, as a dweller in the daylight, and went to breakfast with Nicholls.

"You were talking about Homer, last night," he said, as he sat down, anxious to recreate the illusion that here they were, dining on the terraces in some Alps, watching sheep-herders going about their business, wondering when the wireless might broadcast the latest stockmarket quotations.

Nicholls glanced at him sharply. He, also, had taken the time to shave, to change his clothes and brush his hair.

"Was I?" He poured Don a cup of Andy Williams' coffee.

"Something about Ulysses and Telemachus."

"God, I must have been drunk."

"Or suffering from food-poisoning."

Nicholls relented. He decided to let the boy into his thoughts.

"It's frightful, isn't it?" he said. "I can never get used to their culinary manners, try as I might. And any white man who reckons he can is a liar. Are you a scholar of the Greeks?"

Don shook his head.

"You know Murray? Hubert Murray? Administrator of these fair islands before McNicol?"

Don nodded, appreciating his coffee, the sun's sharpness, the feel of his clothes and boots.

"His brother Gilbert is one of the century's leading Greek scholars. Incredible, isn't it? Two sons of a country solicitor in New South Wales, making his circuits on horseback, from one starving outback town to the next. And one son grows up to be Lord Almighty up here, in the land that time forgot, while the other returns to the very cradle of civilization and re-interprets it for us."

He shook his head, smiling at the paradox.

"Does this expedition remind you of Ulysses' journey?"

174

"Like I said last night, I haven't read it. I'll tell you what..." Don hesitated, and then committed himself to the confession. "It reminds me of a novel by Rider Haggard ..." He caught the flicker of contempt on Nicholls' face, but decided to finish the sentence, any rate. "*She.* Do you know it?"

Nicholls shook his head.

"Don't laugh. I know it's just a romance; but the way he hammers on about the death, the dying, the decay and, in the middle of it, this woman, larger than life . . ." He shook his head as his voice tailed off. He was aware that Nicholls was watching him sharply.

"Have you read Conrad's *Heart of Darkness*?" Nicholls asked.

"No, I thought he was just a romancer of the sea."

"He's a damned sight less romantic than bloody Rider Haggard."

"Look, all I meant . . ."

"You should read it when you get back. It's the only story I've ever come across that comes within a mile of describing this kind of life, accurately. And it's reasonably factual. He was involved with Roger Casement in the Congo, in exposing the Belgian atrocities."

"I'll get a copy," Don promised.

"I'll lend you mine. I can't have someone on my team reading that kind of trash you just mentioned."

Nicholls rose and beckoned to Baranuma to clean up. He hitched his pants and looked across the village to the stream.

"What we'll do now," he said, "to really impress them, to strike even deeper fear in their hearts than a few gunshots can, is to hold a census, and look in their eyes and ears, pull out a few worms, lance the odd boil, and make them build us a latrine."

He grinned, waiting for Don to arise, nodding his approval at Don's appearance. He felt his own chin. "I'm glad one of us is not going native."

"How do we go about impressing them?"

"We got hold of the Lu-lui, who is actually old Barum, and get him to put on this peaked cap." He showed the cap to Don, resplendent with a brass badge. "He's top dog around here, and what he says carries a lot of weight—particularly when he's wearing something like this. Clothes do make the man, you know . . ."

Don caught a moment of hesitation as he spoke. Their eyes had met as Nicholls made his joke, and suddenly Don had caught a flash of something there.

"Are you all right?" he asked.

"Come on," Nicholls said. "Let's get a move on."

Ludwig woke shivering with cold, hunched into a ball, returned in his sleep to the foetal crouch. He stared across the ground, to the white ashes and the remaining sticks like wheel spokes. He undid his arms and pushed the sticks in further and waited, but they did not catch. The fire was out.

He could not stop the shivering. When he pushed himself upright, it set him dancing. It prevented thought. His body, where it had lain on the ground, had been drained of all heat, exhausted of its life, so it was now numb. He lurched across the interior of the hut, his muscles uncoordinated, grabbed for the wall and dragged himself outside.

The day had broken. The fog was draining from the mountains. The rim of the world was becoming lighter as the fire of the sun burned through.

Still hunched he shuffled to a patch of light. His eyes filled with tears as he stood there, shuffling his feet to start a flow of warmth, crouched, hunched, naked, and frozen.

The sun struck his face and made him squint. Its heat unfolded him with warmth. He could feel, way inside his skull, the process of thought begin again—the respiration of his nervous system. Like breathing, once it had started it went on.

At first he thought in simple modules: warm; hungry; numbness leaving. The modules rose up through his warming brain and grew complexities as they did. The sun was the warmth, but he must conserve his body heat; the niggers

176

used ash and fat. Hunger was acceptable; he could live with it; it cleared his head; but he needed water. Feelings returned; ache in legs and hip from the hunched sleep; belt missing; where was the belt?

He turned and lumbered back to the hut. The daylight blocked in through the low door, and filtered through the decaying roof. He found his belt where he had thrown it off some time during his fever sleep. He picked it up and looked again at the coals.

He stirred them with his hand. There was residual warmth in them. Carefully, he knelt down, buckled on the belt, then scooped up a double-handful of warm ash and took it outside. He left it by the wall and returned for more.

When he had enough, he sat down, removed the belt again, and began to rub the ash into his flesh, trying to force it into the pores.

He became aware of the forest around the abandoned village. There were no leaves on the crouched, jagged trees. The limbs were green and grey with fur. The forest floor was the same colour. Runners of the grey-greenness advanced across the village floor and reached into some of the huts, pulling them towards it.

Moss forest, his mind told him. He glanced into the warming sun as it rose clear of the final mountain ridge. High up, he told himself.

He discovered he had a memory. It showed him the riverbank in the darkness, his feet first encountering the brittle softness of the moss as he struggled from the river.

For a moment it showed him something else. He saw the eyes, a sudden glimpse of them, projected onto the waiting trees. He gasped, and flattened himself against the wall. But he had seen, at the same moment as he saw the eyes, the bubble of thought that produced them.

They're not real, he told himself. He repeated it. They're not real. He looked at the trees. The eyes were still there. They merged behind the tree, into a dark, nigger shape. He dragged himself upright and took his knife from his belt and shuffled towards them.

They're not real, he repeated.

But they still watched him.

Sweating with fear now he grabbed the tree trunk and swung the knife behind it. The knife sliced through lichen and moss.

He grinned.

He laughed.

They're not real.

Now, he had to walk.

He holstered the knife and examined the village.

The bone he thought he had seen when he stumbled in through the rain and the dark, fixed to the ridge-pole of the men's lodge-house, was still there. He walked over and stared up at it.

The skull was ancient, mouldered to a grey-black. The eye-sockets held a fine cover of ash and mud. He grunted and walked around the building, stopping when he found a long, thin bone. He pressed it with his toes but did not pick it up.

How long have they been gone? he asked himself.

There was no ready answer. Longer than a month, but not a year. They would be somewhere nearby, in another village, waiting for that one to fill up with pig-shit and people-shit, and then moving along again. By then, the moss would have turned this village into a heap of mounds, almost indistinguishable from the frozen jungle.

He grunted again and turned downhill, blinking as the sun crossed his face, smiling at its warmth.

He knew the spot the sun had risen, and that gave him his Easting. He turned through a circle, establishing the other cardinal points on the furthest mountains. He examined the whole of the horizon again, deducing where the rivers broke through to the plateau.

With the map fixed in his head, he began to walk.

"Your Mr. Haggard and my Mr. Conrad . . ."

"He's not *my* Mr. Haggard. I simply said I read a book of his."

178

"Yet, here you are, replicating the heart of that story, through the trackless jungle, in search of the mystic barbarian princess."

"I'm not! You put words in my mouth! It was you who began talking of women!"

"As I was saying, about our respective authors . . ."

"Am I to take it that you are here because of Mr. Conrad?"

"He's part of the reason. Yes. He, single-handed amongst authors, wrested attention away from the decay of Europe to focus on the decay of the Pacific. He was both poet and adventurer, and when I realized I could never be a poet, I realized I could still be an adventurer."

"You wanted to be a poet?"

"As I was saying. The point of contact between the two, and bearing in mind that Conrad wrote directly against, to undermine, the whole cycle of romances of the jungle, but nevertheless . . ."

"More coffee, Bwana?"

"What? Oh, yes. With a dash of J.W."

They grinned at each other over Don's joke. They sat in the hissing light of the pressure lamp. If they shut their eyes they could see cavernous mouths, full of destroyed teeth; tropical ulcers burned clear to the bone, like looking into the craters of volcano; hookworm-infested feet; and the eyes, staring, stupid, refusing as if by an act of will to understand hygiene, to see the importance of building latrines.

So they put on their white shirts with the sleeves rolled back and had Baranuma heat up the irons and press their slacks, and they ground some more of Williams' coffee and drew the cork on another bottle of Scotch whisky.

"So what's your point, Bwana Nicholls? Spit it out."

"The point is that neither Conrad nor Haggard understood anything about sex. In Haggard, that's unimportant. Reading him is like reading the confessions of a necrophiliac. The whiteness of She is the whiteness of decay—nothing mystic at all, nothing genetically linking her to the great Aryan race.

"But, in Mr. Conrad, who sets his sights so much higher, the failure to talk openly of sex . . ."

179

"How could he, in those times?" Don demanded, shaking his head to concentrate.

"He wanted to get to the heart of things, therefore he had no choice. So, his characterization of Kurtz is almost unacceptable, because he only alludes to what really held that man in that lonely spot, and turned him into Satan incarnate. He alludes to it with reference to the woman."

"But he only alludes?"

"That's right. She is almost as mythically unattainable as your She."

"Ayesha."

"What?"

"Her name. Ayesha."

"Oh . . ."

They fell silent, staring into their mugs of coffee-with-a-dash. The pressure lamp was dying and Nicholls reached for it, mechanically, and pumped the bellows. From orange-yellow the light grew white, dazzling them, and the moths. They could not see beyond its arc.

"Two white men on patrol is no good."

"Why on earth not?"

"Because we form this little club. We sit here, ignoring what is going on around us."

"Your Mr Kurtz, travelling by himself, didn't seem to get very far."

"He travels fastest who travels alone. If it hadn't been for the woman, Kurtz would still be going."

"Where?"

"Perhaps he'd have been able to tell his own story, and justify his actions."

"Native women mean a lot to you, don't they Nicholls?"

There was a moment of silence. Both men examined their emptying mugs. Then Nicholls lifted his head and turned and looked out to the black night, the clouds half-hiding the brilliant stars. He glanced back, but Harris had his head down.

"They mean a lot to every man in these Highlands, black or white."

"Why?"

"Because they're all we have."

180

"They're like creatures out of a vivid nightmare," Don said.

"She was magnificent," Nicholls said to himself.

"I beg your pardon?"

"Magnificent. Breasts." He indicated their scope with his hands. "Thighs, and her . . ." he hesitated. "Her sex."

"Covered with pig-fat?"

"I washed her. She liked it. Now I can't find the bitch. Old Barum reckons she's headed for another village."

"What happens to them if they sleep with us?"

"Who knows? It probably raises their bride-price, as prospective husbands bank on getting some of our Power at second-hand."

"Or else it ostracizes them."

"What? I doubt it."

"Without her coating of fat? Her virginity gone? I think she'd be decidedly inferior goods."

"Are you criticizing me, man?"

"Yes, I guess I am. You didn't think about the consequences of your actions."

"Don't condescend to me, you little puppy!"

Don waited, watching Nicholls keenly as he got to his feet, pushing his camp-chair back. The sound of raised voices from the Mastas had turned every head in the encampment.

"You understand nothing," Nicholls told him, leaning on the folding table.

"I understand lust when I see it, and I understand that it clouds men's judgement. But I can't understand what you see in these . . . Harpies!"

He stared back at Nicholls. Don was seething with anger. He knew Nicholls was goading him, and he knew he should not attach so much importance to what was said. But Nicholls' lust was so crudely vivid. It made him nervous. He could see the veneers of civilization falling away from Nicholls as they penetrated further and further into the mountains, as if the clue to Nicholls' success in these mountain valleys was a mental transformation he made, to think and breathe and lust like a savage himself.

"One day," Nicholls said. He spoke thickly. "One day, sonny . . ." his voice trailed off.

181

Don waited, but it did not resume. Instead Nicholls shook his head sorrowfully. He glanced at Don and smiled, as if Don were an infant, who could not be taught, who would have to wait until he reached the age of reason.

"Good night, Harris," Nicholls said. "Don't forget to put the cat out."

And he stumbled off to bed.

· CHAPTER NINE ·

The man came running for the ridge-top village, stumbling as he looked behind at something pursuing him. He slipped in the darkness, and struggled to his feet, and kept running for the stockade, yelling as he ran.

"Let me in! Let me in! A ground-spirit! There's a ground-spirit on the loose!"

But laughter greeted him from the gates.

"A ground-spirit, Garaban? Sure it wasn't the Earth Goddess herself? Eh? Lying there with her legs apart?"

"Stop fooling! Undo the boards!"

"A friendly little earth-spirit you had an assignation with, eh? Who was it?"

"Probably that loose woman, Merin, you remember her?"

"Do I remember her? What breasts! Mmmm! Now, there was a ground-spirit."

"Come on, rubbishmen! Open this stockade."

Samura decided it had gone on long enough. He left the entrance to the men's house and walked to the gate and began to untie the boards.

"Come on," he said. "Give me a hand."

The terrified runner came scrambling in.

"The colour of ash, it was, pale and grey, with one glittering claw that tore at the earth."

"That's right, Garaban, and a big hole between her legs."

"Quiet!" Samura ordered. He stared closely at the terrified man.

"A ground-spirit?"

"Yes, Samura. Rising up out of the earth itself."

"And where did you see it?"

"In amongst the big trees on the edge of the forest."

The others had stopped their joking, seeing the intensity of Samura's questions.

183

"Do you think it's true?"

"The women down in the valley have been working sorcery with the ground-spirits, with the semen of the Kiap. The Kiap will be coming here. A man sees a ground-spirit near our village. What do you think?"

"Do you think these Sky People can be overcome with sorcery?"

"We can't overcome them in battle."

The boards were refastened. They all stared at the stockade, and lifted their heads to try and see beyond it, into the night, the darkness; into the abode of spirits—whether of the dead, or of the earth itself, or of rocks and gardens and streams.

Every object they saw — stakes, boards, trees, huts, men themselves — was suddenly luminous with spirits. Men stared at each other in fear and awe, feeling the power all around them, poised, ready to strike out where they directed it. As if the whole village were sorcerers.

"Split the patrol?" Harris said.

Nicholls poked at his lunch. Tinned beef and glutinous rice. He avoided Harris's angry stare. He looked out at the village and the ever-present small boys watching solemnly, silently, fingers in mouths.

"Because we need to. Because I'm in charge and it's my decision."

"Oh, come on!" Don felt Baranuma lifting his head from his seated position, and lowered his voice. "That's how they got us up the coast. Divide and conquer. I thought you were a student of strategy."

"I've had a damned sight more experience of this business than you, my boy."

"Don't be bloody patronizing, Nicholls!"

Nicholls blinked and looked at his companion. Harris stared back, unafraid. Whatever had been unsure, unformed in him, was falling away, like puppy-fat. Nicholls rubbed his forehead. He was drinking too much lately, and getting into silly quarrels.

"We've got to," he said. "We're isolated from what's going on. And something damned funny is going on. I can smell it. It's too peaceful. Yet all we do is sit around arguing about literature or whatever."

"You argue about it. I never bring the subject up."

Nicholls waved his hand to silence the interruption. He tried to think clearly.

"We have two objects: apprehend Ludwig; and chastise the people who ambushed Wallace and myself. We arrive, armed to the teeth, ready for battle. We are met with cordiality, with speeches and pigs and the whole production. Barum seems determined to take all the fight out of us."

"Maybe he's learnt his lesson?" Don said.

"He'll never learn his lesson. He's a warrior. He can't afford not to fight, or he will lose face." Nicholls stared soberly at Harris. "And the only way to make him fight is to draw him out, make him think we're weaker than we are."

"And that's your rational assessment, sir?"

The sarcasm in Harris's voice made Nicholls blink.

"I beg your pardon?" He leaned closer.

"I mean that this whole scheme doesn't have anything to do with you chasing after this woman you've been talking about?" Harris was now openly contemptuous.

"You bloody prudish little puppy!"

Nicholls was on his feet. He realized the solemn eyes of the village children were on him. Baranuma was watching surreptitiously. He breathed deeply and sat down.

"Look," he said. "We're at each other's throats. It's no good. I'm only going to the next village. It's less than a day from here. They're trading partners of these people. They'll not try anything."

Harris was shaking his head in disagreement.

"For Christ's sake!" Nicholls said. "At least entertain the idea. Why are you blocking it so vehemently?"

"I'm not blocking . . ."

Looking at him, Nicholls suddenly understood.

"You're afraid," he said. He saw the shaft strike home.

"You bastard!" Harris said.

185

"You're afraid of the responsibility, aren't you?"

Harris didn't reply, but his face was white with anger. He pushed back his chair and stood up, knocking the chair backwards, sending it scuttling. Now Baranuma came hurrying over, eager to pick up the chair and be where he could hear the argument better.

"Piss off, Baranuma," Nicholls said.

"Savvy, Masta?"

"Ahh . . . raus, sakwip . . . get to hell out of here!"

"Savvy, Masta."

He watched the servant leave.

"See that?" he said. "We're doing more harm sitting here arguing."

"All right," Harris said. "All right. We'll split the patrol up."

He looked down. His face was set, clamping in the anger.

"I'll leave you Sergeant Bukato. He's a bloody good soldier."

"Won't you need him if you have trouble?"

"I'd like to break in the new boy, Giram. I can handle whatever trouble they come up with."

Harris's stare was sharp. He avoided it. Something was nudging at him, telling him to listen, but he wasn't going to. For some reason he was sexually aroused. He needed a good old-fashioned fuck. Harris needed one, too. Harris's need, in fact, was far more urgent. He needed to lose his cherry, Nicholls decided. Maybe that was the fear he could smell on him. If he stayed here, alone, unchaperoned, one of the village girls would get him.

He stood up and clapped Harris on the shoulder.

"Come on," he said. "I'm sorry we've come to loggerheads."

He felt Harris tense, and then relax.

"Bukato worries me," Harris confessed. "I'd feel more at ease with Giram."

"Bukato's all right. He's a bit taciturn. But he's intensely loyal, and the best soldier on the island. I'd rather have him than anyone. Come on, let's talk with him."

"OK," Harris said. "I'm sorry we had words."

"Two white men in the bush. It's the worst possible combination."

186

He pushed Harris ahead of him, smiling to himself. He almost chuckled, thinking of the solution to the lad's problems.

He watched them as they left his encampment. Harris walking forcefully, striding out with contained anger. Nicholls following, almost shambling. He felt a sudden warmth for the old Kiap. They had been through a lot together, and now he could see that Nicholls was close up to the end. Nicholls himself couldn't see it, but Bukato had survived longer than any other Police Boy because of the sharpness of his senses. There was something in him that could forewarn him of approaching death. And death was approaching the Kiap, there was no doubt of it.

He looked around the village. Death was not here. The subliminal signs reassured him. Peaceful tamed jungle hens, slumbering pigs, little boys playing with their genitals as they watched the Sky People. Nicholls' danger lay elsewhere.

He had not protested when Nicholls effectively demoted him to nursemaid. For him the object of war was to survive. If survival meant holding the hand of the new Kiap, then hold it he would.

Sergeant Bukato had been recruited as a boy by the Germans at Finschhafen. But he was not from the coast. He was from the valley of the Watut River, his people related to the "bloodthirsty Laewomba". Together they would sweep from their river valley homes to raze the settlements along the Huon Gulf shore. Their attacks on these fatted people, made timid through contact with the Germans, had decimated the coastal population, and disrupted the attempts of the Germans to win a profit from, and save the souls within, the area. So they, in turn, had attempted to bring war to the Laewomba and their kin.

The war had not been a success for the Germans. The

187

boy, Bukato, had been old enough to be included in the meeting called by the Kiap to discuss the state of war and to argue and sue for peace. His brothers, his father, the men of his people, were full of glee when they set off. What possible bargaining could the Germans offer? The price they would have to pay for peace would be very high.

Eagerness drove them to set a hard pace. The boy, Bukato, laboured to keep up. But the harder he walked, the harder it became to walk. His legs became rubbery. There was a feeling inside him, his heart beating harder, nausea, that finally made him stop and rest.

He had no idea why he should feel sick. Images swam before him. The blind eagerness and greed on his people's faces as they raced to meet with the Kiap, in the Lutheran church that had been established down the valley, and then abandoned in face of the raids. Then the face of the Kiap who had come to meet them. A brave proud man. Brave enough to come alone with his message. But with something in his face, something of which he was ashamed, which haunted him when he proposed the venue.

Bukato sat down and rested against a tree. He could not get that face from his mind. The calculation in it. The arrogance. The pride. And the shame. He closed his eyes.

When they opened, the afternoon was far advanced. He had to force himself to run to make up lost time. It was close up to sunset when he came within sight of the mission, and he rested to get his breath, seeing that the doors of the church had been closed and that all of the warriors—his father, his grandfather, his brothers and uncles and cousins—were inside.

His breath regained, he was about to move into the clearing when a furtive movement caught his eye.

If the movement had been simple—a man walking up to a window—he would not have noticed it. But because the man stole through the grass, bent almost double, trailing his rifle behind him, he froze, and watched carefully.

The man, a white man, risked a glance through the window. What he saw satisfied him. He looked around and waved his arm.

Other white men appeared, soundlessly, trailing rifles,

carrying planks of wood that they clamped over the outward-swinging doors of the church.

Now he wanted to scream, but whatever had stopped him on the track was determined that he should live. It constricted his throat.

He could imagine his people standing, eager, inside the church. Before them would be the Kiap, with his troubled eyes, and the smooth-faced priest. The Kiap would glance nervously to the window, and equally as nervously to the pit prepared behind the altar. But the Laewomba, in their eagerness, would not read those glances.

The men outside moved to positions by the windows, save for two who knelt by a pile of wood.

The white men stood up. He heard the screams of warning from within. The white men aimed their guns and poured in their fire, shouting themselves.

His people screamed. The doors bulged against the planks.

The two kneeling men stood up, fire in their hands, and swung the fire up against the wooden door, the wood and thatch walls.

The men fell back from the windows, taking up kneeling positions as the fire caught and the screams turned from rage and outrage to fear, to panic, to absolute terror as men began to burn as they fought to slash through the walls of the church.

When it was over, the men moved quietly with their rifles, poking the blackened corpses, twisted arms, bloated bodies from which flesh burst pink and white. Those that moved received a sudden, sharp jolt from a bullet, and were mercifully still.

Bukato ran.

As he ran, he thought. The women and the infants would be next. He could not return to his village. But any other village he sought refuge in would recognize him as from the Watut. They had plenty of scores to settle, plenty of payback waiting. He would not survive.

He slept beside the track. He stayed on it, trusting to that thing which had made his body refuse to go into the trap. He hid from a patrol of whites. He hid from war-parties of other people, intent on redressing the old wrongs now that his

189

village had fallen. He realized that the whites did not need to finish off the women and infants. Other people would do that for them.

He came, at last, in the silent, pouring rain, to the huge lagoon of Finschhafen. He hid in the bush and watched the activities of the copra workers. He watched the whites. When the time was propitious, he presented himself for employment.

The whites had their own war. As suddenly as it had been established, the power of the Germans was gone. Mastas who had sweated out their time along the coast, building their copra empires, raising families of pure white children, and their shadow family of bastards, were suddenly crushed old men, begging for a place on the boat that would "return" them to a Motherland they had well and truly forgotten.

Bukato changed sides again. He knew Pidgin. He knew the Morobe dialects. His skill in anticipating trouble was already known. He became a Police Boy with the Australian Administration. He rose quickly to the ultimate rank: sergeant.

Now he watched the split Patrol move out of the village. His evaluation of the situation was similar to Nicholls'. If an attack had been proposed by the Parap, then it would have come during the festivities. That was why Bukato and his men had not joined in the feasting—though they had recruited a couple of village girls to compensate. His evaluation differed from Nicholls' now. He knew that the brains behind the prospector's ambush were the Gafu—he had heard it from the girls. But Nicholls was no longer listening to him. He was being tugged towards his fate by some sorcery that Bukato could not evaluate.

Perhaps this was because Bukato did not believe in sorcery. He believed in force of arms. So the rumours of sorcery that the girls brought them did not overly impress him. So what if they had some of Nicholls' semen? There was a lot of Bukato's semen scattered up and down the island. It hadn't done him any harm yet.

190

Nicholls had the experience and the armament. And the first meant he would not hesitate to use the second, in an attack. Bukato could not account for his uneasiness as he watched the Patrol snake its way down through the gardens, along the thatched paths, past the garden huts and the shuffling pigs. Then he turned away from it and covertly examined Harris.

The young Kiap was smiling, despite himself, at the departure of his boss. Bukato was willing to bet the lad had a few plans of his own to test. Plans of a carnal nature.

The young Kiap had elected to stay within the village, and Bukato thought this a wise decision. You were more exposed to sudden, sneak ambush. But you were also more aware of its likelihood. You could watch for the sudden disappearance of children and pets, the sudden tightening of the air, the silence and fear. Camped out on a hill, like the foolish prospector, you had no idea what was going to hit you until ten seconds after it did.

Ten seconds was time enough to die.

The young Kiap turned and his eyes met Bukato's. The boy smiled and he grinned back. He read the boy's eagerness, his strength. He had seen the uncertainty fall from him in the confrontations with Nicholls. He nodded his approval and saluted.

The boy saluted back and took the hint and returned to the Haus Kiap. Bukato watched him enter, then went in search of the girls. Sexual favours were the favours most easily granted to a travelling Policeman. But a man, if he wanted comfort, needed something more. He needed someone to cook good food and pick the nits out of his hair. He was going now to trade some access to his power for the loan of a woman. He would let them know that whatever they did to help Sergeant Bukato would be remembered. He was a man of his word. When they ran into trouble with the complexities, the stupidities, of white law, then he would be ready to intercede for them. And all he asked was the loan of a woman, to do her normal tasks around him.

It was a bargain, really. A chance of a lifetime. For, like it or not, and regardless of what happened to Nicholls, the Sky People were here to stay.

191

Diary: 17th May, 1937

I dislike kunai grass very intensely. The fact that it has taken over large sections of these valleys indicates to me that the ground has been over-used, probably over-burned, for grass-seeds germinate quickly after a fire, and get a head-start on the other vegetation.

The Gafu would appear to fire the grassland for hunting purposes, rather than to clear undergrowth for agriculture. What forest we passed through was secondary regrowth—a lot of casuarina—with no really large timber. I know comparable virgin forest with trunk diameters in excess of eight feet, and trees two hundred feet tall. The burns must occur frequently, and must go back many generations.

What I can piece together of the prehistory of the area indicates that the current inhabitants are the last in a series of waves that go back to time immemorial. And each more warlike than the previous. For, in this world, it is the survival of the ferocious.

If we throw out the concept of a Guiding Spirit—and despite Darwin's own views, his work leads inexorably to that conclusion— then what are we left with? Genetic material struggling to survive?

No. Species struggling to survive. For the genetic material, whatever form it may take, has survived quite successfully. We moved across that grassland in a long, twisting snake of humanity. Carriers, policemen, and the Kiap. Of all of us, only the Kiap could articulate the purpose of the journey. We were like a worm or a caterpillar fumbling across an alien landscape, groping blindly in search of something familiar that would aid us in our journey towards? . . . food.

For the Boys . . . adventure, sex, the promise of riches. I have to keep remembering that for many of them this land is as unfamiliar as it is to me. For the Police? Duty? No, that is some crap they learnt down on the coast. They don't believe it. I know what it is for Bukato—power. I must confess I left him behind because, increasingly, he makes me uneasy. There is a depth to him that is locked away from the rest of the world. The depth of violence. He has risen to the top of his career because he has that drive to assert himself over others that marks any good Policeman, in any society. And that drive has its genesis in something that makes me uneasy.

So the caterpillar groped its way across the kunai slopes, each element in it propelled by a belief that they would find something

192

waiting for them on the completion of that journey—and each element's dream different. If it wasn't for the Kiap, in fact, that disparate collection of entities would not have come together. In that sense, He, I, am the Guiding Spirit.

But the thought that nagged me, the whole of the journey—well, one of the thoughts, if you subtract the blister on the ball of my foot, a concern for the safety of Harris, an itch in my groin, some idle speculation on the possibility of war with Japan one of these days—my overriding thought was of that twisting organism. And it struck me that the only thing which has survived, multiplied, and flourished through all of Creation is something intangible. Call it Life. Call it Genetic Material.

It came to me that the species exist for one purpose only: to pass on that material through Time. And with each passing it grows more refined, it moves towards some Aristotelian goal, and that goal emerges slowly out of the dross of existence.

The survival of the ferocious.

The constant burning of these grasslands will have eradicated certain species. Even now, talking to old-timers, they remember when things were different: when bush-rats, possums, could be trapped on the lower slopes. But, inexorably, they are being driven higher up the mountains. All that remain in this environment altered by Man are the species that Man has introduced . . . and Himself, in many areas the major source of protein.

And within Man's tiny history, that variant, that sub-species which has survived has, without fail, been the most ferocious.

Perhaps the dinosaurs died out for the simple reason that they were too gentle? Mammals came, equipped to kill. Out of them grew Man, who learnt quickly that he had to be more ferocious than they. In fact, so ferocious that he would have destroyed them all if he had not turned his energy inwards, to the slaughtering of his own kind. Perhaps that "decision" was one taken by the Genetic Material, too, somehow—assuming it did have some intelligence, or assuming simply that if it didn't, then life on this planet would have ceased somewhere around 1914. But that excess of ferocity was turned inwards. Men stopped slaughtering the wild beasts, and perfected the means of slaughtering each other. The rest is "modern history".

The Sacred Objects here are relics of previous cultures, objects they have discovered that are inexplicable; or else, as in the case of the Mortars and Pestles, so domestic as to create anxiety that the people who are long gone could have, conceivably, been like themselves. And now where are they?

The inexplicable objects are curiously shaped stones, of a type

193

not found locally and not traded anywhere through the Island. They hang from the rafters of the men's house, dangling, whether consciously or not, like a pair of enormous testicles. The Fighting Stones.

Their sense of humour is so ribald that the similarity can not have escaped them.

Barum was right, it was a full day's walk, and he was right that his side of the valley is the better. At the moment he is in the ascendant. But should his manners become less warlike, then the ugly Big Man here, Samura—short and squat, with huge chest and shoulders, like a truncated gorilla—Samura will draw back his lips and snarl, and attack.

There is unease in the air. The children were friendly enough— and I always heed Bukato's warning to watch the children for signs of a fight. But the adults were truculent. They did not remonstrate with those children who raided my camp and attempted to steal whatever bright objects they could. But then the natives never discipline their children. But this time there seemed an air of malevolence to the way they watched me scolding those brats.

Maybe it's knowing I've come from across the valley, from Parap—and maybe they are already scheming to overrun that territory and take all that good land and those fat pigs and glossy women.

The political status quo is very delicate in this valley. The sooner one tribe emerges as the clear leader the better. My presence will have altered the "rules" of warfare considerably, and at the moment I suspect it will be to the advantage of the Parap.

But Samura is younger than Barum, and I suspect tougher and, if possible, more cunning. He is a man with a star in the ascendant.

In fact, to be quite Machiavellian about it, it would probably suit our purpose—which is the purpose of Peace—to subtly shift the balance in favour of the Gafu. Then, upon my departure, there would be a short, sharp fight, and the valley would be consolidated under one tough regime . . . well, that's how Machiavelli would have seen it.

I told Samura we had arrived for census purposes, and to continue the investigation of Ludwig and the "Wallace affair". Properly cheeky he retorted that we should investigate the "attacks" made upon his people by our own Patrols! So I spent some time justifying the "Punitive Patrol" concept. A bit difficult when even I can see it's simply motivated by revenge, and also functions as an excuse to render a tough people harmless—thus civilizing them.

The girl is not here. No doubt they will trot her out when they consider the moment most propitious—when they feel they have the most to gain from presenting her to me.

194

We're camped on the outskirts of the village, hard against the primary forest of the upland, with the poor-soil vegetable gardens spreading down from us, to merge into the kunai slopes. I've never liked camping in kunai grass, with the attendant poor visibility, but the closeness of this timber—up to 120 feet in height, laden with stragglers, vines, thorny creepers, all dark on its floor—makes me even more nervous.

But we're roping the area off, clearing fire lines, lacing up a stockade of our own. I've requisitioned a nearby garden hut, to serve as Haus Kiap and census station.

It's late afternoon and the storm clouds have built up right across the valley. The mountains beyond the Parap have totally vanished into grey mist. The river at the valley's trough is grey. A couple of hawks are circling towards that cloud. The air is still, and the sounds of the village people come to me: the liquid laughter of the women, the screams of children as they run between the rows of vegetables, pursued by indulgent laughter. Old Lik-lik lies by my feet, nose and tail extended in opposite directions, flat against the earth, ears twitching to the sounds of the children playing. It is almost possible to feel at peace here . . . but for the fear that comes up my spine as I relax.

But if I relax, instead of Paradise, this is what I see.

I had come into that other village as a Cadet with Morris. We had moved very swiftly, hoping to surprise them. But they had got wind of us and fled the camp. We came into it, deserted, though still with the smell of smoke, and of grease, hovering in the damp leaves of the forest.

There, in the clearing, something moved. I thought at first a pig. Then I realized it was human. It flapped something that was half an arm. I stepped up to it. It regarded me with eyes made huge with madness—driven into total insanity. The stump of that remaining arm had been caulked with hot pitch. The other arm had been expertly sheared off at the shoulder and caulked. The legs were roped together, and attached to a stake driven into the ground.

I vomited. Morris came up behind me.

"Oh, shit," he said, very softly.

I stared at him.

"Fresh meat," he said. He lifted his rifle. The staring, insane eyes were on me, however. It had once been a man. Morris put the barrel to its temple and pulled the trigger.

The eyes went blank immediately.

I realized what sort of grease I had smelt, intertwined with smoke on the evening air.

And yet now, right here, at this instant, the clouds march across the chequerboard fields. The pigs browse along the trimmed roadways, beside the thatched fences. The streams rush, babbling past the little, thatched houses.

And the caterpillar writhes, blind, unknowing, towards its destination.

They came for her at dusk. She had made the pigs comfortable in the garden hut and was sitting outside, watching the flow of the stream flicking out the trailing runners of the taro. She was sitting there, afraid of the absence of the fear with which she had grown up.

Then she heard their singing, high-pitched, trembling with laughter, and Merin stood, eager to see the women again.

We will take you to your lover,
with his snake that stretches so far;
chasing for you through the valley;
sniffing in the gardens;
feeling at night for your hole.

You will bind it with creepers,
and stroke it with thorn.
You will bury it in your garden.
And he will never leave your side.

The song ceased and the laughter burst out from behind it. She held out her arms and embraced them, letting them run their hands over her breasts and vagina, returning caress for caress as they admired her body and laughed about its coming effect on the young white god.

Shrieking, they dragged her, half-protesting, into the stream, and began to scrape away the warm, protective pig-fat that coated her.

196

Her mother did not join in. She stood on the bank and watched her daughter and her age-mates. She watched the naked flesh emerge from that pale, greyish other skin of ash that was almost the entire clothing of a woman.

She held up her hands and prayed.

"Earth Mother. Mother of women. We, who bleed for you, ask you to take this woman, my daughter, into your care. Let her move freely amongst these Sky People. Protect her from their magic, now that she is naked. Intercede with the spirits of the air so that she may not be stricken in the head, in her chest, or in her arms."

She motioned and Merin's age-mates began to rub each named part of her body.

"And yourself, strengthen her legs. Strengthen them to resist the pull of the Sky People's ways. Strengthen her thighs. Strengthen her belly against their food. Strengthen her sex against their assaults."

As the hands fondled and caressed, her mother stepped into the water, holding aloft now the joint of hollowed sugar-cane. She lifted it high, showing it to the Sky, to the Earth, to the Water, and then broke its mud seal and upended it into the stream.

The fresh menstrual blood was whisked into a quick red runner that dissolved and became one with all the rushing waters.

And Merin, shivering from the cold air on her bare skin, felt what it was like to be entirely unprotected. As her age-mates lifted her from the stream her eyes met her mother's. They stared at each other. She saw the fear in her mother's eyes, the sadness. She could see her mother was on the point of calling out to her, of saying something that had never been said before.

Then her mother reached forward and, for the first time in many years, embraced her troublesome daughter.

Ludwig came awake and the sun was high overhead, filtering down through the canopy of shining leaves and twisted

197

creepers, falling in dulled spots on the litter of leaves in which, the previous evening, he had gouged himself a sleeping hole with his knife. His throat was dry, his tongue was lumpy. His stomach was something the size of a pea within his belly; a hard, aching knot.

He wiped the dirt from his knife blade. Last night he had been too tired to replace it in his belt. He had stumbled to a halt, looking up at the tree that had suddenly appeared in front of him, and a bubble of thought had informed him that here was his resting place.

He had knelt on the dead leaves and slashed through them to the moist earth. He had rubbed that earth into his pores, to replace whatever ash had worked its way out. Then he had slashed at the earth with his knife, watching it rise and fall, like a claw, hacking until he could line the hole with leaves and protect himself from the night.

Something had thrashed through the forest as he worked. He stopped, and glanced up. But any attacking nigger would not have been so clumsy. It was probably a cassowary. He turned back to the job in hand.

Now he wiped the blade and returned it to his belt. He stood up and saw a stump in which water had collected. He scratched himself as he walked to the stump. He knelt and sucked the water from it. He broke off the rotten wood and began to chew it as he resumed his downhill journey.

When he heard the voices he threw himself onto the ground and listened. After a while he saw three figures in the distance.

His brain was cold and clear. He knew these niggers were real. He must be close to their village for them to stroll about so casually. He moved silently after them. They carried no weapons, and no garden implements. Curiosity began to replace caution, getting in the way of his survival instinct.

He followed them to a small clearing in the forest, where a lean-to had been erected. As he watched, they entered the clearing and, out of the shadows, another dozen of them rose up to greet them. The newcomers walked to the bivouac and looked inside it. One of them bent over and picked up something. An axe.

As he held it up and turned it, to admire its edge, Ludwig

198

saw that its head was steel. The nigger grinned and ran his finger along it and held it up to look at the ooze of blood.

Ludwig's heart surged. Niggers did not trade their steel axes. They hung onto them. He was now looking at a tribe that had made "contact". A fierce exultation flooded him. He had made it back.

The niggers squatted down to begin one of their interminable, indecisive discussions. Ludwig pushed himself back into the forest, and traced a wide arc around their camp. He was becoming aware of another level to his thoughts.

What was he going to do now?

He had survived the jungle. Now he had to survive "justice".

"Did you hear it?" Garaban whispered.

Eyes met his, as wide, as full of awe and fear. Samura nodded.

"The spirit," he said. "That was the spirit, walking."

They all glanced to the weapons cache. They could feel the moment approaching them.

"I must return to sit with the Kiap," Samura said, "so he thinks I'm a docile old fool like Barum."

"Be careful of the spirit."

"The spirit hasn't been called for me. It's hunting the Kiap."

He picked up his billum and felt in it and showed them the steel knife he had brought. He tossed it into the lean-to.

"When the time is right," he said.

He knotted the billum over his forehead and walked off, looking like a gardener en route to his vegetable patch. The others watched him go, in awe of his courage. The flesh on their arms crawled, and the hairs stood erect. There was a ground-spirit out walking.

· CHAPTER TEN ·

Everywhere he went a troop of small boys followed Harris, round-eyed with curiosity, keeping several paces behind, analysing his every move—the way he wiped the sweat from under his hat, the way he squinted into the distance, the way he undid his flies to piss.

The land presented itself to him, raw and naked. The light was vivid but not harsh. The colours were raw, primary colours; or else ochre-mixed browns. The clear air was a prism, a lens that allowed him to see features miles distant on the mountain slopes—a man standing sentry, resting one foot inside the knee of his other leg, weight on his handful of spears, head thrown back in profile, jutting beard, flared nose—a woman squatting cross-legged in a field, baby asleep in a net billum on her back, digging stick in her hands as she cultivated the rows of vegetables—pigs rooting up fallow fields with their snouts, lifting their heads to give a sudden shake and chase one another.

He carried his sketch-book with him and worked at mapping the topography. But his hand kept returning to sketches of the naked land; the human-like forms of folded ridges and gullies; the groves of casuarina through which the breeze sighed; bamboos along the creeks, mingled with sugar-cane; and always the patchwork of the fields in their various stages of cultivation, growth, and rest. His eye, following his hand, became conscious of the order that these people had stamped on the landscape—conscious of the far distant edge of forest, the world before Man, that had been hacked away to allow this stand to be made.

It was his second day alone. He had been sketching all morning and was conscious of the raw heat of the sun as it climbed above him. The air was slightly humid and he was sweating. He looked up from his work and realized that his escort of boys had disappeared. He was aware of a sudden silence.

Then, in the silence, a sentry called—a long, drawn-out cry. He looked around but could not see the sentinel. Down the hill was a grove of casuarina, leading to the banks of a creek. He hastened down to their shade and to the water.

As he walked, he heard the call again. Again he looked around, wondering if it might be an alarm. But nothing moved in the heat. He entered the shade of the trees.

The creek was chattering loudly. He squatted by it and cupped up a handful of the cold, clear water, and splashed his face. Then he lay on his belly and scooped it into his mouth.

When he sat up he saw her, downstream from him. She seemed unaware of his presence, sitting on a rock, leaning back, hands spread, head turned to follow the flow of the water down towards the main stream. He stared at her breasts, brown and dark-nippled, firm girl's breasts. She trailed one foot in the water, her legs parted, and he could see her pubic hair.

He stood up slowly. Her flesh seemed to glow, reflecting the clear light that broke through the gap in the trees made by the creek. Her skin was dark, a mahogany brown, but gleaming with highlights.

Then she turned her head and caught him looking at her.

They remained stationary, staring at each other. Her eyes were huge and dark. Her nose was high and flared. His eyes travelled mathematically over her, absorbing the sight. He realized, with a slight shock, that she was not caked with ash, mud, and fat.

The thick lips opened. He saw her tongue for a moment. Then she smiled.

She called out something to him. He did not know what it was, but her voice was teasing and welcoming. He hesitated and she leaned forward. Her breasts shivered with the movement. His penis pushed against his flies. Her eyes remained on his face, still smiling, still inviting. He walked towards her.

201

For a moment, she thought she was going to lose him. She had heard the shouted signal and knew he was coming. She had arranged herself on the rock. Her quick ears had picked up his movements when he stepped onto the carpet of casuarina needles, and had followed him until he stopped, when she knew he must be watching her.

It excited her to be watched so hungrily. She had never felt her power so fully until then. In ordinary meetings with ordinary men the power of your sex was always disguised, turned aside into conventions. But here, with this alien, there were no rules. She drew him towards her, holding his eyes, and his body, by a shake of her shoulders and the subsequent quiver in her breasts.

She felt anger too. She felt it deep beneath her other feelings as he stumbled towards her. She had been chosen, through her fate, and through the active connivance of her father, to be alienated forever from her people. She bit back the anger and concentrated on drawing him to her. She focused the anger into a smile that was going to destroy him.

She saw the desire plainly on his face. She pressed her hands back against the rock and wriggled her toes in the water. She felt the touch of water, menstrual blood, for a moment, of her mother. She saw him, the true Sky Person, fighting with his desires. His body wanting her. His mouth twisting to deny her. His eyes caught between the two, not knowing which way to turn.

"Come here," she said, "and I'll squeeze that snake right off your body."

His mouth opened and spoke something unintelligible.

She said something. He did not know what, but the tone was coquettish.

"Hullo," he said, hopeless with inadequacy.

He saw her eyes leave his face and travel down to where

his cock lunged at his pants. The eyes returned to his face, sparkling with amusement.

A tremor ran through him. Suddenly he realized that there was no precedent for this moment. The little he had learnt at school dances and social evenings was as meaningless as the advice offered in novels, in the chapters that always concluded with three dots.

And then he took her in his arms and passion overcame them...

He licked his lips. He could do anything he wanted! The power available unnerved him for a moment.

She reached up and her fingers grazed his groin.

He flinched.

"You bitch!" he said. He dropped his sketch-book. "I'll show you, you black bitch!"

It swept him up in a wave. He tugged at his belt. His lips throbbed with desire fiercer than any he had experienced. His fingers, the tip of his nose, all his extremities were like his cock, shivering with excitement.

For a moment she was afraid. He ripped his trousers down and his snake sprang out, straight as a spear, circumcised, its one eye staring right at her. She could see his face way up above it. His body had won and now he could be capable of anything. He had felt that same current of energy that she had. At this moment he was capable of anything—lost in the illusion of total freedom, unaware that twenty warriors were waiting for the resolution of this moment, and that one wrong action of his would place a spear between his shoulders.

To bring him back to the matter that was most urgent she leaned forward and took it in her mouth.

He shouted and flailed his arms, but she felt it throb, and then his hands grabbed her head and held it against his groin. Her ungreased flesh met his.

He thought he would explode with the intensity of it. He shouted at her, and then grabbed her by the head, afraid she would pull away from him and deny him the promise. All sorts of wild thoughts tumbled through his mind at that moment.

He could kill her. Wild anger surged through him. Anger at all women. Anger called up by the intense feelings that shook him. In fright at the anger, he pulled away from her. There was an audible sound as he left her mouth.

He stared at her. She waited, calm, composed, the epitome of all that was desirable, alien, unreachable, and available in a woman.

"Jesus Christ!" he said.

He knelt and fell in the same movement, as she lay back. He fumbled against her. Her fingers pointed him in the right direction. Then he was inside her. She was dark, moist, juicy. He slid into her alien flesh, his mind shouting that he could do anything. Anything! He pressed against her half a dozen times, wanting to draw the moment out forever. But he was too quick.

He screamed and exploded.

In the silence he heard the creek tumbling beside them. He collapsed against her and felt her arm come around and clasp him and hold him tight. He closed his eyes.

When he opened them, she was watching him. They stared at each other solemnly. Then he smiled. His smile reassured her, for she returned it. He chuckled and turned over and lay against her, suddenly feeling like an old married man who has had his Saturday afternoon fuck with the wife and now is looking forward to turning on the wireless and listening to the races.

He laughed.

His laughter made the tension leave her body. It was done. She had let the power sweep her up, and she had felt it sweep him up. Now they were locked together, and events were out of their hands.

In the distance a long-drawn cry signalled the success of the operation. Nearby the warriors would stand down and return to the village, grinning, chuckling, already increasing the size of the legendary White Snake with their hands until, by tomorrow, it would occupy the whole valley and her hole would be a cavern that could engulf the mountains themselves. Thus were legends made.

She smiled and nuzzled against him.

"Damn it to hell, Bellamy! I can't afford to have you away from Madang at this moment!"

Bellamy faced the Administrator across the desk. He stood at attention, thumbs down the seams of his trousers, unaware of his stance, automatically assuming it when McNicol yelled.

"Relax, for God's sake."

Bellamy stood easy.

"Patricia's had enough, sir. I had to get her out of there."

McNicol nodded, staring at the files on his desk. He looked up, at the lazy fan in the ceiling that chopped a breeze into the muggy, sulphurous Rabaul air.

"Did she have a good journey?"

Bellamy looked around and found the edge of the chair. He perched on it.

"Fair, sir. Fair. I managed to charter a schooner that was working along the Lutheran coast. But we had to go to Finschhafen first, so we copped the current off Huon Peninsula. That made her pretty sick."

"Where is she now?"

"In hospital, sir. She's very exhausted . . ." He hesitated, the admission to her condition not coming easily. "I guess you could call it a breakdown."

The Headmaster in McNicol won out over the General. He sighed and laced his hands together.

"It happens to the best of us," he said, sympathetically. "Or, at least, to the most sensitive."

205

"She was convinced there was a plot to do her in. She felt they were continually watching her."

"But she's safe now?"

"She's under sedation. She . . . her mind wanders a lot. She rambles in her speech."

McNicol nodded, rubbing his chin with his clasped hands.

"So what do you want to do now?"

Bellamy hesitated. "Sir," he said, "I'll have to leave the outstations. I really will. That's all there is to it."

"I can't offer you a job at your level in Rabaul, you know."

They faced each other across the desk. Both men knew there was a vacancy for a District Magistrate, based in Rabaul. It was Bellamy who looked down, realizing he would not be offered the post.

"There's a secretarial job," McNicol said, after a pause. "Actually, it's Assistant Secretary, in Administration. But it would mean a slight drop in salary."

"That's all you have to offer, sir?"

"That's all I can offer you, Richard."

They were both aware of the emphasis he had given the word "you".

McNicol watched him a moment, and then continued.

"It will be necessary to enlarge our post at Lae, some time in the future. I know it's smaller than Madang, but it is the effective commercial capital of the main island. It's certainly the airways capital."

He pushed himself out of his chair and walked to the window. The great trees of Rabaul's boulevards were below him, thickly green. The harbour glittered coral blue. The broken, volcanic peaks rose at the entrance to the harbour. The air had a tang of sulphur. He glanced back at the District Officer.

"Did you know Lae 'drome carries more cargo than any other 'drome in the world?"

"No, sir," Bellamy said.

"Look, Richard. I don't want to demote you. But, if you must come to Rabaul, then this is all I can offer you. Assistant Secretary, with the promise that any job we create at Lae goes to you. Lae's a different kettle of fish to Madang. It's much more go ahead, really. Some bloke over there's even killing fresh meat, and milking cows. He stirred the freezer operators up, no end."

Bellamy refused to be sidetracked.

"When will Lae be upgraded, sir?"

"God knows. At the moment, down in Canberra, Guinea Airways is lobbying for a monopoly of air transport throughout the island. Until that issue is settled, Lae's future remains in Limbo."

"Yes, sir."

He watched McNicol, whose eyes had turned inwards, chasing up some memo on the airways dispute, or perhaps on the unlicensed killing of livestock within a declared town.

"How much would the drop in salary be, sir?"

"What? Oh, about twenty per cent."

"Thank you, sir."

Spreading mango trees offered Bellamy cool shade on the walk to the hospital. The breeze from the bay was cool, but it stank of sulphur. He climbed the wooden steps to the hospital verandah, and smiled to the duty sister, who nodded that he could enter his wife's room.

Her eyes were darkly circled. Her face had lost weight, the flesh now stretched taut on the bones. Before he had got her onto the boat she had been drinking heavily. There was still a slight tremor to her hand. Her eyes clamped on him across the room, filled with fear.

"Something's about to happen, Dickie," she called as he entered, struggling against her sedative.

He took her hand. It was cold and moist. It clung to him.

"I can feel it building up, all around us. Something's going to happen."

"Don't be absurd, dear." He tried to speak lovingly, but could hear the impatience in his voice.

"You're leaving, aren't you?"

"I'm booked on the *McDieu*, yes. But we won't sail for a day or two."

"Can't you feel it in the air?"

In spite of himself, he listened. There did seem to be a

207

heaviness to the air, a sense of something brooding, even a high-pitched ringing. He smiled at her.

"Of course not, dear. There's nothing . . ."

She saw he was lying.

"Sponge me, please."

He reached out to sponge her forehead.

A wave passed through the room. The bed heaved. She gasped, but did not scream as he pitched backwards, arms flailing as the whole building, and the ground under it, heaved and shook.

Glass shattered. Women screamed. He heard nurses running in the corridors. The room shook a second time and he sprawled on the floor.

"Guria," he gasped, staggering to his feet.

She moaned in reply. The door opened and a chalk-faced nurse stared in. She held a pitcher of water in her hand, but seemed unaware of it. She looked at them, nodded mechanically, and then shut the door and was gone.

He rose shakily to his feet. They stared at each other across the room. Her bed had slid out from the wall. He pushed it back. Neither of them spoke.

Merin had felt the difference between him and the man the moment she had first touched him. Nicholls would not have drawn back from her. This one could have been a boy from her own village, with the same nervousness face to face with a woman, the same clumsiness in his first caresses.

But he was not like them. He did not have that deep chest, those wide slabs of muscle, or the corrugations of muscle down his belly. His legs were not as powerful. Touching him, she was amazed at his slenderness; at how such a powerful being could be so refined.

What she liked was his inability to boast about himself. Because of his failure with her language, he could not regale

208

her with stories of his conquests at war and sexual play, in the breeding of pigs and the making of garden magic.

He had not preened himself for the dance. He was not covered with discs and discs of gold-lip shell. Yet he had more power than any other man in the valley.

She realized that every other sexual encounter she had made had been an encounter with a ceremonial mask. Men and women in the valley made love to fibre, webbing, ochre and mud and feathers. All life between men and women was a series of stylized gestures that culminated in a moment of privacy, when all could be stripped away, and they could show each other . . . nothing but another mask.

But here, stripped of language and custom, they had only their bodies. This touch pleased him. This touch pleased her.

Lying back, in the carefully constructed Kiap's house, where there was even a separate room in which to defecate, she opened her legs to him, feeling him sink into her. She thrust back at him. She teased him with her fingers and her tongue. She watched his eyes and brought him to the brink and held him there.

And she took her own pleasure. He had no need to enslave her for work in his fields. So he did not bully her. He did not try and master her. He simply gave back what she was giving him.

His hand was inside her now, soaking up her juices, his fingers eagerly experimenting. He withdrew, spreading her hole wide, and brought his snake up, sidling it into her. She gasped and wriggled against it.

And the bed she lay on shivered. Then a hand reached up through the earth and pressed against them. She opened her eyes, seeing the fear in his.

The guria rippled through the building and she closed her eyes and convulsed against him, spasming with intense pleasure, close almost to pain. She felt him driving into her, coming himself, and their thighs heaved against each other.

The Haus Kiap rocked on its foundations of saplings. The village street shivered. Life came to a momentary standstill as the distant guria touched the valley.

209

Bellamy grasped the window-sill, breathing deep to settle his fear. From the hospital he could see the streets leading down to the bay, and the jungle-clad volcanic peaks rising around the bay's perimeter. The islands in the bay itself, mute witnesses to the forces of previous vulcanism.

Closer at hand he could see the Chinese-owned hotel, with a small crowd of patrons suddenly gathered outside, staring at the sky as if the guria had originated from there. They had brought their bottles and glasses with them.

A Chinese woman, hurrying by, hastily crossed to the other side of the road. The obscenities of the drunks followed her as she walked, head-down.

Bellamy realized how much he hated this town and everything it stood for. And in the same moment realized how much he loved the life of the outstations.

Then the second shock wave hit. The street lifted and slammed itself into the drunks. There was a tremendous roar. The hotel bucked and buckled. Glass shattered into the street. Chinese women screamed, lurching for their babies. Along the shore the shipyard workers flung themselves to the ground. Already the sea had retreated and was gathering into a wave. The shipyard workers were on their feet and running.

The wave slammed the docks, heaving boats against the piles. Water cascaded into the street, lifting up a car and throwing it onto the pavement. The water kept rising. It picked up the struggling drunks. It burst open the hotel door, sweeping them into the bar as it rose. The water burst back out through the windows, returning itself to the street with a load of whisky bottles and port wine flagons.

Then the water was gone. The shock was gone. People moaned. Bellamy looked down at his locked, white knuckles. He could not move them from the window ledge. He looked over his shoulder at his wife.

"I can't shift my hands," he said. "They're locked."

"Breathe out. Take a deep breath," she said.

He did so. The adrenalin seemed to pierce all the way to

210

his armpits. His left hand moved. He pulled it free and prised the right one away with it. He turned back to her.

"Do you like it here?" he asked her.

"It's better than Madang," she said. "I don't feel the . . . the threat."

He massaged his hands and sat on the edge of the bed. Her water pitcher was shattered on the floor. He kept his feet clear of the wet.

"It's strange," he said. "I feel it much more, here."

"What are we going to do?" she asked him.

"Perhaps we could compromise? We could live in Lae?"

"Lae!"

"You can get fresh meat and milk there now."

She stared past him.

"I would like to live in Rose Bay," she said. "In Sydney," she added. "I would like to wake up to the sound of traffic and pick up our newspaper from the lawn and look down the hill and over the street to the Seaplane Base. I would like to see the harbour. I would like to pick up the milk-pail and carry it inside and make our tea and carry it back to bed and lie there, with you, drinking tea, reading the *Herald*, and know that, in a moment, the children will come bursting in."

He nodded. His eyes were blurred with tears. He took her hand and she pressed it to his face.

"Please, Dickie," she said, "I want to go home."

Inside himself he could feel something, like a cough. He tried to clear his throat. But the cough began to shake his shoulders. The tears welled from his eyes. Ashamed, embarrassed, he tried to stop it, but he couldn't. He began to sob.

She pulled his head onto her breast and he tensed. But the touch of her hands was too much. He let go and began to cry.

When the moon was finally caught and devoured by the forces of the dark, and was reduced to a sliver like the blade of an obsidian knife, the Crocodile met.

211

The parts of the Crocodile lived far from each other, held together by the bond of Sorcery. The Snout lived closest to the home of the great Guria, on the island that the Whites had taken as their capital. The Eyes lived on offshore islands. Alo was one of the Front Legs, and he and the other Front Leg lived in coastal villages. The Rear Legs lived on the edge of the mountain escarpment, while the Tail curled up the Ramu River Valley in braided streams.

They had travelled by sailing canoes, three men each in two boats. They travelled by night as much as possible. They came to meet on the island that most people avoided. It had grown out of the deep lagoon, thrusting up from the water, demonstrating the power that the Guria still possessed — power that was content to slumber until the time was exactly right. An island that still smoked and that trembled whenever, deep beneath, the Guria turned around in his sleep.

They rode out the twin shock waves of the earth tremor, eyes never leaving each others' faces. The Snout listened, one hand firmly on the earth, feeling the Guria shiver, the tremor running down its ancient spine.

He was an old man. He had learnt his Sorcery in the shadow of the first wave of Sky People — the harshest, most violent of the men from the Sky. As a young man he had seen the Sky People try and kill the Crocodile. They had broken its Front Legs: Alo's father. But like its namesake it had submerged, until only its watchful eyes could be seen, and it had waited.

He had felt many a guria come and go. This one was as sharp as any he had known. His body felt it through the earth. He felt how close it was.

The fact that, when the Sky People arrived, they had first settled across the water on the main island, at the town they called Madang, but had then reconsidered and come here, to the home of the Guria, was evidence enough of their Divine origin. How else would they have known that here was the source of the power of the Earth Spirits? Here was the entrance to that Underworld where the ancestral brothers had journeyed in search of Cargo.

The Snout had come to believe that these Sky People were renegades, on the run from a rebellion amongst the

212

Sky Gods, and that they were trying to establish contact with the Earth Spirits in order to make them allies in a return fight with their Divine relatives. But the Earth Spirits and the Water Spirits had rejected them. Violently.

The Guria had rumbled, and then the mountain had exploded. The island they now sat upon had been born overnight. The Sky People had run screaming to and fro, like ordinary villagers. The Snout had been only a boy then. His own father had been the Snout. The level of the deep lagoon rose and fell. Smoke and steam issued from the ground. A vile smell, as of death, hung over everything. It looked as if the Spirits were rejecting the Sky People.

But they hung on. They brought in their steel canoes, laden with Cargo stolen from the ancestral brothers. They tended their injured. They praised their leader, Jesus Christ, most powerful of the Sky People, and sang songs to him. And they hung on.

The circle of men, seven men, stared at each other, not daring to move. Hard on the heels of the shock waves came the intense smell of sulphur. They heard the sea rushing out, and waited for it to come rushing back in. They felt the island shivering, like a frightened child, as its Father, far down in the earth, growled and flexed. They knew the time was close.

"Front Leg?"

Alo felt the old man's eyes on him. He stared back, waiting.

"Did you do what we discussed at our last meeting?"

He nodded.

"And are you closer now to their power?"

"I have the machinery of their power. I have the book. I have a gun."

The old man nodded, watching him closely. Alo looked away, and felt the immediate reaction from the old man.

"What are you doing?"

"Nothing," he said.

They felt the waves return. They heard the boats tossed against the jetties, and the sound of the water tearing at the town the Sky People had built. The old man ignored it, holding up his hand, drawing their attention back to himself.

213

"You are doing something, inside your head."

"Perhaps we are wrong," Alo said, letting the thought speak.

He released his breath with a sigh. He had said it. He glanced at his Clan Brothers. They all watched him.

"Perhaps we will not be able to master their power. Perhaps it is too different from our own."

"Have you tried?"

Alo nodded.

"And you were unable to work it?"

"I worked the gun, for a while. Then the power left it and it worked no more."

"But it worked for a time?"

He nodded. The old man stared past him, glanced at the others, and then stood up. His hands rubbed at his stiffened joints.

"We are close," he said. "I can feel it. But, when things are at their closest, they are at their most difficult. Front Legs!"

He spun and Alo, his attention wandering, jumped, as did the other Front Leg.

"This Kiap from whom you took the book and the gun will need a new houseboy?"

Alo nodded. The old man's eyes travelled on, and stopped at the other Front Leg.

"The Front Leg," he said, and he smiled, "works for the Mastas?"

Front Leg nodded. Alo watched the old man.

"They will teach you what you need to know, so that the Kiap, when he goes looking for a houseboy, will find the most desirable one to be . . ." His finger extended and he grinned.

"Me?" asked Alo.

The old man nodded. "The Kiap is here, speaking with the Administrator. He will be returning to Madang soon." He fell silent, his eyes piercing Alo.

Alo waited.

"What you will learn, the secrets of the book, and of the gun, will be learnt for us, for the Crocodile. It will not be learnt for other people. It will not be learnt for yourself."

He stared back at the old man. His heart was hammering.

214

He tried to keep his face blank, not to let the old man know he had read every one of Alo's thoughts. And wondering if the old man had penetrated to the deepest, most secret thought of them all.

His deepest thought was: the Crocodile has lost its power.

"No, Snout," he said. "It will not be learnt for others or for myself. It will be learnt for the Crocodile."

For which his own father had died. For which he had killed other men of the islands.

And it came to him then, with a rush, like the Guria-made waves hammering against the wharves, that the Crocodile was killing the wrong men. It was killing black men. It should be killing white. If it would not, then it was time it did lose its power. The old genealogy of power no longer meant anything. It was time a new one grew up.

He kept his face very polite, waiting. The old man's gaze bounced off it, like spears off a war-shield. He must not read my thoughts, Alo told himself.

The old man nodded. He grinned again.

"The Front Leg," he said, "will teach you how to iron a Masta's pants."

Diary: 20th May, 1937

It's going to rain, damn it. In fact, here it comes now. It's been building up all day long. Something fishy is going on here. I can feel it. Sidelong glances. Very little work being done in the fields, as if everyone is waiting for a signal to do . . . what? God knows. Attack me? Sneak down and ambush the women from the next village as they go for water?

That little guria didn't help, either. It probably brought the rain on in point of fact.

There are times when I wonder what I'm doing out here. And other times when I know. I'm here because I can be nowhere else. I'm exactly the same as young Harris. Looking at him is like stepping into Mr Wells' Time Machine. Same background. Same dreams. There's no more than fifteen years separates us biologically.

215

But I've spent that time waiting to be killed, and that ages a man — as well as concentrates his mind, as that boring old fart once said.

Yes, it is like my son has come to take me home. And it is like I'm intentionally marooned on Circe's Island, amongst my Pigmen. There is nothing new under the sun, and unfortunately for our storytellers Homer said it first. So we can never escape him. It is true that tomorrow belongs to the people of the past. My people, the present, have missed their chance. They're like Hawaiian surf-riders who've paddled for a wave and lost it. While it charges to shore they wait, hoping another one will come.

But there will be no more waves.

Australia had its chance, then. Maybe it would have been different if we had fought against England, like the Americans, and declared our independence. We're like a young man who has not had it out with his parents. Has not cut the apron/umbilical cord. We yell about our independence, but we fight England's wars and die like flies, mouthing her patriotic nonsense. We import her Depression and then her Experts to drive us further into ruin. And all we can fight Her with is cricket balls!

The sun is departing. Down the hill, in the gloom, I can see a group of men. For reasons best known to themselves, they carry women's string bags, stuffed with vegetables. Men doing women's work? Something is wrong.

They have halted at the base of my camp. They sit down, in their timeless fashion, hunching on haunches, and begin rolling cigarettes. Probably they are getting in early for tomorrow's census-taking, and will sit there into the night, and eventually fall down asleep. They are not armed.

And the rain explodes out of the sky without warning. No prelude of thunder. No surge of wind. One moment dampness, not even drizzle, the next, thundering tropical rain. But the men sit on through it, stalwart, stolid, as unmoving as the mountain itself.

That is the force which will win history . . .

He laid down his pen and blinked. His eyes ached. He focused on the distant march of rain. Thoughts jostled his mind, quickly, in teeming confusion. He could not capture them all.

One image was of his mother, in the laundry of the farmhouse. It was washday Monday and she had been up since dawn, first stoking the fire under the great copper

216

cauldron, and now stirring the baby's nappies, saved for a week, in a glutinous mass.

She moved slowly. There was another one newly in her belly and it was making her sick.

He sat on the floor, playing with the kittens that the heat had driven from their box in the corner. Their mother mewed anxiously to him.

"Don't sit there like that," his mother said, irritably, pushing past him with the wash-basket, sliding a stumbling kitten aside with her foot, gently.

"I don't want to go away to school, mother," he replied.

She stood there, cradling the wash-basket to her hip, as though it were a child. She looked at him.

"You've got to," she said. It hurt her to say it, but she did. "That's all there is to it. It's your father's old school. You'll be happy there."

She dropped the wash-basket by the cat's box and stepped past him to the door. He pushed the kitten back to its mother and followed her outside.

The paddocks ran down from their stone-and-slate house to the creek, and curved up the slope at the other side, green and flat, denuded of trees by the efforts of his grandfather and his father. Fat sheep now grazed where the wattle used to bloom. He took a deep breath and told her the absolute, rock-bottom truth.

"I don't want to be away from you, mummy."

She froze, pegs in her mouth, and looked at her eldest child. He stared back. He was overweight and pudgy. Her husband said she cosseted him too much. She was beginning to think he was right, and that boarding school would, indeed, make a man of him.

"Don't be ridiculous," she said.

He saw the anguish in her face, and saw her mask it with anger and turn back to her chores, removing the pegs from her mouth.

"Look," she said, sharply, "we've all got to stand on our own two feet, some day. Stop acting like a baby. There's more than enough of them around here already."

"You always want me to go away," he said. "Or else you go away from me."

217

The truth of it made her angrier.

"Go and get your jobs done!" she shouted. "Do you want your father to belt you again!"

She glared at him. His lip quivered, like an infant when its sudden resolve to be masterful breaks down and it howls for its mummy. But, as she watched, he fought it. He nodded soberly and turned away from her. She felt a gut-wrenching feeling and clutched at her belly, thinking it was that child moving. But it wasn't.

Seeing a kitten staggering into the doorway, he walked to it, picked it up, and returned it to the safety of the box. He watched it nuzzle amongst its less adventurous kin, and then turned away. He was careful not to look at her, but he could feel her watching him. He knelt and laced his boots, and then walked past her. He felt her turn to watch him. He opened the back gate and walked down to the pigsties.

He thought he heard a sob. But he did not turn back to verify it. He thought she half-said his name. But he was full of cold anger. He stopped at the feed bins and mechanically began to make up their mixture . . .

Now, he wrote as the first rains fell.

Standing on my own two feet. That could have been the family motto. Grandfather stood on them, and left Aberdeen. He and father stood on them and cleared the hills. I stood on them and walked away from the family.

The pattern is interesting. More and more I believe that our behaviour is inherited. It's the only explanation when you analyse what happens over a number of generations. With such a closed gene-pool as you find up here, society fails to generate new behaviour, because there is no input of new genetic material.

He broke off writing and looked up. The thought that came to him was sharply carnal: the image of a naked village girl.

In a way, the introduction of half-caste bastards to village life is an introduction of new behaviour patterns. It is probably the only way to move these people effectively into the twentieth century. I know the armchair theorists are pooh-poohing Evolutionism.

They're the ones who've done their field work sitting on their bums. All they're observing is the growth of haemorrhoids.

We had a small earth tremor this afternoon. Its epicentre would be somewhere out to sea. It's interesting how the villagers sensed its advent. They were all out of their huts when it arrived, waiting for it. I think they can sense subtle atmospheric changes, and probably behavioural cues in the domestic animals. We could certainly do with such an early-warning system, particularly in loveless Rabaul.

It's interesting how, in that town, the one totally forbidden topic of discussion is the fact that you're living on the lip of an active volcano that last blew its lid in 1878, creating Vulcan Island, an entirely new ash island in the middle of the harbour.

Correction. There is another forbidden topic. That of a native rebellion. No one talks about the unsuccessful native wharf labourers' strike. Or about what they did to the "ringleaders"— "union delegates" would be the description if they were white. But call a person a "ringleader" and you can do what you will. Don't they know what happened to the British in India?

Probably the two taboos are linked in their minds. We live by metaphors. The metaphoric association between subterranean vulcanism and native power is so straightforward that it takes a conscious act of will not to point it out—and hence not to act to alleviate at least one of them . . .

And Nicholls felt the desire to write leave him. He had said what was on his mind. Cleansed, he watched the ink dry; then he folded his journal and stood up. He capped his pen and stretched and yawned. While he had been writing the sun had slipped behind the folds of the mountains. Night had come quickly and blackly. He dropped the journal into his travelling case, on top of the armour.

Seeing it, he hesitated, glanced around and, seeing no one watching, pulled it out. He laid it at the foot of his bed and stroked it thoughtfully.

Standing there, feeling the murmur of the earth beneath her, whispering the tremor of the streams, the push of grass and

219

trees to be born, the clutching of the forces of dampness like the clutching of an infant for her knees, both to drag her down and lift her up, Fogeo listened to the wind. It bore the cadence of village voices, bird-calls, the squeal of pigs. But, above that, it bore the whisper of the Sky Gods, massing now in thunderheads over the ranges, waiting to fall on the fields, to mate with the Earth Goddess and produce new growth, new vegetables, and from them new pigs, and from the pigs more Power to her husband, Barum, and through his Power more Power to herself: Fogeo, wife to the principal Big Man of the valley.

In her hand she held the glazed leaf. She powdered it between her fingers. It spoke to her of its donor. Holding it was like holding an infant's penis—soft and malleable, unaware yet of desire and the Power it contained. It conjured up the image of Nicholls, and his lost, haunted eyes.

The first time she had seen him, sitting beside her husband, she had seen his hunched shoulders and that expression, deep within his eyes—both fear and longing—and she had known he was marked already for death. She knew that now she was simply the mediator between him and the Gods, perhaps hastening the process, perhaps not—perhaps it was already moving and her actions were irrelevant. But, either way, Fogeo would go through with the sorcery.

She had been born to the Gafu, so long ago she could only dimly remember the village—and what she remembered was not borne out by the reality whenever she returned to it. She remembered clear light, water, laughter, huge distances. But what she saw were stunted fields, hemmed in by the wild jungle that was always pushing closer and closer, seeming to drive the Gafu further down the ridge, out of contact with their Power, making them into a lost people, people searching for a way to replenish that Power. Thus, dangerous people.

Women are much closer to the source of Power than men. They, she, felt it with each birth. Women knew who they were and what they had to do. They felt the new life growing inside them, and they saw how it ate them up, and in the end destroyed them. But they loved the children that came forth from their bodies. They loved them, knowing they would be their death. That was life. It was something that came and went and you were simply the path it chose to follow for a short while.

There was no way men could feel this. They tried, with their ceremonies, to be like women. They made themselves bleed, slashing open their penises in a show of bravado that fooled no woman. They yelled and fought and strutted and danced. They challenged life. They destroyed it. In the end, it destroyed them.

But all their posturing was not in vain. Some men, very few, caught hold of the Power and, when they had it, they shared it with a woman. Together the pair produced children. The children grew and helped increase the man's wealth. The woman shared in it. The Power was held in check, was channelled like a stream down an irrigation ditch.

She knew he would achieve that when she first saw him. The young men from Parap at the dance, raking all her age-mates with their eyes. But, amongst the whole tossing, beplumed mass of dancers, she saw only one. She saw the discs of muscle across his stomach, his powerful chest, his thick legs and arms like knotted vines. He was the dance leader, already a recognized Big Man. He made her sex weak. It fluttered inside her, like unborn children.

Her age-mates giggled and nudged each other. There were girls here prettier than her, with longer legs, tighter behinds, firmer breasts. They were already running their hands down those supple thighs, pushing their thighs at him. She knew she had only one chance.

Breaking precedent, before all the males were assembled on the ground, she had run to him. Her elders, her mother in particular, gasped with shame. Her age-mates tittered with embarrassment—and with anger that they had not made the move. Her father and his mates glowered with anger at how she had shamed the village—how she had effectively said, "Look, everyone, this stranger is far more desirable than any man in our own village."

And he had seen her and grinned at her and laughed, a full male laugh. He strutted, confident, proud, for the moment supremely powerful, gesturing to his mates that she had

221

demonstrated what everyone knew but no one had yet said: the Gafu were lost, the Parap had the Power.

Now the season was changing. The Parap had grown lazy. The Gafu were hungry, with a hungry new Big Man. The coming of the Sky People had altered everything and, in the new shift of Power, she could see that the Gafu were on the ascendant.

Just as she had shamed her mother, now her own daughter had shamed her — by refusing a husband, by letting any snake drink at her hole, by giving herself to the Sky People. But her daughter, Merin, had not clutched onto the Power through her shamelessness. She was adrift, lost, like the Gafu had been — as if she had inherited that from her mother and not her mother's own strength.

This sorcery she was performing was not sorcery for the village, or for her husband, or for herself. It was for her daughter. Nicholls was a dead man. But she felt something different about his young assistant. If she was reading him correctly — and how could a human understand a God? — then he was like her Barum had been, but without the surface show of arrogance. Gods used women, that was clear. People in the valley knew of this happening in other places. The women went eagerly, hoping to become wives to the Gods. But none ever did. After the God had finished with them, they went on to the men who assisted him. From there, they might become diseased. They died. Or they simply disappeared.

The young God was different. He did not look at women simply as holes into which his snake could crawl. That difference marked him out. She thought it marked him as a man of Power. That was the chance she was taking for her daughter.

And, thinking of the young God, she had a clear image of him sitting beside Nicholls, trying to mask his nausea. For a moment there were two images in front of her, fused together. As she watched, they began to separate. She saw him as a God. And she saw him simply as a man. The Sky People, in the end, were men.

Men could be harnessed with sorcery.

· CHAPTER ELEVEN ·

"Jesus!" the Masta screamed. "Jesus! Jesus!"

Sergeant Bukato smiled, hearing the young Masta calling to his God. He was standing under the eaves of the Haus Kiap, immersed in the sound of the rain, its wetness and its smell. He could see nothing of the village but the dim outline of huts. Through the pounding of the rain came the occasional thin cry of a child. All other sounds were muted by the downpour.

But, when he leant against the wall, he could hear the lovers. He turned and inserted a finger in the thatch and wormed it about, until he had room to press his eye against it and peer in.

The Masta had not been praying, though he was on his knees. He knelt between her spread thighs, his fingertips just touching her breasts. The lovers smiled at each other. Her hand returned his caresses. Bukato could see she was biting her lip with the cold of her nakedness. But she was not going to let him see it.

Masta Harris eased himself from the stretcher and stood up, his emptied penis hanging limp and loose. Bukato stared at it, and found himself sad, not amused. He didn't know why. Then the Masta stared up at the roof, his hand clasping his shoulder.

"Water," he said, pointing to the stain beginning to spread across the thatched roof. "It's bloody leaking."

She, of course, had no idea what he was talking about. She sat up and leaned back on her elbows. Her body made Bukato even sadder. He wanted it, at first for sex, but then with such a hunger for comfort that he felt the tears against his eyes. Now it was he who bit his lips, to keep from crying.

She watched her Masta with amusement. He was chattering away, his body pale, gleaming in the light of the central fire.

223

Bukato could see her hungrily assessing him. His thin, elongated body, without the solid, chunky muscle of the Highlands men she was used to. He turned to her and spoke again, and Bukato could see the look of total incomprehension on her face.

For a moment, Harris was angry with her. He raised his fist. He saw her shrink back, and he dropped it and sat beside her. He touched her cheek and she nuzzled against him.

Bukato stepped back into the rain. Part of him wanted, desperately, to cry. But the other part, the stronger part, clenched his fists and gave him anger. He walked through the rain, in search of sleeping sentries to abuse.

Nicholls raced. It was an athletics track marked with white pipeclay, around the school oval. He was on his fifth lap and there were three to go. But his feet seemed to have become encased in concrete. He stared down at them. No, it wasn't concrete. It was like they were wanting to slide into the green turf.

Which is what they did. Now the other runners were catching him. He couldn't hear the crowd. He could only hear the breath of people running. There were only two people. One of them was a girl. This shouldn't have been. It was a boys' sportsday. Why was she running with the man?

He was trapped now. He still tried to raise his legs, but the earth drew them back. Pulling against the earth tore at his flesh. He could see blood. He felt pain in his calves. The running pair were now beside him. They seemed oblivious of him. The sound of their harsh breathing filled his head. He put his hands to his ears to shut it out. His legs screamed with agony.

He was awake. His heart hammered. He thrashed against the sleeping bag and it seemed to wrap itself around his legs.

He cried out and heaved himself upright. The old dog yelped indignantly and slid off the stretcher.

Nicholls saw the thatched hut and knew where he was. His heart quietened and he listened to the rain. It roared all around him. He untangled the sleeping bag and pulled himself from it.

Now he felt something else. A prickle of fear ran across his belly. He tensed and tried to hear through the rain. He isolated its roar and splash, and thought he heard it again: some human sound. The fear was in his mouth, running through his limbs. It cleared his mind.

That was what you came to like about fear, he thought. The clarity it gave you. That's why you went back to it. It made everything else unimportant.

He recognized it as the fear of death; the purest, fiercest fear. Fear that was almost joy. He smiled and picked up his armour and lowered it over his head.

He buckled it tight and sat on his stretcher and laced his boots. He heard the sound again, something shuffling close at hand. Sitting up, he felt a sexual thrill. Excited now, he stood up and strapped on his pistol holster and stepped to the door. His excited penis seemed to lead him. He pushed at it with his hand, but the action only excited him more.

They had caught the sound of the hut floor creaking as Nicholls stood up. They froze. Samura glanced to his left and right. His men were like trees. The rain streaked through the mud and ash on their greased bodies. He looked to the empty door, willing Nicholls to step into its frame.

Something moved in the shadow of another hut. Samura turned his head slowly. His mouth was full of fear. He expected an armed sentry to challenge them. Instead, he saw Nicholls' servant standing there, stretching, yawning, shivering as he stared blankly out the door and urinated.

225

He stepped into the doorway. The revolver was now in his hand. Nicholls caught the flash of movement in the dark and swung the weapon at it.

He saw the half-asleep Baranuma shaking the last drops. The fear left him. Its afterwash was a moment of pure pleasure, so intense he shivered with it. He grinned and watched his servant fumble back into the hut. He replaced the revolver in the holster and turned, himself, for bed.

His peripheral vision caught the movement. He momentarily checked his own movement, then forced himself to carry it through. He let the intense night-sight of the periphery scan the compound.

What had been posts in the murky rain became men. They slipped towards his hut. His heart surged and the gun came back into his hand and he turned to confront them. He glanced down at his dog.

"Come on, Lik-lik," he said. "Let's see what they're up to."

Barum sat with Fogeo against the wall of her house to avoid the rain. He could see the hut where his daughter was with the white man. In his belly was a confusion of feelings: fear and excitement, sadness, and anger. Fear that the mission would fail, and that he had sacrificed Merin, her life and reputation, for nothing. Fear for her future was even stronger than the fear for his own neck, which would be stretched from a tree if the Gafu bungled their part of the action. Excitement, that it was going to work, that through the maze of deals and anticipated double-crosses and counter-deals, the people of the valley could make a stand against the Sky People, could make it clear that they were a power that must be bargained with . . . that they were the equals of the Sky People. And excitement that it was him, Barum, who would be recognized as the strategist who had brought this plan to fruition.

And then the sadness as he watched the Haus Kiap. No

matter what happened this night, his daughter was lost to him. Perhaps he should not have tried so hard to hold on to her. Other men's daughters came and went, and the men felt not a ripple. But he was different. His difference made him the Big Man, but it made him so small when he thought of losing her.

Then the anger. The Sky People were not Gods. That fiction was gone. Only the most ignorant cannibal from the deepest bush could think that—only people who had not seen them eat and sleep, piss and shit, lie down with a woman, and pick their noses. Who had not seen the greed in their eyes and the cunning in their minds.

They were men all right. But they did not treat other men as men. They acted as if they, alone, were the men, and the rest were no better than pigs—to be bought and sold, fattened and killed. They took your daughter without a word of thanks or an offer of obligatory exchange. Some simply killed and kept on going—like a man slashing a vine as he passes it, without thought, without stopping.

Tonight his anger would be vented.

In the Haus Kiap they forgot the rain. They gave up trying to talk about it, in tongues that could not accommodate each other's strange sounds. But tongues that could do so much else. Their bodies touched, parted, and touched again.

She held his head in her hands and looked into his eyes, trying to read their future in them.

But she could read nothing, for he was lost to thought. He had forgotten who he was, and what he was. He was simply a lover in a Stone Age village. Outside his hut, prehistoric rain was falling. The earth trembled with it. The fire smoked and hissed as it dripped through by the central ridge-pole. The smell of water, dust, smoke, entwined for him.

His eyes were now like the eyes of a man. He was no longer a God. She smiled at him and he smiled back and pressed his forehead against hers.

227

His Stone Age love touched his cheek. He felt her shoulders shaking and realized she was crying. He smiled and stroked her thick, kinky hair. It was like wire. He touched her eyes, streaming tears. He kissed her eyelids.

"I love you," he whispered, surprised as he realized. "Oh, God, I love you."

Nicholls stayed inside the compound. The rain had not eased. He had returned the revolver to the holster and covered it with the leather flap. He crossed his arms, conscious of the movement of the armour as he did so. He stared at the silent, waiting men.

When he had first seen them, they seemed to be moving with sinister purpose. Now that purpose had evaporated. They stood there, foolishly, heads down, the water streaming from them, still clasping the net-bags that bulged with vegetables.

"What the hell's going on?" he said.

He singled out Samura, their leader, and walked to him and looked down at him. Samura would not look at him.

"It's bloody-well pouring rain," he said. "What do you want?"

Samura was looking at his knees. Nicholls wondered what he could see there. Then he suddenly realized that his armour covered only half his body. The fear made him weak.

It was such a silly oversight! He realized his fist had opened, palm up, as if he was explaining to someone this simple mistake. He realized Samura had reached into his billum, and that the other men were crowding closer. He turned the hand down and lifted the holster flap and put his hand on the revolver.

"Look," he said. "Come in out of the rain if you want to see me."

There was a steel tomahawk in Samura's hand.

"Look!" he shouted, with such authority that Samura did look, the tomahawk half out of the bag. Nicholls wondered if

228

he had got it in trade or if he had pinched it from Wallace's equipment.

"Look!" he said again. "I am invincible!"

He hit his chest with his fist and they all heard the thump of it. He gestured to one of the men, whose hand was removing a short spear from amongst his taro. He grabbed the spear and jammed it into his chest.

The men gasped and stepped backwards.

"See!" he said, proudly, praying they had forgotten his exposed legs.

The spear shaft snapped off and its carved head fell to the ground. They all stared at it in amazement. The dog questioned it with her nose.

But Samura's eyes turned again to his legs, and then lifted to Nicholls' face. Their eyes met and Nicholls saw himself as they were seeing him. He saw a madman. He shook his head.

"No," he said.

He was a foolish, vain man who had engineered his own death. And who, right to the end, was strutting and fretting, beating his chest, convinced of his own invincibility.

He saw Samura breathe deeply and clench his teeth and swing the tomahawk out of the billum, cascading vegetables as he did, swinging low, like a man cutting vines.

Nicholls did not scream. His eyes opened in astonishment. He pitched forward. A spear snapped off against the armour, as it was intended to. He tried to move, but his left leg would not co-operate. For some reason, he fell over. The tomahawk was lifted above him. It swung down and he saw it slice through his right thigh, and felt it bite into bone. He screamed. He could hear his dog squealing in terror.

Samura struggled to free the axe from the bone. He put his foot on the fallen Masta's thigh and wrenched and the axe came away and, from behind it, bright, red arterial blood erupted. One of his men had killed the Masta's dog. He kicked the carcass out of the road.

Nicholls' hand had hold of the revolver. He steadied it, and fired at his attacker. The gun kicked twice against his hand, and the man hurled backwards, shaking with astonishment as much as pain, not knowing what was happening to him.

229

A stone axe crushed into Nicholls' leg. He fired again, and its wielder dropped away. He tried to claw his way back to the buildings. His attackers were regrouping, ready now to finish him off. He was watching a man twist back to hurl a spear.

The man was no longer there. There was an eruption behind Nicholls' shoulder. It was the sweetest sound he had ever heard, the sound of a 12-gauge shotgun barking. Black legs were beside him, spread apart to take the recoil. He looked up and saw the still-naked Baranuma, firing from the hip. He emptied both barrels. Nicholls rallied and fired his revolver again, and the attackers fled, dragging their dead and dying with them.

And then something materialized out of the wet, muddy gloom. A creature, like a man, naked and mud-splattered, white with ash, but red-haired, wielding a knife in one clawed hand. Nicholls saw the knife slashing, and he saw his attackers flinch away from the apparition and run, as if they were running from a ghost. Then the creature turned and saw the white man on the ground, the armed Boy standing over him, and behind them, the Police tumbling from sleep, rifles already cocked, safety catches pushed forward.

"Don't shoot!" he screamed. "Do not shoot. I am white!"

He had a heavy accent. Nicholls knew who he was. He groaned. He couldn't help smiling at the irony. He was losing consciousness as his body retreated from the pain. He saw Baranuma staring down at him, panic on his face.

"Get him a gun," he whispered. "They'll counter-attack any moment."

And he gave himself up to the numbness, to the cessation of movement, to the freedom from fear and desire. He curled into the mud that was red with his own blood, and with the blood of his old dog.

Samura's body was alive with pains, running like fire through him. He had never experienced such pain. There was so little to show for it. Just two small holes, from which the bright blood was pumping. His hand tried to clasp them, but the blood poured over his fingers.

"Get back to them," he whispered. "While they are still confused with sleep. If you don't get them now, you'll never get them."

"The spirit," someone said. He could hear the fear in the man, close to panic, and he knew it could sweep through them all. "The spirit is there. It is with them."

He thought quickly, aware that he was now dying and would soon be dead.

"If you can kill them," he said, "the spirit will return to the Land of the Dead. It is a restless spirit, probably of someone killed by the Sky People. If you avenge it, then it will not trouble you."

Their eyes watched him, evaluating what he said. Couldn't they see he was dying? He forced all of his will into his own eyes, staring back, forcing them to believe him.

"Go," he said. "My spirit will be fighting for you."

And they saw him relinquish it to them.

They looked at each other. One of them raised his hand.

"I will take my brothers in from the front," he said. "When they are fighting us, the rest of you will come in from behind."

They stepped over the body of their Principal Big Man and ran back to the Kiap's camp.

The Boy brought him a rifle. Ludwig grunted thanks and examined its action. It was a British Lee Enfield. There was a round in the breech and the magazine was full. The Boy still hovered by him and he glanced at him. The Boy was holding out a greatcoat. Ludwig realized the sight of a naked Masta was a bother to him. He grinned.

"Ahh, thank you," he said. His smile reassured the obviously terror-stricken Boy, the one who had been standing over the

231

Kiap, blasting away with the 12-gauge. "You go look after Masta bilong you, eh?"

The Boy nodded and watched him slip his arms into the coat-sleeves. Ludwig turned to face the next assault and looked around at their defences.

The Police Boys had gone to ground, lying behind their Lee Enfields. One of them was watching him. There was one stripe on the Boy's tunic.

"You. Boy," he said.

"Masta?"

"Kiap he die pinis. Na dispela masta he number one." He pointed at himself. "Savvy?"

The Boy's frightened eyes relaxed.

"Yes, Masta," he said, thankfully.

"Name bilong you?" Ludwig asked.

"Giram, Masta."

Ludwig nodded. The Boys looked like they could hold. The nigs would have won if they'd carried their first attack through. They would not be able to sustain the attack against the rifles. He grinned and peered into the gloom, suddenly aware that the rain had eased off, and that all was quiet.

He was thinking that he had made it to safety. Europeans might squabble amongst each other when things were going well. They might talk about "justice" and "fair dealing" with the nigs, then. But when things went badly, then they stuck together. What would matter more in Rabaul? That he had killed a couple of nigs when he was trying to get his work done? Or that he had saved a Kiap from certain death?

The screams erupted ahead of them. He saw the Boys jump with sudden fear.

"Fire!" he screamed back. "Fire!"

The rifles caught them coming through the gap between two huts. The first wave of attackers were the remains of the group that had ambushed the Kiap. They fell, soaking their hands in other men's blood. Looking up, they saw the red-headed spirit, wings seeming to flap from its side as it screamed again at them.

"Fire!"

They fled. The .303 bullets caught some in the back and they died.

232

And, as they fled, the stockade behind Ludwig crashed to the ground and the counterattack hurled against them. Giram and Ludwig turned together, firing together, seeing men go down, but still the attack coming on.

Then the Kiap's Boy appeared from the doorway of the hut where he had dragged his Masta. His fear made his face contorted, like a caricature kanaka. But he swung the 12-gauge again from his hip, blasting into the attacking warriors. The unexpected assault checked them long enough for Ludwig to rally the other Police Boys.

Don Harris woke to what he hoped was thunder. He wanted it to be distant thunder. It was raining again. Thunder was the only thing it could be. It was not shooting across the valley.

He turned to her. Her eyes were wide with fear.

"Thunder," he said. "It's only thunder." But his words meant nothing to her. He smiled reassuringly and touched her forehead. Her eyes watched him, evaluating his response to the noise. He got up and pulled on his trousers.

Sergeant Bukato was already at the door. Don thought irritably that the man must never sleep, but then he felt glad the old warrior was there.

"Thunder, sergeant," he said. "That's all."

But the sergeant's eyes told him the truth. They were black, like twin rifle barrels, the double-snout of a shotgun. His head shook slightly, to deny Don's wish.

"Shotguns, Masta," he said. "Rifles. Revolver."

God damn it, he thought. He can't tell all that from the noise. He's just guessing. He's hoping it's trouble.

Then the noises rumbled again, distorted by distance and rain, but they were unmistakable. The double woof of the shotgun. The flat crack of the .303s.

"Oh, Christ," Don said, and sat down on the bed. She tucked her knees away from him. She was not watching him, though. She was staring at the sergeant.

233

"We go now, Masta," the sergeant said. "Catch the Gafu by first light. Kill them dead."

They both watched the old sergeant. They could see the hunger on his face, the lust for blood beneath his "official" concern for the Kiap. Don looked around the hut. He suddenly wanted to escape. But the only exit led past Bukato. He stood there, aloof, a black avenging angel, wide-nostrilled, high-cheeked, black-bearded, his eyes glinting in the dull firelight.

"We go now, Masta," he said, simply.

"All right," Don said. He sighed and felt all the energy leave his body. He wanted to sink into the earth. But there was no escape. The only exit led past Bukato. He made a gesture to rise, but he didn't have the means to push himself off the bed. He placed his palm against it, but nothing happened. His body had decided not to listen to his brain.

Bukato still watched him. Merin watched him. He smiled nervously at her. He frowned at Bukato.

"Sergeant," he said. "You get the men ready. I'll be out shortly."

Bukato read the fear in Don's body. He shrugged scornfully. He let Don see all of the scorn.

"Me go now," he said. "Catchim Gafu."

As Baranuma nicked the top of the morphine ampoule the shock hit him. His hands began to shake. He clenched his teeth and bore down on the clear liquid with the syringe. He was aware of Nicholls on the floor beside him, trembling, dancing with shock; his eyes crazed and staring, his swollen tongue protruding, bleeding from biting on it. One of the Police Boys was holding the severed artery, his fingers pinching it off, his eyes solemn, watching Baranuma as if Baranuma were the Masta.

He could still feel the kick of the 12-gauge against his hands. The web between right thumb and forefinger was lacerated. The fear that he had not felt during the battle consumed him now.

234

The Masta's left knee was smashed open, and the lower left leg was hanging by sinew. The bones of his right leg were crushed by stone axes. But the steel axe had done the real damage, slicing through the right thigh after it had almost severed the leg below the knee.

And it could have been himself! It was this he had fled from when he was a lad. He had seized the opportunity to escape all the violence that was mapped out for him—son of a Big Man. Already in boys' play he had become aware of it. They snapped spears at one another, flicking them aside with small shields. If you were slow, you were cut. They went with the men to see ritual blood-lettings. Men standing in streams, trembling, blood pouring down their thighs, eyes glazed like Nicholls' eyes were now, refusing to scream as they sawed at their penises with cutting-grass. This he had fled.

And it had been chasing him in all his time with Nicholls. Now it had almost caught him.

So that he felt an immense relief that it was himself crushing the ampoule, forcing his hand to guide the needle to the trembling arm, to slide the needle in, to sponge the arm with methylated spirit and withdraw the syringe. And then to mop the sweating face and rigidly locked chin; the whole time avoiding those crazy, shock-flared eyes. But he also was crying for his Masta, for the man he knew. The stubborn, proud, pig-headed, arrogant, sensitive man he had lived with and fought with and even been drunk with.

He kept seeing the night Nicholls had taken the girl from the nearby village. He found himself between laughing and crying, remembering how the bed had caved in beneath them, and how he had been beating himself as the lovers thrashed and twined together. He remembered the amusement on Nicholls' face when he discovered the hung-over Baranuma that morning in Madang—the look of complicity between two equals that had flowed, for a moment.

And he knew that, when the Masta was dead, then he would no longer be a man of importance. He would be another bush kanaka, another houseboy. Someone else would take up his services; some Rabaul White Missus; a drunk gold-miner. He would be away from the centre of the

235

Power, and away from the only chance to make himself Big in this newly ordered universe.

He unwound the gauze bandages and began to bind the wound that the Police Boy was holding, binding as tight as he could to stop the blood. He knew the risk of gangrene, but he also knew that the leg was as good as lost no matter what happened.

Barum watched the Patrol pulling out of his village and knew that the plan had failed. The second burst of rifle-fire had told him that. If the Gafu had succeeded that would not have occurred. They had lost the element of surprise. He had watched the old sergeant lead his men, snapping orders to them, flicking them with a stick into a shuffling run, rifles held across their chests.

There was nothing anyone could do now but flee. The Gafu would be fleeing, at this moment, to the safety of one of their razorback ridges. Women would be straining under the weight of babies and piglets. The old men would be crying as they shuffled away from their warm huts. The old women would go silently, having seen sons and grandsons killed before. It was time for the people of Parap to be gone from the area, to hide away until the anger of the Sky People cooled and the reprisal raids were finished.

But flight indicated guilt. If they did run, they would forever be implicated in the ambush. Their reputation with the Sky People would never recover.

There was a possibility that the Gafu had been successful, and that they had killed Nicholls. If they had, then the only man who could put all the pieces of the story together was gone. It would be possible, then, if they had the right connections, to become allies with the whites, to work with them to bring the criminals to justice.

He thought with their terms, grinning as he did. The

236

answer now lay with his daughter, and with the man she had been working sorcery on.

He walked to the Haus Kiap. The rain had blown away. The clouds were parting above him and he could see stars. It was an omen of hope.

But he saw no hope when he entered the building. His daughter sat on the stretcher, watching him as he entered. Sitting next to her, his body sagged, arms on knees, hands dangling, head down, was the young Masta.

"What have you done to him?" he asked her.

She shrank back from her father, shaking her head to deny everything. He advanced into the room. The boy looked up and stared at him, not recognizing him, not recognizing anything.

"What love magic have you used? Eh? Adulteress!"

She kept shaking her head. She pushed herself off the stretcher and stood up, waiting for the blow from his clenched fist.

"He is useless to us now," her father said. "He is a rubbish-man amongst his people now. Maybe you will be a rubbish-man's wife."

"No," she said. "I did nothing at all."

He couldn't hit her, he realized. He shook his head and lowered his fist. He prodded the boy with his foot, savagely, derisively. The boy flinched, but did not protest.

"What are we going to do with this? Eh?"

"Father, don't. He is in pain."

"He is! How do you think we will be when they catch up with us?"

She went to go to the boy, but he stopped her with his hand.

"We need to knock him on the head," he said. "He will be able to tell what happened if we don't. He is useless to everyone, now."

Then the boy turned and looked directly at them, one at a time. They could not understand what he was saying, but they could hear the accusation in his voice. She shook her head to deny it and fell on her knees and clasped his legs.

He kicked her aside and pushed himself up and went to the door.

"It was a trap, wasn't it?" Harris said.

Their faces confirmed it for him. He could see it now, coldly, clearly, logically. He leaned on the doorframe and stared out. The villagers had assembled in front of the hut. He watched them and they watched him with equal silence.

"God," he said. "I'm for it now."

The night sky was black and clear and cold. There was no wind. The silent warriors stared at him, bows and spears hanging easily from their arms.

"I've had it," he said, shaking his head to clear it, to drive thought back into it. "The bastards," he added.

Ruefully, he admired their scheme. Just as Morris had been attacked when his force had been divided. They were learning about tactics.

There was a scream and he cringed forward. She collided with him, knocking him through the door. She was shouting at her father. He stumbled to his feet. The old man was coming at him with a stone axe. She threw herself at him again, interceding between him and her father.

The old man hesitated, not wanting to hit his daughter.

The other warriors were coming to life now, at the sign of action. Don glanced at them, then at Barum. He grabbed her hand.

"Come on," he said. He had his revolver in his hand. He stared at it, wondering what reflex had put it there. He fired a quick shot over the heads of the crowd. He tugged her with him and ran into the black night.

The first thing, Bukato had all his men cock their weapons, and then he checked that each safety catch was in place. He had six Police Boys, each with a Lee Enfield .303 rifle. He had ten carriers. Two of these he armed with the two spare rifles that the patrol carried. He had his own rifle.

He glanced back towards the village. He could hear the

238

locals yelling. They would be looting his stores, and that would gain them twelve steel tomahawks. He grunted and jerked his head to his men, pointing them downhill.

During the idle days waiting while the Mastas did their business, he had made it his job to learn the terrain. He had lounged around the fields and estimated the local fighting force, and knew they could bring thirty men after him.

He knew the river crossing was the obvious place for them to hit him, and he figured they would take the track down through the fields, hoping to beat him to it. He also knew the ridge between his own position and the creek crossing. The track curved around it. He knew he could put his men along that ridge and they could sweep the arc of the track.

Some of the carriers were frightened. He urged them up the slope gently—patting their arms and their shoulders, soothing them with his voice. Without packs on their backs they were lost men. The two he had issued with rifles carried them at the high-port, nervous but proud.

He could see the track below them when they crested the ridge. He kept his men crouched low, so they would not show any silhouette. He placed them individually, putting a Police Boy between each carrier. He had the unarmed carriers cut stakes and sharpen the ends, knowing they would not use them in an ambush, but that a man needed something to clench in his hands while he waited.

Satisfied, he moved along his line, checking that each man had now released the safety catch and was pointing his gun down the track.

Then they all heard the urgent slap of bare feet running towards them.

It was very quiet now, and dark. The sky was clear. Ludwig touched a body with his foot and looked around the compound. The Police Boys were dragging other bodies to the perimeter. He stepped over it and walked to the hut.

He stared at Nicholls in surprise. The Kiap was wearing a

239

strange suit of armour, quilted with cotton, that covered the upper body only. The cotton had been ripped by axe-blows, exposing sheet tin beneath.

But the damage was in the naked legs. The Kiap's Boy was trying to clean them, moving almost blindly, mechanically dipping a rag in a pail of water and swabbing the wounds. Nicholls' eyes were wide open with pain, but unfocused.

Ludwig brushed the Boy aside and knelt by the Kiap and took his wrist. The pulse was still there, racing violently, but strong.

"Masta is dying," the Boy said.

Ludwig shook his head impatiently.

"He'll live," he said. He ran his hand across the flesh, watching Nicholls' eyes for reactions. He found the severed artery and checked the clamp on it.

"The Police Boy said there's another Masta, what happened to him?"

"Masta Harris is with the Parap. He's got the rest of the Police Boys, and the carriers."

Ludwig nodded and stood up and gestured for the Boy to go on swabbing. He walked to the door and leaned against the door-post, looking out at the night. He thought that if Nicholls was dead, and the Patrol divided, then it was possible the other Kiap would get it, too. He might yet lead the Patrol himself!

Then the guns across the valley erupted into one short, savage salvo.

It was Barum's track and country, too. He knew he could beat the sergeant to the river. He knew that, if he hit first, then surprise would work against the sergeant's superior firepower.

He wondered where she had taken the young Kiap. Probably to her hut down by the stream. Something would have to be done about them. Right now, though, the important thing was to stop the sergeant rejoining Nicholls.

240

He could hear the river babbling ahead of them, surging with energy. It covered the sounds of his approach. He stepped aside, to let his men run on, nodding to them, touching them as they passed him, smiling to them as they ran.

Feeling for the fight flooded him with excitement, but he kept his mind clear and alert. He checked the last man by and followed him down to the water.

The dark hillside beside him erupted into flame along its entire length.

For a moment he was in the air. For a moment he could hear screaming. It was his own. He twisted, struggling to notch an arrow to his bow. Then he fell forward.

He was dead.

· CHAPTER TWELVE ·

Ravuva Tearooms and Baths was the perfect location for a cocktail party. Bellamy stood out on the lawn and he could look across the harbour, back to the town of Rabaul three miles away. Orange, yellow and blue electric lights swayed on overhead wires, faintly illuminating the throng, casting their reflections in the still waters of the bay. The lights of the SS *Montoro* and an American ship could be seen shining on the black water. He could see the volcanic peaks against the dark background of the water.

"A martini, Masta?"

One of Mrs. Garton's well-trained Boys stood beside him, bearing his tray on an upstretched hand.

"I'd rather have Scotch, if you don't mind," he said.

The Boy stared at him, frowning. For a moment, Bellamy felt a twinge of panic. Then the Boy remembered the correct sequence of actions that followed on this particular request. He turned away and searched the crowd for one of his compatriots, another Boy of at least forty years, in a red lap-lap, with a frangipani flower behind his ear. He waited until the other Boy looked up. He caught his eye and gestured with his chin to the nervous Masta beside him.

Bellamy watched the red-skirted Boy cleave through the crowd, bearing his tray and its bottle of Johnny Walker Black Label.

What he liked about Scotch was its ability to isolate you in a comfortable glow, so you were at peace with your loneliness, so it seemed the natural thing, and all this bright gabbling about him—the women in their mail-order frocks, and those dressed by Chinese seamstresses from *Rabaul Times* instructions; the men in starched shirts, starched shorts, starched minds, with clipped moustaches going grey—all this was unreal, nonsense, the dancers on the deck of the *Titanic* as she went down.

"You've got a Scotch, Bellamy! Where the Dickens did you obtain it?"

He found himself addressed by Howard Roberts, Doctor Roberts, Chief Government Medical Officer, a man carefully grey-haired and grey-moustached. Bellamy's solitude wavered, its glow less rosy at the prospect of company.

"There's a Boy wearing a red lap-lap and an orange frangipani, he carries the Scotch. The Boy in the blue lap-lap and red frangipani has the cocktails."

"What I like is a man who observes the important things in life. Where is the bugger?" He looked across the crowd and located the orange flower. "Hey, Boy!" he bellowed, and held up his hand as if it were wrapped about a glass.

Bellamy watched the Boy return. He accepted a top-up from the bottle.

"Damned well-trained these coons of old Ma Garton."

Bellamy nodded, smiling pleasantly. He stared back out at the water. He kept remembering the earth tremor of that morning. He frowned, wondering what it was that kept the people here tonight from mentioning it at all. The stink of sulphur was still hanging close to the ground.

"I looked in on Patricia," the doctor said, misinterpreting his frown.

"Oh, thanks."

"It's too rough for any woman worth her salt, up here, if you ask me. That's why I sent my missus back down South. They've got too much idle time."

"What did you think of the guria?"

"What? Oh, that. It was a bit stronger than normal, wasn't it? Still, you get used to them."

"Do you think we could be building up to an eruption?"

"No! Never! The tremors relieve the pressure, don't you know? Look, have you heard any more about Nicholls' search for that Ludwig character?"

Bellamy shook his head.

"The Chief's been asking me to bone up a likely 'not guilty owing to an unsound mind' type of defence. It's about the only one he'll be likely to use."

"Do you think he'll defend himself?" Bellamy asked, mildly interested.

243

"I'd imagine he'll get Kelly." The doctor searched the crowd for a sign of the lawyer. "He's got a reputation now from defending Spleen cases. He got Eustace's charge reduced from Unlawful Killing to Assault, six months, which the bloke had already served, waiting trial."

"The Chief's sure he'll stand trial, then?"

"Absolutely. The League of Nations will demand it. A public trial, and we can guarantee that the carpenters will be building him a platform the moment he steps off the boat. I've been looking at the medical technicalities."

"And do you think he'll be found of Unsound Mind?"

"I think he'll be found of quite Sound Mind, and I think he'll hang by the neck until dead and everyone will breathe a sigh of relief: the Coons, the Kiaps, the Coconut Barons, the Citizens . . . even the Chinese."

Bellamy laughed. "That's what I like," he said, "an impartial justice system."

"God, you don't think he's innocent, do you?"

Bellamy shook his head and smiled. "I've been involved in the case," he said. "I know what he did. Did you know about the death of his son?"

"That can be ruled as Inadmissible Evidence. It happened in Uncontrolled Territory. Look, there's damned Johnson, with his pair of lovebirds. Excuse me, Bellamy."

He watched the doctor push eagerly through the crowd to where Johnson was drawing the eager eyes of the men, and the darkly jealous eyes of the women, to his pair of lovebirds. Bellamy felt the return of his loneliness as he watched them, remembering the night he had dined at the Captain's table with them. He drained his glass and looked away.

She had taken Don through the dark to a small hut by a stream. There were pigs in the hut, that were glad to see her and squealed and grunted a welcome. Inside the hut it was totally black. He had given himself up to her directions, letting her hands lead him to a corner, rouse the pigs from it, and make him comfortable.

244

All he had wanted to do was to sink down into the earth. He had a wild idea that he might be able to disguise himself as one of them, and to eke out some kind of existence on the edge of the village, playing the part of village simpleton, the Fool.

Then they heard the guns.

In the dark she scrambled to the door. He had been on his feet, too, shouting at her to come back. He tripped over a pig, that squealed and kicked him. He kicked back, swearing. The door opened and the less-dark sky could be seen, with Merin silhouetted against it. She was calling for her father.

He plunged after her. She ran recklessly, heedless of danger, and was lost to sight. He had floundered after her and then given up. She was gone, running up the creek towards the sound of the gunshots. He sat down and got his breath.

He had heard rifles and they had only fired once. He knew it had to be Bukato, and that he had been successful. Now he would be heading to the relief of Nicholls. Bukato's report would seal Harris's fate. It was all over for him.

He roused himself and walked along the bank of the stream, following the foot-beaten path beside the village gardens. The night was cold and he wrapped his arms about his chest and stamped his feet for warmth. He was thinking nothing, just moving.

He found her amongst the bodies. Great sobs were still racking her body. Piccaninny dawn was near, the sky lightening enough for him to see the results of the ambush. He felt sick in the guts.

Barum and his men had not had time to respond to the fire. They had died almost instantly. A few had dragged themselves away, but had died from loss of blood, sprawled further up the track, instinct pointing them in the direction of home.

She lay across her father's body. He had been hit several times by rifle fire. His eyes were open, glassy, coated with dust. His tongue protruded. His hand was locked on an arrow, the bow shattered beside him.

She was whimpering and crying, mumbling words to the cold body. He crouched beside her and put his arm around

245

her. She wasn't aware of him. She plucked at her father's chest, and beat on it, like an infant demanding attention from an adult preoccupied with some adult business.

The dawn was approaching. Don looked up, and saw the light showing him white fog draining down the river-valley. In the nearby trees, a male bird of paradise shook out its iridescent plumage—purple and gold, a shimmering mat of feathers, a lacy white tail—he preened and strutted in rehearsal of the coming day's courtship.

Don stood up and lifted her from the body. Her grief was subsiding. She let him guide her onto the track. The death of her people had decided Don's actions. If he returned to the village, he would be killed. He pushed on to the river crossing.

As they came up the kunai slopes, threading through the man-high grass, Sergeant Bukato felt elated. He was wet through with the clinging dew, but he did not notice it. The sun was beginning to steam the grass dry. He was forcing his men hard, confident that there would be no resistance on this side. If he were the Gafu, he would be holed up now in the mountains, in some well-prepared, impregnable retreat.

His men, too, jogged confidently. The carriers were different to the fearful men they had been before, clinging in the dark to their sharpened stakes, waiting for the ambush to be sprung. They had discovered their power last night. Now they ran through the grass.

In one sense, he was doing wrong to take them all the way to Masta Nicholls. For, once reaching the village, they would have to turn and come back. The only way out of the valley led down the path they were now taking. Some of them could, right now, be beating the gardens for Masta Harris and his woman.

But the effects of splitting your force had been graphically demonstrated to him. He was not prepared to move any-where—even if the Gafu were all in the farthest depths of the jungle—without his force beside him.

246

He thought about Masta Harris. The girl had obviously worked love-sorcery on him. It happened all the time. It was why the best approach when on patrol was one of simple rape. It was a time-honoured custom, but the Mastas, for their own strange reasons, chose to nominate it as bad. Well, the evidence now existed of what its alternative led to.

If the Masta had simply taken her, then all would have been well. But he believed it was necessary to court her. In courting, a man turned his power over to the woman. There were good social rules that made sure he got it back, after marriage. But they could not cover the awkward time in between.

That was why he never courted. He would never place himself in a situation where someone else had power over him. He was determined that only he would rule his life.

Closing his eyes for a moment, he saw the Lutheran church, the men filing in, the jungle leaning towards it; within the jungle the Germans waiting, rifles already cocked—as he had learnt to do, so as not to advise the enemy of your approach by working the action—and then . . .

He jerked his eyes open, refusing to see it.

Ahead he could see the village defences of stockades and ditches. But the stockade was down.

His men slowed of their own accord. He ran to the head of their line and examined the entrance to the village.

On the ground were women's billums, their contents— vegetables, fruit, bark—scattered. Stacked in an untidy heap beside the fence were the bodies of men. As he watched, he saw a man move, in the distant interior of the village.

He signalled to his men and dropped to one knee. He watched as the man walked towards the gate, dragging a body with him. The man was naked, caked with mud and ash. He assumed it was one of the Gafu, and that he was cleaning out the bodies from Masta Nicholls' ambush. He pushed the safety catch on his rifle forward.

Then the man turned and Bukato saw he was white, with a red beard. The man stared down the road at the troops. Bukato smiled and stood up and slipped the safety catch back.

247

So he was still alive, Nicholls realized.

The thought gave him no particular pleasure. He floated in the cocoon of morphine. The cocoon was slowly unravelling, into a caterpillar, into a clump of caterpillars writhing their way across the plains, intent on a slow, laborious journey to nowhere.

He could sense the jagged, ragged edges of the caterpillars. They were composed of pain. He kept his mind away from them.

A naked white man stood before him, daubed with mud, his raggedy red beard grimy. He held a rifle in one hand and one of Nicholls' overcoats in the other. His penis was uncircumcised. His pubic hair was red. The man's eyes were intensely blue, clear, and mad. Nicholls looked at them.

"You're Ludwig?"

The man nodded.

"Why don't you get dressed?"

Ludwig looked with interest at his own body, then at the rifle, and finally at the overcoat. He appeared to have difficulty making up his mind which should be worn. He frowned and looked down at Nicholls.

"Your Boy gave me the coat, but it's too big," he said.

"Sorry."

"Why did you wear this?"

He pointed at Nicholls' armour.

"I thought I was Ned Kelly."

The joke was lost on the German, who simply stared at him, assuming he was delirious. Perhaps he was. He'd never seen the connection with Kelly before, but it made sense now. Until now he had seen himself always in the light of Greek mythology. Perhaps it would be more instructional to examine that of his own people.

"Australians always celebrate their defeats," he explained.

"You're not defeated." The German did not grasp his meaning. "You're saved."

"Thank you," Nicholls said, with heavy irony.

Ludwig shrugged and came to a decision. He leant the rifle against the wall and placed the overcoat beside it.

248

"Europeans always stick together," he said.

Nicholls nodded. He wasn't quite sure what Ludwig was driving at. And he was more interested in his discovery of the Kelly myth. He glanced quickly at Ludwig. He could not cast him in that story, at all. In Australian history, Germans were the mad explorers who perished in the desert in search of something ineffably transcendent.

Words! He loved words. Maybe they were his downfall? Maybe an intellectual should not attempt to be a soldier. Maybe he would have been better off studying other people's battles, not making his own.

When he next focused on the outside world the German was gone. For a moment Nicholls thought he might have dreamt him. He tried to sit up, but couldn't. He found himself looking at Sergeant Bukato. He smiled when he recognized that stolid, emotionless face.

"Bukato," he whispered. His hand reached out and touched that of his sergeant.

"Masta?"

"Where's Harris?"

He saw the contempt on his sergeant's face.

"The girl turned his head. He weakened himself fucking her. Now they're both gone."

"Oh, Jesus." He lost his drugged objectivity. He felt sudden despair, and now shame, realizing Bukato was eyeing the torn armour. The villagers had used a girl to get Harris.

"The young Masta's finished," Bukato said, simply.

"Dead?"

"Finished, Masta. Out there." He gestured dismissively at the night.

Pain sprang from Nicholls, like pus from a sore. He screamed at it. A hand appeared at his forehead. It was Baranuma's, with a cloth. Nicholls jerked his head and got his teeth onto it, so he could hold onto something as the pain obliterated everything but itself. Through the pain a voice, darkly.

"The nigs have all gone." It was the German. "If we're getting out, it should be now."

He tried to nod in agreement, but had no idea if anyone in the room understood the thrashing of his head. He willed

249

himself still and opened his eyes and focused on them. The sweat poured from his body.

"We go now," was all he could say.

Motion gave him some relief. It was like being an infant, rocking in your pram as your mother pushed it along the road. Lying there, you felt so warm, so secure. If you looked up, you could see her face, distorted in perspective. The world began and ended in that small frame: mother, pram, a child.

But you pushed; for that was your nature. You were like a kitten. Starting in a box in the laundry, warm by the copper fire, you staggered to the edge of the box, then darted back to your mother's fur. Then you stepped outside the box, onto cold stone. A noise somewhere beyond your hazy field of vision sent you scurrying home.

So you pushed. You kept pushing, looking for your own limit. At first you accepted the proposition that other people set that limit, beyond which you must never step. Then you thought there were no limits, that you could push yourself into a new world, one of mythic characters, where you, too, could be such a character. You were like Ulysses descending into the Land of the Dead. You were magically charmed. You could not be hurt.

Then why did you grow so afraid?

And why did you think of Ned Kelly, the great Australian hero who didn't protect his knees?

He jerked his head back and forth, trying to stop the thoughts from pushing him now, finally, to his limit. He did not want to see it. He would rather retreat to the Land of Ordinary People, to live in fog again, not to see with such cruel clarity.

Something dabbed outside his body, sponging his sweat. He opened his eyes. Calmly, not looking at him, Baranuma moved his hand, his lips pursed in a tuneless song, a native lullaby.

Above Baranuma was the cloudless sky. Over his shoulder were the spears of kunai grass. Beside him were other men, bare-backed, flesh glistening mahogany brown, arms holding up the litter on which he was travelling. He closed his eyes again.

250

Immersed in the simple task of sponging the face on the stretcher, he was only half-conscious of their slippery scramble back down the slopes to the river. Mostly, Baranuma relived the battle.

The shotgun hot in his hands, bucking against him, slashing the web between thumb and fingers without his noticing as it recoiled. The violent surge of fear that he had fought against, willing his hands to move in obedience to his conscious mind—and not to that part of it that wanted simply to drop the weapon and flee. That surge which, when overcome, became a wild excitement that lifted him onto his feet and hurled him into the doorway, the gun now an extension of himself, cutting down the warriors.

The Masta's face relaxed. The muscles around the eyes let go and the mouth, held tight to stop itself moaning, fell open. Baranuma returned to the moment.

"Stop!" he called, grabbing the stretcher to prevent forward movement.

The old sergeant, at the head of the Patrol, turned back, frowning, but Baranuma had no time to argue the niceties of who was in charge, or of what section of the Patrol.

"Put the stretcher down," he said.

The carriers obeyed him gladly and stood up, flexing their arms and rubbing the aching joints. Bukato came striding back, his uniform swishing against the kunai grass that crowded them onto the narrow track.

Baranuma knelt and placed his head against the Masta's chest, and heard the breath still there.

"What's going on?" Bukato demanded.

"The Masta's in great pain."

He looked up and their eyes met. He stood up, slowly, not letting go of Bukato's steady gaze.

"We need to rest him," he added.

Bukato looked away from him, at the leaves of the kunai spearing above them. He shook his head.

"Not here," he said. "We're dead meat if we get caught here."

251

"And the Masta's dead meat if we keep going. What good will that do us?"

"We need to cross the river. We can rest in the village. It'll be deserted by now."

"No," Baranuma said.

Bukato looked at him carefully. He looked at Baranuma's eyes, that did not drop from his stare. Then at his mouth and his neck. Then he saw the dried blood on his hands.

"How did you cut your hands?"

"On the shotgun. When it kicked back."

"You fired it?"

"Yes. If we don't stop here, we must stop before the river."

"Did you get any of them?"

Baranuma nodded. "Yes," he said, "I got a few."

Bukato looked at him and smiled.

"I agree that it is too dangerous just here. But I need to make him comfortable again," Baranuma said.

"You've got to hold a shotgun very firmly. You clamp it hard against yourself, and if you're firing from the hip you must keep your hand away from the recoil."

"I'll remember that."

"I'll show you when we get some time."

Baranuma realized that the old sergeant, too, was riding the battle-high.

"We'll stop as soon as we're clear of this kunai. I was caught in this sort of place once before. We'll stop at a stream and you can bathe the Masta," Bukato said.

He turned away, checking his troops.

"Thanks," Baranuma said.

Bukato walked back to the head of the Patrol, lifting his hand in acknowledgement. Baranuma saw the sergeant stop beside the naked white man with the red beard. Words passed between them. He could not tell what, but he could see that the white man was speaking sharply and that the sergeant was replying deferentially—but not deferentially enough. Then Bukato must have said something insolent, for he saw the white man react. For a moment there could have been trouble, but the white man recovered and nodded

252

sharply, storing the insolence in memory, and Bukato walked on.

There was going to be trouble before they were clear of this country. He had seen men who went mad, before. Inevitably they took off their clothes, as if that somehow made it all right to abandon the rules other men lived by.

The stretcher-bearers glanced at him and he nodded. They bent and lifted their fragile load. He looked down at the Masta, whose breath was shallow and intermittent. He put his hand on the forehead. It was icy cold. They began to move forward. Baranuma felt the tears behind his own eyes.

Music. Sad, sweet music. Yearning saxophones and the rustle of wire-brushes on the drum. A girl, dew-fresh, smiling past his shoulder as they moved around the dance-floor. His hands were sweating and he was afraid of staining the delicate dress she wore. He did not know what to say to her. The tune was ending. Couples applauded. He had to let go of her.

The cessation of movement roused him. The rough edge of pain returned. He became conscious of the smell of his leg, and he knew what it meant. The leg was beginning to infect the whole body. In order to save the whole, a part would have to be removed.

He could hear water close by. He was close to the ground, looking up at the patterns cast by a giant tree. It was a ficus, he decided. Then he saw Harris moving towards him, slowly, uncertainly. And he saw the woman at Harris's shoulder.

He recognized her immediately. She saw the look of recognition and glanced down. She wore a bark skirt, beads, and a shirt that must have been Harris's, for he was bare-chested.

"You bitch," he said, softly.

"Sir?"

Harris squatted beside the stretcher.

253

"So, they got you, too, Harris?"

"I'm sorry, sir." The expression on his face was earnest, with the look of someone humouring a man whose mind, and speech, was wandering.

"They used the same bitch on you that they used on me."

"I don't understand, sir."

"The girl."

"She's not involved, sir."

Nicholls saw the look in the boy's eyes. Anger gave him the strength to half-sit.

"She set it up, you bloody fool."

"That's what I thought, sir. But then old Barum attacked me and she saved my life."

He had used too much strength. He fell back. His eyes left the scene, searching in his will for some strength. All he had was anger. He clung to it, like a flame in the dark, and opened his eyes.

"So, you're going to hang onto her?"

"I want her with me. Yes, sir."

"Harris. You fuck them. Everyone fucks them. I've fucked her. But you do not live with them. Is that clear?"

"You made love to her?"

"I fucked her. They gave her to me for a night. They gave her to you for a night, in order to keep you in that damned village, so their allies could chop my leg off."

"I don't think so, sir. She put herself in danger for me. She's cut herself off from the rest of her people . . ."

Nicholls closed his eyes. What did it matter? If the boy wanted to hang himself, that was his affair. If he wanted to take her back to the coast and join the beachcombers and the trade-store owners on the edge of town, with their bastard children, what did it matter? What did it matter if there had been a plot, and it had worked?

Here was the music again. The trumpets were muted. The crooner stretched his neck to the microphone.

There's a rainbow on the river,
romance is calling . . .

He looked across to her table and saw her turn, giving him a profile, and she smiled up at the other man and gave him her hand and rose, her skirt drifting about her. She smiled

254

and held her hand out from her body and the other man took it and they spun onto the floor with practised nonchalance.

Let's you and I go drifting . . .

Nicholls and the other trainees hefted their beers. Their course was finished. Sydney would soon be behind them. The great adventure to the Pacific Islands was about to begin.

· CHAPTER THIRTEEN ·

Gloria found it hard to relate the Rabaul of that day with Rabaul of the earthquake. She almost felt as though she was losing her mind, for she had come to expect the earth to open up, any day now, and swallow the whole town.

"It was only yesterday," she reminded herself. "Yesterday it happened. I was standing on the verandah of that house." She looked away from the harbour, up the hill, trying to locate the building, but couldn't.

And last night, she thought. The absurd cocktail party in the prettiest spot on the whole island. Jennifer, as always now, on the arm of the aviator. Jennifer with her lustrous black hair and her slim figure and her doll-like features.

She touched her own cheek. It felt rough. She tucked a loose strand of blonde hair back under her hat. In her present mood she thought of it as "mousey hair". She stared irritably around the wharf, conscious of the old doctor standing beside her, only just managing to keep his hands off her. He looked like a character from a Noel Coward play, she thought, with his grey moustache and grey wings of hair and his pompous manner of talking.

She could see the Administration man, Bellamy. In true English fashion he had not volunteered his Christian name. She had seen him through the throng at the party and tried to catch his eye. She had heard that his wife was ill, and he had brought her here to Rabaul to the hospital. She had wanted to go and tell him how sorry she was, but Johnson had taken her straight to meet the doctor.

She was beginning to think that they would never leave the island. What had begun as a pleasure cruise had become a prison for her—and all because of Jennifer's infatuation with the bearded pilot. It was their third week in the islands

256

now. The time had gone fast, and been enjoyable. With the pilot they had been able to visit all manner of places the usual tourist would not have seen.

But she was growing tired of the continual presence of the "eyes"—the feeling of being watched at every moment, and not just by the natives. Their appraisal was, in some ways, more honest and bearable than the covetous looks of the planters and Administration clerks. When the infatuation had run its course, and Jennifer was back to normal (except normal for her consisted of falling in and out of love), they would still be faced with the wait for a ship capable of transporting them back to civilization.

It wouldn't be the one waiting at the docks now. The SS *McDieu*. A tiny, coastal trading boat with a dirty deck and a constant stream of dirty water running down its side, down a well-worn rust track. A flimsy plank connected it to the shore. She was watching, with the doctor, as Bellamy and the other passengers for the north coast of New Guinea queued to step onto that plank.

It was as if these people had taken a collective vow, upon arriving in Rabaul, to not mention the earthquakes, to not speak about the smoking volcanic peaks that surrounded the harbour. As if the cocktail party had been called specifically to enable them to forget the day's "guria". So that it had been necessary for the women to wear more perfume than normal, to apply more rouge; for the doctor to preen his moustache with extra vigilance . . .

He touched her. She glanced quickly at him and smiled mechanically, and took a step to the side. His eyes followed her, wanting her. She then felt someone else watching, and looked up to find herself the focus of the burning gaze of a native. She stared back at him, refusing to be humiliated.

He carried a net bag, as they all did, and he was wearing a striped cloth, a "lap-lap". He did look quite smart. The cloth had been washed and pressed recently. His flesh seemed to glow. She smiled at him, and he looked away.

She realized his real centre of interest was Bellamy, who had shown his ticket to the white-coated steward by the gangplank and, satisfied that all was in order, had stepped back to take one last look at the hospital, high up on the hill.

257

He could see the hospital verandah, but it was too far distant for him to make out any figure on it. There was the usual crowd of idle spectators at the wharf, watching the ship load, as they watched every ship load—waiting if they were European for the day when it would be the one that would return them to Sydney. If they were native? He couldn't speak for them, for their obsessive interest in the comings and goings of the ships, and their chatter in which the most distinct word was always "cargo".

He caught the doctor's eye, and nodded to him. The doctor had the attractive blonde girl with him. Bellamy felt a touch outraged that such an elder member of the community would make such a blatant play for a girl as young as that. But this was the Tropics. If he wasn't chasing her he would be secretly sending his Boy out to round up a few village girls.

She looked at him and smiled, and he smiled back, feeling a sudden surge of happiness lift the load of misery that had enveloped him since his meeting with McNicol.

Then he became aware of the native approaching him. A man of middle height. From one of the north coast villages; clean shaven, mahogany brown. He carried a billum. He wore a washed, starched, and ironed lap-lap, and his woolly hair had been artfully combed.

"Masta," he said, smiling a smile of greeting.

Bellamy waited.

"Masta needs a Boy?"

"How did you know?" he asked; as always, surprised by the rapidity of the bush telegraph.

"A cousin of mine, Masta, from Madang, said your Boy died finish."

Bellamy examined him critically. He had the look of someone who knew his way around Europeans.

"I need someone to wash and iron, to make tea," he admitted.

"Ah, Masta," he spoke as if he were the Fairy Godmother herself, Bellamy thought. "Ah Masta, I can do all of these. Washing. Ironing. Tea? India tea? China tea?"

258

He couldn't help smiling at the chap's eagerness to oblige. Of course they would all tell you they could do whatever you wanted, just to get a foot in the door, and then rely upon you either teaching them or beating them into knowledge of the mysteries of Service to a Masta. He stopped smiling and made his face severe.

"When you iron, what is the first thing you do?"

"Ah, Masta. I make the irons hot." He touched the fingers of his right hand to his outstretched left hand, in imitation of a Boy testing temperature. "I have the water ready, too. I have the ironing board, smooth . . ." He pressed down to demonstrate how smooth it would be.

He sounded almost too good to be true. Bellamy stared at his lap-lap. It was an excellent advertisement for his abilities.

"We cast off in five minutes, Mr Bellamy," the ship's officer, at the gangplank, said.

Bellamy looked around. The doctor was leading the girl away, his arm firmly on her shoulder to prevent any other man getting close. He decided to make a decision.

"Can I get a ticket for this chap?" he said, nodding at the Boy. "He's my new washing and ironing Boy."

The officer nodded. "Take him aboard, sir. I'll fix him up when we've cleared the harbour."

Bellamy turned back to the Boy.

"Well," he said, "that's it, then. Come on, hop aboard."

"Masta?"

"Come on. You're hired."

He was conscious of the remains of the crowd, the drifters and the idle plantation managers waiting around for their copra quotations. He remembered the cocktail party and the stiff and formal manners of the "well-trained" Boys there. He heard, again, snatches of dialogue.

"Damned coon didn't take the cigarette from his mouth when I spoke to him, so I knocked it out."

"They don't even step aside now, when you walk towards them . . ."

". . . Chinese are no better. They want to educate their brats . . ."

He smiled at his new Boy.

"What's your name?"

259

"Alo, Masta. I am Alo."

He held out his hand and the Boy stared at it, and then took it and pumped it, eagerly, up and down, like he was pumping water.

"Thank you, Masta. Thank you."

They smiled at each other, both knowing they were doing more than seal a contract. The attention of the whole of the wharf crowd was now on that handshake. Bellamy withdrew his hand, with difficulty, and put it on the Boy's shoulder, and escorted him up the gangplank. The officer nodded to them, his face unreadable.

"Outstation Johnny," someone in the crowd remarked. "If you're in the bush long enough you stop seeing the colour of skin. They should be sent back to civilization every now and then, to remember how to act with the damned coons."

In the clear, thin air of late afternoon, under the shadows of the casuarinas, fear seemed to breathe. The trees made the only constant sound. Their needles whispered back and forth as the evening breeze picked up. The men worked silently, feeling the fear all around them, conscious of the darkness closing in, and within that darkness, the possibility of attack.

Occasionally there was another sound: the girl sobbing sporadically. She sat outside one of the abandoned huts, clutching in her hands a few of the scattered objects left when the villagers had fled: a child's carved bird, a wooden flute. She sat amongst broken billums that had proved too heavy when laden with household effects, that had been left for the pigs to break apart in their eternal quest for food. The door behind her had been firmly shut with boards, and two staves had been tied across: magical staves that would bar the entry of unwanted spirits that now could come to plunder the deserted village.

From the edges of the village a few abandoned pigs were creeping slowly back to inspect the new occupants and

260

decide if they were worth cultivating. The pigs behaved as if nothing had happened. They grunted with annoyance when a Police Boy crossed their forage path to lay out a trip-wire, or clear a sight-line.

Smoke was collecting again from the fire Baranuma had kindled. It combined with coming darkness to make the air dense once more. The fear they had all felt when the first scouts had entered the village and burst open huts at random, to discover no ambushes, no warriors, no spears, was intensifying. They needed an attack to clear it, to turn fear into action. But the air grew heavier and the shadows more pronounced, and nothing happened.

Except that Ludwig ordered Baranuma to make up a pan of hot water and sat down in the middle of the village, oblivious to everything, and scrubbed himself free of all the accumulated ash and mud of his travels. He called Baranuma in to wash his back and to pour the water over his head as he lathered. As he washed he even began to sing to himself. Around him Bukato's men stacked up an improvised stockade; the old sergeant measured out distances to reference points; the carriers butchered a pig, with a great deal of squealing and grunting from both parties; and Nicholls hung on to his life in the stretcher. But Ludwig washed and sang and dried himself before the fire and bawled out Baranuma—as if he had reached a decision to no longer act the part of the mad German, and instead had determined to be a Kiap of the First Order.

In the end Don could not resist his manic good humour and had volunteered some clothes for him. Ludwig had accepted them as his due—and in accepting allowed his eyes to meet Don's, so that Don had seen he was not suddenly sane; the eyes were blue and staring, but cunning too, and they jumped around the village, ceaselessly, catching every movement of tree and leaf.

Finally Ludwig had unfolded Nicholls' own folding chair and settled it beside the fire and bawled again for Baranuma to bring him whisky.

Now he sat on the chair, feet up on a biscuit tin, with a glass of Nicholls' whisky nursed in his hands, wearing Harris's trousers and shirt.

261

There was nothing for Don to do. In Bukato's face was open contempt for him. Baranuma watched him uneasily, not knowing how to play a Masta who had acted so un-Masta-fully. In the end he had to withdraw, playing out his version of Ludwig's charade. Watching as the Patrol made ready for a fight, and admiring the skill and efficiency of Bukato as he checked his defences.

Other evidence of Bukato's skill lay back down the track. Don had found it necessary to carry the girl past the bodies—some already scattered by pigs, by the skulking dogs—that lay stretched along the road where Bukato's ambush had been sprung. She had tried to fall on her father's body, and mourn him, but they did not have time to indulge her feelings. Fear drove them on to the village, anxious to have themselves defended before night fell.

Don had tried to help Baranuma make up the kerosine-tin of rice and tinned meat for their evening meal. The pig would have to wait until next day—if they survived the night. There was not enough time to get it cooked. But Baranuma was obviously on edge, with a mad Masta usurping his own Masta's place, and this lost Masta trying to do a Boy's work. Don realized it was better that he not interfere, and he had finally withdrawn to sit beside the girl.

Where he sat now, as darkness fell, watching Baranuma give the mess of food a final stir and pronounce it ready.

Don's attention strayed to the Boys, the carriers. He had not paid any attention when they ran down one of the larger pigs in the village. He had heard it squeal when they butchered it. They didn't have the expertise that Barum and his men displayed and it took three blows with a steel axe before the beast was silenced.

Now it lay, seemingly forgotten, in the middle of the open square at the village's centre. Don wondered vaguely if they shouldn't hang it up and gut it and let the meat draw for a while, or at least drain off the blood—though by now it probably would have congealed in the veins. Instead, they left it there and turned their concentration to collecting as many rocks as they could and dumping them on the fire. Beside the fire they built up a pile of large, thick leaves from various plants.

262

Other Boys constructed a little house of bark and shovelled dirt up near it.

They all worked with intense concentration. The humour of the chase was gone. This was serious business. They tested the heat of the stones from time to time. Occasionally one would stand by the pig and prod it with his toes.

Don forgot them and turned his attention back to what Nicholls had said about the girl.

Nicholls claimed to have "had" her. Was he telling the truth? Don wondered. Or was he simply trying to shock him? He remembered the conversations with Nicholls, where Nicholls teased him about the native women, insinuating that he had his way with many of them. Don glanced at her, in her mourning like a child as she clutched at the toys that were all that was left of her family. He had no way of knowing if what Nicholls said was true. He realized how much on his own he was. There was no one to advise him now. The only person he could converse with was Nicholls, and he no longer trusted the older man—not just because of his attempt to manipulate Don's feelings, but because he had failed.

Don realized that, despite the feelings he should have for the hideously wounded man, he felt anger and contempt. Because of the way Nicholls had presented himself—as the acknowledged expert, as the tactician, as the wily elder statesman . . . as Ulysses himself. He shouldn't have let it happen, Don kept telling himself. He should have seen it coming. The man was a fool.

Ludwig saw Baranuma stand away from the food at the fire.

"Hey, Boy," he called. "How about it? How about some food?"

Don saw Baranuma stiffen, and he saw, on the camp's perimeter, Bukato stiffen too. Don saw the two natives stare across the fire at each other. Whatever passed between them, he could not read. But the result was that Baranuma filled a plate with the mush and walked past Ludwig, who watched him the whole way, and knelt beside Nicholls' stretcher where it was placed under the lee of the men's house.

Ludwig laughed to himself and poured some more whisky. Bukato watched from the shadows. Don felt the tension in the air.

Nicholls eyes were open. His face oozed sweat as fever and infection raced through him. He looked at the plate and managed a weak smile for his Boy. He shook his head.

"I'll just have a whisky," he said.

Baranuma nodded and stood again. Don wondered how much Nicholls was aware of the undercurrents in the camp. He watched Baranuma walk back to Ludwig's place by the fire and, unsmiling, hold out the plate.

Ludwig took it, giving him a sly grin. Baranuma held out his hand.

"Masta Nicholls would like some of his whisky," he said.

Ludwig smiled mockingly and held out the bottle.

"My compliments to the Kiap," he said. "His whisky is excellent."

Baranuma nodded and took the bottle, stopped at the pack of utensils and found a glass, carefully measured out two fingers, recapped the bottle and set it down well out of Ludwig's grasp, and took the drink to his Masta.

Ludwig giggled and spooned the food to his mouth; eating, Don realized, like a man who has seen no food for a week.

Fear had returned, clothing her, as of old, and Merin didn't want it. Her father had been all-powerful. He had rescued her, once, picking her up out of the stream as she stumbled away, fleeing the people of her brutal husband. Now he was dead. But he had not died like men ordinarily die. He had died from contact with the Sky People. And now the Sky People were in disarray, scurrying to build themselves shelter from imagined attacks.

Where was her mother? Where was the infant brother who had made her life miserable with his ceaseless demands? She wanted him back. She wanted her mother to be nagging her, sending her to do child's chores to humiliate her. She ran the carved wooden bird against her cheek, feeling the indentations it made, remembering how her father had lost himself in an afternoon, cutting it out for the amusement of his new child, the son, in whom he took so much delight.

And what did her man think now? Nicholls would have told him about the night she spent in his bed. Was that why he squatted beside her without saying a word? Without even glancing at her? She had no way of guessing how the Sky People reacted to infidelity. Were they as jealous as ordinary men? Would he beat her?

And what did it matter? It came to her that she, like her father, was now dead. Her family was gone. Her valley would never be the same again. And she was captured by the Sky People. They would take her somewhere with them, perhaps to a mountain top where the Baloose would come down out of the sky and carry them off. Perhaps they would take her with them to the Land of the Dead. Perhaps the arrangements that their helpers were now making were to guide the Baloose in.

In the night, they waited for attack. Firelight lit the camp. The Boys who were not on sentry duty were now preparing the pig for cooking. They cut off its belly fat, but that was the only dressing they did. They dragged it to the little bark house and pushed it inside and arranged the strips of fat around the body. They closed the house up with more bark, and piled bark on top of that.

Still they worked silently, all seeming to know what was called for. Don had the feeling that each man, in his own way, wanted to carry out whatever ceremonial acts were necessary in his village, but that each was conscious that he was amongst strangers who did not share his form of worship. In order to offend no one, no ceremonies were carried out. They would simply cook the pig, like a Masta might. But they were sad, remembering how it should be done.

The stones glowed redly. Men dragged the fire aside with

265

sticks and dropped the thick, green leaves onto the stones. Smoke billowed forth immediately. Baranuma stood to one side, watching closely. He held a bucket of water in his hands. He watched the first man lean forward and grab the bark-covered stone. He ran, juggling it, to the bark oven, and dropped it against the little house.

The next man gave a yell and grabbed his stone and ran with it. Now life was returning to the Patrol. The transport of stones became a test of endurance. Each man, in turn, grabbed up the red, glowing object in the thick, green leaves and, smoke billowing from his hands, ran, or staggered when the rocks were heavy, to the bark oven. The stones rained around it, building up on all sides until it was covered. Men swore and shook their hands and looked at the blisters on them. Their mates laughed and teased them and they shook their heads ruefully. Occasionally a man would shout and drop his stone and plunge his hands in Baranuma's thoughtfully provided bucket.

Even Bukato came out of the shadows of his self-imposed sentry duty to watch. He smiled at the antics and shook his head at their silliness.

When the stones were all heaped into a glowing mass, the Boys piled dirt around them. The smoke still poured up through the dirt, but less and less of it as the pile of earth mounted higher, until only angry wisps of smoke escaped from the incongruous little volcano in the middle of the village. The Boys fell silent, staring at it, each one remembering a similar oven in a village far away. They turned, one at a time, and returned to their duties, or to bed, leaving only Bukato, Baranuma, and Harris.

The three men glanced at each other, realizing they were alone. Don nodded to them, and they gestured in reply. Bukato walked back to the camp perimeter. Baranuma took his bucket over to the stretcher, where Nicholls lay. He set it down and searched in the medical kit and brought out the ampoule of morphine.

Don hesitated, and then walked over to join him.

The firelight bathed Nicholls' face. His eyes seemed to be growing darker as the flesh on his face tightened. Don watched Baranuma ration the morphine, knowing there was not enough to last the distance back to Mount Hagen. He watched the parched mouth open and accept a little water.

Then Nicholls' eyes turned to him and held him. He knelt down beside Baranuma, who glanced at him and slid the needle into the slack flesh of a protruding arm. Baranuma removed the needle and tenderly bathed the spot where it went in, and then began to bathe the leg with long, slow, tender strokes. Don suddenly caught the first whiff of decay from the shattered, weeping limb. He turned away and looked at the steaming mound of rocks and earth.

"Harris. You, Sergeant Bukato, take ten Police Boys, and get ready for Patrol tomorrow."

Don looked into his face. Nicholls paused between phrases, summoning up the energy to keep talking. His eyes wandered past Don to the sleeping Ludwig, aware of the power-vacuum that existed, and aware that only action would fill it.

"Yes, sir," Don said. He smiled. He would be able to keep the girl here, in her village, safe from contact with the outside world, safe from retribution from her fellow-countrymen.

"We can base ourselves here, sir," he said.

He glanced around the village, his eyes coming back to her, hunkered down by the hut, crying no longer, staring unseeingly ahead.

"The girl will be coming to Rabaul."

The thin voice whispered to him. He stared down at the hot, luminous eyes, opening his mouth to protest. He felt a pause in the rhythm of Baranuma's gentle massage.

"She is a material witness, possibly even an accomplice, in an attack on a Government Patrol."

"But we've lost no one, sir."

"That remains to be seen."

Don flushed, realizing what he had said.

"Is that the only reason you're taking her, sir?"

"What's your relationship with her?" Nicholls demanded of him.

Don stared into the fire, watching the play of flames and coals. The voice needled at him, like the wind in the casuarinas. But he could not bring himself to say what he had come to realize: "I love her".

267

"She's come to mean a lot to me, sir."

"Even though I fucked her long before you did?"

"I don't necessarily believe you, sir."

In the silence, the coals of eyes stared at him. He felt his strength gathering and he stared back at them, no longer ashamed of himself and his feelings.

"I love her," he said.

Now he felt an enormous strength, a power, like he could fly. He grinned at the dying man, who stared back, unwavering.

"You can sleep with them, Harris. You can let them live in your house. But you can't marry them. Is that clear?"

He did not reply. He stared into the eyes and they turned away from him. As they turned he saw, lurking within, guilt, even shame. He took advantage of it.

"I hear what you're saying," he said. "And I want you to know that I find your motives very suspect . . . sir. You have the power to do what you want, but I, and she, will be returning to Madang when all this is over."

"And I . . ." Nicholls tried to sit up. His servant stroked him down. Nicholls hit at him to be left alone. "I shall make a full report of your cowardice, Harris. I'll see that you are sent a long way from these islands, if you do not do what I order you."

"And what is that . . . sir?" The final word cut heavily with sarcasm.

"You and Sergeant Bukato will administer some Native Administration before you return. Before you run off with your lady love."

"What do you mean by Native Administration?"

"Teach the bastards a lesson they'll never forget."

The whisper ceased. The eyes closed. Don glanced to Baranuma, who felt in the medical kit by the stretcher and pulled out a small mirror. He placed it under Nicholls' nose and they both watched the twin streams of condensation.

Don got up and looked around the camp. He saw she had not moved.

If only the bastard would die, he thought, staring back down at Nicholls. If he dies in the night . . .

For a moment, Don saw himself returning to this village,

268

this valley, with the girl, with his "lady love". He remembered the Patrol Officer at Mount Hagen and his scheme to grow coffee. That was possible. Anything was possible. All it hinged on was the death of the man on the stretcher.

He walked to where she sat and looked down at her. She glanced up at him. He could not read her expression. He remembered how he had first suspected her of setting him up. If he could have spoken, he would have accused her then.

But she had warned him of her father's attack. That wasn't the action of someone who wished you harm. It was a deliberate defiance of the man she was now mourning, the father she had presumably loved.

Perhaps she had been his unwilling accomplice — or even duped by him; her own feelings for Harris used without her knowledge.

He knelt down in front of her, still watching her eyes. He smiled at her. She smiled back hesitantly. He needed to believe she was innocent, or he would go crazy. He needed someone to trust. He reached out and took her hand in his.

They stared at each other, their hands clasped tight. As they stared, they both could smell the aroma of cooking pork.

Ah, God, it was good to be warm! To be full of food! To be drunk on whisky! To be the only white man of any consequence. He was king, now, sitting on the usurped king's throne. The Boys scurried at his command, Ludwig saw.

The fire warmed him on one side only. He turned the chair so he could toast the chill down his right flank. He could see the stretcher on which the Kiap lay dying. Already he could smell gangrene in the air: that and steaming pork.

He looked further afield. The white boy was kneeling by the ugly Highlands woman, with his head in her lap. Ludwig felt a rush of outrage. As leader of this expedition it was up to him to maintain correct standards from his men. Rudi should be brought to task for this behaviour.

269

No, it wasn't Rudi! What was he thinking?

And there it was, as sharp as the day it happened, unfaded by time and jungle and dirty fighting. He sobbed and jerked his head to drive it away. He closed his eyes, but it was still there. He opened them again.

So tall and lean and brown, well-muscled, wearing only a pair of shorts, as red-haired as his father. He looked up from the sluice-box, grinning from ear to ear.

"Walter!" Ludwig called. "Walter, my boy!"

But the boom of the hurtling stream was too much for them to hear. His heart surged with love for his boy as he stood up, holding aloft something to show his father. And Ludwig knew what it could only be. What it had to be. It had to be colour.

Like an infant who has discovered something of exquisite wonder—a leaf, a dead beetle, a feather—some part of the miracle of the world, and now is holding it up with excitement, with love, to his father's approving eye.

Walter stumbled forward, as if he had tripped. On his face there was an expression of shock, surprise, and then mortal fear. His hand grabbed behind him, and the second spear took him in the side, caved him in, and he crumpled, screaming soundlessly against the pounding river, and Ludwig had his rifle up and was firing blindly, without knowing he was firing, while the Boys screamed and ran willy-nilly, throwing themselves to the ground, leaping across the stream, only to fall and be swept to death as the cannibal bastards now came out of their hiding places. So it was only Ludwig standing against them, jamming another magazine into the Mauser, killing as many as he could.

The body that had been his son fell backwards. It tried to stand again. It tried to crawl. He could see its open mouth. But it was too deeply hurt. It began to crawl, but it had lost sense of direction and was scrabbling backwards. He shouted to it, but he could not stop it. It slid into the sluice race. He saw a momentary return of consciousness, of realization of the mistake it had made, and its eyes called to him, pleading for its father to help. But the water was too strong. He was gone.

270

He crouched by his Masta, watching the thin, steady flux of breath. Nicholls' hand had found his and was clutching it tight. There was a sound from near the fire and he looked over and saw the other white man clutching the arms of the Masta's chair as tightly, knuckles white. He could see the wild, staring eyes as the man rocked his head back and forth, as if he were trying to deny some accusation. He felt the pressure in his hand change and looked down.

Nicholls had stored up some more strength and was now ready to expend it. He tilted his head towards the fire, towards the chair.

"Get Bukato and Giram . . ." the voice gave out. Baranuma waited, watching the condensation on the mirror flicker and then return. Nicholls' brow furrowed and he found more breath. "Arrest him . . ." He jerked his head again towards the chair where the other man had now fallen into a stupefied sleep, the sleep of a drunk. "Irons," the thin, wavering voice said. "Arrest him in irons. Charge of murder."

For a moment the condensation vanished from the glass. Baranuma leaned close to the mouth. Then it flowed again weakly, then gaining strength.

Baranuma looked around the camp. The other Masta was sitting beside his woman. Now she had her head in his lap. He stood up and walked past the fire, locating Bukato where he sat, cross-legged, with Giram and two other constables.

Bukato looked up and nodded to him. They must have been discussing Police business. Baranuma squatted next to them.

"The Kiap has ordered us to arrest the madman," he said. "He has asked you and Giram and me to do it."

Giram looked startled. Bukato studied Baranuma's face, then looked across to the Kiap's stretcher, and then to the dozing man in the chair.

"We are to put him in irons," Baranuma added. Bukato's eyes came back to him. Now the sergeant was startled.

"The charge is murder."

Bukato stood up and hitched at his belt. Giram looked to him and he nodded to the young man reassuringly.

271

"All right," Bukato said. "You know where the cuffs are, Giram."

As the constable went to get them Bukato looked again to Baranuma. His face was troubled, but it was excited, too.

"He said put the white man in irons?"

Baranuma nodded, knowing what Bukato was thinking. They had never seen such a thing. The arrest of a white man was always carried out apologetically, if a native constable was present. The Kiaps preferred to do it by themselves.

Bukato nodded to himself and jerked his head to Baranuma and they walked to the chair, approaching it from behind. Giram joined them.

Ludwig seemed so helpless that Baranuma felt a pang of guilt at doing it. He was drunk and full of food. Baranuma felt Bukato and Giram looking at him, and realized that the old sergeant was waiting for the signal. Baranuma was in charge.

Baranuma nodded and they grabbed the white man's arms.

He came awake, feeling them on him. Fear sprang in his eyes. He opened his mouth to protest.

"In the name of the King," Bukato said solemnly, "I am arresting you on the charge of murder."

"Nigger bastards! Leave me alone, you coons!" The oaths shattered the uneasy peace of the camp. He thrashed wildly, but the sergeant wrestled the irons onto his wrists.

"You monkeys! Apes! You cannibal bastards!"

The sergeant's expression was strange. He moved slowly, eyes turned inwards. Baranuma winced at the flow of insults.

"What the hell are you doing?"

They looked up and Harris was standing by them, staring in astonishment.

"The Kiap ordered it," Baranuma began.

"Nicholls? He ordered what?"

"That the man be charged with murder and arrested, Masta." Baranuma was uneasy. He glanced to Nicholls' stretcher, but his Masta made no movement.

"You! Harris! Stop these gorillas, for God's sake!"

Harris stared at the wild-eyed white man and then at the distant stretcher. Bukato looked up at him solemnly.

272

"We should gag him, Masta. His noise will bring the warriors straight to us."

Baranuma could see Harris's confusion. He knew that, on Patrol, the white men liked to act as if they were in perfect accord on all matters of policy. He could see the argument in Harris's eyes. Harris turned and looked to Bukato and nodded.

"Very well," he said. "Follow the Kiap's orders."

"You're a fool, man! Can't you see what's going on? Do you want these niggers running the show?"

Harris stared at the white man. Baranuma could see him thinking. Then he looked again to Bukato and again nodded.

"Gagging him seems like a good idea," he said.

"You'll live to regret this! You nigger-loving little . . ."

Baranuma saw the white man's eyes pop as Bukato got the cloth around his mouth. He saw the teeth bite into it. Bukato and Giram picked him up, his heels drumming on the ground, and dragged him across the dusty village floor and threw him into one of the huts.

Harris stood the chair up again and looked around the camp. He poked the coals together and placed another log on the fire. Baranuma waited for the Masta to request something, but Harris stared at him, vacantly, preoccupied, and merely nodded.

"Good man," he said.

"Thank you, Masta."

"The girl would be more comfortable in a hut, I think."

"Yes, Masta," Baranuma said.

He could see Bukato standing by the hut where they had thrown the white man. He was methodically sealing the entrance with boards.

"Help me make up a fire, will you?" Harris asked Baranuma.

"Yes, Masta."

They broke away the magic staves from the door of the hut she was leaning against. She did not seem to notice them. Baranuma kindled a fire on the central hearth. He watched the young Kiap carry her in and wrap her in a blanket. She stirred and he murmured to her. Baranuma felt suddenly embarrassed and backed out of the hut.

273

He went to the dirt oven. Smoke still seeped from it. He could feel the heat coming through the dirt. The smell of pork was nostalgic rather than attractive to his appetite. The thought of eating it made him faintly nauseous. But it reminded him of his own village and his brothers; of nights when the cold winds came off the mountains, slicing into your kidneys and you crouched closer to the fire and tried to tell stories that would keep the spirits away, and turned to the fire, first one side, then the other, keeping warm.

The thought of his brothers and his cousins strengthened his resolve. He looked across to where Bukato crouched by the fire, staring at his hands as he held them out to it. He was lost in thought, and Baranuma could guess what the thoughts were about. It was the first time the sergeant had done this to a Masta. He was starting to realize that the structure of the world was not as ordained as he thought it was. He was starting to see that the Europeans did not have it all their own way.

Baranuma placed his palm on the mound of earth, feeling its temperature. The pig would be done by mid-morning. He turned and walked to where Bukato sat.

He picked up the whisky bottle as he passed the pack. Bukato glanced to him as he approached and he handed it to him. Bukato looked at it in surprise. Baranuma nodded, giving him a quick, reassuring smile. Bukato took a swig, and coughed. Tears sprang to his eyes. Baranuma took the bottle from him and expertly tossed down a shot.

The camp was quiet again. The boy was in the hut with his woman. The Kiap was asleep. The sentries were back at their posts, staring into the jungle, waiting for the attack that both Baranuma and Bukato were certain would not be coming.

"These are strange times we live in," Baranuma said.

The old sergeant nodded, feeling the whisky steady his nerves.

"I remember when the whites first came to the Highlands," Baranuma said. He glanced at the empty chair, but neither he nor Bukato moved to sit in it. "We were too busy fighting amongst ourselves to stop them. Just like these people.

274

Black men need to work together if they are to keep their Power."

Bukato looked over at him, his face beginning to relax, letting a hint of the strange excitement he had felt begin to show.

"When they came, my father lost his eminence, because he would not take a risk. I took a risk, and now I am making my fortune." Baranuma stared, musingly, into the fire. "What can you do, now you are a sergeant? Where do you go next?"

Bukato jumped at the sudden directness of the question. He looked away, uncomfortable, and finally shrugged.

"You've reached the top, haven't you? Black men don't become Patrol Officers. Black men wander around the bush, doing the whites' murdering for them. In the end, if you don't get an arrow in you, or end up like him over there . . ." he gestured to Nicholls with his chin . . . "they get rid of you when you're too old to work."

He had the sergeant's attention now. The aging face watched him apprehensively.

"There are a lot of pigs in this village," he went on, seemingly at random. "The villagers won't be back for a long time; perhaps never. The Kiap has ordered you and Harris to do some 'Native Administration' with your guns. The pigs will wander off, or they will die. It's a shame to see such fine pigs die."

Bukato looked around the village. He was beginning to pick up Baranuma's drift.

"My people come from Mount Hagen, where the Patrol Post is. It would not be too difficult for some of them to walk here . . ."

He watched Bukato closely. The sergeant listened, cocking his head to one side. He stroked his chin. Then he began to smile. He reached out his hand.

"Give me another shot of that whisky," Bukato said, "and let me hear your proposition."

275

Merin slept, curled in peace like an infant. The fire in the hut sputtered as Don stretched his hands to it for warmth. When he was a boy he had done the same thing, staring into the coals for witches and dragons—safe, then, in the solid, four-square walls of the North Adelaide home.

Nothing made sense. He needn't be here. He need not be faced with the decision ahead of him. It was possible to get back to Mount Hagen, to find Johnson waiting there with his plane, his popsies, his silk scarf and pirate's beard; to get in the plane and fly down through the mountain valleys to the coast. On the coast you would wait a day or two for a boat that would get you to Rabaul.

There you were safe. You did not have this decision staring at you. You would sleep within four-square walls, not curved walls that made you think you were inside an animal's gut—or in the open where you would be totally exposed. Yes! In the morning, a Boy brought you tea and toast. You got up and went down to the wharf and there was the boat, probably the *McDieu*. It took you to Rabaul.

You went to the tearooms, perhaps. Or you had a drink in one of the pubs. You strolled past Chinatown, or through the Botanic Gardens. You met the Administrator at a reception. And you heard the mournful, bass sound of the steamer's whistle and picked up your grip and walked onto the broad, white gangplank.

A steward saluted you and asked if you were comfortable. The ship's orchestra played a foxtrot. You asked a girl to dance . . .

No. He shook his head. It wouldn't be like that.

He reached out and stroked her hair. Rough, crinkled. On her cheek the first tattoos. How would that go, back in Rundle Street? No, she would wither and perish in that alien environment. And so would he.

What would happen? They would reach the coast. They, of course, would be shunned by the "pukka" whites. But a few would still associate with them. Bellamy, for example, and his missus. They were all right. He would make the acquaintance of that world he had ignored up until now—

276

schooner skippers, traders, prospectors, labour contractors. The men who lived half in the native world and half in the white world—who sneered at Patrol Officers and disdained ever to visit Rabaul—unless they infringed some Administrative order and went under detention.

They would settle down amongst them and their Marys. His half-caste kids would play with theirs. And with the Chinese. He would take up drawing again, and painting. Perhaps they could live off the tourists.

And there was agriculture. Too little of it was practised with any degree of science. They could grow coffee, or even vegetables for the towns. Wasn't there someone attempting to start a dairy at Lae? That was enterprise. That was where the real business of the future lay—not in "Native Administration"; not in gold.

But first he had to face the decision. As it was, now, Nicholls was going to hang on. His will was unbeatable. It had to be admired. Darwinian survival was at work here. If, after five years in the bush, a Patrol Officer was not dead, then he must be made of iron, and he would survive. But the inflexible iron that kept him alive drove him to act as Nicholls was now acting—to risk other lives simply to keep his own will imposed upon the Patrol. He would take the girl with him to Rabaul. He would leave Harris in Madang. If Nicholls had not already slept with her then someone in Rabaul would be bound to. All she had to barter was her body. If some white did not take her into his concubinage then she would go to jail. There she would have to barter her body to native warders.

She would not know what had happened to him. Nicholls would not tell her. Nicholls would work to destroy him in her eyes, and in the eyes of all the world. She would assume he had deserted her.

So the choice was to obey Nicholls, or not to obey him. If he obeyed, then Nicholls would not "report" him. If he disobeyed, then he would probably lose his career. And if he obeyed Nicholls, he would lose her.

He thought of Nicholls, lying on the stretcher, cheeks sunken, eyes glowing, breath whispering in and out, flickering moisture across that glass. He thought of the glass, the

277

nostrils above it, the life flowing there. In his mind a hand appeared and clamped the nostrils. Another covered the mouth.

The body began to heave and buck. The eyes stared. The feet thundered on the ground, waking the camp. The hands were hastily removed.

The hands took the syringe and measured out the remaining morphine. Nicholls' eyes were closed. The hands slid the syringe into the flesh of the arm. Nicholls murmured, but the prick of the syringe was familiar now, and welcome. The pain-racked body relaxed. The hand returned to the nostrils. The moisture still flared on the glass. The fingers pinched off the flow. The body did not react.

He got up, shaking his head, and stepped to the hut entrance. But he had forgotten where he was. In order to leave, he had to go down on hands and knees and crawl through the narrow opening. He emerged and saw that Baranuma and Bukato were still by the fire, staring thoughtfully into it. Or, at least, Bukato was, while Baranuma talked to him. They had Nicholls' whisky bottle.

At first he thought of bawling them out. But then he realized he was no longer against them. When he got to the coast with his bride they would be in the same social register.

Baranuma looked back, and then glanced at the bottle. He was caught. Don smiled and walked over to them and squatted beside the fire. He picked up the bottle. They watched him. He nodded to them.

"Cheers," he said.

He tossed down a shot and handed the bottle to Baranuma, who took it, watching him all the time, not knowing what to do with it. Bukato relieved him of it. Bukato, too, watched Don. He nodded and lifted the bottle.

"Cheers, Masta," he said, and drank.

"Masta," Bukato said, handing the bottle to Baranuma, who drank, "Masta, we must send a runner to Mount Hagen, as soon as it is light."

God, Don thought. Why didn't I think of that? It's the first thing that should have been done.

"Yes, Masta," Baranuma added. "Send someone straight

278

to Mount Hagen, so the Baloose can come for Masta Nicholls."

"How is Masta Nicholls?" he asked, aware of the tension in his voice — and also aware of some other tension in them, that he put down to fear.

"He's very strong," Baranuma said. "But his wound is very bad."

"The leg has to go," Bukato growled.

Don saw Baranuma wince. He realized that Baranuma's fate was inextricably locked with Nicholls. To be the Personal Boy to such a powerful Patrol Officer was to control a lot of local power. To be Personal Boy to a cripple was a totally different proposition. And to be Personal Boy to a dead man would return him to the jungle.

But if Don was to survive then Nicholls had to die.

"He might not make it through the night," Don said, carefully, and Baranuma looked straight to him. "We must face it," he added. Then he reached out to comfort the other man. "You have done a splendid job of saving him, so far. I will write it up in the Patrol Report."

"Masta Nicholls will write the report," Baranuma said, stiffly.

"Masta Nicholls has ordered you and me to find the villagers?" Bukato asked Don.

Don stared at him. What was going on here? He felt he was on the edge of some native conspiracy. But he was dealing with the two oldest and most trusted men in the Patrol. They had not said anything untoward. Was it their manner?

"I beg your pardon?" Don said, frowning at Bukato's knowledge of Nicholls' order.

"I told him the Kiap's order," Baranuma said, hurriedly.

"The order was for my ears only."

"I'm sorry, Masta. I spoke without thinking."

"We should send Giram," Bukato said. "He is a reliable man, and he is fit. He should leave at first light and not stop until he has told the Kiap at Mount Hagen."

Don nodded. Giram was a good choice.

"Fair enough," he said. He picked up the whisky bottle again. "You organize him, Bukato."

279

"Shall I choose the men for our punitive Patrol, Masta?"

He looked carefully at Bukato. Something glimmered in his eyes. He spoke carefully, but his face was eager. Bukato had scented blood.

"Are you planning on killing the villagers?" he asked.

"If that is what the Kiap orders."

Too careful. Too hooded. And the eyes too eager.

"And if I don't order it? If I order, instead, that Masta Nicholls is too sick to lead, that I am leading, and that we all return to Mount Hagen as fast as we can?"

"It would be a mistake Masta."

He had caught the glance between them.

"Why?"

"They must be taught a lesson they will not forget."

What was it in the sergeant's face? It was both pleasure and pain—a memory and an anticipation. It was, Don realized, the sex of killing. That was what attracted Bukato. That was what made him so efficient a soldier.

"I think it would be best if we got some sleep," Don said, standing up. "We will decide in the morning."

Baranuma glanced towards Nicholls.

"It's all right," Harris said. "You go to bed, Baranuma. I'll sit with the Masta a while. You need sleep."

"Thank you, Masta," he said.

"Good night, Bukato."

The sergeant hesitated.

"Good night, Masta."

They read each other. He saw Bukato acknowledge that Don knew his motives, and he saw that Bukato was not ashamed of this knowledge. Bukato assessed Don as a man assesses an equal—not a Masta—and an equal who is standing in your way.

Don nodded, picked up the whisky bottle, and walked over to Nicholls. He grabbed the chair as he passed it and took it with him. He planted it at the head of the stretcher and settled himself in it. He took another swig and, as the other men walked to their sleeping spots, he stared down at the sleeping face, and the breath flowing in and out, flickering like a silver flame on the cold, dark mirror.

"If it were done, then best it were done quickly." Who

280

said that? he asked himself. Someone in Shakespeare; but he couldn't remember which play. Nicholls undoubtedly could. He remembered himself as a schoolboy, reciting lines of poetry that he understood emotionally, but the meaning of which grew slippery as the teacher struggled to "explain" them. "Is this a dagger I see before me?" Wounds that were "poor, dumb mouths".

He began to remember the magic and the violence of the plays; the thunderstorms that always raged when emotions grew hot, when blood was about to flow.

But the night here, on the mountain, was calm and cloudy. There was a faint moonlight.

He had played Brutus in the school production of *Julius Caesar*, because he'd had a well-fed, solemn look about him. He could recall dusty boards and the yellow stage-lights and his clumsy movements as he tried to remember his lines, remember his actions, remember how his voice should sound. It was all so false.

Nicholls, though, had immersed himself in all that. It was Nicholls who spoke of Ulysses and Telemachus. Don had forgotten everything he knew about that story. But Nicholls had explained how Telemachus was Ulysses' son who went in search of him after Ulysses had got lost somewhere in his wanderings. Nicholls wanted to interpret their relationship in those terms. He was a man who liked to approach life obliquely, through literature. Yet, somehow, he had managed to live a far more exciting life than you'd expect from a bookworm.

And now he was dying. But he was dying with a great deal of fight. He had felt the tensions in the camp and tried to resolve them by having Ludwig arrested. That had been the original purpose of the Patrol, that and to chastise the Parap. Both purposes had been fulfilled. He could return to the coast.

Don, though, couldn't return. There had been that fatal moment of weakness when Nicholls had been attacked. His body had let him down. He should have sprung from the bed, tossed her aside, strapped on his revolver, and run to rouse Bukato—it should not have been Bukato who came for him.

281

The thought of it physically hurt him. He shook his head to deny it. He drank more whisky, but it would not go away. The dying man lay before him.

Once you have done something, then you have changed the course of your life forever, he thought. Every act from then on has been modified by that act. I cannot take it away. I cannot go back. I have no choice but to do what is necessary.

He got off the chair and fumbled through the medical kit, and found the morphine ampoule. He looked up, but no one moved. The village was as quiet as a churchyard. Once he did this act, then his life would be modified again. But if he didn't do it, it would take yet another turn—a turn where he was forced, against his will, to slaughter more of the villagers, and where he lost his woman. The death of Nicholls was no more than the chance to save those people's lives. He had to do it.

"It's all right, Harris. There's no pain."

He had been down a long way, further down than he had been before. He could smell roasting flesh. He remembered that Ulysses had slaughtered rams before his descent into the Underworld. The trench had run with fresh blood. The hungry shades of the dead had gathered to drink that blood. Who had made this sacrifice for him?

Then he smelt the rotting leg, and it roused him. He remembered where he was and opened his eyes.

Harris was kneeling beside him, preparing him a syringe. He spoke to let him know it was all right—knowing how little morphine they had, and how far there was to go.

Harris jumped and fumbled the needle and glanced at him, quickly and guiltily. Then he set it back in the medical kit and turned. Nicholls saw him force himself to act as if everything were normal. Nicholls' instinct for conspiracy and ambush rang its subconscious alarm.

282

"What are you doing?" he asked.

"Nothing, sir. Preparing your medication."

"Ludwig is safe?"

He nodded and glanced to one of the huts. "In there, sir. The Boys arrested him. I had him gagged, as he was making enough noise to waken the dead."

He flushed as he spoke the last phrase, and looked quickly down.

"It didn't waken me."

"I didn't mean you, sir. There are a lot of dead people in this valley tonight. I guess it's on my mind."

"The girl?"

"She's fine, sir."

"Arrest her."

"Are you totally mad, Nicholls?"

The anger drove out whatever it was Harris had been hiding. The boy glanced around and then glared at him, pushing his chin forward pugnaciously.

"She's done nothing except sleep with me, and that, some-how, has offended you, sir." He used the title like a knife.

"Ambush . . ." Nicholls used each word carefully, conscious that he did not have many more, and wanting to save the Patrol from whatever perfidy she could manage when he next slipped into unconsciousness. "Barum, her, the Gafu, clearly linked."

"You're not well, sir. Your mind is confused."

This time it was Nicholls who felt the anger. He pushed himself as far off the bed as possible.

"Arrest her. Go and wake Bukato and bring him here. If you won't lead this Patrol, then he will."

He fell back, his chest heaving, his heart pounding. He looked inwards, and when he looked outwards again he could see Harris's hands over his face. He could see Harris's face. It was calm, almost dreamlike in expression. It smiled at him.

"I couldn't have done it cold," Harris said. "But I can do it now."

The hands clamped over his face.

283

This was it. Although his mind was clear, something was shrieking, like an alarm, a siren. It tingled in his armpits and down into his groin. Nicholls thrashed against his hands, almost like the girl bucking with passion. Don felt the same surge of power through his body as when he pressed into her.

He had seen the sex in Bukato's eyes when he spoke of killing. He realized he had seen it because he had recognized it in himself, and that was why he was here, in these mountains; not because he was forced, by a power greater than himself, to do this act; not for his own pleasure; not for the greater good of the people in the valley, or the girl; not even for history. It was simply for himself.

This valley. These mountains. Where man had established a foothold and shown himself superior to all other life by his ability to kill. The mountain people believed they, too, were in the grip of a power far greater than themselves, and they had no option but to do what was "necessary". To redress the old wrong with another death.

He let go. He was breathing hard, as hard as Nicholls whose eyes stared, whose mouth gasped like a fish out of water, sucking air into his dying lungs.

". . . bastard. Finish the job," the dying man said. He looked up and saw Don, glaring anger at him, that and contempt.

Don realized that the contempt didn't matter any more. He stood up and shook his hands. He stared at them.

"Get Bukato," Nicholls gasped.

"Get fucked," Don said.

He laughed. He doubled over and put his head in his hands, laughing and crying. He glanced at the man on the stretcher; the red, staring eyes like the eyes of a jungle spider watching him.

"Why the hell should I listen to you?" he said. The eyes blinked. The fire was going out. They were receding again into the security of unconsciousness. "If you want to kill every man, woman, and child in this valley, do it yourself. Just don't give me any of your Classical shit to justify it. Just admit you want to kill. Just admit you want my woman for yourself, you slimy bastard."

". . . don't understand . . . Law is bigger than us. We must punish . . ."

"Law is as small as the men who administer it. Go to sleep, Nicholls. I won't try and murder you again. I'll get you back to Mount Hagen, and there you can write up your Patrol Report, and we'll let the Administrator decide if I deserve to continue in the service."

The eyes had closed. Pain had returned, drawing the cheeks in, the brows together. Don wondered if he should give him a little painkiller, but decided against it. Let the bastard suffer a bit, he thought.

He walked away from the fire. He shook his head, his shoulders. He felt as if a great weight had been lifted from him. He didn't have to kill anyone. He didn't understand why, but somehow he had come to these islands with that intention. Well he had done it once already. He might have to do it yet again before he was safely out. But he didn't have to go out of his way to look for the opportunity.

What an ideal spot this was for a European who wanted to try his hand at killing! He had every sanction for his acts! He was upholding Law, not breaking it. As long as he could keep abreast of the lawmakers—so he only killed, in those times and places, those people it was acceptable to kill; unlike poor Ludwig, who had got confused and thought he could do it anywhere, any time. No. You had to study very carefully, but the payoff was enormous. A licence to kill.

Now he remembered the decision that had brought him here. He remembered the Exhibition Hall at the South Australian School of Art. He remembered the axe in its display case. He remembered the erotic combination of sex and death there, in its ornamentation, in all the art works displayed for the unsuspecting students to browse through— not knowing what it was that thrilled them about this stuff. Well, in that way he and Nicholls indeed were similar. They both had distrusted the scholars and come to find out for themselves. In that way, he and Nicholls were related.

He saw the mirror on the ground and picked it up. He held it under Nicholls' nose. The breath was still there. He turned

Nicholls' head to one side and drew the blanket over his shoulder, tucking him in like a sleeping child.

He was conscious, again, of the smell of cooking pork. He pocketed the mirror and walked over to the mound of earth. It had ceased smoking. The soil was too hot to touch. He stared at it, thinking of the roasting animal inside. He smiled and turned towards the hut where his woman lay sleeping. He realized how tired he was. He walked across to his own stretcher and sat down on it.

He glanced once more around the camp, swung his feet onto the stretcher, and was asleep.

· CHAPTER FOURTEEN ·

Diary: 23rd May, 1937

Nicholls used to do this and I could never understand why. Keeping a journal was simply a bore for me; an Administrative necessity. I mean, if I look back in this book I can find entries on arrests and inquiries and statements by indentured labourers and lu-luis and whatnot. They're like the ingredients of a fanciful romantic novel. Yes, they are like the bits you find in Rider Haggard, but not strung together by any novelist's imagination. The raw details. They became part of Patrol Reports, collated, typed up, submitted to an office somewhere in Rabaul, and forgotten.

But they changed me. I didn't realize it at the time. I filed them and thought I'd forgotten them, but they were building up inside me, to the point where I actually began to behave like them, like the people I was arresting.

If some North Coast lad thought his uncle was seducing his fiancee, then he'd wait till the uncle went down to get in his canoe, follow him, and spear him. Then he'd pretend someone from further up the coast did it. There'd be a fight. Some woundings, probably another killing. That killing would have to be paid for, and so it would go on.

Enter the Kiap. The Kiap stops it. He takes all the statements. He doesn't have to be a detective. The Boy admits the killing. Why shouldn't he? That's what life is all about, after all. The Kiap takes him away, to Salamaua or Rabaul. The Boy stands in the dock and listens to words he can't understand—but he stares at the incredible machinery of the Kiaps. He is awed. He is on the most fantastic trip of his life. He gets five years' hard labour. He gets three meals a day and his ulcers cleaned out, tablets for his worms. He learns Pidgin from another inmate. He learns how to cook the Kiap's way. When he gets out, he's an indentured houseboy. His career never looks back.

And the Kiap goes back on Patrol. He takes more statements. His back gets more bowed, his brow more deeply furrowed. It all is poured into him, every drop of murder, rape, kidnapping, intrigue.

287

He tries to mediate. He tries to explain his concept of Law. He goes on filling up with it.

Until it becomes too much for him and he starts to unload it. He unloads it like this, in his journal. Like Nicholls would do—scribbling far into the night. Like I'm doing, right now. Scribbling into the morning, as the Patrol waits around me. Waits for Nicholls to make up his mind about living and dying. As Bukato tries to decide if he will obey me or start his own insurrection. As Baranuma and the Boys cook the pig they killed yesterday. As my woman mourns her dead father.

Until there's even too much for the journal, and the Kiap snaps. He begins to act it out. Every murder story he has listened to. Every fight over a woman. Every bit of intrigue.

Nicholls tried to stop it happening to him. That's what his Classics were all about. He kept trying to turn his life into literature, in order to stop himself doing what he could feel was rising up inside him. Or maybe so he could let himself do it, and not feel bad about it—because Ulysses killed people, but always with good reason; just as Macbeth thought he had good reasons; as Brutus thought he was doing good.

But he never thought about love, did he? That's interesting, because the Literature he kept quoting was always loveless. His Conrad story. Where was the love in that? His myths of power and fighting. He never mentioned Mr Somerset Maugham and his stories, but I bet he's read them all, and believes fervently that Mr Maugham's view of "love" is the correct one.

So, I guess I'm a "young puppy", eh? I've made a fool of myself over this girl. Christ, I don't even know her name. For all I know, I could have made her pregnant by now—I should have, the amount of sperm I've put inside her . . . there I am, talking like a New Guinean: sperm, shit, blood, guts, maggots, death. But it's all around us, how can we not be affected by it?

"The Kiap wants to talk, Masta."

He stared up from the page, blinking, trying to remember where he was, even though he had been immersed in the inner details of it. But writing had removed him from the present. He looked up at Baranuma's kindly face, written over with concern and care for his Masta.

"He's awake?"

Baranuma nodded. "He's very weak, Masta. Last night I think he suffered a setback."

288

Harris nodded, not being able to think of anything to say to that. He stood up and rubbed his knees. He was getting used to sitting on the ground, like a native. He closed his journal and looked around. He placed it on the ground where he had been sitting. Baranuma looked down at it.

"Masta Nicholls had me keep his journal wrapped up, in a pack. Shall I look after yours, Masta?"

He examined Baranuma closely. He was getting the distinct feeling that the Boy had decided that Nicholls was going to die, and was now trying to ingratiate himself with Harris. Was that too cynical a construction? Or was he simply a Boy who needed a Masta?

"Thank you," he said. "That won't be necessary. The girl is still in there," he pointed to the hut. "She is still mourning her father. Take her some food."

"Yes, Masta."

He nodded to the Boy, who hesitated, with something else to say.

"Masta?"

"Yes."

"You were asleep at first light, but Bukato was awake. So he sent Giram."

Oh, shit, he thought. It slipped my mind entirely.

"He did what!"

"I'm sorry, Masta. But you did say, last night, while we had our whisky . . ."

That's right, he thought. Remind me of my complicity.

". . . you said we should send Giram to Mount Hagen."

"What message did you give him?"

"That the Kiap was badly wounded. That the Baloose should come."

There was something else, but Baranuma was not going to say it.

I'm learning fast, Harris thought. I'm learning how to be a Kiap. I'm starting to smell conspiracy at every turn.

"In future, Baranuma, I will make the decisions."

"Yes, Masta."

He glared at the Boy, who looked away guiltily and went to arrange some food for the girl. Harris walked over to

289

Nicholls. He put his hand on the chair, but did not sit in it. He stood, looking down at the Kiap.

He stared into the eyes and saw what Baranuma had seen.

Nicholls had given up.

The eyes had the confusion you saw in old people's eyes when their minds were wandering. The lips moved, but for a long time no words came. When they finally did they were thin and reedy.

"Are we moving out?" Nicholls asked, uncertain and confused.

"I'm resting the Boys, sir. I want to move out tomorrow."

Nicholls nodded, his eyes far away. Then Don saw them focus on a thought. Nicholls frowned and stared at him, concentrating on speaking clearly.

"You've arrested that girl?"

"She's in the hut."

"She's no good, that one. She led me on. She'll lead you on."

Again, he didn't reply.

"Trust Bukato . . . good man . . ."

The eyes closed.

"I've sent a runner to Hagen, sir. Young Giram."

The head nodded. The lips opened, but no words came out. Then there was a sound. He leaned closer.

"Sorry, sir. What did you say?"

". . . Kelly."

"The solicitor, sir? In Rabaul?"

". . . his knees . . ."

He waited, but there was no more. He felt a cool, clinical detachment, watching Nicholls die. The ramblings intrigued him. He would have liked to have understood them.

Feeling pain meant that he was still alive. And the pain was incredible. It absorbed all thought into trying to keep it at bay. Yet the more he concentrated on it, the more he felt it. He needed something else to take him away from it.

290

They must be saving the morphine for the journey back.
That would be hell. He would not think about it.

He would think about centipedes. Caterpillars. No, a
kitten. Warm and secure in a box by a fire. Blue eyes staring
at the world with wonder. Stumbling on its unsteady feet,
watched by its self-satisfied mother, the sound of her purring
vibrating the room. A little boy kneeling down to see them
there, to see the kitten beginning to stumble forth in its
quest; to see its mother watching with pride, with love.

It wasn't pain that swept him. It was anger. It was the
intense rage of an infant; wordless, screaming, shouting as it
twisted its small body. It hurled itself at some other object,
large, amorphous, and mothering, that soaked up the raging
blows, so that the rage was useless, for it did not effect any
outcome.

The small boy picked up the kitten. It mewed in protest.
Its mother's purr became an inquisitorial mew. But she
recognized the boy and relaxed. The boy carried the kitten
into the bright daylight. The boy carried it to the drum of
water.

"I don't want you," the boy said. "I wish you were dead."

The kitten flailed in the water. The boy watched it. Then,
seriously and slowly, he sat on the side of the drum. He
dangled his legs in the water, feeling the bottom with his
toes. The kitten clung to his leg. Gently, he disentangled its
claws and pushed it underwater. He felt it thrashing in his
hands. The feeling was intensely exciting.

So that he would not get his sleeves wet, he put his feet on
top of it and pressed it to the floor of the drum.

"I love you," he said, experimentally.

And there was that rage again! It had never left him. It
had lain there through all the years, until now. Now it was
discharging. It was centred in his legs. It was a rage as
intense as pain. He felt it pressing against the soles of his
feet. It flailed and scratched him. It bit at him. He was
infant, boy, and man.

And then it was gone. No rage. No pain. No feeling. He
drifted like a cloud. The images receded into his bloodstream.
Peace came drifting down his veins. Peace, blackness, but
not death. Not yet.

291

The drab brown bird scuttled along the branch, twisting its head inquisitively. It looked down into the clearing, straight at her, and Fogeo inspected it. The bird turned its head to the other side, examining her from the perspective of its other eye.

Female, she thought. You're just like us. Our men kill your men for their plumage, for beautiful feathers to decorate themselves. Then they dance for us, like yours do. And you hide in the branches, hatching the young: girls who will grow up as drab as yourself, and boys to boast and fight and flaunt themselves. And they go on being killed because they're so beautiful. But they won't stop being beautiful, will they?

The bird tensed, listening, and turned to look across the other side of the clearing. Granite rocks thrust up through the humus kept the jungle from closing the sky out. The second woman stopped by the rocks and looked around uncertainly. She was younger than Fogeo.

"Over here," Fogeo called, keeping her voice low, watching the green walls of the clearing for movement.

"There's no one around. You needn't worry."

"Old habits are hard to give up."

They smiled and tentatively embraced each other.

"How is he, your husband?" Fogeo asked her.

"Dead. He got to the Sky God and wounded him, but the Sky God killed him."

They stared into each other's face, into the grief.

"And your man?"

She nodded wearily. The younger woman reached down and stroked her thighs.

"He went after that black devil, and he, and all the men with him, died."

They leaned against each other, bringing their foreheads together.

"My daughter has gone with the other one," Fogeo said.

"She is still alive?"

Fogeo nodded and straightened up. She looked for the female bird of paradise. It was still watching them.

"Merin did well," she said. "Perhaps she did too well. She

292

may have turned his head too far." She tapped her head to signify madness.

"If only the sorcery had worked on Nicholls."

"It may yet. The wound he received would have killed a mortal man."

She led the younger woman to the rocks and they leaned against them, arms about each other, looking up to the sky, from where the troubles had come.

"But, whether he lives or dies, we must continue. Whether he lives or dies they will come after us. Whether he lives or dies we must get back our own lives."

"Half our men are dead."

"I asked you to come here to beg a favour."

The younger woman did not look at her. It was not easy for Fogeo to admit that the Power had left her, wife of the Biggest man in the valley. She realized how her loyalties had become his loyalties in the years of their marriage. This woman beside her, wife of Barum's rival, was a blood relative, yet Fogeo identified herself with the people of her husband.

"You have a good hiding place, along the ridge. You can sit out their attacks. But us, we have nothing . . ."

"You would like to come with us?"

They faced each other again. Fogeo nodded.

"How would your men feel?"

"We don't have many left. Those that have survived are . . ." she hesitated, not knowing what was wrong with them. "The Sky People have worked sorcery on them. They are not men any more."

The younger woman nodded. "It's the same with us. They saw too much when they attacked Him. They saw the Power too close."

"So, you will consider my plea?"

"Of course I will. The women will agree. The men will have to agree. In times of emergency, other people have banded together. Mingled their pigs, and shared their land. What is more important, for women, pride or life?"

"Thank you," Fogeo said. She couldn't see properly and brushed at the tears. She felt a hand on her cheek, a gentle caress, and didn't look up. She heard the younger woman leave.

293

When she did look up, she was alone in the clearing. She looked again for the bird, but it had gone. She turned, and then saw it at the far end of the clearing.

And there, shimmering on another branch, was a dazzling rainbow of plumage. He strutted along, and fell, clinging with his claws, cascading his brilliant tail as he spun on the branch. Upright he let her see the purple on his chest, and turned again, spreading out the mantle of colour.

And the female watched him, bright-eyed, critically eyeing the display.

Fogeo wanted to laugh, but found only tears. He was too like her own man. She turned away, blind, for the track.

Ludwig had been right all along. The knowledge of his rightness gave him no comfort, though, because he was trapped in it. He had been unable to communicate it to Nicholls—who was too immersed in his own legend—or to Harris, who was too immersed in the girl. And now he, Ludwig, the only European left with a clear mind, was a prisoner of the nigs.

He had seen that the whole history of the island pointed towards this collusion between the Australians and the nigs. Once the nigs had reigned supreme. Then Europeans had reigned supreme. Now, for a brief moment in history, the Australians—who were neither one thing nor the other—had the upper hand. But they were simply a force in history. History would move on. The nigs were using them to re-establish their own position.

Except that nothing stands still. Whatever happened, the nigs were now out of the Stone Age and loose in the twentieth century.

He was caught in the middle of it. His arrest was one incident that would push them to their next step. He could not believe Nicholls had ordered the arrest, for Nicholls had more sense than that. Yet the nigs had said it was Nicholls' doing.

294

And his arrest had broken the unwritten law that established white supremacy. A nigger had been allowed to assault a white man.

The ramifications stretched all the way from the hut in which he lay in his own shit to the coast, to Rabaul, and from there to the rest of the civilized world. All the way to the League of Nations, the League of pious missionaries led like puppets by their American masters.

A shadow blocked the light from the doorway. He wrestled himself around to see what was happening. A figure crawled in and squatted on its haunches, watching him.

It was the old sergeant. He moved into the interior of the hut, moving fluidly, like a snake. He kept his eyes on Ludwig. Ludwig twisted his head to keep watching him.

The old sergeant stopped and settled his bum to the ground. He frowned. He leaned forward and stretched out his hand. There was fear in his eyes.

He cuffed Ludwig, quickly, snatching his hand back. He watched for a reaction. Ludwig glared at him, but couldn't move, couldn't speak. The old nig grinned and this time hit him across the face with all his might.

The fear was gone. He studied his fist and looked again at Ludwig. Ludwig shut his eyes, not wanting to watch the next blow.

But it didn't fall. He opened his eyes and the sergeant was standing up. He walked around the hut, looking at the ornaments and the knick-knacks left hanging when the occupants had fled. He found something in a corner and grunted and squatted down to examine it.

When he stood up again, Ludwig saw it was a crude stone axe. Its handle was too short for battle. It had been left behind in exchange for one of the good, steel axes, probably. The sergeant grinned at him and walked to him and stood there, swinging the axe back and forth and looking at a spot behind his ear.

"Bukato!"

The sergeant jumped.

The young Kiap crawled into the tent. He had taken the precaution of getting his revolver ready.

"Get to hell out of here!"

The sergeant stared at the Kiap, hefting the axe, watching the gun barrel.

"I mean it, sergeant! Drop that axe and get out."

The axe fell beside his face. The sergeant looked down and dropped to his hands and knees and crawled out.

The Kiap knelt down and undid the gag. Ludwig gratefully flexed his mouth. He jerked his hands, to suggest they be undone. The Kiap shook his head.

"You're still under arrest," he said. "I want you back in Rabaul, standing trial for your murdering."

Ludwig got his mouth working.

"I saved this Patrol. You know that," he said.

"I'll testify on your behalf. Have no fear, Ludwig. I'll see that you get a fair hearing."

"What about the niggers? The sergeant?"

"I'll speak to him. Everything's a bit tense at the moment. But once we move out it'll settle down."

"How's Nicholls?"

"Dying."

"So, you're in charge?"

The young Kiap nodded, looking at the axe.

"For God's sake . . ." what the hell was his name? "For God's sake, you're a white man. We're on the same side."

"I'm on no one's side, Ludwig. I'm representing the Law. If Bukato had killed you, I would have prosecuted him with the same rigour you'll be prosecuted."

"And I'd be dead, either way."

"It was your choice, Ludwig. You needn't have come into the mountains. You needn't have killed anyone."

"I'm a prospector. I go where the gold is."

"You're a killer, and you go where the killing is. I'll get you some food."

Harris wrinkled his nose and looked, with disgust, at Ludwig's soiled clothes. Harris's borrowed clothes.

"What do you expect, when I'm treated like a nigger?"

"I'll get you cleaned up," the Kiap said, but the look of disgust was still there. In the young Kiap's eyes, he was lower than the niggers.

Ludwig watched him crawl back out of the hut, taking the axe with him, his revolver holstered. Ludwig closed his eyes.

296

He was reaching the point where nothing mattered any more. He had pushed as far as he could. Now fate was pushing back.

The Patrol had collapsed into anarchy. Here it was, midday, and the only activity was around the cooking trench, which was now being opened in preparation for a feast of stolen pig. Bukato watched.

He didn't object to the stealing of the pig. But he did object to the almost complete loss of discipline, even of common sense. The new Kiap wasn't interested in keeping guard, or in pursuing the villagers—and they could be no further than half a day away. He wrote up his journal. He watched the dying man. He was like someone on holidays, like one of the tourists who came sometimes to Madang and hung about, watching men at work.

As was all the camp. Police Boys lounged about, smoking, laughing. Carriers stayed asleep by their fires. The looted packs still lay open, contents strewn about.

The life of the Patrol had gone. Its shape. Its firmness. Its comfortable security.

He watched the young Kiap crawl from the hut. He was not afraid of him. He had his measure and knew that, in a showdown, the Kiap would hesitate to use force, and that would be his undoing.

Bukato was intensely excited by what had happened. He had never considered killing a white man before. But now . . . it was easy. In a sense he could practise on Ludwig. That was no harder than the killing of the pig yesterday.

Baranuma was very smart, a very clever man. Bukato had acquired tremendous respect for him, watching him manipulate the Patrol so that his own interests always came out on top. But Baranuma's weakness was his fear of violence. He had shown he was capable of acting in an emergency. But he couldn't coldly and logically plan it out.

297

Baranuma thought that he could manipulate Harris into doing what he wanted. But Harris's strong point was his refusal to go all the way with Baranuma's schemes. Bukato could see him growing more and more suspicious of Baranuma.

Now that Nicholls was on the point of death, the balance of power was tilted Bukato's way. Once Nicholls was dead— or at least indifferent to life—and Ludwig was trussed up, then only Harris stood in the way.

Baranuma might not like this new twist to the plan. Too bad for Baranuma. He had begun it. He had put the possibilities into Bukato's head; had questioned the meaning of a sergeant's life. Baranuma would have to go along with it. Events were overtaking him.

The young Kiap looked around the camp, frowning at the disorder, but obviously incapable of taking action against it. Then he saw Bukato and his frown deepened. He walked over to him.

Bukato came to attention and waited.

"What were you doing in there, sergeant?"

"I heard movement, sir. I thought he was trying to escape."

"And the axe?"

"He was trying to get it, sir, to help him escape."

The Kiap held up the axe.

"Would you call this a killing axe, sergeant?"

"No, sir."

"Why not?"

"The handle's too short. There's no balance in it." He reached out for it. In surprise, the Kiap gave it to him. He demonstrated how it would not swing easily. "See the binding, sir. It is too frail. I think someone made this axe for the amusement of a child, to give him something to play with."

"Play at killing?"

"Probably, sir."

The Kiap frowned at the axe. He looked up at Bukato, sharply.

"Sergeant. I want us to understand each other. I am in charge of this Patrol now that Kiap Nicholls is wounded. I am not going to administer any 'Native Administration'. I am not going to kill people. Is that clear?"

298

"Yes, sir."

"Tomorrow, when the men are rested, we will begin the trip back to Mount Hagen. We will go as fast as we can. We will not be stopping for rests. We will not be sidetracked into fighting."

"Even if we are ambushed, sir?"

The Kiap stared him down.

"Especially if we are ambushed, Bukato. I want to get Nicholls to a doctor as quickly as possible. Is that clear?"

"Yes, sir."

"Now, take yourself off duty. Get your energy back for the walk out of here."

"We may be attacked here, sir."

"By whom? By women and children? You killed all the men in this village."

"Yes, sir."

Now the Kiap looked away from Bukato's clear, level gaze.

"I want to write up my journal. Dismiss, sergeant."

"Yes, sir."

The Kiap walked away. He had suddenly acquired again the load of worry he seemed to have shrugged off that morning.

Baranuma looked on as Boys tossed dirt and cooled stone from the oven. They were excited now, talking as they worked. The gloom that had descended last night was gone. The aftershock of battle was receding. One of them knelt down and flicked away the still-hot bark with his hands. Someone laughed at him.

And there was the pig. They threw away the last of the bark. It lay there, its flesh black. Its head faced him, eyes burnt out, lips blackened and drawn back, so the teeth and tusks protruded fiercely. One of the Police boys drew out his bayonet and stepped up to it and slit it open.

Steam burst out, and the smell of the cooked intestines. The Boys crowded forward, picking up leaves to serve as plates. The Boy with the bayonet was kneeling in the hot ash, slicing away, up to his elbows in guts.

Someone else attacked from the rear, with another bayonet, expertly slicing off a leg. Someone tried to grab it from him. There was a shout of protest. The leg of pork flew through the air. Other hands grabbed it. One of the carriers had it. He sprinted away, juggling the steaming meat.

A Police Boy brought him down. There was a loud cheer. The leg of pork kept on moving. Back at the carcase, the other hindquarter was sliced away, to accompanying cheers. Baranuma was on his feet, grinning hugely.

"Over here!" he yelled. "Get it to me!"

He had no idea why he called for it. He didn't want to eat the stuff. But then he had it and was running. Someone swore at him and grabbed him. He twisted free, laughing. He hurled the leg of pork to someone else. It didn't matter who. For a moment it looked like the Police Boys would take on the carriers. But now it was every man for himself. The pork was greasy with fat. It slid from man to man. One carrier managed to get a leg, get his knife out, and slice off a handful. But that was snatched from him, with a shout of triumph, by someone else, who gobbled it down on the run.

He looked up, and saw Bukato on the outskirts. Bukato was studying the state of play, seriously, intently. He felt Baranuma watching and nodded to him. Then he dived into the melee. Men swore at him. Someone kicked him. But he grabbed the leg of pork and charged through them, shouting wildly, crashing towards the outskirts of the village.

Until the burliest of his Police crashed him against a thatched hut. They both fell through the wall, fighting for the leg of pork. They were lost to sight, then the Police Boy emerged from the entrance, on hands and knees, pushing it before him. Before he could get up, Bukato dragged him back in.

As they fought a carrier snatched it away.

The Kiap came out of the woman's hut and stared in amazement. He looked over to Baranuma, shrugging a question.

300

"Bush kanakas," Baranuma said. "They go crazy when they smell pork."

The Kiap stared at them, and then began to laugh.

Diary: Same Day, PM

I think of all the things I have seen, the game of football with the pig was the strangest. The circumstances had something to do with it. After what we have all been through in the last couple of days, it was a tremendous relief. I guess it was a return to normal. Man can't be all bad if he can laugh at himself.

The pig is eaten now—though they have not touched the head, which lies where it was cooked, black and blistered, with a fixed, hideous grin. Behind it is a charred skeleton, a few scraps of blackened meat, and the debris of the oven. And the Boys loll about the camp in a state of satiety, of food-induced stupefaction. The image of that camp oven, the steam, the smell, will remain with me a long time.

Nicholls is no better, no worse. If I am honest, I expect him to die on the trip back. If we waited here, and could get the plane in . . . perhaps. But there is no space flat enough for long enough to get a plane down. Perhaps they could drop us medical supplies—but they would have to drop a doctor as well.

And what if he does live? What if he does put in his report on my "cowardice"? My refusal to arrest her? My refusal to declare war on the villagers? Can I handle the Inquiry on my own? I think not. I'll need to write to my father as soon as I return and get him to find a Brief for me. He's got the contacts.

I haven't thought about him for a long time. He was always such a nonentity. A harmless man. The exact antithesis of a Nicholls. But he's a man of peace, and I think at last I have come to respect that.

So we sit here now, in the gathering gloom. The fires are low. The Boys are indolent. I have spent the last hour with her, simply lying together, arms about each other, foreheads close. We lay in the hut, faintly aware of the sounds of merriment outside. When I had seen them carving the pig I had gone to Nicholls and, with Baranuma's help, moved him out of harm's way. I had got Baranuma

301

to feed Ludwig and make him comfortable and clean. God, I was becoming the proper Kiap—looking after all my Boys, my charges, my prisoner, before my own comfort.

She would not give up the carved toy she clutched. She made a sound as she held it, something like "papa", the equivalent her tongue has for that first syllable. I wanted to comfort her, to tell her I loved her, to explain my dream of a life together, but I had to be silent.

Perhaps it is for the better. What if I could talk to her and she refused me! She has spirit, that I know. But grief seems to lay them so low—far lower than us when we grieve. They seem to revert to such simple dependency. And I think I prefer it to the stolid mourning of Anglo-Saxons. I think it is more honest.

But lying there with her—and now, as we both sit here outside the hut, together on the ground, our flanks touching—it became obvious to me that these people are the same as myself. They are people. They hurt like us. They laugh like us. And even the distinction into "they" and "us" is blurring. We are all people in this spot, with the same problems. That is something she has given me, without the need for words. Our common humanity.

Which brings me to my future—to those paths forking ahead of me. For again I have trotted out onto a new one, aware that in doing so I have closed off others. And this one is very little used. It is a simple bush track—as opposed to the broad highways I had contemplated before. If I had killed Nicholls I would have joined the most used highway of them all. If I "go bush"—join the beach-combers—I suspect the road will become a dead end. What faces me is the choice of doing something worthwhile, but on my terms, not on the terms of "Rabaul" or even Nicholls' enlightened "Evolutionary Racialism".

So why even do something "worthwhile"? I don't know. Except that I have stared into the face of anarchy up here. If you don't keep the tracks cleared, the jungle grows back over them. Yes. I do believe, despite everything, that my background can offer these people something good, even something better than they have. And I speak of agriculture, of medicine, and a concept of Law that goes beyond simple retribution.

I know that this Law is more honoured in the breach than in the observance. I can't help that. I only know that I can hold to it. I know that we weren't born to kill each other—for if we had been, the species would not have survived; despite Nicholls' arguments regarding population control in areas of low protein. All right, so if protein is low up here, let's increase it. Let's grow pigs worthy of their breed. Let's bring in beef cattle. Let's investigate vegetable protein. God, I know nothing about any of this. I'm an art student. I know perspective and colour wheels and the History of Western Art. My education has been unique in fitting me out not to survive.

So I'm going to have to learn. If Williams can grow coffee, I can grow beans and corn. I can learn to kill a pig—properly, draining the blood, letting the meat hang. If we can train these natives in simple hygiene, in hookworm control, then I can learn about Pasteur's work.

She stirs and nestles against me, wrapping her hands around my arm. I feel such peace! I watch the night coming down. My love is beside me. I have had to go to the ends of the earth to find her. I have had to unlearn everything I had learnt. I have had to strip myself bare and plunge into the darkness. I have had to face myself and see the worst that is in me.

I'm going to have a shot of whisky, if Baranuma hasn't pinched it all, and do a round of the camp, and then turn in. Tomorrow the Great Trek begins.

He took her hands gently, and removed them from his arm. He smiled at her and placed his lips against her forehead, and then he stood up. She watched him cross to the fire and rummage in one of the packs. She felt content, watching him. She rubbed her belly, wondering if all that lovemaking had done its business. Then wondering what the child of a God and a woman would be like.

Her father's spirit had not come during the night, even though the stakes had been broken from her mother's house. That meant he was not roaming restless, unhappy, a desolate dead man, but that he had gone straight to the Land of the Dead. He had died as he had lived—a Big man, doing Big things, daring to challenge the Sky Gods themselves.

Her mother and her brother and sisters would be safe in the mountains. When the Baloose came to take her and the God back to the Sky, then her mother would return. She would be safe. Her daughter was with the Sky People, and would intercede on behalf of the people of the valley.

303

Everything that had been planned was coming about. The Kiap might not die, but Merin was placed there with the people of the Baloose. Her man had not disowned her. He had not believed Nicholls' accusations—choosing, instead, to believe the feelings in his own belly, and the feelings in her belly.

She felt, again, her destiny. She remembered the stream, the women, her mother anointing her. She remembered her anger at being singled out for the task. Now she felt a quiet achievement. Life with her man would be no worse than life with one of the valley people. It might well be better. In any event, it would be something good for her people. She would bring the Sky God down to earth. She would be the bridge between Earth and Sky. On her body they would run back and forth—delivering the good things from one place to the other.

He found what he sought in the pack and lifted it up. He took one of the clear, shiny receptacles and poured liquid into it. He lifted the receptacle in his hand, lifted it to the Sky, holding it up to show his People. Then, when they had taken notice of him, he saluted them and drank—like someone drinking a sacrificial drink, an offering for the Gods of the Sky. He stood there, in the light of the fire, calling down his Power.

Then she saw something in the shadows. A shadow itself. For a moment she thought it was her Father's vengeful spirit. It was watching her man closely, watching him salute the Sky. It turned, and she saw it was the old soldier, the one with the violence in his eyes. He stared across the fire at her, his eyes black and flat. Then he glanced to the next hut, where the door had been recently refastened stoutly. He looked at the remains of the pig feast, and then he looked back to her man.

She felt his violence. She felt his desire for killing. She moved, to get up and warn her man. The soldier saw her, and seemed to melt back into the shadows. She blinked and stared after him. There was nothing to show where he had been. Perhaps it had been a spirit. Perhaps it had been her own fear, imagining the worst. She stared after it, but it did not return.

· CHAPTER FIFTEEN ·

Bellamy trudged the mile from his house to the Administration offices. The house, high on a headland, had been built for the previous District Officer, who had expected to stay on, but had received a lucrative offer from a burgeoning hotel chain operating through Fiji and the Solomon Islands. It had been built by Tom Flower, whose pragmatic, square, verandahed designs squatted across the goldfields and along the coast. Now he had abandoned the islands to rebuild a city somewhere in Asia that had been destroyed by earthquakes.

He thought about Flower's luck in getting the contract. That led him to thinking about Rabaul's tremors and, of course, his wife. She would have to return to Sydney. He must write to the children and explain what was happening. They, at least, would benefit from the circumstances. Like Flower benefited from the Asian disaster.

He let himself into the office. It seemed undisturbed, but he stared around it uneasily. Although he would not admit it to Patricia, he was well aware of reported larcenies, systematic pilferings, and the breaking and entries that went on. And he knew that his revolver was still missing since the night of Peter's death. That and his Bible, leaving a gap in the tight order of his bookshelf.

It was the disappearance of the Bible that bothered him the most. A gun's use was obvious, but what motivated the mind that would steal the book? He opened the louvres and smelt the sudden gust of ozone. Glancing at his watch, he went to open the radio room.

The set gave him a quiet satisfaction. In the midst of primitive magic and blood feuds, to have technology at your fingertips; you could banish the magic by doing as he did — touching the tuning dial and feeling its well-damped movement. He checked the battery levels and switched open the circuit.

The speaker gave him static. He squelched it and checked his watch again. Mount Hagen outpost was due to come in. He spun the tuner past the frequency, waiting for the squeal of the carrier wave. The static sounded like surf.

Then the squeal, rising as he tuned towards it, blipping out, and squealing again as he passed over it. He finetuned back and caught the position between either side of the carrier wave. He turned up the volume, frowning to hear through the static.

He heard a microphone being pressed. Then a voice.

"Bellamy? Bellamy? Williams here. Do you read me, Bellamy?"

Williams was always careless of proper procedure. Frowning, Bellamy pressed the Transmit button, speaking slowly and distinctly into the microphone.

"VK9AB to VK9 Mike Hullo. Receiving you 3 and 3. Over."

Williams did not take the hint of his example.

"Bellamy? Bellamy? There's been a big fight. One of Nicholl's Policeboys has just got in."

Bellamy kept his voice calm and grabbed the log-book to him.

"Go ahead, Mount Hagen. Make your report please. Over."

"Nicholls has been badly chopped up. The Boy doesn't think he'll live."

"What about Harris, Andy? How's he?"

"The Boy left at piccaninny dawn. Bukato sent him off. He said that Harris and Bukato were organizing a punitive patrol."

The signal faded and he couldn't hear the rest of Williams' report.

"Sorry, Andy. I lost your signal. Can you give it to me again?"

Andy frowned and checked his battery levels. He pressed the Transmit button and checked the meter. He was receiving quite well, and he appeared to be transmitting. But that didn't mean he had to be being heard. He waited a while in

306

case some outside interference was passing. A thunder-storm in the mountains perhaps.

The Boy had staggered in the previous night, totally exhausted. Andy had got the information out of him and then run him a bath and fixed him a decent meal. He offered him a bed, but the Boy seemed too in awe of being inside the Haus Kiap, being treated like a white man. He wanted to go and camp with Baranuma's relatives—which puzzled Andy a bit, as he was so obviously a coastal Boy. But he seemed to remember that Baranuma had been introducing him around his relatives before the Patrol pulled out. Perhaps he had a girlfriend down there.

Anyhow, it didn't matter. The news was too important. He checked his own medical kit and didn't think he could handle what sounded like an amputation case.

He pressed the Transmit again.

"Bellamy. Bellamy. Nicholls is badly wounded in the legs. Bukato thinks that he may have to lose one of them. The Patrol was due to leave the morning after the Boy left, and they should be here in a couple of days."

"Roger, Mount Hagen. I received that. Message under-stood. I will organize a plane and a doctor, and I'll confirm with you at fifteen hundred hours. Is that clear?"

"Got you, Bellamy."

"VK9AB closing down. Over and out."

He felt mildly irritated again at Williams' lack of proper procedure. Then he spun the dial to the Rabaul Administration frequency, hoping to hell that Johnson and his seaplane were available. He wanted a pilot who knew the route perfectly, even if he would have to change planes at Lae or Madang. Johnson would probably be out joyriding some-where. And what the hell was wrong with Harris that he had left everything to Bukato?

To say Giram was scared was an understatement! Surely, it was an honour to be chosen as the messenger. But then to

307

run for three days and nights, knowing he'd be too scared to sleep, through the country of these people who had killed the Kiap! He hadn't signed the paper with that in mind!

And there was the business that Baranuma wanted him to transact. After his sergeant had given him the message about the Kiap, Baranuma had led him aside and described to him two good-quality gold-lip shells that were to be his. They could be had from Baranuma's brother, whom he remembered meeting, and they would be had on delivery of another message.

So while the Mount Hagen Kiap talked on his magic machine to Rabaul, Giram walked into Baranuma's village and stood there, looking around unsurely. Finally, he was recognized, and Baranuma's brother came up to him— smiling a greeting, but clearly suspicious.

"We met before," Giram said. "With Baranuma."

The brother nodded. He looked tough, Giram thought.

"He has asked me to give you a message, in return for two good-quality gold-lip shells, that he has asked you to show me in his stock."

"Baranuma has no stock of shells here."

"Baranuma told me they are wrapped in bark and are buried in a garden shed on a field, near the stream."

The brother studied him a while, then nodded.

"Supposing that was the case, what would the message be?"

"He said you are to show me the shells, but that only he will give them to me."

So they had to find a couple more male relatives and walk down to the shed. There the brother again looked at him suspiciously, and took a digging stick and began to probe in the dirt. Giram was impressed at the power Baranuma could command—that he could entrust relatives with knowledge of his treasure, and they would respect it and not steal it.

They showed him two shells, no more. Giram was satisfied with them. There were no worm-holes.

"Baranuma said that, when he was last with you, he spoke of certain things—certain acts. How a man could become Big in these difficult times."

The brother nodded. "He did," he admitted.

308

"Baranuma said he told you that the Sky People disturb the relationships that exist between people, and that others may benefit."

There were four of them listening intently. The brother was the eldest, probably about twenty years old. The youngest would have been only recently admitted to the men's house.

"He says you are to take your comrades," he nodded to the other three, "and leave immediately for the valley of the Parap and the Gafu."

"Those headhunters!" the youngest said, scornfully.

"There has been a big fight and they have all fled into the mountains leaving their pigs behind."

Some kind of comprehension began to dawn on the brother's face. He smiled and put his arm on Giram's shoulder.

"What about the Kiap?" the brother asked him.

"The Kiap is badly wounded, perhaps even dead by now."

The brother chuckled.

"That Baranuma," he said. He grinned at Giram. "He thinks of everything," he added.

He had been on the radio most of the day. From Rabaul he had found that Johnson's plane had departed that morning, probably at the time Williams was calling him with the news. Doctor Roberts was off-duty, and could not be found. He had left an ambiguous message about "visiting friends", but had not stated which friends.

Bellamy had then got through to Guinea Airways at Lae, to discover that Johnson's plane was sitting out in the bay, off Salamaua. Guinea Airways would make a Junkers available, and they would contact Bulolo Gold Dredging and get the doctor from Wau flown down. Bellamy was a bit unsure, knowing the man they meant—who was only just finding his way into bush medicine and, to Bellamy's knowledge, had not carried out the sort of operation that would be required, under the primitive conditions he would find at Mount Hagen.

He then remembered Roberts and the girl, the girlfriend of Johnson's woman, and put two and two together. He got Guinea Airways to try and raise Johnson's plane. And that was where he found the reluctant Doctor Roberts.

At last it was finalized. Johnson would fly the Junkers himself. This would suit Guinea Airways better, for they would not lose any airtime; they could schedule a standby plane, and keep their own pilot on the goldfields run. Johnson's "party" would stay at the hotel in Lae. Johnson himself would dash back to Rabaul and pick up emergency medical supplies. He would leave immediately and be back at Lae that afternoon. He would probably get the Junkers into Madang the next morning.

By then Nicholl's stretcher-party would be almost home, Bellamy calculated. He couldn't help smiling at the thought of the two girls trying to make do in the Lae hotel—where the "rooms" were divided off with hessian screens from one another, and you could lie awake all night, first listening to the revelry downstairs, then to the fornication upstairs, and then to the vomiting and urinating into the small hours. He had a feeling that Doc Roberts might be getting out of his depth with the two women on his hands, and hoped he wouldn't try anything that would lead to a heart attack.

At dusk he got back to Williams. Reception was deteriorating as storms gathered, but he got through. Williams, too, was puzzled by the lack of word from Harris. The boy who had brought the news had gone bush it appeared, so he couldn't be questioned. All they could do was wait.

Bellamy shut up shop, closing the windows against light-fingered night-strollers. These days he locked the important files in the office safe, until recently always left open. Locking it, he realized the incident with Peter had affected him more than he had first recognized. That, and the information just received that a Japanese training ship would be docking at Rabaul, apparently intent on visiting every port in every island—and discharging hordes of midshipmen with little cameras.

Intrigue was everywhere.

He walked home. He liked Madang. The climate suited him, and the location, with a coral reef close inshore, and the sandy islands with the palm trees hanging over the calm waters of the bay, and the backdrop of mountains folded against each other, becoming bluer and bluer with the distance.

He walked past the huge copra stores by the wharf, where the year's harvest from all the outlying plantations along the coast, and on the offshore islands, was stored. He climbed the hill to his house.

The new Boy opened the door for him, smiling eagerly. He fixed the Masta a Scotch and water. He showed the Masta how he had washed and ironed. Bellamy employed a separate cookboy, who had some knowledge of European cuisine—admittedly gained on a trading boat where the diet was fish-and-rice or tinned meat-and-rice, and occasionally just rice.

The Masta sat on his verandah and watched the enclosed bay turning bluer and bluer, towards black, hearing the voices of villagers going about their business. He turned his radio on and got the voice of Radio Australia—aware how Alo came to listen, staring in awe at that disembodied voice, and flinching when suddenly a dance band was there, in the room with them.

Diary: 26th May, 1937

Evening. This is the first chance I've had to draw breath! We have been marching from sun-up until well after dark—but the stretcher, the prisoner, even the girl, have slowed us. I try to help her as much as I can, but she is obviously afraid. She is well outside her own territory—probably in the land of some sworn enemy. She is having to learn to live like one of our carriers, placing all trust in the Kiap and the Patrol, to be a little world all of their own, immune to the natural laws of the area they happen to be in.

311

Ludwig is being deliberately obstructionist. I unshackled him for a while, and he promptly made a break for it. So he is back under guard, back in handcuffs, and feeling indignant over it. He is trying to win me back to the cause of white supremacy, whispering, when I get close to him, of conspiracies he can observe.

I made the mistake, last night, of stopping by to see if he was comfortable. He drew me into a discussion. At first it seemed quite rational, and I took the bait. Did I think the League of Nations, a body set up to administer after the effects of the last European war, could possibly have a mandate to dictate the terms of existence up here, fifty thousand years away from them?

I suggested that perhaps the League of Nations could learn from these people—in that the battles were localized and stopped after one or two people were killed. I didn't pursue my darker thoughts, regarding the way homicide is structured into the core of their lives—so that battle is the outcome after far nastier killings. But, hell, Europe can't boast any better behaviour, really.

Well, Ludwig wasn't going to have it that the nigs could teach the flower of Western civilization anything. He's a real colonial. More German than someone from Dresden or Hamburg. Just like the Brits out here are more British than their comrades at Home. And the Australians? To our shame, we become secondhand Colonial British, one further step removed from reality. But that wasn't Ludwig's argument. No. He pressed me to agree that the League of Nations was an American dupe. I don't know enough about it, really. But he could convince me. It's true, what the hell do any of them know about life in these mountains?

They censure, for example, Mick Leahy, because he shot first and saved the lives of his Patrol, at the expense of some of the people who were shooting, or about to shoot, at him. They don't censure the behaviour of the British against the Boers—the death of women and children in British camps. I pointed out to him that that was well before the League was in existence. But there was no stopping him now he was in full flight. There had always been a League or its equivalent: nations watching nations, people watching people.

Ludwig kept talking. I was tired. I mumbled my replies, not that they mattered. He was off now, and I had trouble keeping up with him. The Americans were watching New Guinea and the islands. They wanted to take the world's eyes off the way they treated their own nigs. (Well I couldn't argue with that.) So they had declared themselves Policemen of the Pacific. They would promote the "rights" of the nigs over those of white men all the time. To do that they were putting pressure on the League of Nations—through, of

312

course, their financial superiority—to force the Australian Administration into prosecuting whites (like himself, though he did have the courtesy not to point it out to me). For example: the penalty for a white man murdering someone was always more severe than for a black man murdering someone. (I demurred: the penalty for a black man murdering a white man had been exacted down the track, by Bukato.)

But that brought him to the crux. The Americans had agents here, in this Patrol. Specifically, Bukato and Baranuma. I had only to watch them and I could observe them conspiring. They were spies for the League of Nations. Bukato could sacrifice a dozen bush kanakas, because his long-term aim was more important. (And what was that? I inquired, yawning now with boredom.) The death of all whites in the island.

I laughed. Ludwig grew indignant. What did I think Bukato had been doing, in the hut, standing over him with the axe? Bukato would get him, Ludwig, first, because Ludwig could see through him. And then he would get me. Then Nicholls. Then, there would be Bukato at the head of an armed force. He could wipe out the Mount Hagen Patrol Post, capture the Baloose, and descend on Madang.

I suppose I was rude. I walked away laughing.

And what I saw, when I did so, was Bukato and Baranuma arguing together, fiercely, whispering, Baranuma's hand on Bukato's arm, restraining him. They caught me looking and stopped.

So who knows? Maybe Ludwig is right. Maybe it takes a madman to see his way clearly through a mad world.

Nicholls is no better; no worse. He has not fully regained consciousness. We have run out of painkillers. I am hoping the plane can find us and drop us something. But so far we have not heard it. As we are backtracking exactly along the path that Nicholls brought us in on they will know our position. But Giram would only just have returned, and it will take time to organize relief.

Her name is Merin! How about that! We are making progress now towards understanding. We walk together, when possible, chattering away at each other—pointing at things, at vegetables, at parts of our bodies (and here, like all of her people, she can become most lewd!), and we recite our names for them. She has trouble pronouncing Don Harris, coming up with something like "Arap". Mrs. Arap, indeed!

Once a thought is put in your mind it stays there. It colours all your observations. I had dismissed Ludwig's ravings, last night. But all today I watched Bukato. He walked alone, brooding, plaiting

313

some kind of artifact. He kept away from me and I could not see what it was.

And Baranuma was unusually solicitous, all for showing me a better track—one that would involve fewer river crossings, flatter ground. In fact almost to the point that I was wondering if there actually was something going on. Perhaps they had engineered an ambush with some locals—all of whom were most conspicuous by their absence—and intended to draw us onto a sidetrack.

Naturally, I refused. And, in the end, Baranuma gave up and went to argue once more with Bukato.

Now we are camped on a small ridge. There are a few old, abandoned huts, but no one is making use of them. They seem to shun them, with good reason—they would have been abandoned when the land became unproductive, and the village full of excrement, breeding fleas and hookworm and God knows what. We camp down the ridge from those decaying grass mounds.

Bukato seemed to have recovered his composure enough to nag me about the possibility of ambush. To placate him I sent him off with two of his fellows on a scouting patrol around the perimeters. That will keep him quiet.

But now Merin wants to massage my feet! Ah, what luxury! What gentleman abed in England ever had it so good!

Tomorrow they would meet Baranuma's relatives on the road. There was no way they could avoid that. Baranuma kept telling Bukato he could handle the situation—he could fool the Kiap. But the Kiap was getting harder to fool. When he had first taken over from Nicholls, then he was uncertain. But he was settling into the job. And there was always the possibility that Nicholls would regain enough consciousness to again be the acute observer of old. Baranuma would not be able to withstand questioning by Nicholls.

And the prisoner had to be watched as well. Bukato could feel the man's eyes on him all the time. Last night the prisoner had got hold of the Kiap and begun twisting his mind with his fast, plausible tongue. The Kiap had laughed

314

at him, but today the Kiap had been brooding on the prisoner's words.

Bukato kept away from the Kiap. He had work to do. Harris had forgotten about that clumsy axe he had found. Bukato had saved it and stripped off the old handle. As he walked, he plaited a new one to the stone. The stone was dull, and would not take an edge. But that didn't matter. The force of the blow was in the leverage of the handle. The new handle he had taken from an ornamented digging stick he had found in the village. It was carved with a bird design: long beak, stretched wings running the length of the handle, and feet ending at the sharpened end. He had reversed it—so the sharpened end was out and the blunt end against the stone. The bird's head was covered by the braided fibre he used for plaiting. It looked like a blinded bird with its head in a hood.

The axe was now with Bukato's possessions, buried in with his change of clothes and his sleeping blanket. Right now he carried his rifle. He had taken the Patrol down the ridge and was now sweeping around the side of it, ostensibly looking for ambush, but with the real purpose of convincing the Police Boys with him that they were being watched, to set in their minds the possibility of attack. Once a thought was implanted in a man's head it grew. By midnight the sentries would be convinced that someone was out there, waiting.

He would take out Harris first, because he was the most dangerous. Then he would finish off the prisoner and Nicholls. Harris would be sleeping next to the girl. Bukato didn't want to kill her. He wanted her alive. But if she was in the road, then it would be necessary.

The important thing was the planning. Baranuma hoped they would muddle through. Baranuma's belief was that you lived in the middle of fate. You scented out what fate was doing, and you went with it. Or you withdrew and waited until it changed.

Unfortunately, a soldier couldn't live like that. Not if he wanted to stay alive. Perhaps he, Bukato, was Baranuma's fate. Perhaps he was the instrument of it. Baranuma had started this business, and now the business was moving out

315

of his control. That was too bad for Baranuma. He would not suffer, if he kept his head and kept his loyalties clear. Bukato needed him.

When all the whites were dead, then Bukato would take his steel knife, and slash his own arm. He would scream out. The sentries would start, shit themselves, and fire into the bush. They would pepper the bush with bullets for ten minutes. When they got control of themselves they would discover the attackers had fled, leaving Bukato wounded in defence of the Mastas, and leaving an axe, covered with blood, by the bodies.

They would carry all the bodies in to Mount Hagen, so the Mastas could see that the Boys had been faithful to the end.

Meanwhile, Baranuma's relatives would be stealing the pigs.

All his life Bukato had been a man on the run. But now, with this action completed, he would have bought himself a family: Baranuma's family. The thought warmed him. He could marry and settle down, with an honourable discharge, an honourable wound, a partner in the great new enterprise. He would be running away from that old, Lutheran church no more.

"Masta will teach me to read."

Bellamy jumped, spilling whisky. He stared at his new servant, who until then had blended so perfectly with the background that he was as forgotten as Patricia's chair — not thought about, but part of the mental map of the room. His face now gleamed as he stepped into the circle of light from the pressure lamp, eager and uncertain, guileless and still holding something in reserve.

"Why do you want to read, Alo? What good will it do you?"

"To learn about Jesus Christ, Masta."

Bellamy studied him carefully.

"Why?"

316

"To go to heaven, Masta."

The reply was too "pat", too much what every other Boy said. Somehow, Bellamy thought it wasn't the real reason. He probed a little further.

"Is that what the Mission taught you, Alo? Learn to read, read about Jesus Christ and heaven?"

He saw Alo frown and concentrate—obviously aware that the conversation was not heading in the right direction. Bellamy realized how hard it must be to try and express yourself in a second-hand language like Pidgin English, to a person whose way of life was so incomprehensibly different to your own. He thought of his children, when they were two years old, with the same earnest, puzzled frown and carefully watchful eyes as they tried to negotiate the pitfalls of conversation. He smiled and leaned back in his chair.

"Don't talk about Jesus Christ, Alo. Talk about what you want."

"To serve you, Masta?"

"You mean to work for me? To perhaps be able to get a job in Madang?"

The eyes studied him soberly, and assessed the drift of the dialogue. Alo nodded and smiled broadly.

"Yes, Masta. To get a job."

Bellamy frowned, but only with concentration. The request pleased him, in a way flattered him that he was the sort of person that a native would approach with such a monumental request. He glanced along the rows of books, and saw the gap where the Bible had been. He glanced quickly at Alo, who had seen where he had been looking. But the native smiled on.

Bellamy rubbed his forehead. If you let it, conspiracy blossomed out of thin air.

"Alo?"

"Yes, Masta."

"Sit down over here. No, here, beside the desk."

Clumsily, his servant sat down on the chair, leaning forward, staring avidly at the papers on the desk, the books, the pen and ink. Bellamy took a sheet of paper and placed it before him. Alo drew back momentarily, his eyes fierce with concentration, with wonder and awe, as he stared at it.

317

"I'll teach you . . ." he said, reaching for his whisky glass, and discovering it empty. "Here, take this glass," he said, "and pour some more whisky into it."

He waited while the Boy, the man, was gone. He grinned to himself. Maybe he would yet become a schoolmaster and give up Administration.

He let Alo see the grin when he returned and resumed his seat. He took the whisky and sipped. Alo watched closely. Too closely. He saw Bellamy's need for the drink. Bellamy put it down and pushed it out of easy reach.

"To read, Alo, you must learn about the letters." He began to draw the alphabet before his pupil. "Letters make up words. Words make up sentences. Sentences make up . . ." He glanced at his servant. Alo still stared avidly, but this time at Bellamy's wristwatch.

"Would you like a wristwatch, Alo?"

The man stared at him, his face saying "yes", but his mouth saying nothing.

"I'll give you a wristwatch of your own when you have learnt to write and say, and understand, the alphabet. Is that clear?"

"Masta?"

Alo seemed confused. Bellamy reviewed his previous utterances. The word "alphabet" may have caused trouble. He found himself looking at the whisky glass and made himself look away, towards Alo.

"When you can say the letters, know them, all of them . . ."

Alo's fingers touched his wrist and felt the watch. Bellamy jerked it away.

"Not now!" he said. "Not now, Alo. You will have the watch when you can say the alph . . . the letters."

"Masta will teach me to tell the time?"

"Yes!" He bit his lip and smiled to show he wasn't as angry as his shout indicated. He stared at the man's eyes: they were clear and confused. Bellamy realized he would have to go back a bit further to find some common ground.

Clumsily, he drew a pig. He printed the letters P I G beside it.

"P I G," he said, pointing at each letter. "Pig."

"Yes, Masta, Pig."

318

"These letters, this word, means Pig."

Already his head was beginning to hurt from the concentration. Maybe he would have that whisky. No! He shook his head and printed the word again. He then handed the pencil to Alo.

He turned the object gravely in his fingers, staring at it, feeling its power. He had seen how it acted for the Masta. It created pigs, and through pigs it could create wealth. It could create the marks of power that seemed to store up the Masta's knowledge. He felt its tip. His head hurt with the effort of following the Masta. He pressed the pencil into the paper.

The lead snapped. He glanced quickly at the Masta, who smiled and took it from him and worked at the end with a little knife whose blade could be folded away out of sight.

"Gently, Alo. Gently," said the Masta. "Now, one more time, make a P."

His hand trembling with the effort of controlling the stick, of holding it lightly, of tracing the intricacies of the design, he leant forward and snapped the lead again.

The Masta sighed and sat back. Will he beat me now? Alo wondered. The others had all explained how Mastas beat you as part of the learning process. There was nothing to be done but endure it. The Masta looked at his whisky glass, but he did not reach for it.

"Alo?"

"Yes, Masta?"

"Make us a pot of tea. It's going to be a long night."

She couldn't sleep. If she wanted to desperately enough then she could take the tablets. They were on a porcelain tray on

319

the locker by her bed. She looked at them. But then she shook her head and swung herself clear of the white hospital bedclothes.

There was nothing wrong with her, she thought. She wasn't a hospital case. She was just a woman who was missing her children and their father. She stood up, listening to the silence of the sleeping hospital.

Then she realized there was more to the silence. It was that same brooding, ringing silence she had felt before the guria. It was as though she could feel the tension in the earth transmitted into her feet. She frowned and walked to the window.

The town lay bathed in moonlight. The lagoon showed back the halfmoon and the brilliant stars. The water was black, as still as glass. She didn't know what time it was, but it was late enough for the last drunk to have gone home, for the lights to be out in Chinatown, and the fires to have burnt to embers in the coastal villages.

She turned back to the moonlit room. The brooding stillness made her restless. She pushed her hair back from her face and opened the white hospital closet and stared in at the clothes she had worn on the little trading boat, on the voyage across. She reached into the closet and took them out and began to dress.

The white, powdered coral of the streets was a ghostly grey in the moonlight. The flaming red hibiscus were neutral. She walked into the darkness at the base of the mango and fig trees that lined the street, heading downhill, towards the harbour.

The water did not move at all. Its stillness was unearthly. There were no wavelets slapping the beach. There was no gentle rise and fall against the pillars of the wharf. She walked along its edge, looking down at it, unable to see her own reflection, looking into blackness that contained unfathomable depths.

She thought about Richard and the proposal of a job at Lae. She felt the tug of her children, inside her, where they had grown. She wanted to be with them. She reached the end of the wharf and looked up.

She did not cry out, even though he had startled her. She

320

stared at him. His eyes were on her, black and watchful. Then he nodded and turned to look over the lagoon, towards distant Vulcan Island and its black, polished volcanic sides.

He was an old native. He wore only a piece of bark, and he carried nothing with him. His face was wrinkled and reptilian, like a crocodile with its watchful, hooded eyes. The tattoos on his cheeks were like crocodile scales. His bearing was erect, though, younger than his face, and he seemed to strain forward, towards the distant island.

He was listening, she realized. He could sense the tension, too. She took a step towards him and he glanced at her.

"Can you feel it?" she asked him.

He stared at her, and then he nodded slowly, soberly.

"Guria?" she asked.

His eyes evaluated her; a Missus who could sense its approach. His chin and his face nodded. She smiled and stepped back.

And then it hit them. She screamed as the wharf threw her towards the black, now broken, mirror. But he grabbed her and pulled her back, swinging them both onto the oily boards. The boards shifted under them. The water slammed against the pillars and threw itself on the beach, breaking up the reflections into shimmering kaleidoscopes.

For a moment she tensed away from him. Then she let herself go and leaned against the old man. She began to cry. His arm came around her and held her, comfortingly, one hand stroking her head. She let him hold her until the shock had rumbled away into the mountains, and the smell of sulphur had burst out of the fissured earth, rising up like steam. Then she smiled and pushed herself upright and looked at him.

"Thank you," she said.

"Something nothing Missus," he said politely. His eyes were still watchful, black and unreadable.

She stood up and dusted herself off. A cacophony of voices arose from Chinatown: women's cries, children's cries, men's shouts. They both listened to them, both smiling. He shook his head.

"The Guria is not finished," he told her.

She stared at him, not knowing whether to allow this

321

strange intimacy to continue. She nodded her thanks and smiled politely, then turned and walked back down the wharf, treading carefully over the gaps in the boards. She could feel him watching her depart.

He's not a man, she thought. He's the spirit of a crocodile in human form.

Nicholls was warm and quiet and seemed to be lying up against her breast. He closed his eyes again, smiling to himself. There was no difference between himself and that mountain of warm flesh. They lay together, their joint blood roaring. His little fist clenched and unclenched, fingertips discovering themselves as independent from that out of which they grew. Then they forgot themselves and were reabsorbed into the moment of total warmth.

Fear coursed through the whole body. It slammed him into the pain. The infant in him screamed with panic. Contact with the mothering flesh was gone. She, too, was on her feet. She was running. His infant eyes came open. The world flashed around him: disjointed, disconnected. It was attacking her. It was trying to reach him. Pain erupted.

Violent pain. He screamed, but silently. His eyes were open. He could sense the vibrations receding through the mountain. His eyes focused on the darkness, the low cloud, the stain of moonlight through the cloud. He was alive.

Death receded from him, still beckoning with its warmth, with its return to the mothering earth. It promised him an end to the pain. Again he tried to scream, and felt how his lips did not move, his tongue did not twist. He clung to the pain. It was his only ally against that smothering drift.

A guria, he told himself, forcing the world back into his mind. A tiny guria from far out to sea. His heart was hammering. There, through the pain, was that old elation, the feeling when you had beaten the enemy by a second — and regret, knowing that he had been led back to the point of discovery, back beyond all his life to a moment that had shaped a form for that life. But he had to let it go if he was to live. It dimmed: mountain, mother, warmth . . . and then violent fear and life. He clung to his pain like he was clinging to a lover. The pattern, so clear, was dissolving. It was a haze. Then it was gone.

It was fate. It had to be fate. Fate in hand with sorcery. These valley people had tried to work their simple sorcery and Nicholls had beaten it. Now the Sky Sorcery was turned against him, Bukato. The guria should never have happened. He clung against a tree-trunk, trying to merge himself into the bush. He saw something happen to Nicholls. The guria had broken through his illness. Bukato saw the eyelids quiver and knew he had to strike.

He printed the order of stretchers on his mind. There, almost at his feet, was Nicholls. Beyond Nicholls was the prisoner. He could see the chain holding him to the lopped poles that formed the stretcher-frame. The other side of the prisoner, the young Kiap and his woman slept side by side. Beyond them, keeping a discreet distance, but ready to be called, lay Baranuma.

He let go the tree-trunk and swung up his axe, and then realized the prisoner was watching him.

It was all wrong. It was fate, after all. He sidestepped Nicholls. The prisoner's eyes were on him, wide and bright, but as yet not registering the importance of what was happening. Perhaps it would be all right, after all. He swung the axe back.

Now the prisoner knew what was happening. Bukato saw the shackled hands coming up. He saw the mouth opening to scream. He was aware of Nicholls' moving closer and closer to the world. The axe had a lovely balance to it. All a steel axe had was a superior edge. Its handle was far too short. That was why the bush kanakas threw away those bright, white handles and shaped their own. As he had with this; his axe. He brought it down, over the top of the upraised hands.

323

Now the woman was stirring too. Fate was so close. He could just keep ahead of it. The skull split like a coconut, ripe, ready, bursting with a loud noise that roused her, and roused Nicholls, but did not rouse Harris.

Nicholls was staring at him, understanding, fully awake, his soldier's instinct not letting him down. He smiled at his old boss and heard the woman screaming. Nicholls' hand moved for where it always knew the revolver would be. Bukato swung the axe from the hip, but it was constricted by the stretcher. He swung back again, staggering. The sentry nearest him had come awake at that scream, and had yelled and fired into the bush. Now the other sentries were firing.

Attention was taken away from Bukato. He would do it, yet! He commenced the downswing, angling to follow Nicholls as, fully awake, he tried to roll from his stretcher. Nicholls was dead meat.

The revolver shot threw him across the stretcher. He struggled for balance. Then he fell onto Nicholls' legs. The man screamed. Bukato found his knife and got it out. The steel flashed. He bared his teeth and lunged again for Nicholls.

The second shot killed him.

The sentries were screaming "Ambush! Ambush!" He woke to the rifles discharging into the bush. Merin was yelling, too. But she was not looking in the direction of the attack. She grabbed him and turned him towards Nicholls' bed.

There was a man with an axe. A nuggety native warrior. The man was between Nicholls and Ludwig. The axe had come down and the sound of Ludwig's skull bursting had preceded the explosion of .303 fire. Don saw the axe swinging again, from the hip, like a scythe, and his hands were fumbling, still uncertain with sleep, for his holster, opening the flap, finding the handle, all the time hearing Merin scream, the sentries shout, the rifles boom.

He shot the man. He had to shoot him twice, seeing the

324

knife come out and seeing Nicholls' screaming face twisting away from it. He rolled himself out of bed and faced into the bush, waiting for the rest of the attack. Baranuma flung himself down beside him.

"Where's Bukato?" he asked.

Baranuma shook his head and shrugged.

"See how Nicholls is."

Don saw a moment of fear in Baranuma's eyes, before he sprinted across the gap and threw himself down behind cover of the body. Where were the arrows? The spears? What were the Boys firing at, Don thought.

"Masta!" Baranuma called. He stood up.

"Keep down, Baranuma, for Christ's sake!"

"Bukato, Masta."

It took Don a moment to understand. Baranuma grabbed the body and heaved it off the stretcher and Don saw the man's face and recognized it.

"Cease your fire!" he bellowed. "Stop shooting!"

He saw Nicholls, now fully awake, eyes huge with the pain, face white as a sheet.

"Cease fire!" he bellowed again, and dimly heard the shooting taper off.

He walked over and looked down at Nicholls. Nicholls' eyes focused on him.

"What happened?" he asked.

"Bukato," Nicholls said. "He tried to kill me."

Then he heard Merin give a grunt of disgust. He turned and saw her looking down at Ludwig. He realized Ludwig had no face. His body ended in a mass of blood and tissue.

"Cover him up," he said to Baranuma.

"Put your gun away," Nicholls said.

Don looked at his hand and held it up. His finger was still locked inside the trigger guard. He had to prise it out with his other hand. He snipped the safety back on and dropped it on his stretcher. He squatted beside Nicholls, who lay in the dirt.

"How are you, sir?"

"Alive. Hurting like hell."

"We've got no more painkillers."

Nicholls nodded.

"Thanks," he said. "That was close."

Don nodded, looking around the camp as Baranuma went from Boy to Boy, calming each. As he told them what had happened, they all turned and looked to where the Kiap lay, and to the sergeant's body beside him. Don stood up.

"Well," he said, "dawn must be close. We might as well get moving." He glanced down to his Kiap. "We'll get you into Hagen a couple of hours sooner."

Nicholls nodded his thanks. He could not speak, concentrating on the pain. Don saw Merin staring at him. He smiled at her and beckoned her over. He embraced her. Looking down his eyes met Nicholls'. Nicholls nodded to him and lifted his hand in a gesture of reconciliation. Don nodded back to him and then turned to her and laid his head against hers.

· CHAPTER SIXTEEN ·

She woke late, with sunlight flooding the hospital room, and wondered if she had dreamed what had happened that night. It had the confused clarity of a dream. She saw the sleeping tablets, still untaken, in their dish beside her bed. She smiled and put her feet to the floor.

She had no advance warning of this one. It buckled the floor under her and threw her back, across the bed, against the wall. She yelped, and then covered her mouth with her hand. She could hear the pandemonium in the rooms around her.

The smell of sulphur was constant now. The tension in the air was not diminished by the tremor.

Bellamy, at the airstrip, watched the Junkers circle, when suddenly he was flat on his back. He heard the guria coming, like an express train, roaring across the ocean-bed. On his back he heard it flail through the bush. The plane was coming in now, and he picked himself up and looked around. Other people were doing likewise. They were laughing with relief. A few bush natives looked scared, but were being reassured by the wisecracks of their more sophisticated comrades.

He thought of Patricia and looked towards the ocean, in the direction of New Britain and Rabaul. The guria must have been centred out that way. He realized that his new Boy, Alo, was also staring out there.

"That must have shaken Rabaul?" he said to the Boy.

Alo nodded thoughtfully.

"He turns over," he said. "He is waking up."

Bellamy looked at him sharply, but could learn nothing from his face.

First out of the plane was one of the girls, the blonde. Bellamy had not been expecting them and he sucked in his breath angrily. She looked back and gave her friend a hand. They both stared at the Boys rolling out the drums of fuel. Then he saw Johnson grinning at him as he climbed down. He got Johnson aside.

"What the hell did you bring them for?"

"Easy, Dick. Easy." Johnson brushed his hand aside and untied his scarf. Close up, it was oil-stained. "We couldn't leave them there, old boy. Have you spent a night in the Lae pub? Jesus!" He shook his head in disgust.

"I thought you stayed there regularly?"

"Not with a lady, I haven't."

"Lady? Look, Johnnie, I can't let you take them up to Hagen, you know. We need all the space we can muster."

"I thought they could stay here with you?"

"I'm coming on the plane."

"You're leaving the Station? What will McNicol think of that?"

"I wouldn't have a clue. I've been unable to contact him. He's up in the goldfields on some jaunt."

They both watched the two girls, with the doctor eagerly following them, cross the airstrip, keeping their eyes down, conscious of all the men lined up, grinning in expectation.

"We've just had another bloody guria," Bellamy said, dusting himself off.

"And one last night," Johnson added. "Something's about to happen."

He nodded in reply. Johnson was distracted, watching the Boys run the fuel lines up to the tanks.

"These Guinea Airways bitches always run rich," he said. "Thank God I'm not at the mercy of their mechanics any more."

Bellamy nodded, not really interested. Johnson studied him carefully.

"I can get Patricia onto a steamer out of Moresby," Johnson said suddenly.

"What? What good's that to her? How's she going to get there?"

Johnson grinned at him and took his arm.

"Easy. After we've sorted out poor old Nicholls, I take this crate back to Lae. I then fly my plane to Rabaul, pick her up, then back to Lae. In Lae she gets on one of their regular flights to Wau. In Wau there's a weekly connection to Moresby—straight over the top. In Moresby there's a steamer loading for Rockhampton. In Rockhampton there's a train. She'll be in Sydney within the month."

Bellamy stared at him, wondering what the price would be. Johnson gestured at the crowd at the edge of the field, falling back to let the girls through.

"About the girls," he said.

"OK," Bellamy said, nodding wearily. "Take them with you. I'll stay at the Station."

"You're a white man, Dicky."

"Just get Patricia out of these bloody islands."

Diary: 27th May, 1937

Just one more sleep! That's what I used to tell myself as I lay in bed, on Christmas eve. Just one more sleep! And we're out of the mountains, we're in Mount Hagen. Bloody old Williams is there, grinning away, cooking up a dinner party for a few strange Kiaps— though Johnnie, or one of his breed, will be there too, smelling of oil and pistons and the twentieth century. I wonder what happened to those girls? Who cares? Me, once.

Women are the great civilizers; that's what we were taught to believe. So maybe I don't want to be civilized? Maybe if I'd had a sister, maybe I would have learnt how to get on with them.

It was strange, being an only child. My life was so ordinary; but it was lived in such a vacuum. They never talked about having other kids. Did they try? Did something go wrong?

I look back from here, all the way down from the mountains and the Stone Age, to North Adelaide bungalows and the workmen's terrace houses and the big mansions of the rich. It's like looking at a fossil, or something caught in amber. I look at it and I see that I am doing the exact opposite—not just a little bit different—the absolutely total opposite—of what went on there, behind the white

329

lace curtains that, in turn, were behind the black iron-laced fence. There's my frightened little father, and my grim, silent mother, and me. I sit apart from them, squatting beside a chair—pretending the chair is a mountain. I push my toy tiger across the mountain. My father smiles nervously. It will soon be time for him to kiss me goodnight. Tomorrow he will be doing the same things as he did today, and yesterday, and next year. The rose-papered walls crowd in on me.

And here I am now, not knowing what will happen tomorrow. Maybe we'll make it into Hagen. Maybe Baranuma and Bukato have set up some deal with the locals and I'll be dead, gone finish. Maybe Nicholls will give up entirely.

We're out of painkillers. Maybe they can airdrop some, assuming they can find us.

In the mountains I can think. Who said that, or something like it? He was right, though. Thought becomes so clear as you press on through the fear. That's the trap, isn't it? Nicholls was a man who thought clearly. What is he now? His eyes watch me. They hang on my movements. They have softened. Intense pain has done something to them—like reheating tempered steel, the temper goes out of it; it softens and becomes good for nothing any more. Nicholls is no longer a Kiap. But I am. I shot Bukato. I shot straight, clear, clean. It was him or Nicholls. Bukato was clearly in the wrong. Nicholls? He brought Bukato up here. He trained him. He wound him up and pointed him at the valley people and told him—Kill! So Bukato killed.

One more sleep. But I can't. Everyone else is asleep. Even the sentries. I sit here, surrounded by the stretchers of the dead: Bukato and Ludwig. Over there, the stretcher of the not quite dead.

Merin sleeps. I watch her. I can see her, touch her, feel her. I can't understand her words. We will have kids. I know it. Lots of them. My own tribe. We will people the mountains with them. Boys and girls. God, I'm so happy. Maybe I'll try again to get some shuteye.

He watched Harris close his journal and unfold his sleeping bag on the stretcher next to the girl's. He felt no emotion. It simply was. He, Nicholls, had fucked her. Now Harris reckoned he was in love with her. So be it. Harris had tried to kill him—but he had goaded Harris into it. He had wanted to die, from shame at being a cripple. To not stand on his own two feet any more! The shame of it was far worse than that of being found in his armour. But what did that matter any more? Life went on. There were patterns to it, but you only caught glimpses of them.

When he had been at college, he had been a good runner. Now that caused a flicker of dry amusement! He knew about his feet then! Watching Harris curl into his sleeping bag, he remembered a Sports Day. A clear, spring day. The track laid out in white powder by the groundsmen. And he running the second leg of the relay. The feet pounding on the green turf. The vague, distant sound of the crowd. Arms pistoning. Lungs gasping. Legs thundering. Legs. Muscles. Feet. Ankles. Toes. God, my legs. The cramp waiting in his thigh. It was only paces away. And they were now level as they came down to the turn, and he could see his team-mate already springing, looking back, hand trailing. Now he was in the box. One foot in. The team-mate was clearing, heading for the end of the box. He was running up to him. The hand took the baton. The end of the box was a pace away. His own hand was clear. The third man had the baton. He changed it to the other hand. His arms began to pound. Nicholls felt his own legs buckle under. He felt the cramp spasm his muscles. But it didn't matter. The baton was moving.

There was moisture in his eyes. He tried to reach down to the leg. But what was the point? There was no going back from it. He was the only one left awake in the camp. No one would know.

Alone, silently, Nicholls cried.

That Jennifer was a dish! The glossy, black hair. The soft, brown eyes. The generous mouth. When she was around, you didn't notice that the other one, Gloria, was a fine

331

looking girl—but a bit prim, a bit "horsey". She obviously was not keen on old Doc Roberts. Well, he was old enough to be her father, and a bit. If Europeans went in for it like natives, he'd be her grandfather. And she wasn't helped by the way Jennifer was obviously having a great time with Johnnie. Gloria wanted to share a room with her girlfriend, not with the Doc.

Andy had done his best by her. He was the sort of chap who felt uncomfortable for his guests. He really ought to be running a guest-house. Better still, managing a hotel somewhere. Now there was a job. Who had taken such a job recently? Tommy, that was it. Ex D.O. at Madang. Andy figured he had to keep his ear well and truly to the ground. He didn't want to miss another opportunity like that.

But, Christ, what a man does when he's too long in the bush by himself. He blushed now, thinking about it. You heard about natives doing it—well, he had got the idea from a case down in Rabaul.

Because, when the Baloose landed, he had expected Johnnie, the Doc, and Bellamy. Bellamy had said he was coming. So Andy had got all excited and fixed everyone up with a bed. With a bit of pushing and shoving, there was a room each. And then, of course, he had got all ready for a bit of a dinner party.

And the Baloose lands and these two girls get out! He had been beside himself with excitement. But he hadn't known what to do, or where to look. He was all right with Gloria; she had that easy, level way of looking at a chap. But Jennifer. She flirted. She did it automatically. When she finished speaking, her lips came together in a little puckered bow. Her eyes dropped momentarily, and she looked up under her lashes . . .

What he had done was, he had assigned her the room next to his own. And, when he knew they were out there looking at the natives carrying on, and that his own Boys were out there getting an eyeful of the girls, he had taken a gimlet and he had bored a hole in the thin partition wall.

Then he'd played the host to the hilt. He'd got them whisky and gin. He was going to do all the dinner by himself, but the girls seemed uneasy in the presence of a man who

332

liked cooking. Jennifer had wanted to "whip something up"—and he had suffered in the kitchen with her bending over, letting him see down her front. Gloria had been jolly, making him laugh, but brushing against him in the confined space of the kitchen. One wore perfume. The other smelled of soap and cleanliness. The presence of both of them had been so hard to take—Jennifer's conscious femininity and Gloria's easier womanliness. He was afraid of making a fool of himself.

So he'd excused himself and gone out the back, out to the outhouse and, well, he had jerked himself off. He'd had to. When he came he nearly blew his brains out!

That way he'd got through dinner, but now getting excited, thinking of what he'd done with the gimlet, looking at Jennifer as she teased them all—at the old Doc swelling like a bullfrog as she turned him on and he turned it on to Gloria. Poor girl, she didn't want a bar of it. She was glaring daggers at her friend by now.

His original intention had been just to spy on the girl. He hadn't thought he'd be watching Johnnie, too. That made him ashamed, spying on a mate.

The lamplight gave her a warm, soft glow. When she bent forward to take off her stockings her hair fell forward too, across her cheek, in a lovely, romantic gesture. She brushed it with her fingertips. She looked up at Johnnie, who was lying back on the bed, smiling the smile of a man who owns a girl like that.

"I'm going to sleep, Johnnie," she said.

"Oh, yeah," he said. He laughed.

"I'm serious."

She took the other stocking off. She stood there in her petticoat, or slip, whatever. Now she brushed her hair back. But the movement just made her breast stand out. Everything she did was a flirt. Andy was quite hard again. He opened his pyjamas and took hold of it again.

She sat down and frowned.

"I've had enough, Johnnie."

"Don't bullshit me," Johnson said.

The language shocked Andy. He would never have used words like that.

Johnson was on his feet and tugging at his belt. She put out her hand to ward him off.

"Look, I don't want to be here, with you. I want to sleep."

"You didn't want to stay in Lae. You didn't want to stay in Madang. You wanted to come up here, to Mount Hagen, you bitch."

"I wanted to get away from this! I'm not a . . . a whore."

"Yes you are, and you know it. You're just too hypocritical to take honest money for it."

He grabbed her hair and bent her head back.

"You bastard," she said.

Andy was stroking furiously now. He bit his lips together to stop from making any noise. There was a sound in the corridor, of someone walking. He stuffed it back in his pyjamas.

Gloria stood there, staring at him, her face chalk white. With her hair down, wearing a cotton nightdress, she was girl-like. He kept his hand in front of his crotch, but she was watching his face.

"Mr Williams . . ." she began, "I don't want to . . ."

"Look," he said, hastily, "I'm sorry about . . ." He waved his other hand, leaning against the wall, so she couldn't see the hole. But through the partition they both heard the bed creak. They could hear Jennifer saying, No! Don't! Johnnie was telling her what a whore she was.

"Come away from there, please," Gloria asked him.

He felt it was safe to move. "Let's go into the kitchen," he said.

Leaning against the kitchen table, on which there was still a fine coating of white flour, he shook his head ruefully. She stared out through the window, into the blackness.

"I shouldn't be shocked," she said. "I'm a nurse. I've seen all these things. But Doctor Roberts is just too old for me. I told him I wasn't going to do it with him and that I would sleep on the floor in your room."

"God!" he said. "What sort of host do you think I am? You must have my bed. I'll sleep on the floor."

She turned and studied him closely. He looked past her, at his own reflection in the dining-room mirror; a thick-set, clumsy man clutching his striped pyjamas together.

"What about the Doc?" he said. "How's he taking all this?"

The look in her eyes changed. She smiled and leaned closer to him.

"He's probably asleep by now," she said. "He was almost too drunk, anyway."

He was getting that erection back, close to her warmth. She must have seen it in his eyes, because there was a moment in her own where she backed off and thought about it. Then, to his amazement and delight, he felt her hand on his thigh. He felt her fingers stroking him. He let go of the pyjamas and the cloth sprang apart.

CHAPTER SEVENTEEN

He had made it through! There, he could see Mount Hagen base on the hill. The galvanized iron roof glinting in the sun. The four-square fibrolite walls out of place amongst the rounded, woven huts and the fenced fields.. He checked Nicholls, who had slipped into a fever sleep, into unconsciousness. Then, in the distance, he heard the plane and looked up, searching the sky, and saw a tri-motor, a Ford or a Junkers. A Junkers. It roared down towards them.

Merin screamed and threw herself off the track. He laughed and went to her and knelt beside her, stroking her back. He looked up and laughed and waved as it roared overhead. It waggled its wings in reply.

The boys were cheering wildly, slapping each other on the back. He looked to Baranuma, who was laughing openly. Their eyes met. They grinned at each other. Whatever had been going on between Baranuma and the four boys they had met on the track early in the morning seemed unimportant.

He had thought, when they had seen those boys, and seen Baranuma's furtiveness, that Ludwig truly had been right, and that some kind of attack, engineered by Baranuma, was imminent. But that was just patrol-induced paranoia. Baranuma had relatives all over the place and was engineering some kind of native business. Let him.

"We've made it," he called to Baranuma. "We've bloody-well made it."

He got up and went to him and slapped him on the back.

"Come on," he said. "Another hour's walk and we're there."

That hour was the longest of the patrol. He was as hungry as hell—and thinking of a Williams-style spread. The house on the hill grew no larger, no matter how hard they pushed. The pace was hard on Nicholls. The stretcher rocked and jolted. But the boys were callous with impatience. They let

336

him murmur with his pain. They wanted to be finished, to be free of the burden.

In the distance he saw the Baloose touch down, and felt Merin start beside him. He murmured soothingly to her. He stroked her hair and smiled at her. But her eyes were wide with fear.

The local people, Baranuma's relatives, now lined the track up the hill. They, too, were cheering, throwing flowers at the boys, who were grinning like the heroes they were. Girls wriggled their buttocks and breasts at them. Young boys ran along the crowd of adults, wriggling through the legs to get a solemn-eyed stare at the returning party, and then racing along to watch the progress of the three stretchers —two of them carrying bodies tightly shrouded, and the third the body of a dying man.

Williams came down the track to meet him, grinning all over his face. He seemed smugly, secretly delighted.

"Good-day, mate," Williams said. "I thought you might be dropping in."

"I wasn't going to," Don said, smiling back, standing aside to let the stretcher party carry on up the hill, to where the Baloose was waiting. "But then I heard about your cooking."

Andy Williams frowned and put his arm on Don's shoulder.

"You're out of luck," he said. "Old Doc Roberts wants to get him into the air and back to Madang quick smart."

"Not even a chicken sandwich?"

"I can do you a sandwich." Andy glanced at the black girl standing beside Don.

"Great," Don said. "Is Bellamy here?"

"No . . " Andy hesitated. He looked like he was going to tell Don something, and then decided not to. For a moment Don caught a whiff of some other conspiracy. He closed his eyes. He couldn't handle any more.

"All right," Don said. "When do we take off?"

"As soon as she's loaded."

There it was again, the reluctance in Williams' voice. What the hell was going on. Then Don realized Williams was studying Merin out the corner of his eyes. Don reached over and put his arm on her shoulder.

337

To hell with you, mate, he thought.

"I'll get you some food," Williams said, but Don didn't acknowledge him. He gently steered Merin to the boundary of the airstrip, climbed over the rope barrier, and went to where they had laid Nicholls' stretcher in the shade of the wing.

As he did, he saw, behind the plane, Johnson shepherding the two girls to the cockpit.

She knew it was Saturday morning when she woke, because the orderlies had been late. She had lain in bed, listening to the silence, and smelling the faint odour of sulphur. She thought about the old man down by the wharves and wondered if he had kept his vigil through another night. She thought about the lagoon and shivered, thinking of its black depths and whatever lay down there, that was trying to rise up out of the ancient volcanic pipes and come back to life.

She waited all morning for something to happen, but nothing did. The sulphur smell hung there, almost like smoke close to the ground. When she joined the other patients on the verandah, none referred to it. It was as if the collective will of all Rabaul's residents had reformed reality, had rewritten yesterday so there was no guria in their memory of that day. Friday? they seemed to be thinking. It was an ordinary Friday in Rabaul.

And the smell. What smell? Patricia was imagining it.

They watched the morning unfold. The sun glinted on tin roofs. Chinamen and natives came and went in the shaded streets. The mountain peaks hung over the peaceful, blue lagoon. Boats moved on the water.

She took lunch in the hospital dining room. The ceiling fans seemed only to spread the sulphur smell further. She could not eat in the thick, heavy silence, with that aroma in her nostrils. She feared she was about to experience some sort of attack, something that would definitely indicate she'd had a "breakdown". The tension in the air was unbearable.

338

It was so obvious that she began to suspect there was a conspiracy on the part of all the hospital staff and all the patients not to refer to it—and thus to isolate her and truly drive her crazy.

She drank a glass of water and forced herself to push back her chair and stand up. No one watched her. But then they might want to make her think they were not watching her. With a forced smile she navigated between the tables. She glanced at the clock above the door. It was showing one-fifteen.

And the guria exploded through the dining room. Plates shattered. Glass splintered, falling from windows in cutting shards. She found herself on the floor and scrabbled under a table for safety as she heard the clock itself come smashing down.

As the shock-wave passed, she got to her feet. Expecting it, she was the least shocked of the dining room's inhabitants. She stepped over the broken glass and hurried outside. As she did, she heard a rending, tearing rumble. She looked around in fear, and saw a section of hillside moving, shaking the coconut palms and tearing them down. She grabbed a verandah post and looked over the bay. Matupi Island oozed viscous black smoke.

She could see people in the street staring at the island. Ships in the harbour rocked as the water receded. She could see deck-crew trying to keep their balance, trying to watch the smoking island and the landslides on the hills, and watching the water level in the harbour recede, and then come rushing back.

She looked towards Vulcan Island, remembering the old man of the previous night. But Vulcan was calm and serene. Looking back to Matupi, she saw cracks opening along its flanks.

The world was coming to an end! That was why the Baloose had come down for them. That was why its nest had been made on this hillside, and why they had rushed back so fast, ignoring the pain of the Kiap, and dragging the dead weight of the dead prisoner and the dead soldier who had gone mad. The Baloose would take them all to the Land of the Dead, where they would all be reunited.

Two Sky People had emerged from the Baloose when it had finished its terrifying descent. When she, like so many other people, had flung herself to the ground in fear of its booming roar, the wind of its wings. She had seen her man go up to it and she screamed to him not to leave her, but he had gone under its wing and helped the other Sky People emerge from its body. They spoke with her man. As they spoke, another guria shivered the mountain and all the Sky People looked, with obvious alarm, towards the distant mountains, as if seeking reassurance that everything was well in Sky Land.

Then her man showed them the two dead men. They got the carriers to load them inside the Baloose, whether as food or simply to transport them, she could not say. Very carefully they lifted the stretcher on which the other Kiap lay, and transferred that to the Baloose's belly.

She frowned and concentrated and tried to interpret what was happening. She tried to fit all the events together and find a pattern that could be understood.

They had left the camp-spot by first light, dragging with them the three stretchers. They had set a terrible pace, that caused the men holding the stretchers to groan and swear and curse as they stumbled along. Her man had become withdrawn and coldly angry. He kept watching the wounded Kiap's face and trying to ascertain if he were dying—she could see the concern on his brow. She understood it and knew why he was so angry, fighting to get this man he so clearly loved, back to meet the Baloose. Perhaps the man was his own brother, or an uncle. It was even possible he was her man's father. Arap's father. She practised the name as she walked.

Along the track they had come to a party of men, intent on getting in the opposite direction just as fast as they. The Kiap's servant had spoken with them and interpreted their intentions for Arap. Arap was suspicious. He could sense

something not quite right in their story, their speedy journey
—without provisions, lightly armed, as if they knew that
ahead of them lay a valley where only dead men resided.

She, too, could tell that something was wrong. But they
had no time to stay and puzzle it out. The Patrol stood aside
to let the four men through. The men kept their eyes
downcast, fearing to look up and have their intentions read
by astute people. They murmured their thanks as they
shuffled past the Patrol—whose members were glad of the
sudden, unexpected rest. They stared down into the face of
the wounded Kiap and respectfully saluted him. They looked
away from the shrouded dead men.

She watched them disappear up the track. There was a
relationship between those four young men and the Patrol,
but she could not figure it.

Now Arap came out of the Baloose and looked around and
saw her, standing beside the Kiap's servant. He beckoned
them both over. She held back, but the servant took her arm
and murmured reassuringly to her. Arap smiled at her and
came and took her hand and he, too, spoke reassuring words
and said her name: "Merin. Merin."

And he forced her into the Baloose's belly.

And so she died. Yet she felt no different to when she was
alive. The Baloose's belly closed on them. Black men, white
men all jammed together. One of the Sky People peeling off
the soaked bandages from the wounded man's legs with a
knife—so their stench filled the whole belly and all the other
men in it turned aside. And Arap himself going up to the
wounded man and the wounded man reaching up and finding
Arap's hand and holding it tight—the first time she had seen
one Sky Person embrace another.

The Baloose flung itself across the ground, shaking and
snarling, shivering and rattling. She realized they were flying.
She panicked and flung herself at the side of the belly. The
servant grabbed her and held her and tried to talk to her. He
brought her to a place she could see through the belly, under
the wing, and she saw how high they flew.

They flew close to the mountains, their wings seeming to

341

brush the jagged rocks, the tumbling waterfalls. She felt the Baloose straining with its load, lifting itself higher and higher, scraping through the cloud that clung to it, moist and dark. The wounded Kiap screamed and she saw Arap kneel by him and stroke his forehead.

Then movement made her look up and she stared in disbelief, and then in recognition.

A partition had opened in the Baloose and there, staring at her, was her own soul. They stared at each other: soul and body. The body was dark-skinned, black-haired. The soul was deathly pale, its hair yellow, almost white. It wore fine, funereal clothes. It opened its mouth to speak to her but she could not yet understand the words of the soul. It stared out with its fine, clear blue eyes; seeing the wounded Kiap and Arap and the other Sky Person all together in the centre of the Baloose's belly; and seeing all the men squatting, like her, against its ribs. Then her soul looked at her. They stared at each other. She lifted her hand to greet her soul. Soul hesitated and then she smiled and lifted her hand, too.

Merin smiled. She beamed with delight. She closed her eyes.

When she opened them, the partition was closed. Her soul had gone. She looked out and watched as the Baloose climbed to the top of its flight and began to ease itself down. She could see a braided river beneath them, and mountains clothed with green, like moss—but when she looked closer saw it was trees, and they were high in the air, flying on and on.

Gloria shut the door, leaned against it and stared at Johnson in the pilot's seat, and Jennifer beside him.

"Oh, my God," she said. Jennifer looked back and smiled at her, and then saw how white she was.

"What on earth's the matter?"

"I got such a shock. There's a girl back there."

"A white girl?"

"No. A black girl."

"Oh," Jennifer said, and lost interest. She bit her lip and

342

looked down at her hands folded in her lap. This morning she seemed like a little girl.

Gloria could see the jungle beneath them, and the mountains along their side. But she was thinking about the girl in the body of the plane—with the fear in her eyes, and the wonder, and then the delight when Gloria had returned her greeting.

God, she thought. She was like a black mirror looking at me. And that young man who had tried to flirt with me on the ship a month ago, kneeling there by the wounded man. How can he be so close to that stink and not show it? What's happened to him? He looked up and saw me and his eyes just moved through me. He looked at the black girl and he saw her properly. But me, I was just like a ghost. What's going on?

Then, rising out of the land, she saw the sea. Blue and glittering, studded with tiny islands. Johnson gave a grunt of satisfaction and corrected his course.

"Do you think Nicholls will live?" she asked him.

It always made her nervous when he looked over his shoulder while he was flying, and the mountainsides wobbled closer.

"Yeah," Johnson said, grinning. The man was unable to help himself, she realized. Whenever he looked at a woman he looked first at her breasts, then at her thighs, and finally into her face. "He's as tough as old boots."

"What about that dreadful smell?" Jennifer said, with a delicate shudder.

"The Doc'll get the leg off when we land at Madang."

"Oh, my God," Jennifer said. "The sooner I'm out of this horrible place, the better for me."

"I can get you onto a boat out of Port Moresby," he said.

Listening, Gloria realized that there was relief in his voice. He was not going to persuade Jennifer to stay. The romance had run its course.

I might stay a little longer, she thought to herself. It would be nice to be out from Jennifer's shadow. She looked at the back of Johnson's neck. In her memory last night was unreal, a dream. But the thought of Andy made her smile.

"OK," Johnson said. "Let's take her down."

343

It had finally penetrated the thick hides of Rabaul residents that something of momentous importance was about to happen. Since midday the gurias, the sulphur smell, the landslides and the gaping cracks in Matupi Island had been impossible to ignore any longer.

All movement, all normal Saturday activity, had ceased. They waited.

And at twenty past four it happened. For Patricia it was a relief.

There was a series of gigantic explosions that shook the harbour. But they did not come from Matupi. Then over Vulcan Island rose a plume of dense smoke and steam, mixed with dust.

From the hospital verandah she heard the fire sirens. She saw activity begin again as cars started up and, the first time she had ever seen it, white men ran down the streets. She could see Vulcan in the distance now, like a model from a museum, with its papier-mâché smoke and steam. She stepped off the verandah and walked down the hill.

It all seemed so peaceful, so anti-climatic, after the prelude of earthtremors. A car passed her and a man called out, but she did not catch what he said. He stopped a little further down the street and waited for her.

"Where are you going?" he asked her.

"I don't know," she said.

He opened the passenger door and she got in beside him.

"My family's out at Ravuva. I'm going to pick them up."

"I'll come," she said. "I'd like to see it."

He looked at her searchingly. Then shrugged and engaged gear again.

"We need to get over to the North Coast," he said, "to be really safe. Can I take you?"

She nodded. The idea seemed reasonable. They were passing natives fleeing in the opposite direction. They ran in the centre of the road, women carrying babies, men carrying older children and a few belongings. They seemed oblivious to the Masta's car. Angrily, he hooted at them, and they moved aside, staring up almost blindly, too immersed in

344

their own fear to understand that the Masta wanted his right of way.

"Bloody coons," he said.

She nodded. The sky was getting blacker. For the first time since the eruption, she began to be afraid.

"We'd better hurry," she said.

"I'm going as fast as I can. These bloody natives . . . and Chinamen," he added.

She stared at him and decided he was not her type, most definitely.

There was a gigantic explosion and suddenly pieces of rock began to fall on the road. Some hit the car and bounced off. She realized it was pumice. It rolled down the bonnet, smoking. He cursed and leaned forward, trying to see through the thickening dust.

"I told them not to go," he said, "but my daughter wanted to take a swim. I thought if there was any trouble it would come from Matupi, not Vulcan. Ravuva Baths are too close to Vulcan,"

She nodded.

"Look out!" she said, and he swerved, just missing a native who was trying to shepherd two pigs down the road. He put the lights on, but the dust scattered the light and they could see no further.

She saw the tree before he did and yelled. He twisted the wheel and drove straight into it.

In the silence afterwards she stared at him, slumped against the wheel. She looked at her hands and saw they were shaking. She felt her legs. She seemed unharmed.

"Can you hear me?" she asked him, nervously.

He said nothing. Oh, God, she thought. He's dead.

There was another explosion and the blackness was complete. Hot dust swirled around her. She found a cloth and covered her face with it and pushed the buckled door open.

She stumbled in a ditch and groped blindly with her hands. Then, with her feet, she felt the edge of the road and began to shuffle forwards. Every step was into the unknown. The heat was growing suffocatingly intense.

Stones fell somewhere near her. A pebble hit her on the shoulder and she cried out and fell down. She crawled ahead.

345

She crawled up against a wall. She explored it with her hands. She could hear a high-pitched peeping, a sound of anguish. She followed the wall along.

In the darkness her hands encountered a feathered body. A beak slashed at her and she pulled away. She could just see a white, dust-covered hen anxiously shepherding a clutch of yellow chickens. She stood up and felt along the top of the wall and then saw Ravuva Tearooms and the lawn. She pulled herself over the wall and fell onto the grass.

She got inside the building, stumbling against empty tables and chairs. No one was about. She called out and her voice was swallowed up in the dust.

Then she saw him again. It was the old man from the previous night. Except that now he was carrying something. He was stumbling blindly towards her.

She called out and he looked around and located her. He held out the bundle as he walked. She could see the tears streaming down his eyes.

It was a tiny, dead infant. It looked as if it had been scalded in steam. The old man's shoulders were shaking. She didn't know what to do. She looked further and saw there were other natives trying to shelter in the relative safety of the building.

Then they all heard the sound and stared at each other in fear. It was a roaring, rushing sound, accompanied by loud vibrations. It came from the direction of the bay. She realized it was the sea returning.

She grabbed the old man's hand and dragged him out to the stone wall. He resisted, trying to cling tight to the dead baby and stay inside. He and the other natives acted as if the European building was somehow charmed. Angrily she tore the scrap of cloth that covered the infant, and the infant itself, from him and laid them on the ground. She had no idea why she wanted to save him, except that she did not want to be alone in the blackness. She urged him over the stone wall.

The huge wave struck as she dropped. She heard the others crying out. She heard glass shattering. She was aware of the absurd fairy lights bobbing backwards and forwards

346

above them. She felt the wave slam against the stone wall, shivering it but failing to smash it.

Water swirled around its ends and grabbed at them with hot, liquid hands. Together they ran into the blackness, aware that the sound of struggling voices had ceased as the giant wave swept back out into the harbour, back towards the exploding island.

They clung together, hand in hand, fighting into the dark. They bumped into another man, another native, and she took his hand, too, hoping that they could meet with other people and form a human chain. But he stared at her and wrenched himself away and disappeared.

They pressed on. The heat was waning, but the evening was coming on, compounding the darkness. Then, in the distance, they could see lights and hear a sound.

They found themselves beside a mission church. Inside it was packed with natives. Standing at the altar was a white priest, clothed in all his vestments. Lighted tapers kept the darkness at bay. They all sang, staring at the priest before them, whose head was upraised to the protecting arms of the Cross.

Yea, though I walk in Death's dark vale,
Yet will I fear no ill,
For Thou art with me, and Thy rod,
and staff me comfort still.

Her companion gave a sudden tug and dragged his hand from hers, and plunged back into the blackness. She leaned against the outside wall of the church and regained her breath. The hymn rolled on, sonorous and comforting.

Now she was aware of the sound of trees crashing down in the forest as rocks plummeted from the sky. The volcano was still erupting, still thundering. Lightning suddenly flashed—showing her the moon-like, dust-covered landscape, the tossing trees, the distant, pumice-covered bay. Then blackness returned, even more dense.

And rain fell with the thunder: hot, steaming, dusty rain.

She pressed her way along the wall, fell against the door and stumbled inside the mission church.

No one seemed to notice her. The hymn had ceased and

347

they were all on their knees now, heads unbowed, staring at the priest, whose eyes acknowledged her presence but then ignored her, as he began to intone a prayer.

"Oh, God, Father of Jesus Christ, who gave His life that our sins be redeemed, return to us the light of Thy presence. Wash us clean of this dust of our evil. Call off the mighty wrath of Thy Spirit.

"For we have erred from Thy ways, and we acknowledge it. We have turned aside from Thy worship. We have sought vainly after earthly goods and forgotten the sanctity of our Heavenly souls.

"But Thou, Oh God, art all Wise. Thou art all Good. Thou dost understand our deepest hearts. Forgive us our trespasses, oh Father. Cleanse our hearts . . ."

She began to cry. She knelt down next to a woman and put her head in her hands and cried.

The rain beat on the thatched roof and stones fell from the sky and the voice of the volcano roared again.

He couldn't raise Rabaul on the radio. All frequencies were awash with violent static. As night fell they could see, from the shore, sheet lightning blazing along the horizon. Whether brought on by the eruption or not, he didn't know, but a violent storm burst onto Madang. Forked lightning replaced the sheets of flame on the horizon. The sky was totally black, split by sudden orange and blue fire. The thunder reverberated through the earth. At first there was no wind, but then one sprang up, blowing in from the sea, bringing with it hot dust and the smell of sulphur.

They worked by oil and pressure lamps in the improvised operating theatre in the Administration Building. The roof rattled and the sound of rain drowned out all easy speech.

Johnson had gone in the Junkers, heading back to Lae, and he had left his two women in Bellamy's charge. One of them, the blonde, turned out to be a nursing sister. The brunette had mentally withdrawn herself from the proceedings. Bellamy had left her sitting in the guest bedroom of his house. But Gloria was now there at the doctor's side.

It was she who went through his staff files and found that Nicholls and Harris had compatible blood. She got Bellamy to sit with Harris as she siphoned off a pint into a sterile jar. In the background, Baranuma watched, the strain obvious on his face as he saw his Masta given more painkillers in an attempt to knock him out enough for the Doc to remove the gangrenous leg. Beside Baranuma was Bellamy's new boy, Alo, watching, noting, learning everything he could about the Mastas.

"You did a great job, Harris," Bellamy shouted to the young man, nervously patting his hand. Contact didn't come easily to Bellamy. "If he pulls through, it's you he'll owe his life to."

Harris stared at him. His face, drained of blood, was pale. Bellamy saw him think of something to say, and then decide not to say it. Bellamy smiled at him and patted his hand again.

"You're a brave man, Mr Harris." The nurse was there, checking on her charges. She felt Don's forehead and took his pulse. Both men watched her lips as she silently counted.

"How's it going?" Bellamy asked her, jerking his head to the screen they had erected, behind which the doctor was now at work.

"As good as you could hope," she shouted. She was no longer the uncertain blonde. She was the brisk nurse, efficient, comfortingly bossy. Harris's eyes followed her movements.

"This place . . ." she said. She gestured at the roof, the thunder of rain.

Bellamy grinned at her. She shrugged her shoulders and returned to the operating tent with the blood. Harris tugged at his sleeve and he bent close to hear him.

"Merin . . .?" The beating rain snatched away the rest of the sentence.

"Sorry, old man. Merin what?"

"Where is she?"

He didn't understand. He looked around and Baranuma came over and knelt down beside Harris. He repeated the word to the Boy, who nodded and stood up.

"What is it, Baranuma, what does he want?"

349

"His woman."

"*His* woman?"

"The girl we brought back."

"Oh, Jesus." He stared down at Harris. Harris did not look away.

"She's in the lockup, Harris," he said. "I couldn't think of anywhere else to put her."

An explosion of thunder and a stab of light hit the building and, for a moment, all four men—Bellamy, Harris, Baranuma, Alo—were frozen in a tableau, staring at each other, as vivid, flickering light ran around the room, pulsing with blues of every shade. They heard glass shatter and wind and rain swept in on the heels of the dying light.

The sulphur smell engulfed them, drowning the scent of decaying flesh. The sheets of the operating tent billowed and swayed, like a ghost come to haunt them. The nurse appeared, throwing her arms around the sheets, pulling them back from the lamps.

Bellamy yelled to the boys and the three of them ran to the broken window. Baranuma upended a table and they scrabbled it into position.

"*His* woman?" Bellamy asked Baranuma, again.

Baranuma nodded, looking down with embarrassment.

Bellamy and Alo dragged a filing cabinet up against the unbroken windows. Through the glass he could see nothing. Then a fork of lightning showed him the lagoon, water lashed; along the island shore palms whipped by the wind. Christ, he thought, it's like a bloody cyclone. Then he thought he saw someone running, staggering against the wind, towards the sheds, the stores, and the lockup.

He whirled around. Harris had gone.

"Mr Bellamy! Mr Bellamy!" the nurse called.

He turned to the operating tent. She had a bucket in her hand. She pointed at it and then to the fire that Baranuma had kindled on a sheet of galvanized iron, against the far wall.

Bellamy nodded and took it from her. In it were the doctor's instruments, bloodied.

"Hurry up," she shouted. Then she added, "It's off. We've got some stitching to do. I think he's going to pull through!"

350

· CHAPTER EIGHTEEN ·

Diary: 30th May, 1937

It's all over. The sky's as blue as can be. No wind. Just that dirty great stain along the horizon. All the pundits are saying how they knew the time was ripe for an explosion, and how all the gurias had warned them. Poor old Bellamy's in a state, worrying about his Missus. He took off with Johnson as soon as he got back with his seaplane, and they headed for Rabaul, taking along the nurse, Gloria. She's a pretty good sort. The Doc's had it. He's gone and collapsed up at Bellamy's house.

That leaves me in charge of Nicholls. Not that there's much to do. Change his dressings. He's shot so full of morphine I doubt if he'll ever come down. And, if he does, he'll probably be an addict. But that's the price of survival, isn't it? I would have thought the Doc'd have used ether, but apparently he was too scared to, couldn't measure it accurately, or something, and was worried that it would be more likely to kill him than getting the leg off. Gloria got rid of the bit and pieces somewhere.

When I found Merin she was cowered in a corner of the lockup, no blanket, no mattress, crouched there with her head in her hands, whimpering, scared out of her wits. At least she was dry. I was bloody furious. I had the choice of taking her down to my quarters, and risking the stares and comments of the blokes—and I wasn't having them jeering at her—or I could take her up the hill to Bellamy's.

Maybe I should have checked it with him first. But in the middle of a storm like that you don't think too clearly. I couldn't leave her alone in my quarters. There'd be some smart type make a pass at her. I knew there was the other woman at the D.O.'s, and I assumed she'd be like Gloria, able to take it in her stride.

I got to the house. It was still pouring down great buckets of rain, but the wind was easing off. I found her, Jennifer, in the guest room, in bed, with the covers over her head. I guess I scared her. When she saw Merin she became hysterical. I tried to explain that she was exactly the same as her—a scared girl a long way from

351

home. It was no good. She was shrieking and screaming. I didn't know what to do.

I guess you could see it as funny, afterwards. The white girl, very good looking, too, a stunner in fact, sitting up in bed screaming at me to get that nigger out of here. And Merin not understanding a word of it, but knowing it wasn't good, cowering in her corner, rolling her eyes and moaning. And me in the middle of it, going from one to the other, trying to calm them down. And I was starting to feel a bit woozy, too, from the lack of blood. So, right in the middle of it, I passed out. Just for a moment. I just sort of sat down on the floor and put my head in my hands. I was feeling quite sick.

That's how we were when Bellamy arrived home, boiling mad. One shrieking, one blubbering, and me in the middle looking like I was trying to crawl into the floorboards. Bellamy gave me a kick, actually. Then he saw what was going on, and he started to laugh.

He gave Jennifer a brandy. Then he and I had a couple of whiskies. He told me Nicholls was sleeping. Gloria and the Doc were bunking down there. He gave me a bit of a lecture, about my responsibilities; if I'm going to keep Merin I'd better toughen my attitudes up, and I'd better stick by her, because Jennifer's reaction was going to be pretty typical of a certain segment of the populace.

I told him I was going to marry her, and that made him nod and look earnest. I also told him I wanted to go back into the Highlands, with her, either as a Kiap or as an individual. He said he'd speak to the Administrator . . . but that it would probably be best if he didn't mention I would go back as a married man.

I got a bit angry at that, but he stopped me by offering Merin and me his double bed. He would take the other bed in the guest room, next to Jennifer. Well, I couldn't refuse, and I could see that he was looking further than me, to the actualities of living in this place, not just my boyish fantasies.

I'm not so sure about that. Bellamy and Nicholls are both good sorts, but they're too scared of "opinion"; they think too many steps ahead. You can be too devious, you know. Anyhow, here I am with Baranuma, listening to old Nicholls breathing easily at last. Merin is sitting by the fire they made on a sheet of tin. It's almost like being back on patrol—except that out the windows you can see the lagoon and the palms.

I told Baranuma I wanted to go back to the Highlands and he was quite enthusiastic. He spoke of us doing "business" together, whatever he means by that. I've a feeling he'll go a long way, that Boy!

352

They couldn't land in Rabaul harbour. Vulcan was still belching smoke and ash. Matupi had erupted, showering the city itself with mud and dust. The whole of the harbour was a mass of greyish-white pumice stone, through which shipping tried to move, almost like ice-breakers caught in the floes. The city was unrecognizable. It was like the moon. Derelict, the mud and dust coating everything. The big mangoes and figs broken under the weight of debris. The wharves had been battered by tidal waves.

They flew along the coast, seeing the destruction of villages as they got closer to Vulcan. Ravuva Tearooms had been smashed beyond recognition. They could see figures moving slowly amongst the debris.

"Looters?" Johnson said.

The nurse shook her head. "They look like survivors to me, looking for lost relatives."

Johnson snorted and raised an eyebrow to Bellamy, but he refused to be drawn. He was almost too frightened to think where she could be. Johnson examined his face and nodded.

"We'll find her," he said. "They'll have evacuated the hospital first off."

"Where would they go?" the girl asked.

"Across the island, one of the other settlements. Kokopo, perhaps. Look, there's a mission station."

"Bloody hell!" Bellamy said.

The roof of the church had been smashed in under the weight of falling mud and rocks. Other mission buildings had been similarly destroyed. The survivors moved slowly through the debris, pulling at it in search of their kin.

"Oh, God," the nurse said. "How can we help?"

"I can't put down," Johnson told her. "This is a seaplane, remember?"

"Well, put us down in the sea then. We'll walk in. It's not that far."

Johnson looked at her, then at Bellamy. Bellamy nodded to him.

"Good idea," Bellamy said. "We've got a bit of medical kit here, and the mission'll have some."

353

Johnson nodded and banked the plane once more over the mission, this time bringing it down as close as he could.

"There's the priest," he said.

Bellamy stared out. He could see the priest and a woman beside him, probably a nun. She was kneeling by one of the injured. Then she looked up.

He felt a shock of recognition; of love.

"Patricia," he said. He laughed. "It's Patricia."

"I'll be buggered," Johnson said.

"It's my wife," he told the girl. She smiled and grabbed his shoulder and squeezed it.

"She's unhurt. I thought she was dead."

"All right," the girl said. She was laughing, too. "It's all right, Mr. Bellamy."

"Richard. My name's Richard. God, I thought she was dead."

Johnson took the plane back up and turned for the ocean. They could see the sea shimmering blue, glittering in the distance. But under the billowing clouds of ash it was an ugly brown.

"I'll put you two down and then fly on to Kokopo," Johnson said. "God knows when we can get you out, though."

"That's all right," the nurse said.

"You'll miss your steamer out of Moresby."

She smiled. "I'm sure I can find work here," she said.

"What about you, Bellamy?" Johnson called. "What about getting your missus out?"

"We'll go together, after I've resigned."

"You're leaving the Service?"

Bellamy nodded.

"You're the only sane man on the island then," Johnson said. He gave a snort of laughter and brought the plane low over the beach, looking at the water, searching it for snags. He could see a native path leading to the sand.

"I'll set you down there," he said. "Less chance of feeding the puk-puks that way."

The girl and Bellamy smiled at each other. They watched the water rushing under the hull of their plane. They felt the bump, the skid, and then the backwash of the prop. They were down.

354

Production by
Cobb/Dunlop Publishers Services, Inc.
Printed by the Maple-Vail Company on acid-free paper.